# THE MASTERS FILE

## Jack Dickson

Zipper Books

## Also by Jack Dickson

### Erotic Fiction:
*Still Waters*
*Out of This World*

### Thrillers:
*Oddfellows*
*Freeform*
*Crossing Jordan*
*Banged Up*
*Some Kind of Love*

First published 2002 by Zipper Books,
part of Millivres Prowler Limited,
Spectrum House, 32-34 Gordon House Road, London NW5 1LP
www.zipper.co.uk

A catalogue record for this book is available from the British Library

ISBN 1-873741-75-8

Distributed in the UK and Europe by Airlift Book Company,
8 The Arena, Mollison Avenue, Enfield, Middlesex EN3 7NJ
Telephone: 020 8804 0400
Distributed in North America by Consortium,
1045 Westgate Drive, St Paul, MN 55114-1065
Telephone: 1 800 283 3572
Distributed in Australia by Bulldog Books,
PO Box 300, Beaconsfield, NSW 2014

Printed and bound in Finland by WS Bookwell

# One

He ran mornings and evenings.

Every day, rain or shine, the pound of each trainered foot on tarmac, the steady thump of his heart. Each breath was at first an effort, then something his lungs did for him. The first mile was warm-up.

The second, muscle loosened and stretched, was pace.

In the third mile he found his rhythm and settled into it.

By the time he was on the fourth, one-mile circuit of either the park or the grid of streets around the tube station, his body was moving by itself. The rhythmic motion gathered all stray thoughts together and focused them.

This particular morning it was the park. Dressed in shorts with a jock beneath, hooded sweatshirt and baseball cap, and wearing well-padded trainers, he maintained the distance between himself and the runner in front.

He'd not seen the guy's face. He didn't really care about the face. He never remembered faces anyway. Or names – on the few occasions they insisted on telling him.

Some suggested a drink sometime, or a shower, back at their flat. He invented some pressing engagement or appointment.

Some even scribbled phone numbers on scraps of paper and thrust them at him, saying 'Call me'. He waited till they were out of sight before tossing the slips of paper into the nearest litter bin.

And it wasn't only randy fellow runners. When the building beside the tube station was under renovation, he'd been followed

1

on two separate occasions by two different brickies – both wearing wedding rings.

One had called him a filthy poof, then nearly sucked Gav's cock down his throat in the alley behind W H Smith. The other burst into tears when Gav's hand moved to his crotch, sobbed on his shoulder while Gav held him, cringing.

But today was different. This morning was different – and yet it was not different. Arcing away from the tantalising rear view of the runner in front, he slowed. Gavin came to a halt opposite the park bench, hauled off his baseball cap and leaned against the trunk of the tree.

The guy was still there. The guy in the suit. With the briefcase.

Sweeping a hand over his skull, he loosened tangled, sweaty ponytailed hair and pushed it back from his face.

The guy was still watching.

Throwing his head back, Gav rested his hands on strong thighs and let his breathing even out.

Gav knew he was watching. Staring at early-morning sky, he angled his crotch, pushing the base of his spine back against the rough bark, clenching the cheeks of his arse and thrusting his obvious hard-on out towards the guy in the suit, who sat smoking on the park bench opposite. Smoking and staring. Gav didn't meet those eyes.

He had no need to. He felt them on his body, roving over his sweat-sheened arms and shoulders. His heaving, well-muscled chest. Abs honed by years of running.

Releasing one thigh, he repositioned his cock, casually stroking the engorged curving outline as he did so.

Now Gav was making sure the guy knew exactly what he was seeing. What was on offer. In one swift movement, he turned and braced both arms against the tree. Fingers splayed on the rough trunk, he arched his back and extended his right leg behind in a long, languid hamstring stretch, tendons elongated. A shiver ruffled the hair on the backs of his thighs.

And the hot stare of this stranger in the suit burned into his arse.

Gav changed legs, tightening muscle. Hands pressed against the tree. Trainered feet pushed against the still frosted ground. On the air in front of his face, his breath condensed in a cloud of smoky steam. Sweat was cooling on his calves, on his arms. He widened his stance and repeated the stretch.

Icy morning air drifted up the flared legs of his running shorts, chilling the sweat on his balls and in the crack of his arse. Held tight by the jockstrap, his cock flexed against the fine fabric mesh.

His hole clenched. A film of fresh perspiration broke out on his forehead, trickling down to gather in his brows. Gav narrowed his eyes. He straightened up and turned. Shoving the baseball cap back on his head, he stared straight at the suit on the park bench opposite.

The supporting feature was over. Now it was time to see if the audience would stay for the main event.

The guy met and held the stare, cigarette gripped between thumb and forefinger. Mid-forties, buzz-cut hair. Gav narrowed his eyes.

The guy tossed the cigarette to the ground, stubbed it out under the sole of a well-polished shoe. Then he stood up, took the brief-case, which had been sitting on the bench beside him, and strode off towards the park gates. Gav watched him go, dragging the rem-nants of the cigarette smoke into his lungs. He'd given up years ago, but he still wanted one every day.

Standing there, the head of his cock pushing painfully against the elastic mesh of the jock, he waited until the suit was almost out of sight. Then he followed.

He followed him across the road and down Singleton Street. He jogged on the spot, outside an early-opening chemist.

When the suit emerged, he let him get a bit ahead, then picked up his trail again. The suit walked briskly. Gav upped his own pace. The suit turned left. Gav turned left. The suit slowed. Gav slowed.

Eventually, fifteen yards in front, the guy swerved in through the entrance to the Holiday Inn, pausing briefly for a whispered word to the doorman as he did so.

Gav made up the distance between him and the suit, swerving smoothly to jog up the steps and through the hotel door, which the uniformed security man was now holding open for him.

Inside, 6.30 a.m., the foyer was quiet. The desk clerk glanced up briefly, then past Gavin to the doorman. Then returned his gaze to the computer screen in front of him.

Now walking, Gav swiftly determined the location of the lifts. He arrived just in time to catch sight of the back of well-tailored shoulders between closing lift doors.

He waited, watching illuminated numbers blink up to six. His cock throbbed against the jock's sweat-soaked mesh. When the lift returned, he boarded and pressed six.

Seconds later he emerged at the end of a long, carpeted corridor. Closed doors punctuated the walls. Gavin scanned. His eyes paused at a half-open door, three-quarters of the way down. Adjusting the hard-on inside his running shorts, he padded towards it, the soles of his trainers sinking into the carpet's thick pile.

His skin flushed hot and cold by turns under the hotel's central heating. The back of his throat was rough with the taste of freezing air. And when he reached the half-open door a suited arm on the other side opened it fully and ushered him in.

Gav refused the offer to sit and the drink. He noted the half-full tumbler of whisky the suit poured for himself. And the quarter-empty bottle that sat on the night stand.

When the guy grabbed Gav's shoulders and pressed a hard wet open mouth on his, he could taste the stuff on his breath.

And the need.

Gav returned the kiss, cupping the back of a bristly neck and pushing his tongue into the older man's mouth. His other hand moved to the suited arse. Eyes open, he started at the closed lids of the eyes inches away.

Beneath both palms, the guy was rigid – totally rigid.

Gav altered his stance, closing the distance between their bodies. Bare legs shadowing grey-suited thighs, he ground his crotch casually against another. Gav himself had been half-hard when he'd left Gerry sleeping back at the house at 5.30 a.m. Glancing beyond the creased features of the face so close to his, his eyes brushed the sheets of an undisturbed bed and wondered vaguely where the suit had spent last night.

The guy moaned into Gav's mouth, hauling his mind back to the matter in hand. A desperate grip tightened on his shoulder, fingers digging into sweat-sheened deltoids.

His own light stubble rasped against a newly shaved chin. Altering the angle of his face, Gav deepened the kiss and slid his cock up parallel to the suited one a little less casually.

The guy thrust back this time.

Gav spread his fingers out over the man's arse, drawing him in, holding him there. Kissing him. Fucking the suit's cock with slow languid movements of his own.

Before he could manoeuvre the man further, the suit was taking matters into his own hands. Breaking away, he tore his palms from Gav's shoulders and spun round.

Gav grabbed the hem of his running vest and hauled the damp garment over his head.

Still fully dressed, the suit snatched at the small chemist's bag that sat on the bedside table. Fumbling, he tore the paper in his haste. A boxed tube of K-Y and a slew of packaged condoms tumbled to the floor.

Gav lowered his head and stuck his thumbs into the waistband of the nylon running shorts. To the accompaniment of beginner's nervous fingers scooping the tools of the causal pickup into a sweaty palm, he eased the thin nylon down over glowing thighs.

He heard the suit groan over the rustle of the running shorts as he kicked them to his ankles and stepped out of the thin nylon garment.

Standing there, in jock and trainers, Gav raised his head. The suit's face was flushed. Semi-glazed eyes couldn't tear themselves from the front of Gav's jock. A film of sweat slicked his upper lip, half anticipation, half panic.

Gav's shaft flexed under the intensity of those glassy eyes.

The guy struggled out of the suit jacket, tossing it onto the bed in a heap. On the periphery of his vision, Gav saw it fall onto the bed and cover the worn leather briefcase the man had been carrying in the park.

The guy with the buzz-cut hair and the scared eyes was tugging at his tie now, trying to lever off his shoes at the same time. Gav could hear his breathing, ragged and shallow. He could see the outline of his cock, straining against the expensive, if old-fashioned, tailoring of the trousers.

Somewhere, in the distance, vague hoovering could be heard, and the sound of hotel-room doors opening and closing. Beyond that, the revs of engines, honking horns and the squeal of brakes.

Outside, London was stirring into life.

Within the four walls of an anonymous hotel room, time was standing still. The more hastily the suit tried to get out of his clothes, the more his fingers refused to obey him. The harder he tried to stay calm, the more they trembled and tripped over buttons and belt buckle.

And the more Gav's hard-on flexed.

But time was of the essence. Neither of them had all day. Gavin wandered over and covered the man's hands with his and eased them away. Taking the tongue of the guy's belt, he fed it back through the buckle, loosening it, then deftly unzipped him.

The suit's head lolled forward to lie on Gav's shoulder. His arms hung loosely by his sides.

As he lowered the guy's fly, the businessman's cock pulsed against his fingers. Unzipping him completely, Gav slipped his hand inside and hooked what he could of the jersey-sheathed length.

The guy's body shuddered.

Good and thick. Easing a thumb up and over the waistband of the knitted underpants, he slipped them down and allowed the man's cock to spring free. Gavin curled his fingers around the shaft

The suit's body shook violently. Lube and condoms tumbled to the floor and arms threw themselves around Gavin's neck.

He could feel every ridge and vein on the cock within his fist. Feel the way it pulsed against his palm. Feel more blood flee from the suit's business brain to swell the thick length further.

They stood there. A runner in jock and trainers. A businessman, white-shirted arms tight around the runner's shoulders, cock, warm and tacky, gripped in the runner's fist.

Then pressure on those shoulders. Gav went with it. Bare knees impacted with deep shag-pile. One hand still around the suit's prick, Gav's other fist slid down to the solid curve of the man's arse. The top of his head brushed against the guy's stomach.

The fingers on his shoulders splayed and tightened. A deep sigh echoed in the room as Gavin ran his fist down to the root of seven thick inches. He dragged the foreskin right back.

The cock in his hand flexed violently. He could smell the guy. A mixture of soap, sweat, fresh piss and the sour musky odour of arousal. Young guys had a sweeter, almost unripe scent. Like a good wine, men in their forties were tastier.

Stronger. More mature.

Somewhere around the suit's knees, Gav's own cock was leaking pre-come onto the mesh of the jock. He inhaled deeply, lips parting.

He tightened his fist around the root of the suit's shaft.

The suit trembled.

And, when Gav flicked his tongue over the guy's gaping slit, the body above him tried to smash itself against his face. Gripping the fabric of the guy's trousers, he held him steady and flicked again, drawing the clear liquid into his mouth and rolling it around.

The suit was panting now. Small sounds from deep in his throat filled Gav's ears.

He choked back a whimper of his own, dragging his tongue over the piss-slit again and licking it around the rim of the suit's thick velvety glans. He tilted his head, drawing the edge of his tongue along the channel of flesh, round to where the foreskin joined the head, then back around the other way.

In the distant recesses of his mind, Gav remembered the lube and condoms the suit had hastily purchased in the chemist's shop on their way to the hotel. As he slipped his lips over the engorged head of the man's cock, he vaguely wondered whether the guy had wanted to fuck him.

The gold band on the third finger of the suit's left hand pressed into the warm skin on Gav's right deltoid. Married men got enough of doling it out at home. More likely, the guy wanted Gavin up his arse. And, Gav had to admit, it was a hot prospect.

But sucking was faster.

Tightening his lips, he moved his mouth down to meet the curled fingers of his own fist, before sliding back up again. Gav splayed his fingers around the cock, reaching down with his pinkie to stroke the guy's heavy bollocks.

Faster than either of them knew.

The soft hairy skin clenched under the touch of Gav's smallest finger. The suit grunted, bucking with his hips. The sudden movement took him by surprise. Tacky with pre-come and the sweat from Gav's hand, the suit's shaft pushed up and out of his fist.

Gav gagged wildly, the head of the guy's flexing cock curving past his lips to impact with the sensitive flesh of his soft palate. His eyes watered. The guy's pubes smashed against his nose and cheeks.

Then he was sprawling backwards and the suit was astride him, pumping his cock between Gav's tight lips.

It took seconds – less than seconds. Both hands now on the man's thighs, Gav held on and opened his throat.

Fucking Gav's face in short, frenetic jabs, the suit roared his release. And Gav was choking for real. The cock in his mouth shuddered. One violent twitch later, hot spunk hit the back of his throat.

He couldn't taste it – too far back for taste. But he could feel it. Feel the hard mash of the suit's balls against his chin as the man astride his chest shot a second time.

The hot mass of spunk slid slowly down Gav's throat. He gripped the guy's thighs, head and shoulders, leaving the floor as his throat opened further.

Then two hands hit the floor, somewhere beyond Gav's face. Arms braced, head lolling down between hunched shoulders, the suit let the receding waves of orgasm roll through him.

Eyes open, cock still hard and itchy inside his jock, Gav stared up at the man's stomach and almost smiled.

The suit didn't ask his name. Gav had no need to ask his. The suit, a.k.a. Sir Norman Springfield, was married, with three grown-up children. He was also chairman of Springfield Electronics, down from company headquarters in Birmingham for secret merger talks with representatives of a Pacific Rim conglomerate.

No interviews. None of the media were even supposed to know Sir Norman was in London at all.

As the man hauled himself up and drew his softening cock out of Gav's mouth, Gavin eyed the briefcase, which now lay on the floor. Within, he knew were details of exactly what financial problems Springfield Electronics were facing – problems that Sir Norman's whisky consumption and habit of cruising Battersea Park in the early morning already hinted at. Problems that the editor of *Business Today* would pay highly for.

'Take a shower, if you want, son.' A gruff, Midlands accent coated the first words Sir Norman had uttered. Awkward words.

Gav levered himself onto one elbow. 'It's OK, I'm fine.' He watched the man step out of his trousers and go to toss them onto the bed.

He watched Sir Norman pause before thrusting thrust one hand into the pocket of those trousers and withdrawing a slim wallet. He almost laughed when Sir Norman Springfield withdrew two ten-pound notes and held them out uncertainly. Instead, he smiled and shook his head. 'But I will have that drink now.' He nodded to the three-quarters-empty whisky bottle.

The man's face flushed scarlet. 'On you go, um, er...' Sir Norman stuffed the money back into his wallet and kept hold of it. He threw rumpled trousers onto the bed and waved a vague arm towards the *en suite* bathroom. 'I'll just...' He began to loosen his tie, had more success this time.

Gav nodded, his eyes on the underarms of the guy's sweat-soaked shirt as he reached casually for the bottle. He knew Sir Norman wanted him out of here. He knew the guy was feeling that same guilty embarrassment he himself often felt after casual encounters. And Gavin had no intention of hanging around.

Blinking rapidly, Sir Norman turned and staggered off towards the bathroom. Gav waited until he heard the sound of the shower, then lunged for the briefcase.

No, no intention of hanging around. After he'd got what he'd come for.

# Two

'How's it going?'

Sitting at the kitchen table ten hours later, eyes fixed on the laptop's screen, Gavin Shaw was only vaguely aware of his boyfriend's hands on his shoulders. His fingers moved smoothly over the keyboard, typing in the final couple of sentences.

A sigh from somewhere above him, then, 'Can't you finish it tomorrow?'

Gav depressed a key, then brought up JPG files while the spellcheck flew through the two-thousand-word article on Springfield Electronics' financial problems.

The hands tightened on his shoulders. Gerry's lips brushed the top of his head.

Satisfied the picture files were adequate, Gavin activated the modem connection and leaned back in his chair. The familiar stream of digital tones filled the kitchen.

Gerry's hands slipped down, his arms curling around Gav's neck. 'You work too hard.'

Gavin laughed. 'Work hard, play harder, though, eh?' Tilting his head back, he looked up at the younger man.

The shadow of a frown crossed Gerald Nelson's handsome face. Gavin registered it. Pre-empting another inquisition, he raised one hand to stroke the man's back and changed the subject.

'How was your day?' A futures dealer with one of London's largest investment bankers, Gerry had a strictly eight-to-four job and clashed again and again with Gavin's less structured freelance activities.

Brown eyes rolled. 'Same old same old.'

Gavin winked. 'That same old same old pays the rent, though, eh?' A beep from the laptop told him the spellcheck had finished. Returning his attention to the screen, he closed the document, moved it into the same folder as the JPG files and sent the whole lot off to *Business World*'s editor – he glanced at his wrist – a good three hours under the deadline.

Another sigh from behind. 'Gavin?'

Work finished, he flipped off the laptop and ran large hands up Gerry's arms. 'What, hot stuff?' Pushing the chair back, he stood up and turned.

Gerry's expression was sombre. 'Are you happy?'

Gavin grinned and nodded behind to the article on screen. 'If this bastard pays me on time, I'll be delirious.' Palms stroking the rounded swell of Gerry's deltoids, he moved his hands on up and over the man's shoulders.

'That's not what I mean.' Gerry tried to hold Gav's eyes.

Gavin ducked the attempt, leaning forward to nuzzle the smooth neck. His hands came to rest on the hard muscle of Gerry's Stairmaster-tightened arse.

'Are you happy – with us?'

Gavin bit back a sigh. The man he'd been sleeping with for six months, living with for the past two, was not about to let the subject drop. He dragged his tongue up towards Gerry's right ear.

What was there not to be happy with? The Kensington muse house was luxury incarnate. Gav kept his small office-cum-bedsit in King's Cross going for tax reasons, but Gerry's place was much more pleasant to work in. He had it to himself most of the day. And he genuinely liked the handsome twenty-eight-year-old.

If Gavin had decided to settle down, after all these years – and, as far as he was concerned, this *was* settling down – it might as well be with someone like Gerry.

'Gavin?'

He heard the worry in the man's voice. The doubt that was always there. Splaying his fingers over the solid muscle of Gerry's arse, Gavin drew the man's crotch against his. His lips brushed a warm earlobe. 'Course I'm happy, hot stuff.'

Gerry stiffened in his hands. 'I wish you wouldn't call me that.'

'Why?' Gavin laughed and kissed the side of the sleek blond head.

'It makes me feel like...'

He heard the hesitation. He knew what was coming. And wanted to avoid it.

Just as the words 'like a piece of meat' formed on Gerry's lips, Gav dragged his head from the man's neck and covered those lips with his. Inside his jeans, his cock flexed. Hauling Gerry's crotch against his, he held him there, grinding his half-hard-on against the other man's.

Gerry moaned and returned the kiss, the doubts momentarily dispelled. And, as the futures dealer's eyelids slowly closed, Gav knew it was safe to open his.

He deepened the kiss, widening Gerry's lips with his and feeling his own cock harden further. Blood fled from his brain, pumping straight to his crotch.

Gerry's cock pulsed, parallel to his.

Gav pushed his tongue into the man's mouth. Gerry sucked on it, feeding on him, his arms now tight around Gavin's neck.

Gav's fingers were moving on the man's arse, massaging, kneading, feeling the clench of muscle. Feeling Gerry push back into his hands, then thrust forward to drag his erection against Gavin's. His mind flashed momentarily back to earlier that day, and Sir Norman Springfield's suit-clad arse. Gav's eyes narrowed.

Sometimes he got the impression he was just going through the motions. Marking time. It was all so easy. All of it.

The sex was there for the taking – either with Gerry or with any of countless others. His reputation as a freelance journalist was firmly established, and the assignments came regularly.

Work. Fuck. Work. Fuck.

Gerry's lips were warm and urgent under his, and so Gavin pushed these thoughts away. Then he was moving, walking the man backwards. Past the expensively fitted kitchen and its dozen state-of-the-art gadgets, across the quarry-tiled floor, passing though the doorway, his bare feet cold on the polished beech, which was fitted throughout the rest of the house. Still kissing, still watching, Gavin manoeuvred Gerry backwards down the hall to the bedroom.

If it had been up to him, he'd have made Gerry take him there and then, over his precious butcher's-block table, surrounded by bottles of balsamic vinegar and extra-virgin olive oil.

But Gerry wasn't into fucking. Gerry liked to suck. Either in a bed or on one, at that. So that was what Gerry got. His palms cupping the hard cheeks of the man's arse, his lips never breaking the kiss, Gav glanced briefly at the alarm clock, seconds before he felt the back of Gerry's legs impact with the edge of the futon.

It was 7.03 p.m.

They could still be at James's by eight, easily. His tongue deep in the man's mouth, his erection itchy and throbbing against an equally needy length, Gav bucked with his hips. And they both fell back onto the bed. Gerry grabbed Gavin's T-shirt, struggling to haul it up over his chest and shoulders without breaking the kiss.

Gav's fingers dived straight down between their twined bodies, to the fly of his own jeans. He hurriedly unzipped.

As Gerry hauled his T-shirt up, Gav wriggled one, then both, arms free of it. The garment hung around his neck in folds.

A sudden frisson shook his strong, sinewy body.

Gav ignored it, rolling onto his back and breaking the kiss. His head hit fine linen-encased pillows. He grinned up, bare feet planted firmly on the bed and knees raised. Lifting his arse from the two-thousand-pound Osaka-manufactured futon, Gav dragged his jeans down over hips and thighs.

Apart from the jock for running, he never wore underwear. He enjoyed the way, when he got hard during the day, the rough denim rasped against his stretching cock. And he liked the time it saved, as far as a quickie was concerned, if he wasn't wearing briefs.

The futon dipped as, kneeling on the bed, Gerry elbowed his way out of the Armani jacket and leaned forward to kiss Gav's nipples.

Gavin arched his back and ran one hand down his shaft, stroking himself a couple of times. The fingers of his other hand edged to the folds of semi-sloughed T-shirt, still around his neck. The looped, crumpled garment was far from tight. It wasn't even heavy. But something about the way it lay against his throat shot an unexpected frisson into his balls.

Then Gerry was mumbling something, easing his way between Gavin's splayed thighs and covering the head of his cock with firm lips.

Gav's back arched again. One fist still around the lower half of his shaft, he pushed the first two inches into Gerry's eager mouth.

Gerry's arms slipped under Gav's thighs, curling around them as his tongue flicked around the swollen, purple glans.

Fingers stroked his thighs. The tongue flicked on, the lips moved down slowly, impacting with the ring of Gavin's thumb and forefinger.

The lips nuzzled, tightened briefly before beginning their glide back up to the head of his cock.

Gav moaned. He rolled his hips, his pinkie and ring finger stretching down to caress his own balls. Lying there, he stared at the ceiling, focused on the tiny inset pin spots that bathed the room in diffuse light.

Gerry dragged his mouth up Gav's cock – tightening, then

relaxing, his lips and trailing the taut foreskin up to the edge of the sensitive glans.

Lips glided over the swollen wedge of blood-engorged flesh, widening, then sliding together and off.

Gav winced, his fist moving up and down his shaft in short, rapid strokes. He bucked with his hips, wanting the mouth back. Wanting it fast. Wanting it hard.

Wanting it now.

Arms curled around Gavin's thighs, Gerry moaned, inhaled and breathed on the sensitive head.

Gavin roared. Warm air drifted over his gaping slit. Something deep in his arse spasmed wildly. He released his shaft and sank a hand into Gerry's expertly cut hair.

The man rebelled beneath his grasp.

Gavin scowled and held on. Changing position on the bed, he raised his head and shoulders, looking down at the figure who struggled between his legs. One hand on Gerry's head, the other holding the noose of T-shirt around his own neck, Gav tightened his grip on both.

Gerry moaned.

Gav battered the head of his cock against closed lips. The breath caught in his own chest. He torqued his fingers in the folds of the T-shirt, winding the fabric around his fist and drawing it up around his throat.

Something clenched in his arse. Gavin moaned, dropping back down onto the bed, the head of his cock bumping and sliding over Gerry's tightly closed lips. Gav squeezed his eyes shut and clawed at Gerry's scalp.

A gasp from between his legs was all the signal he needed.

Gav drove his cock between pain-parted lips and smothered Gerry's cry of discomfort. Then they were both moaning. Gav fucked the mouth hard and fast, using Gerry's hair to drag the man's lips up and down his shaft. His cock flexed. His balls clenched hard.

Somewhere, down the other end of the futon, he knew Gerry had unzipped himself and was stroking his own cock furiously.

His mind zoomed in on Gerry's cock. The feel of it. The thickness of it. In his mouth. In his arse.

But when Gav came, seconds later, eyelids squeezed shut and the collar of sweat-soaked jersey bound around his throat, Gerry was a million miles away.

'James!'

Two hours later, Gerry flushed and smiling in another Armani suit identical to the one he'd come all over, Gavin sauntered across the large room towards their host.

The older man in the well-cut but casual jacket slowly turned, wineglass in hand. A small smile creased the rugged face. 'Well, well – decided to grace us with your presence after all, I see.'

Gav grinned. 'You remember Gerald?' He steered the City trader forward, noting Gerry's eyes sweep the room with undisguised awe. He himself could take or leave James's parties: these days the guy was a business contact, nothing more. Gerry, on the other hand – owing to some puerile fascination with what he saw as a glamorous demiworld – had been nagging him all week about coming.

'Yes – good to see you again, Gerald.' The commissioning editor of *Financial Week* extended a blunt-fingered hand.

Gerry grabbed it with both of his. 'Thanks for asking us, Mr Delany.' He shook the hand vigorously, his enthusiasm palpable.

From behind the babbling form of his present lover, Gavin rolled his eyes at one of his former.

'James, please.' Ever the suave host, James ignored Gav and began to talk to Gerry about his work, complimenting him on the Armani and offering him wine.

Gavin frowned and grabbed a glass for himself from a passing waiter. As he lounged back against a wall, his eyes followed ex and present enamourati as James introduced a, by now, speechless-with-joy Gerry to various media celebrities, including the fashion editor of *Vanity Fair*, the guy from the new *CKOne* campaign and two Spice Girls plus husbands-of-the-moment.

Same old same old.

Gav drained his glass, accepted another from a pretty girl with a shaved head who flirted with him for a while before he wandered off in search of more stimulating company. He cadged a cigarette from an older man, whom he recognised vaguely as someone in films. The journalist in him was sparked, but James had strict rules about his social gatherings.

No business. Only pleasure.

For the next hour or so, Gavin prowled the room. He made faces. Faces made him. From time to time he caught sight of one particular face, now flushed and ecstatic. James had vanished, having left Gerry in the capable hands of Channel 5's new weather girl, who was giggling and hanging on the few words the overwhelmed futures dealer managed to form.

Part of him was pleased for the guy. Gerry worked hard and deserved something in return from Gav, considering what Gavin got from him. But another part was restless. Always restless.

Same old same old.

Despite the fact he'd come less than two hours earlier, a nagging tension refused to leave his body. Despite the fact that, as a freelance journalist, he felt that this was his arena and was at home here, he couldn't settle to anything more than a few half-hearted sentences of conversation. The room was too hot. Too busy. He didn't want another drink. Despite the lavish spread of food, he wasn't hungry.

The smell of too much cologne was making his throat hurt. Swapping his wine for mineral water, Gavin strolled out onto the terrace of James Delany's Wimbledon mansion.

The cool night air was a welcome touch in his hot face. Behind, the buzz of conversation and the tinkle of glasses faded. One hand resting on top of the stone balustrade, he gazed out over the large, walled garden and sucked in the peace and seclusion.

James's job as commissioning editor of one of the UK's leading financial magazines didn't go anywhere near paying for all this. In fact, James had no need to work at all: he came from money. His mother had been some sort of minor aristocrat, and when his parents had died this house plus the grounds, on top of a portfolio shares and options, which he managed as expertly as he managed the rest of his life, had come to James.

Gavin threw back his head and took a deep breath. The scent of mimosa and jasmine drifted into his nose.

James liked to control everything – in bed and out of it. Eight years ago, Gavin had spent some time in that bed. Too much time.

'Wondered where you'd got to.'

'Gerry OK?' Gavin didn't turn.

'Do you care?' There was a little reprimand in James's calm voice.

'I care enough to ask, don't I?' Gavin laughed and braced himself for the usual lecture.

'You know what I'm talking about.' It came, right on cue.

Gav sighed. James was so predictable. It was all so drearily predictable.

'Why him – why Gerry?'

'Why not?' Gavin shrugged. 'I like him – he likes me. We're great in bed.'

'Does he know?'

The casualness of his previous response faded. 'He knows.' Or, at least, had a sneaking suspicion Gav was far from anything that could be considered faithful.

'And he's OK with your... little peccadilloes?'

Gav's hand tightened on the stone balustrade. He tilted the

glass to his mouth and took a long drink of the mineral water. Lying to James was pointless – always had been.

From behind, a sigh.

Gavin stood there, fingering the stem of his glass. He listened to the soft slap of leathered sole on marble as James slowly made his way across the terrace.

'Every couple of months there's a new one, Gav. You collect men like other people collect frequent-flier points.' His ex stopped just behind him. 'I worry about you.'

'Me?' Gavin laughed. 'I'm fine.' He stared out over the expertly maintained garden and tried to ignore the way the mere proximity of the man could still make his cock hard.

'Then do the decent thing: get rid of that poor fool Gerry before you break his heart. He's totally enamoured of you, you know.'

Gav knew. He moved closer to the balustrade, pressing his groin against the hard flat stone and enjoying the sensation of it against his hardening prick.

'Stop messing up his life and take a long look at your own.'

He was aware of movement behind him. In seconds James was standing side on to him, staring at him with those oddly unsettling grey eyes.

'You know what I'm saying.' Gav continued to focus on the garden. 'Your work doesn't stretch you and you're not happy with Gerry – you've never been happy with any of this long line of boyfriends you move in with, whose lives you take over and dominate for as long as it suits you to do so.'

He laughed, but it was hollow, even to his own ears.

'That damned running is such an obvious metaphor, Gav.'

'I run to stay in shape.' His laughter faded until only a forced smile remained. 'You never got over the fact I wouldn't wear your stupid collar, did you?' They'd been here before, many times.

James smiled. 'There are all sorts of collars.' Gav frowned. More word games. The guy had kinky sex on the brain. Gavin, on the other hand, merely possessed a healthy sex drive. 'Some are there, whether we like it or not.'

Why couldn't James understand that for some people – and Gav counted himself firmly among their number – a fuck was just a fuck? And that was all James Delany had ever been. 'Leave it, Jim.' He injected a warning note into his voice. It was ignored.

'Tell me you're at peace with yourself, then.' A hand gripped Gavin's chin, forcing his head round. Odd grey eyes bored into his. 'Tell me you're not looking for something more and I'll never mention it again.'

Gavin's cock flexed violently. He scowled, wrenching himself free of the grip and moving back. 'I'll tell you something for nothing.' He glared at the man with whom, eight years ago, he'd enjoyed an interesting, if unnerving, three-month fling.

'Nothing's for nothing, Gavin – you know that.' The retort was soft but no less insightful.

He was fully erect now. And twice as irritated. The glare hardened into a scowl.

They stood there, three feet apart. James's rugged face was completely calm. Only those odd grey eyes showed any sign of emotion.

Irritation exploded into outright anger. Gavin had never wanted to hit anyone as much as he wanted to hit James now. 'My life is just fine the way it is.' Fists clenched at his sides, he spat the words at the infuriatingly unruffled face.

James held his gaze, a soft smile playing around his lips.

Then Gavin turned and strode away in search of Gerry.

# Three

'She's pregnant again – can you believe it?'

Through the taxi's back window, Gav watched James Delany's smart Wimbledon mansion recede into the distance. He scowled, trying to screen out Gerry. His balls were sweating. His cock dragged against the fly of his trousers.

'We're sworn to secrecy, of course, so keep it to yourself – the tabloids, you know. They'd kill to find out.'

Gav turned and slumped down. On the seat beneath his arse, vibrations from the engine hardened him further. He tried to will Gerry to shut up.

'I wonder if they'll give this one a stupid name, too!' Gerry babbled on, the wine and the thrill of an evening's hobnobbing evident in the loudness of his voice.

Gav caught the driver's eyes in the rear-view mirror. The guy winked. Gav's cock flexed violently. The scowl smoothed itself out into a frown.

'He gives great' – Gerry giggled – 'parties, does your James.'

Gav snorted. 'He's not *my* James.' He eyed the flushed heap of futures trader by his side.

Gerry continued to giggle. 'Whose James is he now, by the way? I didn't see any boyfriend around.'

Gavin could practically hear the taxi driver's ears straining. And something else was straining. Engorging. Pushing itself up towards the waistband of his trousers.

'Must be someone,' Gerry went on. 'He's a good-looking guy.

And that house!'

Stuff James Delany. Stuff the house.

'Not short of a bob or too, either. He's got to be the catch of the century.'

Stuff the money. And the man. Gavin's cock flexed again.

'So – who *is* keeping James warm at night, these days?'

Gerry's voice was an insect that wouldn't stop buzzing around his head. 'Who gives a flying fuck?' Gav's voice was louder than he intended. Catching the taxi driver's eye again, he glowered. The driver looked hurriedly away.

Gerry sighed contentedly and reached for Gavin's hand. 'I'm glad.'

Gav stared at the man but allowed his fingers to be squeezed.

'He's very charismatic – I wouldn't blame you if you still carried a torch for him.' The voice was soft, full of grape-induced sentiment.

An invisible fist grabbed Gavin's stomach muscles and twisted them savagely. 'The only torch in my hand is the one I'll use after I douse the bastard in petrol!'

Gerry laughed. Gav felt the blond head settle down against his shoulder. 'Ah, no – I only have eyes for you, baby. You know that.' Gav felt the soft fingers tighten around his. 'You've nothing to be jealous about – James isn't my type at all.'

Gav almost laughed. So like Gerry to get hold of the wrong end of the stick.

'Those weird grey eyes give me the creeps, if I'm honest – I bet you never really know what he's thinking.'

As the taxi slowed, Gavin was less concerned about James Delany's thoughts and more and more preoccupied with the fact he was still hard. And that James's voice still circled in his head.

They got as far as the kitchen. Gerry was halfway to the Gaggia when Gav grabbed him from behind.

A giggle. 'Whoa, tiger!' The blond head turned, lips parted for a kiss.

Gav's mouth was a hard line. His hands tightened on Gerry's hip bones. He dragged the man back against him, grinding his aching cock against two layers of immaculate suiting.

Gerry grunted, then slurred. 'Lemme put the coffee on, baby.'

Gav pushed one hand down between the Armani-clad legs. His fingers cupped cock and heavy balls.

Gerry yelp-giggled and staggered, widening his stance. His own hands moved up, settling around Gav's neck.

Gavin's forehead impacted with a shoulder. He bent his knees a little. Eyes open and watching, he re-angled his body and pushed himself up between two Stairmaster-hardened arsecheeks.

Two low groans echoed in the state-of-the-art kitchen.

Gav bucked hard against the younger man. Gerry moaned, losing his balance and toppling forward. Hands flew from behind Gav's neck, arms bracing against a marble worktop to break the fall.

Gavin followed, one hand still on a hipbone. The other was fumbling with a belt buckle. Vague drunken mumbles drifted up from the man in front of him. All Gav could hear was the thump of blood in his head. All he knew was the slightly irritating frisson that tingled deep in his balls every time his cockhead dragged up between Gerry's arsecheeks. He wanted more. He needed more. And he needed it now.

'Gavin, oh, Gavin!' Despite all that I-don't-do-fucking stuff, Gerry was pushing back, moving his hips in small circles. A veil of Toni-and-Guy-styled hair hid his face, head lolling between braced shoulders.

'Fuck!' Gav cursed at the belt buckle, then managed to get the tongue loose. Fingers snatched at buttons. Then the rip of zipper lowered.

A gasp from the worktop.

Gav wrenched the Armani suit trousers down roughly. Calvins next. With one hand now up under Gerry's shirt and fingers round a pink nipple, the other was tearing at his own fly. Then they were both standing there, trousers around their knees, and Gav was watching seven inches of hard, angry cock push itself between two pale rounded arsecheeks.

'Bedroom.' The word was low and mumbled.

Gavin stared at his own dick as if it belonged to someone else. He watched the foreskin peel back further as Gerry's arsecheeks quivered and clenched. Someone was moaning. He knew it was himself.

'Bedroom, baby.'

The body in front of his was still moving. But differently. Trying to turn. Trying not to turn. Wanting it. Not wanting it. But wanting it really. Afraid to experiment. Afraid to say yes, but not wanting to say no.

Gavin inhaled sharply as his cock slipped from where it wanted to be, the sensitive head shuddering over a pale, hairless cheek. He frowned, hands leaving those hipbones. Grabbing Gerry's shoulders, Gav pushed down hard.

A grunt. Then more movement. And more sound:

'Listen, Gavin. Please. Come on, baby, let's go to bed and we can—'

Gav shoved Gerry forward. Gerry moaned, a little too loudly, as Gav clamped a hand over the younger guy's open mouth. His other arm was now braced against the Italian marble worktop. He could feel its cool flawlessness under his sweating palm. With one kick, he widened Gerry's stance further and pushed his thighs between the man's legs.

Holding him there with the weight of his body, Gav found himself biting the back of Gerry's neck. He thrust on, knees behind knees. He used his foot to push Calvins and Armani down further, dipping his body and feeling the crinkled rosette of Gerry's arsehole against his thrusting shaft.

Gav's right hand was sliding on Italian marble. The palm of his left was hot and wet with Gerry's moans. He closed his hands and dipped lower, dragging the entire length of his cock up the moist, lightly haired furrow. And on the way back down, he let the sensitive head linger on the tightly clenched entrance to Gerry's body.

He didn't stop. He couldn't stop. He didn't want to stop.

They were both moving. Gerry was pushing – pushing back. Gav gasped at the friction, the inside of his eyelids red and spidery. He managed to move one hand from the worktop. Raising it to his lips, he hawked up saliva into a dry mouth, then spat. Gav slid his hand between their bodies. His own wet fingers brushed his own cock. Then the lubricated pad of an index finger was pressing against Gerry's hole. Gavin moaned. The head of his cock was leaking pre-come against the swell of the man's arse. He moved his hand, catching some of the clear liquid, and rubbed the twice-wet finger over Gerry's hole.

Gerry bucked and Gav's shaft jerked abruptly. He groaned, squeezing his eyelids shut. His balls were heavy and sore, drawn up tautly at the root of his aching prick.

Pain shot through the fingers of his other hand. Somewhere, on the periphery of all the thrusting and the moaning and the grinding and the needing, Gav was aware that Gerry had just bitten him – in passion. For a change. James Delany's taunt refused to leave Gav's head: 'Tell me you're not looking for something more and I'll never mention it again.' Gavin clenched his teeth and rammed a finger into the body of the man he had pinned to the Italian marble worktop. He was thrusting against Gerry's arsecheek now, dragging his cock over the solid, smooth flesh.

He was happy. He loved Gerry. Gerry loved him. He was happy.

Gav barely felt the warmth inside the other man's body. He barely felt the tightness.

He had what he needed. He had Gerry. Gerry had him.

Then fingers grabbed his wrist, tearing his hand away from its position over a now-protesting mouth:

'Stop it! Stop it!'

As Gerry heaved backward, Gav lost his balance and fell. Eyelids flew open. As his spine hit imported terracotta tiling, his balls clenched and he howled, shooting his load into the air. Warm spunk splattered over his own face. He lay there, mouth contorted in release, staring up at Gerry.

'I'm sorry, sweet stuff. I'm so sorry!' Later, in bed, Gavin curled Gerry in against him and stroked his hair. 'I don't know what got into me.' It was the alcohol. He'd had too much to drink, that was it.

Arms tightened around his waist. 'It's OK.' The mouth that had bitten his hand now kissed his chest.

'No, it's not OK.' Gavin sighed. Maybe someone had slipped something into his drink. Maybe it was the atmosphere at the party. Cigarette smoke and noise always put him on edge.

'Shh.' Gerry kissed a nipple. Then half-chuckled. 'You know something?'

Maybe he'd been working too hard. That could be it.

'Gavin?'

'Hmmm?'

Gav watched as the head on his chest tilted itself up. He stared into blue eyes.

'Um...' Gerry blushed slightly. 'It, um, feels sort of good to know you, um, want me so much.'

An icy hand clutched at his guts.

'I mean, I was interested, sure, but I was bloody terrified at the time, too – you know I've never been fucked, yes?'

The icy hand tightened, twisting Gavin's entrails into ropy knots.

'But' – Gerry hauled himself up the bed, nestling back in

against Gavin's shoulder – 'baby, I love you. And I want to show how much I love you.'

Gav was glad he no longer had to look into those open, guileless eyes. He felt Gerry take a deep breath. Then pause.

'And if you, um, want to fuck me, you can.'

Gav groaned and folded this beautiful, stupid man into his arms. What could he say? How could he tell Gerry that what had happened in the kitchen had nothing to do with love? And everything to do with something he couldn't quite put a name to.

He woke, six hours later, to an empty bed and the sound of his mobile. Gavin groaned, rolling into the still-warm space Gerry had left. Last night was fading, a fuzzy memory helped on its way to further fuzziness by the sun, which streamed through the bedroom window.

The phone rang on.

Gav sighed, reaching out an arm to paw at the bedside table. 'Shaw – yeah?' As he clamped the Nokia to his ear, his eyes fell on a neatly written note that had been secured in place beneath the cellphone: 'See you tonight. Love you.'

He groaned.

The caller laughed.

Gav inhaled sharply, immediately recognising the sound. 'What is it, James?'

'And a good morning to you, too!' The voice laughed again.

Gavin dragged himself upright, leaning back against the bed head. 'What do you want?' This was the last person he felt like speaking to.

'Got a bit of work thought might be up your street, but if I'm interrupting anything…' James Delany tailed off, deliberately. The silence was loaded with meaning.

Gav snorted. 'You're not interrupting anything. Go on.' Work was work, and, as commissioning editor of *Financial Week*, James was a valuable contact.

'Good.' The voice smiled. 'How much do you know about' – a pause – 'Derek Masters?'

Gav bit back a 'who?' and searched the recesses of his brain for something intelligent to say. 'The banker?' It was a fair guess that Masters would be involved somewhere in matters fiscal.

'Banker. Investor. Entrepreneur. Millionaire businessman. Philanthropist playboy. Take your pick.'

Gav smiled. Another Richard Branson type. 'OK, so what's the deal?'

'Two thousand words initially. Deadline fifteenth of July, so you've got plenty of time. Depending on what you dig up, we can maybe run to a couple of issues on it. Take your fancy?'

Work was work. Regular work was a foot in the door at one of the UK's top financial magazines, with the potential for worldwide syndication. 'What's the angle?'

In an office somewhere off Fleet Street, James Delany chuckled knowingly. 'You tell me, Gavin. Masters has more fingers in more pies than there are pie sellers! And I think you're just the journalist to let the world see the man behind the public image, as it were.'

He grabbed his notebook and pen, cradling the cellphone between chin and shoulder. 'You mean there is one?' Masters, Masters – he knew the name, definitely. Gavin wrote DEREK MASTERS on the notepad in capital letters, and circled it.

'Well, that's what we'll be paying you to find out, my friend.'

The million-dollar question. 'How much?'

James's laugh was rich and genuine. 'Always looking to the buck, eh, Gavin?'

Gav rolled his eyes to the sun-filled bedroom. 'Guy's gotta make a living, right?'

'Thought all your money worries would be over, with your... sugar daddy there paying all the bills.'

Gav frowned. He'd just about had it with James and these bloody games. 'Give me a figure.'

'OK, OK – how does fifteen hundred sound?'

Above NUJ rates, but Gavin had the feeling there was going to be a catch somewhere: with James, there always was. 'Plus expenses?'

The voice at the other end sighed. 'Plus expenses.'

Gavin grinned. 'Half upfront.'

'Five hundred.'

'A third upfront.'

A laugh. 'Six hundred?'

Gavin was laughing too now. 'Deal! So that's two thousand words on Derek Masters, deadline fifteenth of July, and that six hundred's in my account by the end of work tomorrow.'

'You drive a hard bargain.'

'You wouldn't have it any other way, pal.' Gav circled the name 'Derek Masters' a third time.

'True.' The voice was unexpectedly soft. 'You're worth the struggle, Gavin. You always were.'

He frowned. The moment was ruined. Well, fuck James bloody Delany. Work was work: he would interview this Masters character, get photos from his press office, do a quick bit of background, then dash off the article in a couple of days, no problem. Money for old rope.

'If you could let me see an early draft, that would be great.' The voice was back to its usual, businesslike self.

'Fine.' Gav reached pushed the duvet back and slung his legs over the side of the bed. Naked, he wandered through to the kitchen. 'I'll have it with you – what, Monday of next week?'

'Excellent!'

The Gaggia was still warm. Gavin took a tiny espresso cup from the rack and wandered over. 'OK, thanks for thinking of me, James.'

The voice as good as smiled. 'I'm always thinking of you, Gavin.' His hand shook slightly.

'Oh, one thing you should probably know,' James said. Gav paused. 'Derek Masters doesn't give interviews, so you'll need to be... resourceful. Talk to you later!'

Before he could answer, James had ended the call. Gavin stood there, forehead creased. He'd known there would be a catch. No interviews? Well, he liked a challenge.

Three espressos later and fuelled on pure caffeine, he was still in the kitchen. Now dressed in sweats and trainers, he sat in front of his laptop. After typing the name 'Derek Masters' into the fourth search engine, he leaned back in his chair and sipped thoughtfully while his machine processed the information.

Whatever else Derek Masters might be, he was no Richard Branson – and he really didn't give interviews: a quick phone call two hours ago to the press office at Masters Industries had confirmed that.

'We can send you a press pack, of course,' some menial lackey had offered.

He'd said yes, of course: every little helped. And the press pack had duly arrived – by courier – half an hour ago. Despite the dry uninteresting prose, what he'd managed to glean from reading between the lines of Masters' 'authorised biography' at his organisation's online sites had more than intrigued him.

The guy was of dual British–Latvian parentage.

Gav glanced at the atlas he'd dug out from Gerry's library. Baltic state – that in itself was unusual. Small state: one of those countries everyone from the Goths to the Russians had tramped through, at one time or another. War-torn for centuries, Latvia was now self-governing, apparently, and keen to become part of the European Union: it had even won the Eurovision Song Contest, last year.

The dual citizenship had to be handy, allowing Masters the

advantages of a British passport.

His eyes flicked back to the screen: the site was still loading. Gav glanced at his watch: peak time for US usage of the Net. He sighed and tried to be patient, turning his attention back to his notepad.

He had no idea what age Masters was. Gav picked up the glossy press brochure and peered at the distinguished-looking silver-haired guy on the front. That hair colour could be premature – or dyed – but Masters could be anything from a gnarled early forties to a sprightly mid-sixties. No date of birth appeared anywhere – and Gavin had accessed Somerset House, searched from 1940 to 1960. The guy had a passport, but as yet Gav had not acquired the knack of hacking into Immigration.

In fact, there was nothing on the man's early years at all. When he'd been born, where, to whom: the first mention of Derek Masters anywhere was back in the early 1980s.

One of Thatcher's success stories, apparently.

Gav chuckled, and flicked through the press pack again.

Masters was divorced – so that meant he'd been married. Masters had spent nine years in the army – although whether this was the British or the Latvian army (did Latvia even have an army?) Gavin had no clue. He yawned and stretched, debating something to eat or maybe a run

Finally, the results of his search settled on the laptop's screen. And suddenly running and eating were the last things on Gavin Shaw's mind. Eyes glued to the list of hypertexted links, he grabbed a pen and began to scribble.

It was another two hours before he stopped.

Gavin smiled smugly.

Well, well, well! It was all there, on the Net. If you knew where to look. Derek Masters had a criminal record. At least *a* Derek Masters did: Gavin would have to do me research to establish if it was the same Masters. But the dates looked about right.

Between 1972 and 1975, a Derek Masters had been a guest of Her Majesty, at Manchester's Strangeways prison. The three-year sentence had been clarified, following a quick look at the court records for the Greater Manchester area, for 1971–2.

The laptop had crashed before he could get much further, but at least he'd seen the words 'found guilty of murder' seconds before the screen had dissolved into a mess of blurry pixels. On re-booting, the machine had steadfastly refused to allow him to return to that site.

Murder. Not manslaughter. Murder. And it got better.

Just when Gavin was wondering how on earth Masters Industries' spin doctors had managed to bury this little nugget, the brief three-year sentence was explained.

Hidden away in the Stockport *Evening News* quite considerable archive, Gavin found a report that detailed how on Monday, 14th July 1975, the court's verdict had been overturned on appeal. Derek Masters' twenty-five-year sentence for murder had been quashed. His name had been cleared and he'd walked away a free man.

Five years after that, Masters Industries had been first floated on the stock market.

Gavin licked his lips.

Accessing the archives of *Hello!* magazine, *Time* and *Vanity Fair*, he found that, during the eighties and nineties, Derek Masters had been in with movers and shakers the world over. Cannes, St Tropez, the Hamptons, Malibu beach – the list was endless. He rubbed shoulders with movie stars, dined with maverick artists and attended charity functions with everyone from Shirley MacLean to Francis Bacon.

He'd known the rogue trader Nick Leeson. He'd shaken hands with Jacques Chirac. There was even a photograph of Masters with a sobbing Raisa Gorbachev, at the funeral of some Soviet official or another.

And running through it all was a sense that there was more to this. Far more.

Gavin rubbed his investigative journalist's nose. It had never let him down in the past. It was telling him something now. Beneath the glossy image of self-made man and international playboy, behind the smiles and the beautiful women and the large contributions to various charities, there was something else.

Something slippery. Something darker. Something not quite kosher. Something that Gavin knew he was going to enjoy tracking down.

Gavin was still sitting at his laptop when Gerry returned later that afternoon.

# Four

The evening passed in a blur.

Gerry had reserved a table at some eatery or other. Gavin ate and smiled and nodded over fine French food he barely tasted. Then he took Gerry home and held his head while Gerry sucked his cock and wanked himself off. They both fell into a deep, dreamless sleep, tangled around each other.

It was always the same when he had an assignment. It was all he could think about. Everything else was going through the motions – and, if he was honest, Gavin had to admit he went through the motions very well. Lying beside the still lightly snoring man at 5 a.m., his mind was clear and purposeful.

He'd already started a file on Derek Masters, and had almost enough material for two thousand words. But, before he began writing the article, Gavin knew he had to do one thing.

It was something he always did, if he was profiling. Regardless of his subject. Regardless of whether they did or did not give interviews. Regardless of whether they were the business world's equivalent of Howard Hughes.

He had to see them in the flesh. Whether it was a civilised dinner, a blow job in a hotel or a glimpse caught from the branches of a tree over a twelve-foot electric fence, Gavin always found soaking up the physical reality of a subject greatly enhanced any article he was writing.

When he'd done the piece on skeletoning, for *Sports Illustrated*, he'd managed to find a skeletoning track in east

London and sample it for himself. For the feature on single mothers in Cockfosters, he'd shadowed a local social worker for a week.

And, whether or not Derek Masters would agree to talk to him, Gavin knew he at least had to see the headquarters of Masters Industries in London's Docklands. Having done that, he could dash the first draft off tonight and tomorrow, and have it on James's desk by the end of the week.

Easing himself away from the sleeping Gerry, Gavin slid out of bed.

But first, a run. And where better to run than down by the river?

The roads along the Embankment were already busy with commuter traffic. The pavements were going the same way. Dressed in T-shirt and shorts, with his cellphone nestling against his right side and his voice-activated micro tape recorder against the other – in case inspiration gripped him, at any point – Gavin jogged lightly between men in bowler hats with briefcases heading past him towards Westminster. But Father Thames was his quiet, stately self. The odd scow made its languid way downriver, but otherwise the ancient waterway was quiet.

As he ran, the sun rose further in the sky, warming the air. London in the summer (Gavin turned his head to enjoy the well-muscled forearms of a young road sweeper) – some people hated it. He'd always loved it. He ran on, breathing in the smell of the city. Long hot days and sultry evenings. The haze of smog, which the sun would burn off later, still hung in the air around him.

His mind turned to Derek Masters. What was he doing at six o'-clock on a fine summer's morning? Where did the guy even live? A penthouse somewhere, maybe? Some stately Georgian pile, like James's place in Wimbledon? Or a converted mews house like Gerry's in classy Kensington?

Where a man chose to live spoke volumes about him.

He thought about his own office-cum-bedsit, up in less than salubrious King's Cross: what did that say about Gavin Shaw? He chuckled. When they'd briefly been an item, James had called him an emotional transient, citing the futon couch in a third-floor office in an unrenovated building just along from one of London's biggest stations as proof.

Gavin grinned, meeting the eyes of a passing suit. Held snug inside his jock, his cock twitched at the wordless message. But today he was a man with a mission – and that mission was to recce Masters Industries. Maintaining a leisurely pace, he followed the river east. A cool breeze from the water ruffled his thick dark hair. He hadn't broken sweat yet. Gavin rarely did. His daily runs fulfilled a variety of purposes, only one of which was keeping him in shape.

Tower Bridge loomed just ahead. The hooter of a larger vessel sounded just beyond the famous ancient structure. Gavin jogged on, knowing the more modern but equally well-known buildings of Canary Wharf would soon fill the skyline.

Where ships from all over the world had once disgorged their cargo was now home to the corporate cut and thrust of the capital's economic giants. Many of the big newspapers had their offices here, too. It seemed vaguely ironic that Canary Wharf also housed the headquarters of someone who studiously refused to give interviews.

Something vibrated softly, in its holder under his T-shirt. Gavin frowned – maybe he was due a break anyway. Slowing, he hauled out his mobile and pressed it to his ear. 'Shaw here.'

'Good morning.'

Gav slowed further, walking now. 'Good morning to you – not cancelling my assignment, I hope?'

A laugh. 'Not at all – just phoning to let you know our account department has okayed your advance. It'll be in your bank by close of business today.'

He smiled. 'Ah, cheers – it's appreciated.' It was amazing how well he and James Delany got on, when sex wasn't involved.

'My pleasure. How're you getting on with the piece on Mr Enigma, by the way?'

Gav leaned his elbows on the low sandstone wall above the river and stretched out his hamstrings. 'He's got me intrigued, definitely.'

'Ah, I thought he might – it's all very mysterious, isn't it?'

Gavin craned his head. 'Actually, I'm looking at his office right now.' Staring at the vast, towering structure of mirror and glass, he wondered on which floor the premises of Masters Industries were situated.

A laugh. 'Are you, indeed?'

Gavin lowered his voice. 'Yeah. I know he purportedly doesn't give interviews, but—'

'Well, if anyone can get in to see him' – James was finishing the sentence for him – 'it would be you, my friend.'

Gavin paused in his stretching. His brow creased. He'd not actually considered trying to bluff his way into the guy's office and talk to him, but it might be an idea. 'Yeah, this is what I was thinking.'

'Well, good luck with it – and keep me up to date with how it's going.'

His mind was elsewhere. 'Yeah, yeah. Later.' Gav ended the call and shoved the phone back under his T-shirt. Maybe it was worth a shot. No harm in trying, anyway.

With a new-found enthusiasm, he rotated his shoulders a couple of times, stretched out his neck, then broke into a light jog.

The tall modern structure stood alone, in the middle of an already filling car park.

Gav circled the building for the second time, looking for any fire doors or goods entrances that may have been conveniently left open. None presented themselves. A quick trip into the foyer had allowed him to discover, from a gilt-lettered information board, that Masters Industries had command of the seventeenth and eighteenth floors. He'd nipped back out again sharpish, when the uniformed security guard had started to head in his direction.

Gavin hmm-ed, raising his eyes upwards.

The sun was higher in the sky now, catching and transforming thirty-nine storeys of mirrored glass into a huge sparkling beacon.

He paused back at the side of the building and racked his brain. Maybe if he'd worn a suit – or even biking shorts – he could have bluffed his way up there as either a rep or a courier.

But in this gear?

Gav leaned against a bollard and plucked at his damp T-shirt. The underarms were soaked now, adhering the fabric of his body in dark wet patches. No chance. Watching cars draw up, park and disgorge office workers into the building, he hoped against hope that he might even catch Masters himself arriving – unless the guy flew in by helicopter and landed on the roof.

As he stood there, cursing himself for not coming better prepared, he was aware of movement from the building. Gav watched the same uniformed security guard from moments earlier stride towards him. The guy carried a polystyrene cup of what looked like coffee in one hand. The other gripped a packet of cigarettes.

Gav sighed. It was too late to scarper.

'Bloody no-smoking rule.' The guy grumbled, stuck a cigarette in his mouth, then patted his trousers to locate matches.

Gav watched the security guard light up. 'Those things'll kill you, pal.'

A snort. A cough. Then a noisy exhalation. 'It's a bloke's right to chose his own poison, eh?'

Gav took in the man beyond the blue-grey uniform. Late thirties, five-ten-ish, rugby player's build.

'Not that you'd know it, from the Health Police in that place.'

The security guard blew a smoke ring towards the sky.

Crew-cut brown hair, receding a little at the temples. Oddly blue eyes. Gav lowered his gaze to the name tag fixed to the guy's jacket: HENRY MORTON. Was he a Harry? A Hal?

'Can't take a piss even, without some bastard timing you, these days.' Harry/Hal poked his cigarette accusingly in the direction of the office building.

Didn't sound like any Henry he'd ever known. Gav grunted sympathetically and listened to more tales of work-related woes. As they stood there, something slowly occurred to him. Something that might let him gain access to the offices of Masters Industries. Something with which Harry/Hal could help him. 'Listen, pal.' Gavin moved closer to the stocky security guard. 'Couldn't do me a big favour, could ya?'

Ten minutes later, he found himself standing at less-than-pristine urinals. The staff gents', on the second floor, stank of that usual combination: toilet block and old piss. The elasticated waistband of his shorts drawn down under his balls, the jock twisted out of the way and cock in hand, Gavin tried desperately to pee.

'Always wondered what joggers did if they had to take a Jimmy Riddle.' Harry/Hal laughed from the area of the hand drier.

But at least he'd got into the building, Standing there, staring at five flaccid inches that resolutely refused to pass urine, Gav flinched at the sound of heavy work boots on tiled floor. The sound of a zipper lowering. Then the gush of piss on porcelain.

'Just presumed you guys nipped behind a bush or something.'

Gavin glanced at the source of the torrent and bit back a moan. The cock in his hand twitched. Harry/Hal was hung like a fucking horse!

'Don't suppose you can do that, in the middle of a city, though, eh?' The security guard had to raise his voice to be heard over the sound of the piss-Niagara.

Nicely thick, too. With a foreskin like Odeon curtains, draping what looked like a good broad head and hiding the slit.

'Old Bill and all that, eh?'

'Yeah, don't wanna get arrested for exposing myself!' Gavin dragged his eyes from Harry the Horse's massive dick and tightened his fingers around his own. The action only served to stimulate him more.

He actually did need to piss now: the sound of Victoria Falls from the man at his side had seen to that. But no way could he manage a drop – not with his cock starting to swell further against thumb and index finger. Motion by his side dragged his eyes back again.

The security guard was shaking his dick now, bitten-down nicotine-stained fingernails yellow against the finely veined flesh.

Gav inhaled sharply. He watched the fine golden spray spring from those heavy folds of foreskin. A single droplet clung on stubbornly to a lower lip of skin. He tried to look away. Couldn't. He tried to stop himself hardening. Couldn't.

Just when he was waiting for Harry/Hal to tuck that monster back behind his fly something most unexpected happened.

Eyes still trained on the unusually large cock, he detected a definite twitch. Tearing his gaze from below waist level, Gavin found Harry/Hal's startling blue eyes fixed on his own crotch.

A low chuckle.

Under such obvious scrutiny, his cock bucked violently against his fingers. Gav turned his head slowly and looked squarely into the security guard's face.

Harry the Horse looked back. Then winked. Cock still hanging out of his fly, the security guard pulled a bunch of keys from a pocket and strode across the room. In seconds, the door to the ground floor gents' had been locked and the security guard was striding towards him.

Gavin turned round fully, watching the way the man's dick

swung in a lazy, steadily thickening curve against the front of the uniform trousers. He thought about how that cock would taste. He thought about the thick feel of it swelling further against his lips, and he thought about the urgent thrust of that fully erect monster, battering against the back of his throat.

Beneath his balls, the elasticated waistband of his running shorts was digging in painfully.

Cock throbbing, balls tingling, Gav was on his knees on the pissy floor in seconds. To the background music of a constantly running urinal, he curled his fist around that mammoth shaft and licked the single stubborn droplet of piss from the emerging head.

Somewhere above him, Harry/Hal groaned, long and deep. A rough hand pushed itself into Gavin's sweaty hair and tried to pull.

Gav inhaled the smell of the man and ducked away. He had no intention of rushing this. Maybe Harry the Horse merely wanted his cock sucked. And that's what he'd get. But the Gavin Shaw way. His free hand snaked round to the man's arse. Fingers curled around the belt, holding his victim steady as he rubbed his face against the delicately skinned shaft.

Harry the Horse grunted and tried to ram his horse's dick into Gav's mouth.

Gavin would have smiled, had he not been letting his closed lips move slowly down the thick length towards the hairy root of the man. He traced every vein, feeling the blood throb just beneath the skin. His hand slid up the cock as his mouth slid down. Exploring. Teasing. Enjoying. Controlling.

He flicked his tongue around the base of the man, wetting the coarse hair. He lapped at the underside of the horse dick, then moved his attentions to the area between Harry's shaft and the man's thickly fuzzed stomach.

'Fuck!' The word was more sigh than curse.

Gav paused, tilting his face to look up.

Harry the Horse's eyes were tightly shut. His nostrils flared slightly. Lips parted and slack, need was painted over every inch of those blunt features. Now he did smile, and as he did so Gavin Shaw tightened his fingers around the emerging head of Harry the Horse's massive dick.

Another groan.

Gav's own dick flexed against the front of his T-shirt, leaving a new wet spot. He may be the one on his knees on a toilet floor, but he was also the one controlling this.

Every time, he was the one in charge.

The horse dick was pulsing against his fingers now. The head was thickening further, folds of paper-thin foreskin smoothing out as more blood pumped from the security guard's brain.

Now it was Gav's turn to moan. He couldn't wait any longer: he was torturing himself with the postponement as much as he was tormenting the shuddering man above him. Sliding his hand down the length of Harry's shaft, Gav sheathed his lips and took the half-hard cock into his mouth.

The taste of piss was still there. It mixed with the sweet-sour of copious pre-come and made Gav's own cock buck violently. Slowly, methodically, he let his lips run down the full length of the man. When he reached the bottom, the man's pubes bristled against his nose and he could feel Harry's balls solid and heavy against his chin.

Harry was still not yet fully erect. The guy's glans stroked the roof of Gavin's mouth. The lob of cock lay along his tongue, folds of foreskin unfurling further.

The monster throbbed. Fingers tightened in his hair.

Gavin moaned and let them tighten, this time. Equally slowly, he drew his lips back up the thickening shaft, feeling the foreskin stretch under the motion. He listened to Harry's animal grunts somewhere above his head, his fist curling back around the root of the man.

Harry pulsed in his hand. In his mouth. And, when Gavin slipped his tongue under the receding folds of foreskin, the security guard's whimpers of need filled his ears.

Seconds later, both Harry's hands were in his hair and Gav was speeding up the blow job. His legs were starting to cramp. Pressed into the cold tiled floor, his knees were getting sore. And, much as he was enjoying this, Gav knew he had other things to do.

Fully erect, the horse cock had to be at least nine inches. And thick as a baby's arm. Eyes open, Gav drew his mouth to the very top of the bulbous purple head. He stared at the curving shaft, watching it glisten with his spit. The guy's slit gaped. His entire body hovered on the edge of orgasm.

Gavin jacked his own cock a couple of time, feeling his balls draw up tight against the root of his aching dick. Then, slowly and deliberately, the root of Harry's horse cock held tight in his other fist, Gav flicked his tongue over, then into, that glistening pink slit.

Harry roared, bucking hard against Gav's face.

Gav tightening his lips, just around the rim of the engorged glans. Keeping them there, he gave Harry's shaft a quick couple of strokes.

Then someone was roaring and he was falling backwards onto the pissy floor. The horse cock slipped from between his lips, jerked free by the force of Harry's orgasm.

Gav gasped, head impacting with cold tiling. He lay there, moaning, jacking himself off as Harry's hot spunk splattered down onto his cheeks.

Only after warm milky come filled his own fist did he snake out a pink tongue to lick the other man's seed from his lips.

Gav left Harry washing his cock in one of the handbasins.

Back out on the second floor, he scanned several closed doors. Now that he was inside the headquarters of Masters Industries, he had to be able to remain there unnoticed.

Opening the first door, Gavin stared at a collection of floor-polishing machines. Opening the second, he found a bank of staff lockers. And what he was looking for.

The grey-blue uniform was a bit baggy on him. But it did the job.

Gavin touched the peak of his cap and held the lift door open for two smiling middle-aged women. Watching them giggle to each other, his eyes moved to the smoked-glass panel straight ahead.

Masters Industries. Plus a severe-looking receptionist. Gavin focused his mind and strode towards her. He held out what he hoped was a security pass. If his idea didn't work, he was lost. 'Mr Masters' PA reported the air-conditioning unit in his office was on the blink.'

The receptionist raised her head and eyed him imperiously. Gavin rolled his eyes. 'Jack of all trades, that's what we are – you wait till the union finds out about this.'

The mask cracked and she laughed lightly. 'Mr Masters is in the conference room at the moment. You'll have his office to yourself.' The receptionist nodded beyond the smoked-glass panel and took the extended laminated card. After a swipe and a satisfying beep, a click.

'Third on the left' – she looked at his pass before handing it back – 'Leonard.'

Gav smiled and took it, striding through the parting smoked-glass panels and hoping Leonard wouldn't miss his uniform.

He walked past a door marked D MASTERS, CEO, and kept on walking.

If the man himself was in the conference room, that's where Gavin Shaw wanted to be, too.

The place was like a rabbit warren. And surprisingly devoid of people. Corridors led to other corridors, lined with unmarked and firmly closed doors. No huddles of office workers around water coolers. Hell, not even any water coolers. And it was quiet. Ominously quiet. Just when he was about to give up, voices – from the far end of a narrow passageway. Gavin grinned and tiptoed towards a half-open door.

He was still a few yards away when words became audible.

'Come on, Masters. I'm not going to ask twice.'

Gavin paused. *Masters*? Who had the nerve to address the head of a multinational corporation by his surname name, and in such an aggressive tone of voice? Fumbling beneath the stolen uniform, Gav was grateful he'd had the foresight to bring the micro tape recorder. Hauling the device from its holder, he switched it on and held it out. Then he moved closer to the open door:

'What about copies?' Different voice. Richer. With just a hint of an accent.7

Now flat against the door jamb, Gav risked a peek into the room.

Two men. Both facing away from him. Both in suits. One small, darker. The other instantly recognisable, even from a rear view.

Gavin stared at the back of Derek Masters' silver-grey hair.

'How do I know, even if I do pay up, that these photographs won't appear in the press, anyway?'

Gavin's eyes widened.

The smaller, darker man sniggered. 'You'll just have to trust me, Masters.'

'Blackmail's a dirty game.'

'Don't talk to me about dirt. Two million, and you can stay squeaky clean, pal. Otherwise...'

'Oi! What you up to?' A third voice came from behind him.

Every bone in Gavin's body shuddered. But, like the good journalist he was, he found the presence of mind to shove the micro tape recorder back into his pocket. Turning, he found himself staring into the face of a very large, very angry-looking man. 'Maintenance, pal – looking for some dodgy air-conditioning unit that—' Before he could finish, the large man had closed the distance between them and grabbed Gav by the shoulder.

'You're not Maintenance. Who are you?'

He could feel the strength in the grip. Gavin struggled and wished he'd actually taken time to find out Leonard's last name. 'Mr Masters' PA called down and said—'

'What's going on here, Milo?'

Time to come clean. Gav tried to wrench himself free and turn, but the large man held him fast. 'What about an interview, Mr Masters? Gavin Shaw, freelance writer. Just a few words on—'

'Intruder on the premises, sir. We're dealing with it.' The large man known as Milo cut short Gav's attempt at confession. 'OK, you. Out!'

Gavin yelped as Milo began to bundle him unceremoniously back down the corridor. Glancing around, he stared at the tall, grey-haired man who was now standing in the doorway of the room.

For the briefest of seconds, Derek Masters stared back.

Gavin found himself held captive by the darkest pair of eyes he'd ever seen.

Something vaguely unsettling seemed to pass between them. Something without a name. Something Gavin felt in the pit of his bowels.

'I said out! And be grateful we're not calling the police!' Milo gave him another hard shove.

The eye lock was broken.

But ten minutes later, as he was picking himself up from the dusty tarmac outside the entrance to the building, purloined uniform practically ripped off his back by Milo, Gavin could still feel it.

# Five

Back at the mews flat, a note from Gerry sat, propped up, on top of the kitchen table: 'We need milk. Aga man due at 4.30 – can you be in?'

Gavin swept everything on the table onto the floor and dumped his laptop down, along with the Masters file and a two-litre bottle of mineral water. He knew he should shower: he'd run the entire distance back from Canary Wharf at a fair pace, and the smell of his own body rose around him.

He knew he should at least change. He knew he should probably eat. Reaching under his sweat-soaked T-shirt, Gav unclipped the micro tape recorder, rewound it and hit PLAY.

Two voices filled the quiet kitchen: one English, nasal and smug-sounding. The other rich, slightly accented and decidedly wary.

He rewound, took a long slug from the mineral-water bottle, and hit PLAY again.

And again.

As he drank, he listened carefully to the words. He had to convince himself his ears hadn't been playing tricks on him. He needed to be certain the small dark-haired man whose face he hadn't seen had really said what Gav had thought he'd said. After the eighth replay, he switched the tape recorder off and sat down.

Photographs. The media. Money.

The implication was clear. Having slowed to normal after the run, Gavin Shaw's heart picked up speed again. He stared at the tiny, state-of-the-art, digital device while blood pounded through his veins.

Somebody was attempting to blackmail Derek Masters. Someone had something on the enigmatic head of a multinational company. A run-of-the-mill corporate profile had suddenly sprouted wings. There were obviously reasons why Derek Masters kept his private life very private. But, equally obviously, one of these reasons had slipped out.

Who was the small, dark-haired man. And with what was he trying to blackmail one of the most powerful men in London?

Leaning back in his chair, Gav took another deep slug from the mineral-water bottle. A smile of anticipation flickered across his flushed, exhilarated face. This was going to be interesting; this was going to be much more interesting than either he or James Delay and his readers had ever imagined.

His hand reached down inside the running shorts, adjusting his slowly stretching cock. Dried spunk from the encounter with the security guard was frosting the lip of his foreskin. Gav inhaled sharply, fingering the stiff crystals, which turned to powder in his hand. His cock flexed, stretching further. He thought about glimpse he'd got of Derek Masters just before that thug of a body-guard or whatever he was had grabbed Gavin by the arm and marched him off. He thought about Masters' blunt, slightly Slavic features: the thin lips of that cruel-looking mouth; the almost aristocratic nose; the angular, tilted cheekbones; the broad, unlined forehead; and the shock of thick silver hair above it.

Gav plugged in his laptop, powered it up and reached for his cellphone. He continued to stare at the micro tape recorder as he waited for the phone to be answered. But his mind was full of Derek Masters' dark, unfathomable eyes.

He was put on hold. Twice. 'The Toreadors' Song' from *Carmen* played in his ear. Gav drummed his fingers on the antique-pine table top and tried to be patient. Finally, someone at the press office decided to stop spin-doctoring and pick up a phone.

'Masters Industries. Julie speaking. How can I help you?'

'Hi, Julie – Gavin Shaw here, from *Financial Week*. We spoke yesterday.' They hadn't, he didn't know her from Adam and technically he had nothing to do with *Financial Week*, but a little creativity with the truth didn't do any harm and he was banking on this being a busy office.

Julie walked chirpily right into his trap. 'Oh, hello, Gavin. Good to hear from you. How—'

'Just wanted to say thanks for all your help.' He barged through her question and kept on going. 'The article is going to be great – just what Masters Industries is looking for. Nice bit of PR for the company, what with that important takeover coming up.' He had no clue if there was a takeover on the cards, but it was a fairly safe bet: organisations the size of Masters Industries were always taking over some poor sod or other. 'Now, if we could set up that interview with Mr Masters, that would be—'

'Mr Masters never gives interviews.' The tone of her voice suddenly changed.

Gavin barely broke stride. 'Yes, I know, but he'll talk to *Financial Week*. James Delany has already been in touch with Derek' – it never hurt to feign a more personal contact – 'and I just wanted to let you guys – and his PA – know, any time at all is fine with—'

'Mr Masters never gives interviews.' Her tone remained irritatingly neutral.

Gav switched on the charm. 'Julie, Julie – it's me you're talking to. Gavin? Gavin Shaw? And don't worry: web conferencing's fine.' He knew he had a webcam around here somewhere, and most businesses these days conducted at least the odd meeting this way.

'Mr Masters never gives interviews.'

'OK, a quick word on the phone with him would be great. Just for a quote, eh? Work with me here, Julie.' He managed a laugh. Irritation prickled the still-damp hairs at the back of his neck. 'Just mention James Delany's name to Derek and—'

'Mr Masters—'

'Never gives interviews. I know. You've said.' Repeatedly. Gavin frowned. She was like a bloody recording. 'Listen, love – I'm writing this profile whether the guy talks to me or not, so don't you think it would be better for him to give me ten minutes of his time and make sure I write what Masters Industries wants to see in the financial press rather than—'

'Thank you for calling. Goodbye.' The line went dead.

Gav roared and almost hurled his cellphone across the room. Bloody cheek! Pushing himself up out of his chair, he stalked across towards the Gaggia, then veered away to the kettle.

He grabbed it and filled it under the tap.

Bloody, sodding cheek! Who did she thinks he was? Who did Derek Masers think he was? Without people like Gavin and publications like *Financial Week*, the guy and his two-bit company would still be grubbing around in bloody Latvia, flogging cabbages to the EU or whatever Latvia's main export was.

The kettle overflowed. Gavin cursed it, shook his hand dry, then plugged in the kettle.

If Masters Industries wouldn't work with him, he'd work without them. He'd write the story to end all stories. He'd find out what the little guy with the dark hair had over Masters. And he'd do him a favour, save him some money and get it all out in the open.

Gavin stood there, staring out of the window onto Kensington Gardens while the kettle boiled. The information would be there. Somewhere. It was just a matter of finding it.

Ten minutes later, he was back at the table, a mug of instant coffee in his hand, and starting another Net search for everything and anything on the words Derek and Masters.

By four o'clock, his shoulders were stiff and his stomach rumbled audibly.

Again, nothing. Not a bloody bean. Nothing about where the man lived. Nothing about his upcoming schedule. Gav had managed to unearth publicity photos from a couple of months ago, from Hong Kong, but what Masters had been doing there he'd no idea.

He was about to give up when his cellphone vibrated on the table's antique-pine surface. Gav stared at it. He rarely used text. Gerry never did, and Gavin had no clue who would chose to contact him this way rather than just give him a ring. Reaching over, he grabbed the Nokia, unlocked it and pressed READ. His phone book had no record of the incoming caller's number. Gavin pressed READ again. And stared at the small green screen.

A date: 21st – a Friday. This Friday, in fact.

A place: Reykjavik.

A hotel: the Reykjavik Ibis.

And one sentence. 'If u want 2 c D Masters, b here. 7 p.m.'

The light on his screen went out.

Gav frowned, pressed OPTIONS and reread the message. His first instinct as a journalist was to call the unknown number that had sent the text. He did so, and got a 'number not recognised' message. Grabbing a pencil, he quickly jotted down the details. A smile slowly replaced the frown.

Maybe Julie in the press office had changed her mind. Maybe Masters himself had relented, although Gavin doubted it. But why the cloak-and-dagger? Of course, it didn't really matter who had sent him this information or why. Gavin was just grateful they had. He could have spent endless hours hanging around outside Masters Industries' headquarters in Canary Wharf, trying to get a few words from the guy, only be rebuffed by that bloody body guard again.

At least now, he could observe – maybe even talk to – the subject of his article. Gavin chuckled – as well as get some expenses
money upfront, from James.

They were out of milk. And quite a lot else, as he had discovered
when he'd tried to make a sandwich. Pushing his trolley around
Safeway's towering aisles, mobile tucked between chin and shoulder, Gavin brought James up to date with his progress.

'You want a ticket to where?'

Gav grinned at the incredulity in the normally unruffled voice.
'Reykjavik – it's in Iceland.'

'I know where it is, my friend – just wondering why you want
to go there.'

Gavin chuckled, hefting two litres of milk into his trolley. 'Let's
just say I got a rather interesting tip-off, regarding our mutual
friend Mr Masters.'

'Really?'

He could hear the surprise in James's voice. 'Yes, really.' Gavin
was enjoying this. As he reached over to grab a multipack of still
mineral water, his hand brushed someone's leg. Looking up, Gav
blinked at one of the most gorgeous creatures he'd seen in a long
time.

'Do tell me more.'

Youngish, roughish, in that surf bum sort of way, loose cropped
T-shirt, thin, barely muscled arms, with a rucksack, and wearing a
baseball cap the wrong way round. He sported a well-trimmed goatee on an otherwise still bum-fluffed face. And he was freckled –
bloody freckles!

Gavin's cock twitched inside his running shorts. He smiled.
'Sorry.'

'No problem.' The voice was East End. The beautiful creature
grinned, jaws working a wad of chewing gum. He held Gavin's

eyes a few seconds longer than strictly necessary before wandering off with his own multipack.

'Gavin? You there?'

He watched the way the kid's arsecheeks rolled slightly, inside baggy, low-slung jeans. A chain hung from a front belt loop to one at the back. Its motion emphasised the studiously lazy lope of the boy's gait. Gavin's cock pushed itself against the front of his running shorts. The kid had to be – what? Eighteen? Nineteen at most.

'Gavin? I'm waiting.'

James's somewhat irritated voice cut into Gav's lusty haze. Gavin groaned. 'Sorry, what did you say?' His eyes never left the boy's arse.

'What's this tip-off you've had on Derek Masters?'

At the far end of the aisle, near the corn flakes, the figure paused. Turned.

As their eyes met again, Gavin's cock flexed violently. Then the boy smiled and walked towards the checkout.

'Um – I'll talk to you later. Just get me a seat on a flight to Iceland, for this Friday morning.' He ended the call, shoved his phone back into its holder and hurried on down towards the queues.

Somehow, he got served before the young guy. Somehow, the guy forgot something and disappeared from his queue. Gav hung around outside Safeway, like a fool. After ten minutes, he gave up, more than a little frustrated, and began the journey home.

The sun was shining; everyone else was either in the park enjoying the weather or at work. He was halfway along the street when he became aware of footsteps behind him. Gav's head swivelled.

There, fifty yards to his rear, was the goatee'd creature, clutching his bottled water and working the wad of gum

Gavin paused. So did the young man. Gav smiled. The guy smiled back, continued to chew his gum. But didn't move. Gav took a step forward, intending to close the distance between them. The guy continued to smile, but took a step back.

Gavin laughed. So it was going to be this kind of game, was it? What the hell! He could do with a bit of a leg stretch. Turning back to face the road ahead, Gavin crossed over and headed for the park.

He lingered by the bushes. Goatee-boy lingered some distance away. Gav nipped behind the bandstand. Goatee-boy circled, but maintained a good fifteen yards between them. Gavin even went into the public toilet, the smell of piss and disinfectant hardening him further.

When he came out, Goatee-boy was leaning against a lamp-post, still smiling.

Gav laughed out loud. The guy wanted to play? Gavin Shaw could play more mind games than most. Turning on his heel, he strode out of the park and headed for home.

As he walked along the sunny streets, he imagined what the boy would look like naked. He imagined that lean, barely muscled body, that smooth, hairless chest – or maybe the kid would be hairy, going by that goatee. The boy had no arse, that was for sure. Gavin stifled a groan, refusing to look round and check if the kid was still there. Something about flat, no-arses always got his dick as stiff as a rod.

Gav was still hot from his encounter with the security guard. What he'd wanted to do with Gerry the night before last refused to leave his head. An image of his hands, clamped around Goatee-boy's prominent hipbones as he watched his cock sink deep into that no-arse exploded in his brain. At the entrance to the mews, he grunted and spun round.

The street was empty.

Gavin groaned. Bloody little prick-tease! Oh, well, maybe it was his fault for pushing it. With a sigh, he turned away and trudged on to Gerry's flat. He was ten yards away when he saw the slender figure in the low-slung jeans, lounging against the front door. A multipack of mineral water sat at his feet.

Gavin smiled, drew keys from his pocket and sauntered over.

It was a risk.

His mouth was on the kid's before he'd closed the front door.

It was a big risk.

The kid tasted of mint. Gav moaned, hands clamping to that no-arse and hauling Goatee-boy's crotch hard against his.

Too risky to do it on his own doorstep. Literally his own doorstep.

Thin arms draped themselves around his shoulders. Gav pushed his tongue into the kid's mouth.

But the mews was quiet this time of day. Gerry's neighbours were all either media types or had jobs in the City. They spent all day and most of the night working.

Goatee-boy sighed. Gavin grunted. Inside the running shorts, his cock was a thick, solid curve against his stomach. And nestling alongside it now, parallel, he could feel the surf bum's hard-on.

And Gavin liked risk. Risk gave everything an edge. He pushed the boy back against the door frame, angling his head to deepen the kiss. The baseball cap fell off. Thick blond hair tumbled free. Something soft and slippery slid into Gavin's mouth, along with the surf bum's tongue. Gav choke-laughed and found himself chewing on the kid's gum as he broke the kiss and dived for that bum-fluffed neck.

Goatee-boy was panting now. One hand was in Gavin's hair. The other clung onto a shoulder.

Gav sucked on the nineteen year-old's throat, grinding his crotch against the front of those baggy jeans and widening Goatee-boy's stance with his body. Then words in his ear:

'Can we go inside?'

Gavin's brain suddenly engaged itself. They couldn't fuck in the open – much as he would have liked to. And he couldn't take the kid into Gerry's flat: even Gavin Shaw drew he line at that. Hauling his lips from the kid's neck, he glanced around. Adjacent to the front door, the garage. Praying Gerry hadn't locked it, he gabbed Goatee-boy by the arm and hauled him off the doorstep.

The large gloomy space smelled of oil and had once stabled horses. Now it housed Gerry's Lexus at weekends.

Gavin tugged at the kid's jeans, backing him towards the far wall. The surf bum had both hands in Gav's hair now, his skinny hips undulating and making Gavin's task both more difficult and more arousing. Eventually, his palms cupped hard flat arsecheeks.

Goatee-boy gasped as Gavin ran an index finger down a finely haired crack. His own cock was leaking freely, adhering the swollen head to the mesh of his jock. Then they both hit the back wall. One of the kid's hands freed itself from Gav's hair and fumbled in a jeans pocket.

Seconds later Goatee-boy was on his hands and knees, baggy jeans hooked around one ankle and Gav was hauling his own cock out of the jock, tearing at foil with his teeth. He could hear the surf bum's breathing as he unrolled the condom over seven hard inches.

'Do it, man.' The kid's voice was hoarse with need and came from somewhere beneath a veil of blond hair. 'Shove it in me. Shove it in me now!'

Gav's cock bucked violently between his fingers. Then he was on his knees behind Goatee-boy, one hand roaming over the hard, flat arsecheeks while the other smoothed the last of the condom down to the root of his cock. His balls drew up tight and full. Gavin groaned, the pad of his thumb pausing at the kid's tight pink hole.

The body in front of his flinched.

Gav removed his thumb, licked it thoroughly then reapplied it to the crinkled rosette with more pressure.

The surf bum's murmurs of need filled the dark, oily-smelling space. Something buzzed in Gavin's brain. Still holding his flexing dick, he massaged around Goatee-boy's arsehole, slicking the tender skin. The kid was pushing back, moving those skinny flat buttocks on ever-widening circles.

He wanted to be in there. He wanted to feel the surf bum clamp around his dick. He wanted to feel another man's sphincter strain then, give under the thickness of his cock.

Gav's balls twisted in their sac. Grabbing a handful of that thick surf-bum hair, he wound it around his fist and positioned the throbbing head of his condom-clad cock against Goatee-boy's hole. Breath caught in his throat. They hovered there, on the brink. Then Gavin pistoned with his hips, pushing hard into the warm, yielding hole.

Just as the sound of a roaring engine filled the gloomy space.

With seconds to spare, Gav rolled them both sideways. The surf bum howled. Only half in, Gav was knocked out of the guy's arse. His right shoulder hit the wall, jarring painfully. Arms and legs were everywhere, as the boy tried to pull up his jeans and make his escape at the same time.

The engine died.

'Go, go! I'm sorry. Just go!' The words were a whispered, regretful hiss. Gavin shoved his aching dick back inside his running shorts and gave the surf bum and rough shove towards the raised garage door.

Goatee-boy scrambled to his feet, fell, got up again and tumbled out of the dark space in a blur of blond hair. Gavin heaved himself upright and debated making a pretence of looking for something.

But it was too late. Round the other side of the Lexus, the driver's door was already open. In immaculate Armani styling, Gerry stood here staring into the wake of Gav's departing trick. Slowly, accusing eyes turned to meet his. And, before Gavin could think of an explanation, the Lexus door was slammed shut and Gerry was making his way into the flat.

'Um, I'm sorry I missed the Aga-man. I'll give them a ring, arrange for another time, eh?'

Gerry wordlessly fired up the Gaggia, then moved to the sink.

Gav followed. 'Listen, about—'

'No more lies, Gavin.' Gerry studiously began to wash dishes Gav was supposed to have taken care of three days ago.

He cringed, reached out a hand to touch the Armani'd shoulder.

'And don't think you'll get round me that way.' Gerry moved away, grabbing a dishtowel.

Gav's face flushed up. He hadn't meant for this to happen. He really hadn't.

'I've tried to be understanding. I've tried to give you... leeway. I know there's other men – I've always known. But I thought you had enough... feeling for me to make sure my nose wasn't rubbed in the fact that I'm not enough for you.' Unexpectedly, Gerry looked up from what he was doing.

Guilt drenched Gav's body. He'd heard the hurt in the man's voice, but now he could see Gerry was on the verge of tears. Gav looked away and concentrated on the mug-drying process. He watched Gerry turn it over and over in his hands. He stared at it. Overfocused on it. Looked at it because he couldn't look at the face of the man holding it.

'We need to talk, Gavin.'

He knew it. But he had no idea where to start. And he wasn't sure he wanted to hear anything Gerry would have to say.

'Things can't go on like this.'

He nodded, cursing bloody Goatee-boy and his own constantly

hard dick. Gavin racked his brain for something to say – something that would give him time, breathing space. An opportunity to come up with something that would smooth things over.

'I really think it's about time we went our separate—'

'Um, Gerry?' The idea came from nowhere. Gav raised his head finally and looked his boyfriend square in the face. 'Would you... like to come to Iceland with me – this weekend?' He removed the dishtowel and the mug from immaculately manicured hands, then took those long soft fingers in his. 'Let me make this up to you – we can talk there, talk it all out, if you want, baby.' Gavin squeezed, smiled his most appealing smile and used the one term of endearment guaranteed to turn Gerry to mush.

And it worked like a charm. Seconds later, Gerry was in his arms and Gavin was stroking those Armani-suited shoulders, assuring Gerry he was the only man for him and the others meant nothing and hoping to hell the promised 'expenses' could squeeze an extra seat on the flight to Reykjavik out of James.

# Six

James was remarkably obliging.

Two days later, Gav and Gerry soared 37,000 feet above the north of Scotland, courtesy of *Financial Week*. A double room, at the Reykjavik Ibis Hotel awaited them, a mere hour's flying time away. All paid for.

Gerry leaned back in his seat and smiled happily at Gavin. 'They call it the land of the midnight sun, you know.'

Gav sipped what was left of his complimentary mimosa. Goatee-boy hadn't been mentioned since that cringe-making afternoon in the kitchen.

'From November through to March-ish,' Gerry was saying, 'Iceland only gets something like three hours of daylight per day – and that's more like day gloom, from what I hear.'

He was dreading this bloody talk he'd promised Gerry. With a bit of luck, the guy would be happy with some hand holding and murmuring over a couple of intimate dinners, and they could leave it at that.

'But in summer,' Gerry sighed dreamily, 'the sun never really sets at all. Almost twenty-four-hour daylight. Imagine!'

Gav was imaging what he was going to say to Derek Masters when he finally got his interview. Should he cut straight to the chase and go with, 'Want to tell me who's blackmailing you, sir, and why?'?

A head impacted with his shoulder. 'Thanks, baby.' The voice was low, for Gav's ears only. He smiled and let Gerry's head rest there.

Or would the subtle, open-ended approach be more productive? Something like, 'A man in your position must make a good few enemies, Mr Masters...' And give the guy room to talk.

'You've really got quite a romantic streak, haven't you?' Gerry chuckled. 'I couldn't have asked for a nicer birthday present.'

Gav drained his glass, handed it to a passing trolley dolly, then rested a hand on the futures dealer's denim-clad thigh.

'Here was I, thinking you'd forgotten. But underneath that hard, streetwise exterior there's a thoughtful, caring and considerate man.'

A hand covered his. Gav smiled. Maybe he'd play it by ear. Yeah, feel his way into the situation. Get the measure of Mr Derek Masters, then take it from there. Always the best way, when it came to interviews.

'Know what I want to do first, baby?' Gerry's mouth tilted upwards towards Gavin's ear.

Warm breath on his lobe brought him back to the present. 'What?'

The words were a whisper. 'I want you to fuck me. I want to feel you inside me, baby.'

Inside his cargo pants, Gav's cock flexed. And, if he could get in a little nookie along the way, that would be a bonus. He tightened his hand on Gerry's thigh. 'Me too, Gerry. Me too.'

As the flight began its descent, they both craned their necks for a first glimpse of the terrain below. For at the past hour, there'd been only water. The northern extremes of the Atlantic were deep, sparkling azure, reflecting the clear blue sky above them. Then, out of nowhere, land appeared. Brown, scrubby land. Alien-looking land the colour of brick and with little greenery to speak of. The contrast was startling. This small, most remote of countries defied both their expectations.

Gerry laughed. 'Where's the… ice? For some reason, I thought there would be ice.'

The plane continued its descent, exposing them to more of the land below.

No ice. But mountains. Bare, unforgiving-looking peaks – again, devoid of grass or even a single tree. As they swept over more sea, flotillas of tiny vessels became visible. Then more land. But still no sign of habitation, let alone people. Finally, a collection of squat, disappointingly modern-looking buildings came into view below. The lurch in the pit of his stomach told Gavin the aircraft was losing height fast. As the wheels hit the runway, another sensation knotted his guts.

Anticipation. And excitement at the prospect of finally talking to Derek Masters

Despite the primeval landscape they'd flown over, Keflavíc airport bordered on the futuristic, architecturally. They collected their luggage and wandered though the vast, vaulted arrivals hall towards the car-rental stands. While Gerry efficiently presented documents and made arrangements, Gav gripped the duty-free bags, his eyes roaming irrationally for any sign of Masters. Having collected keys, Gerry led the way outside.

The sun was high in the sky and the air was warm. But it was a strange sort of heat. More like London on a warm spring day than anywhere Gav had ever been in summer. Following Gerry towards an open-topped Jeep, he looked up at the seagulls circling and shrieking overhead. A breeze ruffled the hair on the back of his neck. Then he glanced at his watch and something suddenly made sense.

It was just approaching half past four. But it felt like noon.

Gav stood there, taking in the strange, flat land and the lack of trees while the seagulls continued to shriek overhead. The atmosphere of the place was already doing odd things to him, beguiling him. Even the air smelled different. Cleaner. Wilder.

Then Gerry threw a map at him and broke the spell. 'Come on – you be navigator and I'll drive.'

Gav pulled himself together and clambered into the open-topped vehicle. Seconds later, the Jeep was breezing along broad roads towards a distant huddle of wooden-sided structures.

That distant huddle of wooden-sided buildings turned out, according to Gerry's map, to be Reykjavik. On the twenty-minute drive, the landscape just got weirder. That warm wind tore at his hair, blasting it back from his face as the speedometer inched up towards 50 m.p.h.

'What are those, do you think?' Gav pointed to what looked like washing lines with leaves pegged to them.

'Fish!' Gerry laughed. 'Dried fish – haddock or something. It's the country's main industry – fish and aluminium, would you believe? All that hot water from those natural springs, I think.'

As the city got closer, Gav found himself believing anything. Reykjavik had a crisp edge to it. City-sized and the country's capital it may be, but there the impression of anything urban ended. From a distance, it looked like a toy town, with its painted wooden houses, their sides and roofs every colour under the sun from blue to pale pink. Driving along the capital's wide streets, Gav was reminded of cities as diverse as Paris and Bergen. Archangel and Lisbon. Copenhagen and Portland, Maine. Reykjavik bore similarities to many other places. But it had something truly its own.

The shoppers crowding the pavements, the motorists who passed them driving everything from old VW Beetles to what looked like dune buggies all looked affluent and healthy. They also all looked young. Or, more accurately, youthful. Maybe it was something to do with the climate or all that fish they ate. Maybe it was the international uniform of jeans and sweatshirts, but even the grey-haired Icelanders belied their real ages.

The Reykjavik Ibis was slap-bang in the middle of the city, sitting on the main square. Gerry dropped Gav at the front and drove on down into the underground car park. The hotel was functional and modern – a good basic three-star. And busy: on their way through the streets, Gav had noticed bill posters for various special events. Summer was obviously Iceland's big time.

'I've got a room reserved in the name of...' Gav finally pushed his way through the crowds of tourists, fashionably tatty-looking kids with blond dreadlocks and men in suits to reach the reception desk. He caught the eye of a cool, Nordic-looking blond in a shirt and tie. '... name of Shaw.'

The blond smiled and tapped at a keyboard. 'Ah, yes. Your room is ready, Mr Shaw. Sorry to keep you: we have a convention of skateboarders this weekend. If you could just fill this in.'

Gav took the pen and the registration form, and began to scribble details. Something occurred to him. Without raising his eyes, he injected a studied note of casualness into his voice. 'Derek arrived yet?' There was no guarantee Masters was staying at this relatively lowly, tourist-class establishment, but 7 p.m. at the Ibis had to stand for something.

'Derek?'

Gav scribbled Gerry's address on the form, signed it and looked up as he slid the document back across the desk to the blond. 'Derek Masters?'

'Ah!' The guy smiled. 'You are another of Mr Masters' guests?'

Gav made a noncommittal grunt, which would not have stood up in court but did the job for the moment.

'Mr Magnussen and Mr Sigissen, the gentlemen from Copenhagen, are over there. Their flight was early.'

He followed the blond's eyes to where two middle-aged suits sat, sipping Coke and flicking through a newspaper, respectively.

'We are all very excited, here in Reykjavik, that Masters Industries in partnership with the Greigsson Consortium are considering opening a new bauxite-processing plant in our country. It will be good for local employment. Very good.' The blond receptionist obligingly told Gavin everything he needed to know.

Gav had no clue what bauxite was, except it had something to do with the manufacture of aluminium.

'Mr Masters' flight from Moscow has been delayed.' Moscow? What was Masters up to in Moscow? 'But he has left instructions that his guests be shown every hospitality in the meantime. Can I get you something to drink, Mr Shaw?'

'Make mine a double!' Gerry's breathless voice behind made Gavin flinch. 'God, it's mayhem out there – wouldn't believe it was seven o'clock in the evening, would you?'

Seven o'clock, 7 p.m., the appointed time.

'Mr Shaw? Can I arrange drinks for you and your friend? Something to eat, maybe?'

Gavin barely heard the question. The hairs on the back of his neck were standing on end. As he turned slowly, his gaze swept the busy foyer.

The crowds of guests, diners and assorted skateboarders seemed to have vanished. Or maybe they were still there. All Gavin knew was he didn't see them. He saw only the tall, silver-haired figure in the subtly tailored suit who was striding through the Ibis's main door.

Derek Masters efficiently scanned the foyer, then immediately walked to where the two Danish businessmen were now rising to their feet. Everyone shook hands – including Milo, the bodyguard, who had appeared behind Masters like a second, larger, protective skin.

'Gavin?'

He took in every detail of the ritual: the way Masters clasped each man's hand in both of his, greeting the men more like brothers than the commercial contacts Gavin presumed they were; the way the two Danes deferred to Masters, although one of them at least looked older and more obviously affluent; the way Milo stood in the background, hands clasped behind his vast impressive body, watching everything and nothing at the same time.

'Mr Shaw?'

The four suited figures were now making their way towards the lift. Gav's head swivelled, following them, unable to drag his gaze from the silver-haired figure. Now would be the time. Now would be an opportunity to move casually over and introduce himself – although they had technically already met.

'Gavin? You OK?'

He couldn't move. Couldn't move a bloody muscle. He was vaguely aware of a tight hot feeling in his crotch. A single droplet of sweat made its way from one armpit. Something buzzed in his ears.

They'd reached the lift now, Masters chatting amiably to the two Danes, Milo bringing up the rear. Then, inexplicably, Masters turned and looked right at Gavin.

The hot tight feeling moved to his chest. A band of fire encompassed his ribs. He couldn't breathe. Couldn't stir. Could do nothing except stand there and look back into those dark, pitlike eyes while his cock flexed violently inside his cargo pants.

Masters was the calm eye of a vortex, around which everything spun and whirled.

The ping of the arriving lift was like a gunshot. Derek Masters turned casually away, ushering his guests between the parting doors.

Released from the man's gaze, Gavin gulped in air and staggered backwards into Gerry's arms. The last thing he knew before he passed out was various accented voices offering him glasses of water.

In the hotel room, Gerry was solicitation itself.

Gav sat up in the large, king-sized bed sipping a cup of hot sweet tea someone had produced from somewhere. He'd never fainted in his life. Never.

'I don't think you eat enough.'

He let Gerry fuss around him like a mother hen, rearranging his pillows and smoothing down the sheets. He felt totally fine now. Better than fine, in fact. A little pumping of the blond receptionist later would tell him which conference suite Derek Masters had secured for his meeting. He'd get his interview. But later. For now, he had other things on his mind. Or on his crotch.

When Gerry turned away to get more water, Gav stared at the guy's arse. The jeans showed the futures dealer's prime asset off to best example. And Gav was definitely in the mood for a little... asset-stripping. Slipping one hand under the covers, he pulled his erect cock up flat against his stomach, fleeing the fat length flex against his palm. His other hand reached out and settled on the back of Gerry's neck. 'Wanna... fool around, hot stuff?' He rubbed the channel just beneath the man's hairline.

Gerry moaned and turned round. 'You... sure you're up to... this?'

Gav looked at him quizzically

'I mean, you passed out cold – you gave me a real fright and—'

'And guess where the blood went when it left my head?' Gav eased back the covers, thumb and forefinger dragging down the length of his hard-on. Tightening his grip around the root, he held his shaft steady, watching the thick wormy vein pulse up the underside.

Gerry made a sound somewhere between a whimper and a grunt. He lunged towards his luggage, rifling frantically through a toiletries bag for two items Gav had seen him pack, back in London.

A lube of Astroglide. And a packet of three heavy-duty johnnies.

\*

Gav still couldn't believe Gerry had never been fucked before.

Kneeling behind the naked blond, Gav lowered his face and licked a wet trail up the length of Gerry's already damp arse-crack. Its owner inhaled sharply, then moaned drunkenly.

Not that Gerry wasn't tight. His hole was like a bloody drum. Gav had found that out half an hour earlier, which was why he'd ransacked the minibar and got three stiff gins into Gerry, before a fourth stiffness went in there; and why he was now in the middle of giving the rim job of his life. Holding the guy's arsecheeks apart, Gav lapped down the wet hairy length of Gerry's crack.

Apart from anything else, he bloody loved rimming. The taste of a man. The sweet-sour, sweaty taste of a man's body. The head of his cock was as sensitive as the next man's. But there was something about tongues, something about feeling a sphincter clamp around your tongue that made Gav's balls tingle like nothing else. On top of which, the tongue was one of the strongest bundle of muscles in the body. Maybe a virgin hole could resist a cock – Gav had no intention of ramming right in there and doing them both damage – but no way could any man fight the feel of a tongue.

Reaching the delicate perineum, Gav groaned himself and flicked his tongue over the puckered skin down towards Gerry's full ballsac.

The body in front of him shuddered. 'Fuck me, baby. Fuck me now.'

Gav knew it was still too soon. Although Gerry's hole was wet enough, and had enough Astroglide in it to slip an elephant up there, Gav knew what he was waiting for.

He was waiting for Gerry to beg. He wanted to hear this ninety-grand-a-year futures dealer, with a mind like a razor and a selling technique to match, plead with Gavin Shaw to shove his thick fat cock deep into that virgin arse. Enjoying the feel of the puckered balls skin, Gav closed his mouth and rubbed his lips over the swollen, heavy sac.

Gerry was panting now. Pushing back. Circling his hips like the man-whore he was.

Gav's condomed cock flexed hard, trying to fuck the air between them. He drew back a little, opened his mouth and gently exhaled on the guy's balls.

Gerry roared, bucking like a bronco. He pushed back, trying to smash his arse onto Gav's face.

Both palms were now on Gerry's arse, a hand on each cheek. Gav dug his fingers in and held the man open. The tiny orifice was spasming, opening and closing like a goldfish's mouth. Exerting more pressure with his thumbs, Gavin leaned forward. He watched Gerry's arsehole flex. And stay flexed. He could feel Gerry push back. He could feel the need. He could hear the low groans that had now replaced the roars. Somewhere, on the other side of that Stairmaster-tightened arse, the guy was like iron. Gav visualised Gerry's slender, curved cock bouncing in the air, its surprisingly thick head slick and glistening with pre-come.

As he stared at the arsehole, his own balls knitted together unexpectedly. Gav bit back a groan of his own, lowered his face and ran the tip of his tongue around that crinkled hole.

Gerry grunted. A ninety-thousand-per-annum, public-school- and Cambridge-educated City high flier was reduced to low, animal grunts.

Gav's cock throbbed, pushing at its latex skin. He could taste the telltale vanilla/medical tang of the Astroglide. But there was nothing vanilla about this.

Tightening the bunch of muscles in his tongue until it was as hard as his dick, Gav thrust the fist half-inch between those glistening arsecheeks.

Nothing vanilla at all.

Gerry was panting again, bearing down hard on Gav's face. Gav let his tongue stay there for a microsecond, then withdrew it.

Gerry whimpered. 'Put it back in me, baby. Put it back.'

Gav smiled, ducking his head lower to kiss the man's balls. He knew what he was waiting for. He knew what he wanted.

The touch of his lips had the desired effect. Gerry's entire body started to shake. Huge ripples of lust coursed through the man. At each side of Gav's head, solid thighs quivered with anticipation and postponement. Gav wouldn't have been surprised if the guy grabbed his own cock and started jacking himself off.

Maybe he didn't need to. Maybe the rim job and the thought of another man inside him would bring Gerry to orgasm, all on their own. Before this image pushed him over the edge, Gav dived back between those firm arsecheeks and began to tongue-fuck that hot hole. He shoved his elbows into the backs of Gerry's knees, holding the man firmly onto the bed. Arsecheeks gripped firmly and wrenched wider than ever, Gav fucked the hole slowly at first, savouring the wet feel of the man, the way Gerry's body resisted the attention before bowing to it. The narrow tip slid easily past tight arse-lips.

Gerry rolls his hips in pleasure. But that pleasure was tinged with anticipation.

Gav licked and sucked at the hole each time he withdrew, enjoying Gerry's need. He immersed himself in the double-edged activity of giving.

Giving in order to take.

When he gauged the time was right, Gav broadened out his tongue and deepened the fuck. Pushing further into Gerry's body, his mouth explored the warm, secret, forbidden reaches of the other man.

Rimming was much more intimate than fucking. Or even kissing. There was something almost fundamental about a rim job. And he'd never known a man who could deny him anything once Gavin Shaw's expert mouth had spent any time between their arsecheeks.

Gerry's groans were lower in pitch now. He barely sounded

human any more. The noises coming from further up the bed were ancient and primeval, befitting the strange, primal landscape of this most idiosyncratic of countries.

His throat hurt. His mouth was dry as the barren Icelandic landscape. But his head was full of the taste and smell and feel of the man. He wanted to fuck Gerry so badly his entire body was tense.

Eventually, something cut through the sounds of the rim job and the throb of blood in Gavin's head. From up the other end of the bed, the signal he'd been waiting for.

Gerry was crying. Slow, rhythmic sobs racked that gym-toned body. Then the words:

'Please! Fuck me, Gavin. Please! Please!'

Hauling his mouth from the very heart of he man, Gav leaned the condom-swathed head of his shiny, aching prick against the entrance to the man's body. He wrapped his hands around Gerry's hipbones, holding the man steady.

Three feet up the bed, less than immaculately styled hair hung over Gerry's face. Then the head raised itself, and turned.

Poised there, on the very edge of penetration, Gav stared into red-rimmed eyes. And pushed.

A deeply felt groan split the soft liquid sound of his cock entering Gerry's body. Then the man's head fell forward and Gavin threw himself into what he'd brought Gerry here to do. Gripping the guy tightly, Gav let himself sink into that hot, vicelike embrace. The muscles in Gerry's arse fought him for a second, then admitted the fuck.

No time for finesse now. No time for anything except the thrust and the drag and the stinging friction of the fuck. Eyes closed, thighs taut and quivering, Gavin pushed deeper with each stroke, stretching and widening as he sank into Gerry's pulsing rectum, savouring the throbbing walls of flesh around his dick as he withdrew.

In his mind's eye, he could see them here on the bed, in some anonymous hotel room. Two men among rumpled sheets. One early thirties, the other mid-twenties. One dark-haired, the other blond. One a seasoned cock man, who'd sucked more dick and been up more arses than most people had had hot dinners. The other relatively inexperienced, a romantic who, if he was honest, wanted nothing more than kisses and a bit of a cuddle.

The smell of fucking filled his head: the sickly odour of the Astroglide, the meaty-sweet stink of male sweat, the sour smack of arse and dick.

His balls were slapping against Gerry's with each thrust, now. Gavin moaned, leaning back and changing the angle of the fuck. The head of his cock rammed into the wall of the other man's rectum.

Gerry howled, rearing up off the bed. Arms flailing, he reach around and grabbed a handful of Gavin's loose, sweat-soaked hair.

Then his balls were spasming and they were both falling forwards as Gav's cock jerked violently and filled the tip of the condom with hot milky spunk.

They lay in a tangle of sheets and aching limbs. Gerry's head rested on Gavin's chest. Lips kissed a nipple.

'I love you.'

Half propped up against the wall, Gav stared restlessly across the room to the window. He couldn't believe it was still light. It had to be – he glanced at his watch – nearly eleven.

The action was noted. 'Not keeping you, am I?' The merest hint of irritation in the voice.

Gav laughed and kissed Gerry's sweat-soaked hair. 'Just thinking about your... midnight sun.' Disentangling himself from the man's arms, he slid out of bed and strolled naked to the window. 'Fancy a walk?'

Outside, the centre of Reykjavik still thronged with people. There was a real air of celebration: jugglers, fire-eaters and street theatre vied for the attention of passing crowds – all under an eerily lit sky. Gav had never seen anything like it. He wanted to be part of it – and he wondered vaguely what Derek Masters was doing right now.

'Baby?' A whine joined the irritated tone. 'Come back to bed.'

Gavin continued to watch the crowds below. Sex always invigorated him: the last thing he felt like doing at the moment was snuggling back down beside Gerry and listening to more slushy endearments. 'Come on – we've not eaten. I'll buy you a burger and we can join in the fun.' He spun round, grinning. 'What do you say?'

The face of the man on the bed was a study in disappointment. Gerry sighed. 'Didn't it mean anything to you?'

'What you on about?' Gav grabbed underpants and struggled into them.

'Baby, that was my first time. You're the one and only man I've ever had inside me.'

'Ah.' He scanned the room for their discarded clothes, extracted his T-shirt and cargo pants from around Gerry's and pulled them on. 'Listen pal: don't worry about it. It'll get better. The first time's always a bit of a nonevent.'

'A bit of a... what?' A new note entered the futures dealer's voice: anger.

Gav grabbed Gerry's clothes and threw them at him. 'Come on, I'm starving! Let's go and see your midnight sun and—'

'You bastard!' Gerry caught the clothes and threw them back. 'You fucking heartless bastard!'

A pair of Levi's hit him in the face. Gavin blinked and threw them back. 'What's up with you?' He spotted his boots at the far side of the bed and moved towards them.

Gerry was in there first. In the wake of the jeans came one suede desert boot. 'Get out!'

It just missed Gavin's head. 'Gerry! Calm down!'

The second hit its target, glancing off his temple.

'Get out! Go see your bloody midnight sun!' The handsome face was scarlet with fury. 'Just don't expect me to be here when you get back!'

Gavin stared, rubbing the area above his right eyebrow. 'Will you get a grip, pal?'

Gerry was crying now. Hot tears of rage coursed down his burning cheeks. 'Bloody get out of my sight!'

Gavin debated trying to comfort the obviously distressed man, then thought the better of it. Having grabbed boots, jeans and jacket and shrugged his rucksack over a shoulder, he headed for the door. He had no idea what was up with the guy, but evidently his presence was only making things worse. Halfway out, he paused. 'Um – bring you back anything?'

The responding roar spoke volumes. As did the heavy glass ashtray that impacted with the other side of the door, just as Gavin closed it behind himself and fled.

# Seven

'Mr Masters has left for the evening.'

Down in the hotel foyer, Gav groaned under his breath. 'Any idea where he's gone?' He smiled appealingly at a new blond desk clerk.

'I'm afraid not.'

Gavin sighed and made to turn away.

'Oh, Mr Shaw? Message for you.' The blond rummaged in a pigeonhole, then held out a folded sheet of paper. 'Have a nice evening, sir.'

He mumbled his thanks and took the note. No one knew he was here – well, apart from James. Unfolding the sheet of paper, he wandered across the foyer, reading the small, typed words in the centre of the page: 'Blue Lagoon. 1 a.m.'

He didn't have to ask who: the same tip-off source that had informed him Masters would be here at all was obviously providing further clues. The only question was what and where. A bar? A club? A restaurant?

Gav glanced through the hotel's plate-glass windows at the thronged streets. Just after midnight, and the streets of Reykjavik still pulsed with life. And that odd light continued to drape the crowds of revellers in an eerie half-shadow. Only one way to find out. Passing through the double doors, Gav hit the streets. It took about fifteen minutes to find a taxi. 'The Blue Lagoon?'

The driver gave him a bit of a look, but nodded.

Gav clambered into the back.

*

The first surprise came after the taxi's slow progress through the city centre. They drove past rows of crowded restaurants. Skateboarders spilled out of neon-signed clubs. Cafés and bars heaved with drinkers of all ages. And the taxi kept on going. Soon, Reykjavik was a string of lights, visible through the back window only.

Gavin's brain raced. Was the Blue Lagoon somewhere secluded, somewhere quiet, somewhere for an international corporate magnate to conduct his business more privately, away from the prying eyes of the financial press? Despite the lack of habitation, they were far from the only vehicle on the road. Nearly all the other cars and vans were moving in the opposite direction from the taxi. Few of them had headlights on. No need: straight ahead, a slender strip of dull orange continued to illuminate the midnight sky. It was most unnerving.

'Thought you'd be heading for the glacier – that's where most everyone else is tonight.'

Gav's eyes followed a dune buggy crammed with grungy-looking teens as it cut across the main road in front of the taxi and screeched up into scrubby mountains. Affixed to a nearby telegraph pole was some sort of laminated poster for some sort of festival.

The driver snorted derisively. 'Twenty thousand kids and twenty-four hours of noise – it'll be a miracle if the glacier survives.'

Gavin smiled to himself. No, he didn't see Derek Masters as the rock-festival type. Maybe that brute of a bodyguard Milo: despite the suit and the build, Milo was young enough.

The second surprise came fifteen minutes later: they were still on the move. Leaning back in his seat, Gav stared out of the window at the increasingly barren – and devoid-of-life – landscape. Where the fuck was this bar, club or whatever the Blue Lagoon was? From the meagre research he'd done on Iceland, Gavin knew there were a couple of other settlements apart from cosmopolitan Reykjavik. But they were relatively minor habitations – and they were bloody miles away!

He looked at his watch: 00.44. If he wanted to get there by 1 a.m., they were going to have to get a move on. 'Um – is this place much further?'

'Another ten minutes or so.' The driver's eyes remained firmly on the road ahead.

Gavin continued to gaze out of the window. Despite the mountains where the festival was happening, the terrain through which they were at present speeding was featureless to a fault. The lack of trees was as unsettling as that odd sky. Trees were something one expected. For them not to be there – at all, since Gavin didn't remember seeing a single one – merely served to accentuate the strangeness of the country itself.

The third surprise made itself known to Gavin as he changed position, swinging his legs around to peer out of the other window. A shudder of pleasure tingled in the pit of his stomach. Inside his jeans, the swelling head of his thickening cock brushed against his inner thigh.

He had no idea when he'd started to get hard. Or why.

As his foreskin continued to peel back, he could almost feel the drying spunk from his fuck with Gerry cracking and powdering around his slit.

Was it the motion of the taxi on the smooth, un-potholed roads? Or the low, slow anticipation at the thought of interviewing Derek Masters, which was already drying the inside of his mouth?

Gav moved a hand to his crotch, easing his half-hard-on from against his thigh and repositioning it against his stomach. He tried to get his mind back on this bloody Blue Lagoon place.

The fourth surprise took his breath away. As the driver had predicted, about ten minutes later the taxi slowed, curving left into a tarmacked car park. Quite a few other vehicles dotted the official-looking area. Gavin gripped the back of the passenger seat, peering through the windscreen in confusion. They were in the middle of bloody nowhere – apart from something that looked like a petrochemical processing plant, a little away.

'This do you?' The driver slowed further, then let the engine idle in neutral.

'Um – where's the Blue Lagoon?' He thrust a hand into his pocket for money. Fingertips made contact with dick again. His balls clenched. Gav ignored the sensation, withdrawing a handful of local currency.

'Straight ahead, mister.' The driver pointed to a squat, anonymous-looking structure, which, even by Icelandic standards, looked nothing like any bar, club or restaurant Gavin had ever seen.

But he paid what the guy asked, tipped generously, then got out of the taxi and made his way over to the squat, low-built wooden building. A strong smell of rotten eggs filled the air.

The biggest surprise of the evening was still to come.

The smiling blond behind the desk rented him swimming trunks, towel and flip-flops, then pointed Gavin towards the changing area.

The Blue Lagoon was a real bloody lagoon! In eerie half-light, Gav made his way past men and women of all ages, now totally thrown. Whether it was actually blue or not was difficult to tell. He stared at a vast body of water, at present shrouded in a cloak of steam. Clad in everything from baggy surf shorts to cut-off jeans and full swimsuits, twenty-odd figures chatted at tables around the edges or paddled in the shallows. Just visible further out, a few bobbing heads. Soft music drifted from concealed speakers. If he'd been disoriented before, this was the final, supreme confusion.

What was a lagoon doing in the middle of nowhere? What was

that god-awful smell? Where was Derek Masters? And what was he doing swimming in the middle of the bloody night? Was he here at all? It seemed an unlikely place to find a corporate magnate, but this was Iceland: the unlikely was more than probable. As he walked in the direction of what looked like the changing rooms, Gavin scanned the area for the distinctive shock of silver-grey hair.

And bumped into someone coming the other way.

'Oops – sorry, mate.' His head swivelled away from the steamy lagoon. Gavin opened his mouth to apologise further. And found himself inches from the burly, completely naked form of Milo the bodyguard. His mouth snapped shut and he took a step back.

Milo eyed him, black bushy brows forming a V.

Gavin lowered his gaze, praying the guy wouldn't recognise him as someone he'd physically and not unforcefully ejected from the headquarters of Masters Industries earlier that week. He stared at the thick, flaccid cock that lolled between Milo's massive, well-muscled thighs. Inside his jeans, Gavin's own dick flexed violently. 'Um, sorry.' He moved left, eager to get away.

'No problem.' So did Milo.

Then right. The movement was again mirrored. Unwilling to risk giving the guy more than one look at his face, Gav held his breath and kept his head lowered. His eyes lingered on the curve and sway of Milo's member.

A laugh from in front. Then strong hands gripped Gavin's shoulders.

He found himself gently but firmly manoeuvred aside. As Milo ambled off past him, Gav exhaled in relief and turned: thank God he had one of those faces that don't stand out from the crowd. He watched two solid mounds of muscle make their way down towards the steaming edge of the Blue Lagoon. The encounter had told him something else, as the head of his cock pushed urgently at the waistband of his underwear: Derek Masters was here. It was just a matter of finding him.

In the subtly lit changing room, Gav struggled into Lycra swimming trunks and wished he'd asked for a larger size. Flip-flops on his feet, he scrutinised himself critically in front of a full-length mirror.

The tight, shiny fabric clung to every inch of his dick, enhancing the hard-on until Gav could almost see the thick wormy vein that snaked its way up his shaft. A single bead of sweat made its way from his left armpit.

He frowned. Despite the semi-open-air status of the Blue Lagoon, and the growing chill in the night air, the place was hot and humid. Gavin turned, craning his head over his shoulder and tugging at the legs of the all-too-brief garment. Held captive by Lycra, his arsecheeks were two rounded, well-muscled mounds.

The frown became a sly smile. He had a nice arse, if he said so himself. A real bubble-butt. It was a pity Derek Masters was straight. Otherwise Mr Corporate High Flyer would not have stood a chance.

Gav winked at his reflection, now standing front on to the mirror. With his right hand, he adjusted the curving length of his erection.

Movement behind dragged Gav's narcissistic attention away from the mirror. A young blond with good pecs strolled past him to the bench and began to peel off surf shorts.

Gavin dared not linger: he was aroused enough as it was. And this, after all, was business. Derek Masters' business was about to become Gavin Shaw's business. Head up, cock snuggling against the soft fuzz of hair in his belly, Gav grabbed his denim jacket and slung it over one shoulder, then sauntered back out into the swimming area.

He spotted the subject of his article straightaway.

On the far side of the steamy pool, a silver-haired figure, dressed in a loose-fitting robe, sat at a small table drinking something from a cup. Standing behind Masters, totally naked and with his arms folded, stood massive Milo, scowling and scanning the area.

Gav caught the admiring eye of a slender girl with pink corkscrew hair and small, boyish breasts. She smiled at him, and nudged her darker-haired companion. Gavin returned the smile and wandered over to what he hoped was an anonymous vantage point, near the edge of he steaming pool.

There was a second chair at Derek Masters' table, pulled out and recently occupied, judging by the tall glass and the packet of cigarettes that sat opposite the silver-haired man. One of the Danish businessmen from earlier? Milo?

Gavin glanced at the broad, totally naked bodyguard who stood like a colossus, arms folded, behind his boss.

No, Milo seemed to be on duty. The second place was definitely for a guest of some sort. Having lingered at the edge of the lagoon a good few minutes, Gav knew he was about the only person in the place not either in or just out of the water. The rotten-eggs smell was slowly placing itself as sulphur: traces of the yellow ore tinged many of the rocks and pebbles onto which the steaming lagoon lapped. The water probably came from some underground spring. Taking his courage in both hands, he risked dipping a toe into the cloudy waters.

It was surprisingly warm. Gav smiled and wandered in up to his knees. The deeper he went the hotter the lagoon became. As he waded about, enjoying the sensation of the vaguely silky-feeling water around his thighs, Gav kept a discreet eye on the shore.

Like burly Milo, a couple of the older male bathers had dispensed with their swimming gear and were now lounging at tables. More than a few pink, rounded arses were visible on their way to and from the lagoon. Cocks swung languidly, lazily half-hard from the caress of the sulphur spring. And, behind, the empty place at Derek Masters' table had been filled – by a statuesque red head in full make-up and 1950s-style strapless two-piece bikini.

Gav did a double-take, then found himself unabashedly staring at the woman. Unlike that of most of the boyish girls present, this lady's cleavage was the stuff of legends. High, full and barely kept in check by the boned upholstery of the Doris Day-esque bathing suit, her tits were drawing every eye in the place. Her waist was tiny and cinched, swelling out to full rounded hips. Beneath the table at which she sat, long shapely legs went on for ever, ended only by a pair of the highest, spikiest, peep-toe mules Gav had seen in a long time. No flip-flops for this girl! Each toenail was painted a striking scarlet – matching both her long elegant fingers, the bathing attire and the glossy hair that tumbled down over milky-white shoulders. It was hard to tell her age: she could be fifteen; she could be fifty. There was that timeless quality about her that Gavin had read about, but never actually seen. But, however old she was, the contrast between the woman and her environment was arresting. Here, in the most naturally occurring of lagoons, surrounded by earthy-looking Icelanders with their tanned skins and natural fibres, the lady in red was a vibrant butterfly fish in a sea of drab cod.

Gavin blinked.

A butterfly fish who was now rubbing the sole of a spike-heeled mules up the inside of Derek Masters' hairy calf.

The silver-haired man leaned across the table and lit a cigarette for his friend – or was she a friend? She could be a mere acquaintance. She could be a lover. Digging into the recesses of his memory, Gav recalled that Derek Masters' martial status right now was that of divorcee. Add to this the man's reputation as an international playboy and this woman could merely be one in a long line of lady friends. For some reason, his cock gave a sharp twitch. Gav almost laughed at himself. It was nothing to him where Derek Masters chose to shove his dick.

A couple of teenage boys splashed past him, dousing each other with water.

Gav ducked out of the way, finding himself smiling more broadly. He was in danger of losing sight of the reason he was here at all, so laid back and low key and friendly was the atmosphere. But when he looked back to the Derek Masters' table he caught sight of something that definitely gave him pause for thought. The man himself was just terminating a mobile-phone call. One of the butterfly woman's hands continued to hold a cigarette. The other had slipped beneath the small table – and was discreetly repositioning a very healthy set of cock and balls inside the Doris Day-esque bikini briefs.

Gav goggled.

Looking away from the unexpected sight of such a package on someone so feminine, Gav raised his gaze. And met those dark, unfathomable eyes once more.

Derek Masters held Gavin's stare, smiling slightly. Gav's cock was oozing now. He could feel the warm sticky glue of pre-come join the sweat inside the Lycra swimming trunks to adhere the head of his hard dick to the wiry hair of his pubes.

He groaned audibly.

Unexpectedly, a ringing from the top pocket of his Levi jacket. Now the groan was of annoyance. But he knew he should answer it. Hauling the device free, he clamped it to his ear. 'Shaw.' He stared back towards the table where Derek Masters and his lady-boy had been sitting.

It was empty. They'd gone

'What are you doing up at two in the morning on an assignment, Gavin?' James Delany's polished tones filled his ear.

'Um, working.' Gav scanned the area around the edge of the lagoon, looking for any sign of the couple, or even big Milo.

'I'm impressed.' The commissioning editor of *Financial Week* chucked. 'And how did your mysterious... tip-off pan out?'

Gav groaned. They'd disappeared. Milo and Derek Masters and Ms Scarlet were nowhere to be seen.

'Gavin? You there?'

'Yeah, sorry.' In the strange half-light, and with the smell of sulphur in his nostrils, Gav trudged through the steaming water towards the shore. 'Can I phone you back?' He was breathing heavily.

'No problem, Gavin. I can hear you're' – a sly note crept into the warm, smooth voice – 'busy.'

He snorted in annoyance and jogged towards the way out, aware his clothes were still in the locker room.

In the car park, he arrived in time to see a maroon Range Rover pulling away. Just visible through the back window were two heads, very close together. One silver grey. The other glossy scarlet.

On the flight back to London the next day, Gerry said nothing about the fact that Gav hadn't returned to the room till 4 a.m., but threw him several hurt, kicked-puppy-dog looks.

Gavin's mind was elsewhere. Well, well, well: Derek Masters was into drag queens. Or pre-op transsexuals. Or whatever the dazzling creature with the red hair wanted to call herself.

So what? He wouldn't be the first straight man to like a bit of cock to go with a nice pair of tits. But Gavin wasn't stupid. All those photo spreads in society magazines would take on a somewhat different caste should it be known the glamorous ladies on Derek Masters' arm had a little secret, carefully taped between their long slender thighs. The gutter press would seize on it. Masters Industries' competitors would have a field day, sniggering and pointing. He could lose contracts over this. People – even those in commerce – could be surprisingly judgmental. And, most serious of all, what would happen to confidence in Derek's many businesses worldwide? Masters Industries could sustain a lot of damage.

'Baby?' Gerry's voice seeped into his ear.

Gavin grunted in acknowledgment. His only regret was that he hadn't had the presence of mind to take a camera with him last night: photographs to accompany the recorded conversation between Derek Masters and his would-be blackmailer were all the ammunition he needed.

'I forgive you,' Gerry murmured into his ear.

Not that Gavin would print any of it: he did have some scruples. But it would be very useful to dangle over the man himself, in the interests of becoming the first journalist to get a serious, indepth interview with Derek Masters.

'I know none of those other men mean anything to you,' Gerry's voice continued. 'I know it was me you wanted with you, for the weekend.'

As it was, a couple of heavy hints to Masters Industries' press office over the phone should be enough to convince them it was in their interest to work with Gavin on this one.

'Because I know you love me, even though you never say it.'

And after that? Gavin smiled to himself and slipped an arm around the man beside him. After that, he'd get an interview so hot that James Delany would piss his pants in his hurry to give Gav other assignments.

'Ah Gavin. I do love you.'

As the plane began its descent into Heathrow Airport, Gavin brushed Gerry's immaculately styled hair with smiling lips. 'I know you do, hot stuff.' And he knew this assignment from *Financial Week* was about to get really interesting.


An hour later, the perfect weekend had turned into the perfect nightmare. The door to the mews flat swung open on its expensive hinges before Gerry had even inserted the key.

'Oh no! Oh, please, no!'

Gav dumped their bags on the doorstep and followed Gerry into the hall.

'Oh, my God!'

Gav's eyes swept the mess of broken glass and overturned furniture which greeted them. 'You stay here. Let me...' He motioned to Gerry. But the distraught futures dealer was already running through into the lounge: 'My home! My beautiful home!'

Arriving on Gerry's heels, Gav surveyed the damage. It was pretty bad. Two leather sofas lay overturned, their covering slashed to ribbons. CDs and DVDs littered the polished maple floor. The 52-inch flat-screen TV had been stomped to a thousand, glistening smithereens. A state-of-the-art Scandinavian home-entertainment centre would never entertain again. Books and magazines were everywhere, their pages meticulously torn out, then ripped into confetti. The display case that had housed Gerry's prized investment collection of Third Dynasty Ming ceramics was empty. Its contents crunched under their feet.

Gavin sighed heavily: so much for Gerry's precious hi-tech alarm system. But it was only... stuff. At least neither of them had been hurt. He turned to the man, who was now crying softly. 'I'll phone the police. You're insured, right?' Gavin started to wrap his arms around the distressed figure, to comfort him.

'Get out!' Unexpectedly, Gerry pushed him away. 'Get out of my home – get out of my life!'

Gavin blinked in bemusement. 'What have I done?'

'How many of your little boyfriends have you had here?' Gerry sank to his knees and pointlessly began to gather up tiny shards of Chinese pottery. 'How many of your dirty bits of rough trade have been in my home – casing it?' With shaking hands, he dropped worthless fragments into a palm. 'They want you, Gavin? They want you enough to destroy my home? They can bloody well have you.'

Gav frowned and crouched beside the sobbing man. 'Baby, this has nothing to do with—'

'Fucking get out!'

The force of the shout made him reel back. Reluctantly, Gavin got to his feet. 'At least let me phone the police and—'

'I never want to see you again.' The voice was quieter now. 'Please leave.'

Gavin stood there for a few seconds, watching Gerry's tears drop onto the remnants of three-hundred-year-old ceramics. Then he slowly walked back out into the hall, grabbed his bag and laptop and left through the same door he'd moved in through, seven long months ago.

In the taxi that took him to his small bedsit-cum-office in King's Cross, Gav stared dolefully at the passing London traffic. Gerry was wrong: he'd never brought a trick home, let alone given them keys. The guy was also, understandably, very upset that he'd been burgled. He just needed some space to cool down – he didn't mean any of those things he'd said. Gav would give him a couple of hours, then phone.

That was what he'd do.

Gerry didn't really want to end this. Deep down, he needed Gavin. And, given time, he would come to realise this.

But, as the taxi drew in at the kerb in front of the dilapidated office building, two police cars were already parked there. And, as Gavin trudged up the four flights of stairs towards his office, something told him the voices drifting down from the floors above were looking for him.

# Eight

On the landing in front of his office, two figures in white paper suits and wearing latex gloves stuck labels onto small Ziploc bags. Two uniformed cops stood either side of the door to his office – a door that was lying on the floor, completely off its hinges.

Gav sighed. Talk about bad luck! First Gerry had thrown a number, now this. He had no idea what idiot would want to break into his office: there was little of value and nothing worth stealing. He also had no idea when this had happened: he'd not been back here for weeks, and from the look of things the two other offices on this landing were no longer occupied. Dropping his bags, he made to move between the policemen. The larger of the two held out a restraining hand: 'Sorry sir, this is a crime scene. You can't—'

'This is my office.' Gav looked at the man. He was handsome, in a brutal sort of way. Full, bee-stung lips. Cheekbones any woman would have given her eye teeth for. And a faint but still noticeable scar creased the corner of the guy's right eye.

The cop's expression altered subtly. He glanced left, into the office. 'Sir? He's here.'

Gav followed the cop's line of vision. Just beyond the doorway, he could see overturned filing cabinets, drawers pulled from the desk and their contents scattered over the worn carpet.

'And your name is...?'

The smaller of the two cops was talking to him now. Gav turned, focusing on the slight, blond policeman. 'Shaw – Gavin Shaw. I—'

'Mr Shaw?' A third voice entered the conversation. Deeper. Richer. And retaining the edge of an East End accent.

Gav's head swivelled. He inhaled sharply.

Filling the doorway of his office was the fattest, ugliest plain-clothes policeman he'd ever seen.

'Mr Gavin Shaw?'

Orson Wells in *A Touch of Evil*. Sidney Greenstreet in almost every film he'd made. The sheer bulk of the man momentarily rendered Gavin speechless.

The full, flabby face frowned. 'You can talk, I take it, Shaw?'

The use of his surname made his guts twist. But he did manage to find his voice. 'Er, sorry, um...' He had no idea what to call the man, who obviously no intention of introducing himself.

'You are the registered owner of this office?' Fatboy's frown became a scowl.

'Um, yeah – well, I rent it for business purposes.' Gav fought the urge to back away. It wasn't just the man's bulk, though that was overwhelming enough. The obese cop had a very strong presence, which Gav had a feeling had little to do with the 350-odd pounds he was carrying.

'Business purposes, eh?' Fatboy turned and lumbered backwards, beckoning with a massive hand.

Gav edged forward, following the slow-moving form over the smashed-in door. 'Yeah – I'm a freelance journalist.' He was vaguely aware of the two uniformed cops bringing up the rear.

'Make a lot of money at this... freelancing, do you, Shaw?' A mocking tone had entered the deep voice.

'I get by.' Inside the office, the reality of the break-in came home to him. Gavin stifled a low moan. He could smell splintered wood from the kicked-in door. Shards of glass mixed with the papers and old invoices littering the soiled and stained carpet.

'Any idea what your... visitors were looking for, Shaw?'

Over the far side of the small room – made smaller by Fatboy's presence in it – another figure in a white paper suit was wiping the top of an overturned filing cabinet with a small brush.

'Eh, Shaw?'

Gav could only shake his head. It would take hours to clean all this up – and it was the last thing he felt like doing right now.

'Whatever it was, they didn't find it.' Fatboy's oblique comment was punctuated by a gruntlike sound.

Tearing his eyes from the debris that had been his office furniture, Gav watched the fat face contort into a smile. He frowned: what the fuck was so funny?

'But we did.' The smile broadened into a deep, ugly grin. Fatboy waved hand over Gav's shoulder.

Rustlings from beyond. Gav was still trying to work out what the man was on about when one of the other paper-suited men appeared, holding a Ziploc bag. He passed it to Fatboy.

Gavin stared at it. It was full of something white and powdery. Before his brain could take in anything more, a set of strong hands gripped both of his arms. Gav flinched.

Fatboy continued, holding the Ziploc bag gingerly between a meaty thumb and forefinger. He waved it in front of Gav's bemused face. 'Either you've got a really heavy habit or you've been supplementing your income from the freelancing with something that's a lot easier to sell.'

His head swivelled between the two uniformed cops, who now each held one of his arms. Gav's brain finally began to work. 'I've never seen that before.' He didn't know exactly what the bag contained, but was savvy enough to suspect it wasn't sherbet.

'Gavin Shaw, I am arresting you for possession of a Class A drug. You do not have to say anything, but it may harm your defence if you do not mention when questioned...'

The rest of Fatboy's rote-delivered words faded away. Gav was aware of cold steel around his wrists. Rough hands grabbed his shoulders. Instinct made him resist.

One of the hands fixing cuffs to his wrists twisted viciously.

Gav yelped in pain, but at least he'd broken through the numbness of shock. 'I want to speak to a lawyer!'

The two unformed cops were already pushing him towards the door. Gav stumbled over an upturned wastepaper bin. Arms secure behind his back, he had no way of breaking the fall. He staggered to his knees and toppled forwards, jarring a shoulder as he did so. Strong hands wrenched him back to his feet. 'I know my rights!'

'Do you, now?' Fatboy's rattling grunt-laugh followed him out of the office and down four flights of stairs. He could still hear the sound, ringing in his ears, as the two cops pushed him into the back of a police car.

All his requests to phone a lawyer were politely ignored. In the bowels of Hammersmith Police Station his pockets were emptied. His laptop, cellphone and rucksack full of dirty underwear were taken away. But at least he signed for them. And the handcuffs had been removed. He was fingerprinted. Then he was pushed into a tiny cell and told to take his clothes off.

Gavin stared at Scarface and Blondie. His right hand moved to the belt of his jeans. 'Bit of privacy, eh, guys?' He waited for the two uniformed cops to leave. Right on cue, Scarface moved towards the cell's open door. Gavin breathed a sigh of relief and began to unzip, but the cop had gone only to close it firmly, sealing all three of them in the tiny, claustrophobic space.

'Can't have you disposing of any further evidence, can we?' Scarface grinned.

'Shoes first, please.' More businesslike, Blondie produced a large bin liner from somewhere and waited impassively.

There was nothing to do but comply. Sitting down on the narrow bed-cum-bench, Gav began to unlace his trainers. His fingers stumbled. His heart was beating too fast. Beyond stubborn laces that steadfastly refused to be undone, he could see two sets of highly polished shoes, along with the first six inches or so of navy-serge, regulation-uniformed legs.

'Get a move on, eh? We've not got all day.' Scarface. Sneeringly.

Gavin flinched and tried harder.

'Take your time.' Blondie. Almost reassuringly.

He seized on the encouragement and finally managed to kick off both shoes. Gav stood up, held them out.

Blondie took them impassively, and carefully placed the trainers in the bottom of the bin liner. 'Jeans, please.'

Gav complied, fingers working better now. He unzipped in record time, dragging the denim over his socked feet and holding them out before he was asked to. Meeting the blond cop's eyes, Gavin found himself searching wildly for approval.

His jeans were taken in silence, folded, and placed in the bag with his shoes. 'Shirt.'

A shiver erected the thick hair on his legs. Gav glanced at Scarface, who was now leaning against the cell door, arms folded. The damaged, handsome face wore an unsettling smile.

And something even more unsettling was staking place inside Gavin's white CK briefs. He didn't bother trying to undo the buttons of his shirt. Gav turned away and hauled the garment hurriedly over his head, desperate to hide his growing erection.

Scarface laughed. 'Aw, he's shy!'

Gav's dick twitched again. He held out the garment in Blondie's direction, head lowered. Even without looking up, he knew they were watching him. He knew this was just routine. He knew it was all some horrible mistake. Sooner or later, he'd get to see someone in authority who would let him phone a lawyer and this whole misunderstanding would be sorted out and he would be released.

As Blondie took the extended shirt, their fingers brushed.

Electric shocks coursed through his whole body. Gavin bit his lip and shoved both hands into his armpits. What the fuck was wrong with him? Standing there shivering, in CKs and socks, and with his head lowered, he stared at two pairs of highly polished shoes. Through the buzz in his ears, he could hear the rustle and crackle of polythene as Blondie methodically added his shirt to the rest of his gear. His prayer was silent but heartfelt.

Go! Please *go*!

But it wasn't over yet. 'Now the rest.' Blondie's tones were as detached as ever.

Gav suppressed a groan. He didn't suppress it enough.

Scarface laughed. 'Aw, leave him his knickers, eh?'

Yes, please leave me my knickers.

'You know the rules.' Blondie was sounding cooler by the minute.

'Yeah, I know, but come on – just this once?'

Yes, please, just this once.

'Orders are orders.'

Gav stood there silently as the two men continued to talk around him. He felt like an object. A thing. Something to be refereed to in the third person only – if at all. He could feel his fingers dampening. Sweat was soaking his hair. And between his legs his cock was inching resolutely towards full erection.

'Socks, please.' Back on track, Blondie's cool tones seeped into his confused brain.

Gavin bent over, eager to comply. And, as he did so, the head of his jersey-covered cock impacted with his stomach. He groaned out loud, then tried to balance on one leg to remove the desired item of clothing. And failed. Falling sideways, he flailed to break his fall.

A strong, steadying arm appeared from somewhere and gripped his shoulder.

Gavin moaned, leaning into the support. He held on with his free hand, wrenching off socks with the other. As soon as he'd done so, the arm was abruptly withdrawn and replaced by an outstretched hand.

Scarface was still sniggering.

Gav meekly handed over his socks.

'Now the rest.' Blondie's words were totally emotionless.

Gav raised his eyes from the floor and took a step back.

Both cops now stood in front of the cell door. Scarface was still sniggering. Blondie's deceptively boyish face and frame were deadly seriously. Icy-blue eyes met Gavin's. 'Briefs, please.'

The polite detachment only made it worse. Gav swallowed hard and began to shake violently. The tiny cell was far from cold. In fact, the presence of three adult male bodies – one of whom was sweating profusely – in such a confined space had created a damp, humid atmosphere. Nonetheless, every bone in Gavin's seminaked body felt as if it were about to be jarred free by the jolting shivers that trembled through his broad frame like the aftershocks of a mini-earthquake.

'Gavin?'

The use of his name made his cock shudder. He searched for humanity in the voice. And found only cool, commanding authority. Pinned by glacial eyes, he took his hands slowly from his armpits. Fingers pushed themselves down under the waistband of the CKs. Unable to break Blondie's stare, Gav dragged down his underpants.

They snagged on the head of his hard cock, jerking his shaft.

The sensation made him moan, half pleasure, half pain. All horror.

Face scarlet, he tore his eyes from Blondie's, fumbling in his groin like a schoolboy. On the front of the white CKs, a dark damp spot told a tale for all eyes to see. Gav tried to clench his fists, to stop the shakes. But, without the use of his fingers, he'd never get the damn things off. Eventually, he managed to unhook himself and drag the briefs down over his thighs. He stepped out of them unsteadily, and held the still-warm garment out, head lowered in abject humiliation.

The first sound to greet his ears was a low, snide wolf whistle from Scarface.

His cock twitched, poking further into the warm humid air of the tiny cell.

The underwear was taken. The sound of rustling told him where it had been placed. As he stood there, naked and shivering, Gav's hands flew to his groin. The touch of his own fingers on his cock and balls only intensified his discomfort: he felt more exposed than if he'd stood there, exposed and proud. Heat from his blushing face was spreading lower. He could feel it on his neck, shoulders, then chest and belly. Head still lowered, Gav frowned and tried to pull himself together.

What the hell was wrong with him?

He'd been naked in front of other men before. At the gym, at the swimming pool – countless times. And it never usually bothered him. Never usually gave him anything near the raging hard-on he was at present wildly trying to will away. Gritting his teeth, he tried to figure it out.

Was it because they were cops?

No: Gav knew several policeman – both socially, and through his work. Underneath the uniform, they were mostly ordinary guys. Was it because of the remote possibility that possession of whatever was in Ziploc bag would be pinned on him? The frown became a scowl. Nope. No way. He knew his rights. It was all some terrible mistake, which would be sorted out very soon.

So, if all this was true, why was he, Gavin Shaw – an intelligent, articulate man of the world and as streetwise as the next guy – scared half to death and hard as a rock?

As he cowered there, clutching his tackle and as red as a virgin, a loud bang made him jump. Gav's head snapped up.

The cell was empty. And he was alone.

For the next couple of hours – could have been days, they felt so long – Gav alternately paced, tried to sleep and banged on the door of his cell.

Nothing. No one.

He found a rough, stained blanket on the narrow bed-cum-bench, pulled it off and draped it around himself. They had his clothes. His watch. His cellphone. And they thought they'd taken his dignity. But Gavin Shaw was made of stronger stuff. Clutching the edges of the smelly old blanket around himself with one hand, he attacked the cell door with the other. 'Oi! I want to speak to a lawyer!'

He knew his rights.

He knew he had to be allowed one phone call. Who would he phone? Gav had never felt in need of legal advice before in his life. If things had been normal, he'd have phoned Gerry.

Gerry would know what to do.

But things were far from normal. As it was, Gav had a feeling Gerry was the last person, right now, who cared one way or another what happened to the man he held responsible for the break-in at his beloved mews home.

'Oi! You out there!' Gav thumped his fist against the door again. 'I want to speak to whoever's in charge! I know my rights!'

But who else was there? Gavin scowled in frustration, kicked the door and retreated to sit and brood on his bench-cum-bed. Among his wide circle of vague friends, acquaintances and business contacts, ex-boyfriends, tricks and encounters, there was only one person he'd trust in a situation like this.

James.

James Delaney.

Gav snorted to himself and wrapped his hairy blanket more tightly around his now cooling naked body.

He'd rather chew off his own arms than let James know where he was. Gav could just imagine the guy's amusement if he got wind of this. Bloody Delaney would dine out for months on the story of how he'd had to come and rescue his ex from the clutches of 'those nasty policemen'.

His feet were like ice. His hard-on, thankfully, had subsided some time ago, but had been replaced by a growing urge to use a toilet. All those free mimosas on the flight from Reykjavik had now reached his bladder, causing an uncomfortable pressure in the pit of his stomach. Leaning back against the bare brick wall, Gav drew his knees up and hugged them. He looked up at the single strip light, which was now flickering annoyingly above his head, for something to focus on.

At one end, a fly buzzed onto then away from the cool illuminated length. At the opposite end, a dusty-looking cobweb. And on its edge, a far-from-dusty spider lay in wait.

The fly walked a little closer.

The spider remained motionless. Not a single thread of web betrayed its presence.

The fly paused, buzzed away to circle around the room. Then it was back, a little further along the strip light's plastic cover.

The spider bided his time. And never moved a muscle

Gavin watched, transfixed by a game as old as time itself.

The spider couldn't see the fly. The spider didn't need to see the fly. The spider knew some fly would be along at some time or another. And, when it came, those first fly footsteps on any strand of that intricately woven thread would alert Mr Spider to the fact that dinner had arrived.

Mr Spider merely sat still. And waited. Waiting was what he did.

The fly was mere millimetres away from the edge of the web when the cell door burst open. Gavin left to his feet. 'I demand to see a—' The words caught in his throat.

Two uniformed cops moved into the tiny cell. They were not Blondie and Scarface. One held a set of handcuffs. The other slapped an extended side arm baton rhythmically against his palm.

'Gavin Shaw?'

Something in him started to crumble. But he managed a nod. The hairy, smelly blanket slipped away as one of the cops gabbed his wrists and cuffed his hands once more in front of his body. The other cop thoughtfully picked up the blanket.

Gav was grateful for the gesture.

But the cop threw it over Gavin's head. Plunged into hairy darkness, he felt panic surge through his veins. His legs wobbled. But before he could react further, a heavy hand gripped the back of his neck and Gav found himself pushed roughly forward.

# Nine

He still needed to piss. But it was now the least of his problems.

After hours in bright if harsh light, the darkness was terrifying. As he was pushed along endless corridors for what seemed like miles in total silence, the space beneath the hairy blanket took on a form of its own for Gavin and became something like a fourth entity on this endless journey to God knew where.

His escort didn't talk to each other. Nor did they address him. Gavin could feel the cop's hand on the back of his neck. He could hear the solid clack-clack of the other's footsteps, punctuated by the occasional slap of sidearm baton on palm. He was painfully aware of the old-man shuffle of his own feet, the near-asthmatic wheeze of his breath as it left his lungs. But the thick almost viscous darkness scared him most.

That darkness held smells. Sweat. The ferrous odour of dried blood. The acid stink of old piss. Shit. And the sweet salty aroma of dried spunk.

How many men had used this ancient blanket before him? Wrapped it around themselves as they lay, cold and frightened, in a cell? How many had pissed themselves in it, through sheer terror? How many had moaned and sobbed there, on narrow beds, wallowing in their own filth? How many had wanked in it, in some desperate attempt to find comfort in a comfortless situation?

While his body was stiff from the cold and the waiting, Gavin Shaw's mind raced, working faster than ever. Countless scenarios loomed before his tightly shut eyes, thrown up by an agile brain that still couldn't quite take all this in.

Plunged into a Kafka-esque world where nothing was explained and action took place without reason, he saw himself with a long full beard. Smeared with his own faeces, emaciated and broken, this parallel-universe Gavin Shaw was destined to walk endless corridors for ever. He'd never see day again. He'd never feel the sun on his face, smell new-mown grass or hear birds sing.

He'd become an animal. He'd lose the power of speech because no one ever talked to him and everything he said was ignored. Reduced to communicating in a series of grunts and formless mumbles, he saw himself scrabble for food when it was thrown to him and tear it apart with his bare hands. He slept alone on the floor – any floor. Day would merge into night. Days would slip into weeks. Then months. No one would miss him. Gerry would be glad to see the back of him. He'd rarely known the names of any of the men he'd fucked or sucked or wanked off up alleys, in parks or behind walls. And none of them would remember him as anything more than an afternoon quickie. Perhaps James would wonder, when the commissioned article on Derek Masters failed to appeal. But even he'd probably just chalk up Gavin Shaw's disappearance from the face of the earth to some new boyfriend, and calmly shunt the Masters assignment onto some other hack.

He was alone. Alone in the dark. No one would miss him. No one would care. No one gave a fuck if he lived or died.

Beneath the blanket, in his world of body smells, Gavin whimpered. Stumbling onwards, guided by the hand on the back of his neck, he was vaguely aware he'd got hard again somewhere along the way. With each step, his semierect cock brushed against the inside of one thigh, then the other. Once he became aware of the motion, a rhythm slowly built up. And took his mind off the circles of Hell he'd somehow tumbled into.

With footstep, his cock brushed his thigh. With each slap of sidearm baton on palm, his cock twitched. With each twitch, the paper-thin skin on his shaft grew tighter. As the skin drew tighter, his balls clenched.

Brush, slap, twitch, clench. Brush, slap, twitch, clench.

Slowly, second by second and minute by minute, his cock filled with blood. And, as the blood left his brain, the dark, unsettling thoughts left, too. Some invisible link was forming, between the sound of that baton impacting with a cop's hand and the other stout baton of flesh and gristle between Gavin Shaw's legs. Shoulders hunched forward and aching, arms held in front of his body by the cold metal around his wrists, he inhaled sharply as the head of his stretching cock bumped against the rigid section of forged steel that linked the handcuffs.

He wasn't an animal any more. He was a machine. Switch it on, and the machine began to perform the function for which it had been designed.

Abruptly, the hand on his neck tightened. Gav stumbled to a halt. The other footsteps stopped, too. Through the thick smelly blanket, he could hear the sound of keys. For one delirious moment, he thought his wrists were about to be loosened.

His hopes were in vain.

'Gavin Shaw, sir.' As he was pushed forward by the hands on his neck, another door slammed shut behind him.

At least he wasn't alone any more.

'Sit down, Shaw.' The voice was deep, growly.

When the blanket was whipped from his head, Gav knew he'd merely moved from one circle of Hell into another.

'Christ, did they not give you anything to wear, son?' Fatboy's pudgy face bordered on the sympathetic.

Maybe not Hell after all. Gav moaned and sat down, hands clutched in front of genitals. His head shook slowly.

The fat face frowned. Then the obese policeman was struggling out of a battered sports jacket and mumbling to himself about 'fuckin' rule-bound bastards'. Seconds later, Gav flinched as warm heaviness settled around his shoulders. The small gesture from the big man made his guts clench. He stared at the face of his unlikely saviour in gratitude, raising his cuffed wrists in silent supplication.

Perched on the edge of the table, which sat in the middle of the dimly lit room, Fatboy raised his own flabby hands, palms upwards in helplessness. 'Sorry, they stay on, son.' The doughy features creased apologetically. 'But at least I can get you a cuppa tea – would you like that?'

Gav opened his mouth. Nothing came out. He realised he'd had nothing to eat or drink for at least – eight hours? His throat was dry as a desert. So he nodded, frantically.

Fatboy moved piggy eyes to a point above Gav's shoulder. 'See if you can rustle up some tea, eh?'

The fact that they weren't alone took him by surprise. And sent a shiver of unease up his spine. Head swivelling, Gav watched the back of a faceless white-shirted police officer move swiftly and silently towards the door.

'Now.' Fatboy's growly tones reclaimed his attention. 'Let's you and me have a little talk, eh, son?'

Warm, his nakedness half covered, able to see and relatively secure-feeling for the first time in what seemed like days, Gav nodded vigorously: if this overweight, unattractive police officer had asked for his right arm, Gavin Shaw would have done his best to provide it.


The tea came.

It soothed his throat and gave back the power of speech, but increased the twisting pressure in the pit of his stomach. Gav continued to gulp the weak, lukewarm liquid nonetheless, holding the plastic cup with both cuffed hands. And as he drank, he talked.

About how long he'd been renting the King's Cross office. From whom. The rental terms. His landlord – some faceless business consortium with a bank in Bishopsgate in which Gav deposited his rent every month. His neighbours.

Perched on the edge of the desk, Fatboy listened intently and nodded from time to time. He asked more questions – about Gavin's work.

Gav detailed various assignments, provided names and contact numbers of editors who would vouch for him as an upstanding citizen. 'James'll tell you – James Delany. He's in charge of *Financial Week* – I'm working for him, at the moment, actually.'

Fatboy continued to nod. It was hard to tell whether he believed any of it, but at least he was treating Gavin like a human being. As the interview progressed, Gav couldn't help but notice no one was taking any notes. Nor did any tape machine seem to be in evidence, let alone recording the proceedings.

The immense police officer was now asking about Gavin's movements over the past forty-eight hours.

Snug and safe within the confines of the large man's battered tweed jacket, Gav sipped his second cup of police-canteen tea and talked on. 'See, that's the thing – I've not even been in the country for the last two days.'

Fatboy raised a fat, quizzical eyebrow.

Gav smiled. 'Iceland, would you believe? On an assignment. And, even before that, I've not been near the office for, um, months.' It was the truth.

Fatboy nodded slowly. 'Can anyone confirm this, son?'

Gav opened his mouth to supply Gerry's name. Then closed it abruptly: better not to volunteer an alibi that could well be shot dead in the water, depending on how Gerry was feeling about the break-in at his own flat. His brain raced. James! Of course! James had bought the tickets – James had even phoned him, at the Blue Lagoon. Excitedly, Gav passed on this information, plus the commissioning editor of *Financial Week*'s mobile and personal line number, to Fatboy, who again nodded to the faceless uniformed cop in the corner. Who again left the room.

Gavin shifted in the hard plastic chair, cuffed hands now back in his lap. He looked at the obese detective. 'I've really never seen that – whatever it was you found in my office, before. Ask anyone – I don't do drugs. Hell, I don't even drink much.' He laughed, aware he was babbling. But he couldn't stop. 'Gave up the fags two years ago – I run every morning, you know. Watch what I eat, keep an eye on the old cholesterol.' He knew he was sounding like some sort of health freak, as well as overcompensating like crazy. 'Those drugs could have been there for months – years, even. I just moved in and left the place like it was. Didn't haul up carpets or redecorate or anything...'

Stop.

'I mean, I hardly use the place, you know? Sleep there, from time to time, but it's hardly what you'd call home...'

Stop *now*.

'Maybe you should get in touch with whoever rented it before me, you know?'

Shut up. *Shut the fuck up, you babbling idiot!*

'I mean, anyone could have left those drugs there. We could be talking... years ago! I—'

The sound of the door reopening finally helped Gavin close his mouth. Falling silent, he watched the faceless cop approach Fatboy, lower his mouth to one flabby ear and whisper.

Fatboy looked at the cop. Then looked at Gavin.

Gavin beamed. 'James told you? James confirmed I was in—'

'Mr Delany did indeed purchase two tickets to Reykjavik for you, last week. However, he cannot confirm those tickets were ever used. And, although he admits he did speak to you, last night, mobile phones, as you know, do not confirm the user's whereabouts.' Fatboy sighed heavily. 'So we're back to square one.'

The uniformed cop retreated back to his corner. And inside Gavin's head someone screamed.

*

It went on for hours. And just got worse and worse.

The uniformed cop phoned the airline, who, far from being helpful, informed Hammersmith Police that two open tickets purchased by James Delany had not been used on any flight to Iceland in the past fourteen days. A further phone call to the Reykjavik Ibis astoundingly revealed that no one called Gavin Shaw had ever even reserved a room, never mind stayed there. And passport control at Heathrow had no record of his having left the country in the last two months.

The panic was back. Within the voluminous folds of the fat detective's jacket, Gavin's naked body flushed hot and then icy by turns. In desperation, he gave them Gerry's phone number.

No answer.

Gavin and Fatboy stared at each other, communally sighing. Along with the panic, the urge to piss was now causing severe stomach cramps. But he didn't want to move. He wasn't sure he could. Cold seeped up from the stone floor of the interview room. His legs were stiff and achy. Despite the tea, he had a pounding headache. But at least, here in this dimly lit room with this fat, relatively benign detective, he wasn't alone.

Finally, it grew too much for him. Gav's face flushed up. 'Um, I need to use the toilet.'

Fatboy glanced over Gav's head. 'Take him to—' The growly voice broke off, abruptly. 'On second thoughts, I'll do it myself.' Easing his bulk from the edge of the table, the large detective moved around behind Gavin. 'Up you get, son.' The massive hand on his shoulder, urging him to his feet, was reassuring.

Gav stood up, groaning inside as the blood returned to his legs. His cock twitched against the metal bracelets around his wrists.

But the hand was unsettling, too. It remained there, as Fatboy guided him to the door, reached around to open it in, then ushered a cuffed and shambling Gavin out into another deserted corridor.

Somewhere in the bowels of Hammersmith Police Station, behind some door, a man moaned. Gavin shuddered but walked on.

They passed countless closed and unmarked doors. Inside Fatboy's jacket, Gavin felt his body shrink. He seemed to be growing smaller and more insignificant by the minute. But, while his stature diminished, his cock was continuing to swell.

Piss hard-on. Had to be. He'd never needed to urinate as badly as he needed to now. Everything hurt. His stomach was slightly distended. Even his balls ached. And, deep in his arse, pressure was causing fluttering sensations of something like pleasure.

Finally, a plump arm reached past him and pushed open a door. Gavin whimpered in anticipation and rushed forward into the gents'. Staggering over to the communal urinal, he fumbled for his now almost full erection and tried to aim it at the stained porcelain.

His arms, never mind his hands, refused to obey him. Cuffed and held in front of his body for hours, they tingled from the shoulder down and continued to hang, limp and numb and useless.

Tears of frustration prickled behind his eyes. Gavin bit his lip and tried again. Maybe if he could even wedge the rigid band that linked the cuffs beneath his shaft, somehow, then thrust his hips forward, he could angle his dick in the approximate direction of the urinal. He didn't want to piss down his legs; worse still, he couldn't risk pissing on the fat detective's jacket.

Hunching over, he dipped forward, attempting to hook his tethered wrists over the head of his bobbing cock. But every time he tried his shaft flexed away from him. The floor beneath his feet was wet. Standing in other men's piss and struggling to release his own, he slipped and slid with each attempt.

'Get on with it, son!' Growly irritation from somewhere behind.

Glancing over his shoulder, Gav saw the detective standing

with his back to the door. The pudgy features creased impatiently.

It only made things worse. Gav cringed and turned away. He wanted to please this man. He wanted to piss. And he wanted to get out of this place more than he wanted life itself right now. More desperate than ever, he shrugged, then rotated his shoulders in an attempt to encourage blood flow back into his arms.

Fatboy's jacket slithered to the floor.

Gav moaned, sank to a crouch and made a snatch for it. Too late – the vast tweed garment was already lying in a pool of someone's urine.

'What's the problem?' The growly voice as closer now.

Gav looked at the toes of the large shoes mere inches from his face. Then at the jacket. There was nothing else for it. Using one of the few parts of himself that still functioned, Gavin Shaw, investigative journalist *extraordinaire*, leaned forward, opened his mouth and grabbed the collar of the pissy jacket with his teeth. Slowly, carefully and with knees cracking, he stood up, lifting the wet garment from the floor.

The expression on the pudgy face was hard to read. But he took the jacket from Gav's mouth, shook it and carefully hung it on a nearby coat hook.

Gavin could no longer ignore the burning pain in the pit of his bowels. 'Please – take the cuffs off!' His voice was low with need. 'I can't hold my... my...' He couldn't even say the word, so he gestured with his head and nodded down to where his piss hard-on poked forward from between his thighs.

'Ah...' Understanding dawned on the overweight detective's face. The man smiled. 'Here you go, son.'

One meaty hand gripped his bare shoulder. Gav waited for the other to produce handcuff keys from somewhere. But he was disappointed.

Flesh met flesh.

Then he was horrified as the fat man's other hand curled

around his shaft and aimed it for him. His balls clenched violently. Something that now had nothing to do with the need to urinate tingled deep in his arse.

Using Gavin's cock like a handle of flesh, the obese detective tugged him closer to the urinal. Everything in Gav's body rebelled. Everything he could control at least – which was, right now, precisely nothing.

The hand on his shoulder patted paternally. Standing behind him, Fatboy's legs shadowed Gavin's. The larger man's immense body pressed against his. Gav was suddenly decades younger. He felt like a small boy, although his physical response to this man had nothing to do with father–son relations.

Closing his eyes, he tried. He tried so hard to release a stream of warm steaming urine. It was all he wanted to do. It was his purpose in life. But his hard-on was now part blood, and no way was he going to be able to pass water with this much of an erection. Blushing furiously, he moaned.

A gravely coaxing whisper in his ear: 'Come on, son.'

Gav gritted his teeth and attempted to void his bladder. Nothing. Not a fucking drop. But there was moisture from another source. Somewhere beyond his horror and frustration, Gav became aware that tears were running down his burning cheeks. He could do nothing to stop them. Then the meaty hand moved from his shoulder, and a fat arm was encircling his waist.

'Do it for Daddy, eh?' The deep growly voice in his ear again.

A loud sob tore itself loose from his throat. And urine spurted from his gaping slit. Slumping against the overweight detective's vast form, Gav listened in relief to the sound of the torrent of piss as it splattered against stained porcelain.

The arm around his waist tightened.

He stared at the head of his cock, which protruded from the man's plump, nicotine-stained fingers. Tears were pouring freely down his cheeks now. His chest heaved. Somewhere, just behind his bladder, the vague tingling increased. Along with another, un-expected sensation.

A weird sort of pleasure coursed through his entire body. Like coming – yet not like coming. But a release nevertheless. Of tension. Pressure. And strength.

As the golden stream lessened, the cotton-wool feeling in Gav's legs increased. All the substance seemed to have left his otherwise fit frame. Worse, his limbs has turned to jelly and were now stubbornly refusing to bear his weight. His knees buckled. Gav moan-sobbed. The arm around his waist gripped him more tightly. A gently swaying motion from Fatboy's fat hand shook a few remaining drops of piss from his slit. And the arm around his waist slackened.

Panic surged through what was left of his nervous system.

No way could he walk; no way could he even stay on his feet if that strong, supporting arm was removed. He was completely dependent on this fat, ugly detective. And the thought that the man might leave was suddenly the worst thing Gavin could imagine.

The fist released his cock. The arm around his waist loosened itself further.

Gav scrabbled wildly, helplessly trying to grip onto part of Fatboy. Any part.

Then the arm slipped itself behind the back of Gavin's knees. In seconds, he found himself swept literally off his feet and up into powerful arms.

Whimpering, he managed to raise his own cuffed wrists and drape them around the fat man's neck. His head rested against a huge, bulging deltoid.

The detective was murmuring something to him, in that deep growly voice. To Gavin, it was the sweetest sound he'd ever heard. He closed his eyes, his own mouth formlessly nuzzling the cigarette-smelling shirtsleeve.

Slowly, the man turned, Gav naked in his arms, and strode slowly from the gents'.

He had no clue what happened next. But, when Gavin woke up, he was dressed in his own clothes and lying on a narrow bench.

The door to the cell was open. And his bag and laptop sat against the opposite wall.

A smiling, apologetic face poked itself through the open door. A new face. 'Mr Shaw?' The police officer held a brown envelope and a clipboard.

Gavin shook his head to clear it and swung his legs onto he floor. 'Um, yes?' He sat up slowly.

The cop padded into the cell. 'Sorry it all took so long, sir.' He held out the envelope. 'If you could check your personal possession are all here, then sign for them, you can get off.'

Gavin blinked. 'What about the... drugs?' He snatched at the envelope, emptied its contents onto the bench-cum-bed anyway: cellphone, wallet, passport, watch – it was all there.

The cop laughed. 'That was all a misunderstanding, sir – thanks for your patience.'

Unable quite to believe what he was hearing, Gavin took the pen, signed a form, then shoved his belongings into his pocket.

'That's great – this way, Mr Shaw.' The cop moved out of the cell.

Grabbing his rucksack and laptop, Gavin leapt from the bench and followed the officer. A thousand questions buzzed in his brain.

But, seconds later, he was back out in the sunshine of Hammersmith Broadway.

And his wristwatch showed a mere three hours had passed.

# Ten

Sunshine never felt so warm.

Gav wandered along the road, bathed in a rosy glow.

Smoggy, summer London never tasted fresher. Colours shone so vividly they made his eyes hurt. His skin tingled. The birds sang more loudly. And just for Gavin Shaw.

Slightly dazed, slightly sore and more than a little light-headed, part of him felt as if he'd just been released after ten years in a gulag. Another, bigger part was walking on air. A dopey grin had painted itself across his face. He beamed at the usual assortment of Saturday shoppers as they moved past him like alien beings.

Some of them frowned. Some avoided his eyes. But others smiled back – two girls giggled to each other, and a hunky road sweeper even winked.

Rucksack of his shoulder, and carrying his laptop, he debated getting a taxi home. Gav cut off the main road and into Bishop's Park.

Home. Where was home, at the moment? Not Gerry's place, that was for sure – at least, not yet. And the last time he'd seen his office in King's Cross it'd been lacking a door.

Despite the fact he was technically homeless, the silly grin refused to leave his face. Shoving a hand into his pocket, Gav located some change and bought an ice cream.

Man, powdered milk and frozen colourings had never tasted so good! As he strolled through the leafy park, smiling beatifically at the antics of dogs and small children, his mind slowly began to process the events of the last few hours.

The arrest. The strip. The endless hours in various cells. The smell of the overweight detective's vast, meaty body – had it all, in fact, been a dream? Had he eaten something weird on the flight back from Iceland that had caused him to fall into some sort of stupor? He'd been up most of the previous night: could he possibly have imagined the whole thing, through some sort of sleep-deprivation?

Gav paused at a park bench and sat down. As he raised his ice cream for another lick, the right cuff of his Levi jacket slipped down. He stared.

That angry red weal was no dream. Gav examined his other wrist. An almost identical weal decorated that, too. Whatever had been in that Ziploc bag – coke? speed? – had seemed pretty real, too, as was his memory of his ravaged office. The dopey grin began to slip, and first shadows of anger entered his relief.

False arrest. Inhumane treatment. Excessive use of force. Lack of basic human rights. He'd put in a complaint to the chief of police – maybe even Scotland Yard itself.

Licking melted iced cream from the back of his hand, he stood up, frowning.

At the back of his mind, Gavin knew there was nothing concrete he could actually complain about: he'd been arrested, kept in a cell for a couple of hours, questioned, then released with an apology.

So why did he feel so... violated?

Shoving the remains of the iced cream cone into his mouth, Gav picked up his bags and set off towards the main road. There was so much that didn't make sense. Why was there no record of his having entered Iceland, let alone spent a night at the hotel? Why had the police even thought to break into and search his office, let alone find drugs?

He stuck out a hand. A taxi stopped. He got in.

And was it merely coincidence his office and Gerry's flat had been turned over when they were away?

More mysteries awaited him after he'd paid the driver and jogged up three flights of stairs, ready to call a joiner to make secure what was going to have to be home for the foreseeable future.

On the fourth-floor landing, Gavin's jaw dropped. Irrationally, he closed his eyes. Then opened them again slowly – just in case his mind was playing tricks on him.

Finally, he stretched out a hand. And touched the solid and apparently intact outer door to his office. What the...?

The surface was smooth and unmarked. No boot marks. No splintered wood around the lock – which appeared as old and slightly rusted as he remembered it. Gavin stepped closer, fingertips moving to hinges that, mere hours earlier, had hung twisted and useless. He peered, unable to swear they were the original hinges. Hell, who ever noticed these things?

Gav stepped back and scanned the area. Not a single wood shaving or scrap of sawdust indicated that any burglary had ever taken place.

The possibility that he'd imagined the whole thing returned to break over him in a huge wave. Uncertainty rippled through his sore, exhausted body. Gav hauled up the sleeves of his Levi jacket and stared at the circlets of truth around his wrists.

That was real. The echo of pain in the pit of his stomach was real. A low moan escaped his lips. The memory of his cock held by flabby fingers and his face buried in Fatboy's chest as he cried his eyes out was real. Gav frowned, clenching his fists to steady himself.

It had happened. Of that he was sure. And the police weren't known for the readiness to tidy up after burglaries. So why was someone determined to erase all trace of it here? Fumbling in the side pocket of his rucksack for keys, Gavin intended to find out.

*

The inside of his office was similarly intact. The filing cabinets were upright. His desk was neat and tidy – that in itself was a give-away, since Gav distinctly remembered leaving the place in a bit of a mess the last time he'd been here. Even his coffee machine was OK. He grabbed the jug and filled it with water in the handbasin of the small toilet, then switched the machine on.

Seated on his couch-cum-bed, he replayed the events of the past forty-eight hours.

Two break-ins. His arrest. His subsequent release and the attempted erasure of one of those break-ins.

In the background, the coffee-machine gurgled away.

Twenty-four hours in Iceland, which for some reason had escaped the notice of both the airline that had transported them there and the hotel in which they'd stayed.

Gav's hand reached for his cellphone. He wondered how Gerry had got on with the police. His hand moved away: he had a feeling anything he told Gerry right now would be put down to lies and fabrication.

The coffee machine hissed.

Gav continued to rack his brain. Why would anyone beak into his office? Where did the drugs come from? What were his would-be burglars looking for? Was the Ziploc bag of white powder an attempt to frame him? If so, why? Whose toes had he trodden on? What else had happened in the last day that could prompt such a bizarre series of events?

As he sat there, mulling over possibilities, it suddenly hit him between the eyes.

Masters. Derek Masters. And a certain tape recording of a certain conversation.

Gavin lunged to his overnight back and unzipped it hurriedly. Hurling underwear, toiletries and T-shirts onto the floor, he dug deep until he found what he was looking for.

Right at the bottom of his bag, an ancient pair of sandals he always carried. And not just in case of good weather. Grabbing the right shoe with his right hand, Gav twisted the heel sharply.

Of all people, James Delany had given him the sandals, years ago. He could still hear those sly, half-smiling tones in his head: 'For the man who has everything – should my favourite investigative journalist ever need to smuggle something small but valuable through customs.'

It had been meant as a joke, but for some reason Gav had got into the habit of using the shallow, hollowed-out heel for storing his micro-cassettes. It held three, at a pinch. At the moment, a single item occupied the space.

Carefully, he tipped the tiny object into his hand.

On its own, it meant nothing. But added to what Gav had witnessed, last night at the Blue Lagoon, it obviously bothered someone.

Sitting there, holding a recording on which Derek Masters was clearly being blackmailed, Gav saw in his mind's eye the silver-haired captain of industry and the beautiful lady-boy, playing footsie under that eerie Icelandic sky.

And slowly things began to make sense: Gerry's flat; the break-in at his own office; his arrest; the confiscation of his clothes and belongings – all in an attempt to find and destroy this tiny tape?

A smile crept over Gavin's face. As he slipped the cassette back into its hiding place, the terror and the isolation of the previous few hours were swept away by something much more powerful.

This profile of the head of Masters Industries was going to knock James's socks off.

And it was going to propel Gavin Shaw, freelance writer, into the big time.

After two much-needed cups of strong black coffee and a wash, he finally got around to switching his cellphone back on.

Four missed calls. Plus a text.

Towelling his hair, Gav saw that two of the calls were from James. He smiled, listening to smooth, unruffled tones on his voice mail: 'What have you been up to, Gavin? I've had some cop on the line twice, asking about you.'

The smile broadened into a grin. Part of him wanted to tell James all about it. Another part knew he should wait until he had more on Derek Masters' intriguing private life.

Tossing the towel onto the floor, Gav checked the text. The first thing he noticed was that he didn't have the caller's number. Again. Opening the message, he stared at the Nokia's tiny green screen: 'A'dam. 2night. EU Conference on Taxation.'

To the untrained eye, the message was meaningless. But in the light of recent developments it was gold. Gav chuckled to himself and mentally thanked his anonymous informant. Minutes later, he had connected up his laptop and visited the EU's online site, which conveniently gave him all the details he needed to know, regarding the location of the conference: Amsterdam. There was even a schedule of speakers. And there, halfway down the list, was the name D Masters.

He ran a finger along the man's name. Amsterdam. City of Sin. Derek Masters? This is your life!

James wasn't totally happy about having to pay for yet another flight – let alone one at such short notice. And he wanted to know more about what was going on. Gav assured him he'd submit all his expenses in the proper fashion, and James grudgingly relented.

Laptop on his knee, his rucksack in the hold, he spent most of the short flight from Luton to Schipol airport reviewing the information in the Masters file.

There was so much he still didn't know. The man's age, for a start. Fifties? Early sixties? Rubbing his tired eyes, Gav leaned back in his seat and let his eyelids close.

Despite the silver hair, there was a thrusting virility about the man. Masters could be anywhere between forty and seventy! Abstractedly, he found himself picturing Derek Masters and the pre-op lady-boy together. Gav smiled to himself. A lot of straight guys went for that tit-cock thing – and everyone knew why. Was this another of Derek Masters' little secrets? Did the man bat for both sides? Unexpectedly, Gav felt his cock stir inside his underpants. Not that Masters was his type. Too old, too sober, too... uptight.

The head of his cock pushed against the inside of his thigh. He could almost feel the folds of foreskin uncurl and sense the contradiction in his thoughts.

He was restless, that was all: it had a been a good two days since his last run – or his last fuck, for that matter. Maybe there would be the chance to pick up a bit of rough while he was in Europe's most liberal city. Gav shrugged an incipient erection away, opened his eyes and refocused on his screen. This time, he'd get photographs: he'd bought a cheap digital camera in Luton's duty-free. This time, he wouldn't even bother trying to interview Derek Masters. A picture spoke a thousand words – wasn't that what they said? And pictures didn't lie.

But if the businessman – or his henchman – was responsible for the ransacking of both his office and Gerry's flat, Gav had to admit Masters was onto him. Discretion was necessary. And, if there was one thing Gavin Shaw could be, it was discreet.

Another European city.

Another airport. Another baggage-reclaim hall.

Gav frowned, watching as passengers from the flight after his plucked their luggage from the moving carousel. He glanced at his watch. So much for Dutch efficiency: he'd already enquired twice of different baggage attendants, handed over his luggage ticket and been told politely but firmly to wait there.

Typical – bloody typical!

As the baggage hall slowly emptied, he became aware he was under scrutiny. The way you do. Tuning his head slowly, Gav scanned the area curiously for the source of the attention.

A group of what looked – and sounded – like middle-aged American women were embracing demonstratively. Two pilots stood, chatting quietly. A few tourists sauntered past.

His gaze paused.

Over the far side of the area, a guy in an acid-green cleaning-staff vest with a brush and a rubbish cart met Gavin's eyes.

Gav look in the man. Late twenties. Closely cropped blond hair. Blue eyes. Vaguely Nordic good looks. An open face, at present wearing that inimitably laid-back Dutch smile. Shoulders – big shoulders (his cock flexed), shoulders he could grip onto from behind, as he pushed into the guy's arse. And a pierced lip. Gav's cock flexed again. He risked a returning smile.

Leaning his brush against the side of his rubbish cart, the guy moved one large hand to the crotch of baggy trousers.

Gav watched the floor cleaner reposition what looked like a more than ample package. His eyes narrowed in desire. Man, he could almost visualise the contents of those baggy trousers.

Thick, cut, Netherlands dick. Big balls – balls you could suck on for ever and—

'Mr Shaw?'

Gav jumped and turned.

One of the baggage attendants he'd talked to earlier stood in front of him. Holding Gavin's rucksack. Which he extended, a smile of apology on his face. 'Sorry for the delay, sir. Is this your—'

'Yes, that's mine.' Gav snatched it, shrugging the backpack over his shoulder. 'Thanks.' He spun back round, looking for his floor cleaner.

The guy was nowhere in sight.

Gav sighed.

'Again, our apologies for any inconvenience, Mr Shaw. These things...'

But Gavin was already walking away, striding over to where he'd last seen the guy with the pierced lip. Where the fuck had he disappeared to? Gav had turned away for only the briefest of seconds. His eyes swept the baggage-reclaim hall. Where had the bastard—

Movement on this right made him pause. One of two heavy plastic curtains that screened the service area from the rest of the place was moving. Gav watched a blond cropped head poke from between the folds of industrial polythene. The normally laid-back Dutch features creased in disappointment.

Then their eyes met again. Pierced Lip grinned. He nodded almost imperceptibly. The gesture was more than enough encouragement. Picking up his pace, Gav trotted over, his hardening cock leading the way.

He was barely through the heavy plastic curtains when a hand slipped beneath his ponytail and grabbed the back of his neck. Gav moaned as the guy pulled him into a wet kiss. The rucksack slid from his shoulder. He dropped the laptop, his own palms moving to clamp onto the guy's arsecheeks.

Mouth to mouth, crotch to crotch, Gav sucked on the floor cleaner's tongue. The round metal lip stud dug into his face. And another hardening cock ground parallel to his.

The hand on his neck tightened, angling his head to deepen the kiss.

Gav's response was to push a thigh between the guy's legs. He groaned, rubbing his increasingly itchy dick against a hipbone. He could feel the floor cleaner's hard-on through two layers of fabric. It felt thick and fat and... somewhat knobbly. His mind was still processing this information as his chest met the stranger's.

And the unmistakable sensation of something other than nipple flesh pressed through his T-shirt.

His cock flexed hard. Obviously, the lip-ring was only half the story. Gav adored piercings. Abruptly, he broke the kiss, licking the guy's vaguely cigarette-tasting spit from his lips.

The floor cleaner was breathing heavily. Clear blue eyes looked at Gavin in surprise.

But Gav just smiled and manoeuvred the guy backwards until they both hit a wall. In one swift movement, one hand thrust itself under that acid-yellow work vest. Grabbing a handful of T-shirt along he way, Gav bared the floor cleaner's well-muscled chest. He held the garments firmly just above the guy's breastbone, fingers tight in rumpled folds. And stared.

A tiny ring twinkled in each flesh nub.

A low, lusty laugh. 'You like?'

Gav liked. He liked very much. The floor cleaner's hand settled on his shoulders.

'You English boys, I think you really like.'

Gav ran the tip of his index finger around the guy's left nipple, studiously avoiding the metal circlet.

The guy's back arched languidly. A husky moan replaced the previously cocky words.

Gav smiled. They thought they knew it all, the Dutch did. With their lax laws and their permissive attitude, nothing could faze them. Turning his finger, he reversed the motion, stroking the edge of his nail around the dark pink areola.

The floor cleaner's well-muscled body shuddered.

Continuing the circling, Gav pushed his other arm up further. Holding the vest and T-shirt clear with his wrist, he rested his palm lightly against the man's throat. Just a hint of growth bristled against his palm. Flicking his finger cheekily against the left nipple ring, Gav turned his attention to the right.

Beneath his palm, a prominent Adam's apple bobbed. And, hard against his thigh, the guy's cock was pulsing furiously.

Gavin smiled, tracing wider circles around his next victim. He wondered abstractedly what the guy had expected. A quick blow job from a randy tourist? A hurried hand job from some green Englishman only too eager to take advantage of Netherlands hospitality?

Pausing in his ministrations, Gav suddenly grabbed a handful of firm pec. The floor cleaner gasped. Gav lowered his face to the pierced nipple. He poked his tongue between metal and flesh, tasting the smooth chrome and the warm skin. Deftly, he flicked at the tiny ball, rotating it with his tongue while the owner of the piercings reared up from the wall in desire.

Gav chuckled. Then he closed his teeth gently around the flesh between the metal ring and the tip of the nipple.

A howl of need tore loose from the man's throat. Vibrating growls trembled through bone and cartilage and shivered against Gavin's palm.

His own cock was leaking freely now, straining for release against the waistband of his underpants. He needed to come; he needed to come badly. But the foreplay wasn't over yet – not by a long chalk.

With this free hand, Gav fumbled with the belt of the guy's jeans, his teeth nipping lightly against the hardening bud. Easing back a little, he wrenched baggy trousers and underpants down to the guy's knees. And pulled his mouth from that delicious nipple.

On his shoulders, fingers dug in as the floor cleaner tried to keep Gav's lips and tongue where they had been. But Gavin Shaw had other plans. He continued to hold the man by the throat. Now, however, his attention was firmly focused between strong hairy thighs.

The guy's cock looked more like a weapon than a dick. Curving up, erect and pulsing from a shaggy nest of bristly blond hair, it sported a thick purple head that was studded with a myriad metal decorations.

As Gav stared, one hand left his shoulder and dipped lower. He watched the well-built floor cleaner grab his own balls and hoist the heavy sac up for inspection.

Twinkling among the lightly haired folds of scrotum, two tiny studs winked at Gavin.

Now it was his turn to groan. Falling to his knees, he released the guy's throat and moved both hands to between the man's thighs. Gav rubbed his face against the piercings, savouring the unexpected feeling of metal among the dimpled ball skin.

Another hand left his shoulder and plunged into his hair.

Gav grunted, unzipping himself. Wrapping a fist around his own aching shaft, he returned his attention to his partner's – and began to lick. As he dragged his tongue over, around and down the man's metal-spiked dick, Gavin mapped the piercings. Three niobium barbells protruded from the velvety cut head. Another two decorated the shaft itself. Griping one tiny ball between his teeth, Gav tugged gently.

Fingers tightened in his hair. And the guy tried to shove more of himself into Gavin's mouth.

He inhaled deeply, stroking his own cock while he explored the other. His free hand darted between the floor cleaner's thighs, batting other fingers away and cradling the heavy, studded sac in his palm. Gav's index finger slid beyond, and began to rub the dimpled area between balls and arsehole.

He licked. He rubbed. He nuzzled. He stroked. And, as the man above him was gradually reduced to a quivering mass of need, Gav became aware of noises, just beyond the industrial polythene curtains.

Another flight had obviously arrived. Mere feet away from two men enjoying each other, another batch of passengers now waited to claim their luggage.

Drawing his mouth back up the throbbing shaft, Gav flicked his tongue over the thick-gauge PA that bisected the guy's urethra.

Low conversation drifted into his ears. French. Dutch. The

guttural consonant clusters of rapid German.

The floor cleaner bucked with his hips, both hands now deep in Gavin's hair. Gav jacked his own cock faster. Then he sheathed his teeth behind dry lips, rose up onto his knees and let his mouth descend onto the metal-studded dick.

There was English, too. More interestingly, a voice he vaguely recognised.

He felt every bump and barbell, every ring and ball as he relaxed his gag and took the last few inches of the man deep into his throat. While part of him was totally focused on the feel of this stranger's dick, another part was listening. Ever listening.

'Good to see you again – the boss here?'

'Waiting in the car.'

'Good flight?'

'Not bad.'

Gavin tightened his lips, feeling his mouth impact with the very root of the man. Then he began to draw himself back up the porcupine shaft. He knew that voice – he bloody knew that voice well! But he couldn't quite place it.

'All set for tonight?'

'Yeah – you got the boys standing by?'

The grip on his head tightened. Saliva flowing freely now, Gav allowed his trick to take over. Neck aching, wrist starting to cramp as he worked himself towards orgasm, he found himself pulled into the conversation beyond the plastic curtains.

'The Warmastrasse place?'

'No, we're down by the station now, above the Music Box?'

They moved like a well-oiled machine. Gav's balls spasmed each time the head of the floor cleaner's cock impacted with the hard cartilage at the back of his throat. He was close – so close.

'What time?'

'When's the conference finish?'

'Oh, tennish – wanna make it for eleven?'

'Will do – oh, and tell the boss I've got something really special lined up for him.'

'Great – catch you later.'

The floor cleaner was pounding his throat now. Gav was suffocating on blond pubes, choking on that thick Dutch dick. The taste of the guy's pre-come mixed with his own saliva. The clenched sensation in his balls was impossible to ignore, now.

The floor cleaner came first, nearly knocking Gav onto his back as he flooded his mouth with thick salty spunk. And when Gav came himself, seconds later, he'd finally placed at least one of the voices.

Milo.

Milo, Derek Masters' bodyguard.

# Eleven

He could still taste the floor cleaner's come, sitting on the fast train that connected Schipol airport to Amsterdam city centre. But his mind was on other things.

To hell with some dry-as-dust EU conference on taxation. Derek Masters had some sort of… meeting arranged above somewhere called the Music Box. And Gav felt sure this wouldn't be on his official schedule.

The Music Box.

He flicked through his *Guide to Amsterdam*. Given the city's reputation for catering all to all tastes – and given what Gav had seen in Iceland – was the Music Box a tranny bar?

He checked in his guide book: apparently not. More intriguingly, it wasn't mentioned in any of the comprehensively listings of Amsterdam's many sex bars – straight, gay or anything else.

Maybe it was a record shop. Maybe Derek Masters collected old vinyl. Maybe the place was even a recording studio. The man himself was a bunch of maybes.

As the city's suburbs flashed past outside the window, Gav began to plan his evening. The sun was already low in the sky. He'd put his watch forward: it was now just after 6 p.m. Get his bearings, get something to eat, then head for this Music Box place. And wait.

It wasn't a recording studio.

It wasn't even a club of any kind. And, as he trudged up from the station, through Amsterdam's less salubrious areas, Gav began to see why the Music Box wasn't mentioned in any guide book. The first clue should have been the way the girl in the tourist-information office had looked at him. The second was the location itself, which was becoming sleazier – even for Amsterdam – by the minute. Ignoring the slurred invitations from the slumped, dishevelled women who called out to him from doorways, Gav pressed on. The extreme youth of some of the prostitutes he passed horrified him: but the age of consent for both sexes in the Netherlands was fourteen, after all. Beyond the glitz and seedy glamour of the city's officially sanctioned red-light district lay a less well-known demimonde – a world the tourists didn't visit to gawk and snigger at, a world every city had, liberal laws or not, a world of desperation. Of need.

Other shadowy figures huddled against buildings. Equally pathetic as the tarts but a lot more threatening.

This was a world of drug-related criminality. Night was falling. And the street lighting here was far from bright. Gav squinted at his watch: just before 9 p.m. He peered at street signs for Paardenstrasse and noticed quite a few men on their own, either lounging against walls or walking slowly past him.

Punters? Men who enjoyed a little more edge on their physical thrills? Was Derek Masters one of these men?

Ten minutes later, Gav paused outside somewhere that looked more like an old-style English pub than anything else. The legend THE MUSIC BOX was just visible, in faded lettering, above the façade. A little further up the street, two figures were in engaged in some sort of argument. Gavin watched, eyes acclimatising to the gloom.

One was older, bigger, and looked scarily like the sailor from the back of Lou Reed's *Transformer* album. Gav smiled, remembering the rumours about those two photographs.

The other man was smaller, slighter, a boy, really. But he was yelling angrily at Sailorman in harsh, fast Dutch. Suddenly, the edge of a blade caught what little light there was. The knife in the boy's hand moved swiftly and almost noiseless. But Sailorman's scream was anything but silent.

Horror and fear vied for attention in Gav's shocked brain. He was aware of urgent footsteps as the kid scarpered. Then more footsteps and short, ragged breaths. But these, he realised, were his own.

With the sound of the sailor's scream still ringing in his ears, Gav moved hurriedly towards the Music Box and pushed open the door.

'Not seen you before, dearie.'

The barmaid was big, blonde and blowsy. And English. Gav paid for his Amstel and, still numb from what he'd just witnessed, made a brave attempt to return her smile.

'You here for' – her Devon-accented voice dropped to a stage whisper, still audible over the blare of the jukebox, and she raised overly made-up eyes to the ceiling – 'the party?'

Talk about luck! Gav nodded. 'I know I'm a bit early.'

'Pays to be early.' She giggled. 'I hope you've brought your euros.' One heavily mascara'd eye winked at him. 'And plenty of them.'

Gav patted the inside pocket of his jacket, still distracted by the scene outside, which replayed itself in his head, and tried to look as if he knew what she was talking about. Was the Music Box a thinly disguised brothel? Was Derek Masters into paying for sex? And just what *had* been happening outside in the gloom? Probably nothing more than had happened a hundred times before, he told himself. A street argument that ends in death? An offer of sex with deadly intent? A mugging that goes too far? Probably nothing to do with Derek Masters, anyway.

The barmaid leered at him. 'Just you take a seat, dearie. And when you've made your choice give Ronnie the nod.'

Gav followed her eyes to the far end of the bar.

A fat, balding man perched precariously on a stool, sipping

something pink. An ornate cigarette holder sent smoke curling up into the face of his younger, male companion. Catching Gav's eye, he raised his glass in something like salute.

Returning the gesture, Gav took his change from the barmaid and, thoroughly intrigued, went to find a table. Although it was nine thirty, the place was three-quarters empty. Gav sipped his lager and took in his companions.

A couple of older, smarter-looking men sat, like himself, alone at tables either drinking or smoking. Another blowsy blonde entered, joined Ronnie and his companion. She and the barmaid were the only two women in the place.

The main area of activity seemed to be around the jukebox, where a variety of well-muscled and not-so-well-muscled young men lounged and smoked and sipped mineral waters.

Gav tried to put together pieces of an increasingly fragmentary jigsaw. This place was slap-bang in the middle of Amsterdam's unofficial red-light district. There was obviously sex to be bought: that was unmistakable, from the assorted clientele already gathered and waiting.

But from whom? Were the 'girls' upstairs? Gav certainly couldn't see any of the present assembly handing over money for either the barmaid or Ronnie's overblown lady friend.

As he sipped his lager, various other young men entered. None bought drinks. None talked to anyone else. To a man, they looked sulky, ill-kempt creatures (Gav met a hard, icy eye and immediately looked away) and he didn't envy the poor drugs-ridden tart who'd have to service any of this lot. From time to time, as song after song came to an end, one of the older men on their own would get up, approach the jukebox and pump in a few euros. A few words would be exchanged, with one or other of the lounging group of muscle boys. Then the man would return to his table and his drink.

Gav caught a good few eyes. He also noticed glances exchanged and figures followed with gazes when they disappeared through a door at the back of the bar, confusingly marked HERREN, which he presumed was the toilets. Sometimes they disappeared alone. Sometimes in pairs. Sometimes they were away for ages. Other times, they were back in minutes. But everyone's every movement was noted.

The Music Box was a place where people watched. And were watched, in turn. So Gavin went with the flow, clocking everything. He was in the middle of buying another beer when the door burst open behind. Gav's head swivelled.

A skinny kid, late teens, with a pale unhealthy-looking face and wearing a grubby denim jacket stalked up to the bar and stood very close to Gavin. 'Evian, Sadie!' The English was heavily accented, the voice as rough as his appearance – and vaguely familiar. He scowled at the barmaid.

Gav took in the sores around the young guy's full lips and edged away, instinctively gripping his wallet more tightly. They were the only two at present buying drinks, and there was no legitimate reason why the kid would stand so close, at an otherwise empty bar.

Staring straight ahead, the guy nevertheless closed the gap between them.

A skinny, denimed forearm brushed his. Gav glanced at a dark, wet patch on the boy's jacket sleeve. Sadie brought Gavin's beer. Plus a bottle of mineral water, which she placed in front of the kid. 'Eight fifty, dearie.' Over-made-up eyes looked expectantly at Gavin.

He could smell the guy. A mixture of teenage sweat, cigarettes and unwashed clothes. And that was definitely fresh blood on that sleeve. But prudence made him hand over a ten-euro note, and tell Sadie to keep the change...

The raggedy, junkie-looking kid grabbed the mineral-water bottle, unscrewed the top and downed most of it in one swallow.

... prudence, and the dawning knowledge of what was actually going on in the Music Box.

Ten minutes later, he and the kid had adjourned to a table. And Gav was wondering if James would accept the hundred-euro note he'd just palmed his new 'informant' as legitimate expenses.

'What magazine did you say you work for?'

Gavin repeated the lie. The boy – who introduced himself as Jordaan ('with a double-a') and was now chain-smoking the packet of Marlboro Lights Gavin had obtained for him from a machine in the corner – was as sharp as a knife, despite the undoubted drugs habit and the dishevelled appearance. But he seemed to buy the story that Gav was writing a feature on Amsterdam's rent-boy scene for an obscure and totally fictitious Canadian current-affairs magazine. He'd also agreed to an informal interview, and a tour of the Music Box's upper floor.

Jordaan exhaled, sniffed, wiped a snotty nose on the back of a hand and moved his face closer to Gavin's. 'We get them all, in here. You wouldn't believe it.'

Gav was still trying to process the knowledge that Derek Masters had organised a party at one of the city's oldest, and most infamous, boy brothels.

'Rock stars, movie stars, politicians – the works. I could give you names, my friend. Names that would blow you away.'

There was only one name Gavin wanted to hear, as Jordaan fixed him with mercenary eyes. But he also found himself drawn to this feisty, if pathetic kid. He glanced at his watch: nearly eleven, and there had to be at least as many punters on the upper floor of the Music Box, as there was in the bar, by this time. Maybe Derek Masters was already there. 'Another fifty, after we've done... upstairs.'

The kid chuckled. 'Fair enough – just don't let Ronnie know you're not fucking me, eh? He worries about... negative press.'

Gav nodded, co-conspirator in a double deception. With every eye in the place on them, he got up and followed the swagger of someone probably only half his thirty-five years towards the door marked HERREN.

The upper floor was surprisingly well lit.

Nodding to a large man in a tight white T-shirt who sat behind what looked like a reception desk, Jordaan led Gavin through a bright, almost jaunty-looking lounge area. Several men sat on plushly upholstered leather couches, their expressions ranging from the bored to the nervous. Gav noticed that a good few of them were in expensively cut suits, and wondered if they belonged to the Masters party. But Jordaan didn't hang around, beckoning him onwards. Posters advising safe sex decorated the tastefully painted walls of a long corridor, off which were a series of doors.

'South Seas room.' Jordaan nodded left.

Gav peered in at blue walls, a plastic palm tree and what looked like real sand. From hidden speakers, the cries of seagulls and the sound of ocean waves was audible.

'Nursery.'

A man-sized crib, a pile of disposable nappies and a baby's bottle sat amid a room full of soft toys and teddy bears.

'The schoolroom.'

Larger than the last two – and occupied – this space was full of old-fashioned desks and chairs. A map of the world had been tacked to one wall, a full-sized blackboard rested against another. In front of it, chalk in hand and with the back of his grey school uniform shorts lowered to expose a red-wealed backside, a youthful-looking twenty-year-old was writing, 'I must not cry when teacher canes me.' Gavin glanced away, aware that something about the place was getting to him. One hand repositioned his hardening cock, and they moved on.

Reformatory school, complete with communal showers. Cadets'

barracks, featuring rows of bunks. A doctor's surgery – incorporating examination table, stirrups, latex gloves and a selection of fiendish-looking medical instruments. The Music Box had something for everyone. Boxes of condoms and lube had been thoughtfully placed in every room. Finally, they reached the end of the corridor. Jordaan paused, turned and pressed a finger to Gavin's lips. 'The video suite – and it is in use, at present. I shouldn't be showing you this, but... another hundred?'

Gav's hand fled to his wallet.

The grubby junkie tucked a crisp new note into the pocket of his jacket, then quietly opened the last door and stood back.

This room was in total darkness, apart from a rectangle of light high on the wall facing the door. Instinct made Gav wary: this urchin could mug him, steal passport, credit cards – the lot. Instead, Jordaan seized Gavin's arm and hauled him into the warm, dark space. The door he closed quietly behind himself.

Once inside the room, Gav became aware of vague machine noise. And small, blinking lights.

'Ronnie's offering a new service: video, DVD or CD-ROM of your visit to the Music Box.' Jordaan's rancid breath brushed Gavin's ear. 'At a price, of course.'

Gavin's heart leapt. The fact that Derek Masters was into paying for sex was scoop enough – but the chance of getting digital evidence to back this up was more than he could have dreamed of. Feigning nonchalance, he ran the tips of his fingers lightly over the stack of state-of-the-art computerised recording equipment. 'You know how to... work this lot?' He glanced at the skinny teenager.

Narrow shoulders shrugged. 'Nothing to it – I help Ronnie out all the time.'

The potential of the commissioned feature for *Financial Week* was growing exponentially. Gav could see *Time* magazine maybe being interested – even *Fortune*.

'Come here – look!' Jordaan suddenly giggled.

The childlike sound reminded Gav this world-weary sex-worker was still a bloody kid. He moved where his guide was now standing, at the rectangle of light on the opposite wall.

'I've done him. Three times. He's a kinky bastard – rough with it. But I never knew he was into—'

Easing the boy aside, Gav peered through the narrow slit.

Beyond the video suite, the room in which customers filmed their most private fantasies was as brightly lit as a film set. But there the similarity to any movie making Gav had ever had contact with ended.

The walls were black – they looked like ancient stone, worn and pitted with age. Somehow, whoever had dressed this fantasy chamber had even managed to give the illusion of dark slime and moss on sections of the stone surface. Housed in rusting metal sconces, lighted torches ringed the room, flickering ominously. Heavy shackles were also in evidence, hanging from rusted rings sunk deep into the stone. And they looked real. Chains dangled from the ceiling, attached to what appeared to be a pulley of some sort. In the far corner, a brazier glowed red. Gavin could almost feel the heat from its smouldering coals. And, protruding from the metal fire basket, a variety of implements.

Gav shuddered. While his mind knew this was just some game – like the games James Delany had attempted to get him into, eight long years ago – the torture chamber was incredibly realistic. Or would have been, were it not for the total lack of sound.

Reading his mind, Jordaan darted to the stack of recording equipment and fiddled with something.

A scream tore through Gavin's head. The sudden, very heartfelt noise sent further shudders through his body.

'Better, eh?' The skinny junkie boy was back at his side.

Gav didn't reply. His attention had moved to the room's occupants. Two figures were clearly visible, centre stage. One was a huge hulking man, wearing knee-high leather boots, a tiny black thong that did nothing to disguise his bulging hard-on, and a leather hood. Heavily studded gauntlets also hid his hands, one of which was holding a massive whip. In the harsh, artificial light, the dungeon master's bare torso ran with the sweat of exertion.

And he was not alone in that chamber of horrors. The room's other occupant lay face down, spread-eagled on a thigh-high table. Naked. Held firmly by rough-looking straps, the youth's legs were splayed wide apart. Similarly bound, his arms seemed about to be wrenched from their sockets. He formed a cross of flesh, his skin white and gleaming in the otherwise black room.

Gav swallowed, watching the hulking guy in the hood draw back a bulging arm. He inhaled sharply at the whoosh of the whip as it flew through the air. The crack of leather on flesh made his blood run cold in his veins. And the responding howl of pain turned it to ice water

Gav stared at the prostrate figure. He watched the barely adult body jerk and writhe, wrists scored and bleeding by the rough tethers. The boy's head hung over the end of the table, his face obscured by a veil of tangled brown hair.

Part of Gavin was appalled. Part of him hated the sadistic coward in the hood who was beating this kid's back raw and didn't even have the guts to show his face. Part of him wanted to hammer on the rectangular glass panel and stop this sick game.

The whip landed again. Another scream rent the air. Another jolt shot through Gavin's body in parallel.

And another part of him wondered if the face behind that mask belonged to Derek Masters.

Tranny lover.

Torturer.

He remembered what young Jordaan had said, earlier, about having had 'him'. Dragging his eyes from the scene, he looked at the boy. 'You know the guy in the hood?'

The unkempt head shook. 'No – but I know *him*.' A pale finger pointed just out of sight.

Gavin craned his head. There, sitting cross-legged on the floor, his closely copped head lowered as if in supplication, was the very naked, very familiar form of Milo.

And, if Derek Masters' bodyguard was here, Masters himself couldn't be far away.

Back out in the brightly illuminated corridor, the light hurt Gavin's eyes. He staggered slightly, thrown off balance both by the glare and what he'd witnessed within that torture chamber. A surprisingly strong arm looped itself around his waist. 'Come on – you need a drink.'

Unable to do anything else, Gav allowed Jordaan to guide him back to the plush waiting area. He also didn't object when he detected deft, slender fingers slip into his inside pocket and withdraw another hundred-euro note from his wallet. Sinking into one of the leather sofas, he took the paper cup of water offered and gulped it gratefully. As he looked over to the frowning face of the heavily built T-shirted man behind the reception desk, Gav watched Jordaan pad over and whisper something into the bouncer's ears that seemed to allay the man's suspicion. Around them, beautiful youths were floating past – some alone, some with older, obviously prosperous men.

As his mind slowly gathered itself, Gav knew that, if he hung around here long enough, Masters would eventually appear. And it was also an opportunity to elicit some hard facts from the ever-obliging Jordaan.

For the next few hours, he listened to a whispered account of the young junkie's encounters with various men. Jordaan had no knowledge of any older, silver-haired guy – Gav described Derek Masters in as much physical detail as he could muster – but was well acquainted with his broadly built bodyguard.

'He gives me – how do you say it, in English?' The kid was chain-smoking again, cigarette gripped between badly bitten fingers. 'The creeps?'

Gav nodded.

'He's not interested in fucking – the first time I saw his dick was back there, in the video suite. But man, he nearly beat the living daylights out of me, last time!' Unexpectedly, Jordaan linked a scrawny arm through Gavin's. 'I'm glad you're here – glad you just want to talk to me, 'cos I've got a feeling if Mr Milo had clocked me earlier, I'd have been tied to that table in there and not Pim.' He fixed Gavin with a cold, emotionless stare. 'They like me, people like Mr Milo, because it takes a lot to make me cry.'

Gavin's stomach turned over.

One hour stretched to two. Then three. After a while, Jordaan stopped asking for more money – which was just as well, because Gavin knew he had barely enough left to get him back to Schipol for the 7 a.m. flight. The boy didn't stop talking, though: 'Milo's not the worst, though. Not by – how do you say? A long chalk!' Gav began to wish his cover story about the Canadian magazine hadn't been quite as convincing.

By 3 a.m., the 'party' was in full swing. Milo had reappeared – Gav made sure he turned away as soon as he saw the brawny, grinning bodyguard – and proceeded to shake various older men firmly by the hand, before introducing them to various lithe youths.

Jordaan's grip tightened on his arm. The kid snuggled in closer. His voice sank to a low whisper. And still the stories came.

Tales of life on the streets.

Tales of other parties, for which Jordaan was well paid – although from the constant sniffing the proceeds evidently went straight up the kid's nose.

With the rent boy's saga soft in his ear, Gavin thought about

Derek Masters. Even if the man himself didn't indulge, he was obviously paying for friends and business associates to slake their appetites at the expense of people like Jordaan.

He shuddered. The whole thing was starting to give him the creeps. Part of him wanted to cringe away from the filthy little renter-junkie who clung on to his arm as if it were a lifejacket. Another part pitied the pathetic creature. And another, larger part was angry at the exploitation of it all.

The world should know. The business community had a right to be informed about how Mr Playboy entertained his European colleagues.

Was this the reason the guy was being blackmailed? Had someone else discovered Milo the Bodyguard's little peccadillo and decided to slur Derek Masters by proxy?

The hours slid by. After a while, Jordaan stopped talking. Gavin's eyes continued to focus on the comings and goings between the waiting area and the various fantasy suites.

Five a.m., and the place was emptying. He knew from the weight against him that Jordaan had dozed off. From beneath half-lowered eyelids, Gav watched Milo – still grinning – usher a trio of glowing clients towards the exit door.

They were leaving. Masters himself obviously wasn't going to show – and Gav had a plane to catch. This had been a huge waste of time. Easing away from the slumbering youth, he picked up his rucksack and laptop, then made his way towards the door.

As he passed the reception desk, he caught the eye of the white T-shirted bouncer, who grinned.

'Come back soon, my friend. Jordaan will be waiting for you.'

Scowling, Gav glanced one final time at the sleeping rent boy. Tangled hair hid most of the youth's face. But what was exposed looked heartrendingly vulnerable. Those hard eyes closed, Jordaan was just another kid – who'd given Gavin a lot of information but little he could really use. What young Jordaan and a night at the

Music Box *had* provided, however, was enough to sustain Gavin's interest that there was more to Derek Masters than a suite and a flamboyant lifestyle.

# Twelve

Back in London, he'd barely unlocked the door to his office-cum-bedsit when someone was knocking on it. Gav dumped his rucksack and laptop on the desk and walked towards the sound.

'G Shaw?'

Gav stared at the uniformed courier. He nodded.

'Sign here please, Mr Shaw.' The courier held out a clipboard and pen.

Gav took both, signed, then stared at the small padded envelope that was thrust into his hand. He continued to stare at it, as the courier's footsteps echoed down four flights of stairs. Turning the package over in his hands, he hefted it for weight: heavier than it looked. And full. He saw there was no return address, or even sender's name.

What had taken place in this office a mere twenty-four hours previously made him wary. Gav raised the package to his ear, irrationally listening for... ticking? Then he laughed, pulled himself together and closed he door.

Only one way to find out what lay inside that small, padded envelope. Perching on the edge of his desk, he ripped open the seal and stuck his hand inside. What his fingers tightened around was unmistakable. Gav blinked, hauling the thick bundle of crisp notes from their brown-paper sheath.

The first thing he noticed was they were purple. Fifty-pound notes. Ten minutes later, he knew there were two hundred of them.

Ten grand.

Ten cool, crisp grand.

He let out a long, low whistle. He'd never *seen* ten thousand pounds before – not in the flesh – let alone held it in the palm of his hand. Moving his attention to the padded envelope in which the money had arrived, he scrutinised it more closely. Courier delivery, hence no postmark.

Who would send him ten grand? And why?

Gav sighed and yawned. On top of the all-nighter at the Music Box, the early flight back from Amsterdam had left him drained and sticky-feeling. His eyes were threatening to close. He needed sleep. And he needed it now.

Ten grand.

Ten thousand pounds. The last time he'd stood in this office, he'd been arrested. Now large anonymous sums of money were arriving. When the stick had failed, was the carrot employed?

The amount was four times what he'd get for writing the article on Derek Masters. Was someone trying to buy him off?

Perched here on the edge of his desk and holding more money than he'd ever held before, Gav felt his sleepy eyes narrow. Maybe he should just take the money – after all, what was it to him if Derek Masters liked trannies and rent boys? The man's personal life was really none of anyone's business and had nothing to do with his skill or success as a global entrepreneur.

He was still pondering the unexpected delivery when something small and rectangular vibrated softly against his right arsecheek. Plunging hand into back pocket, Gav withdrew his cellphone. Another text. From another number his mobile didn't recognise. And another message, more oblique than usual: 'Laurel MD 25 B Dennett'.

Gav blinked. What the hell did this mean? MD? Doctor? Dr Laurel? The twenty-fifth of the month was... in three days' time. And who was B Dennett?

The conundrum nudged any thought of sleep to the back of his mind. Minutes later, Gav had hooked up his laptop, filled the coffee machine and was back on the trail of Derek Masters.

MD wasn't a doctor. It was a place – specifically, the US state of Maryland. And Laurel was a small town twenty-odd miles from Washington, DC.

Gav gulped at his coffee. He'd run out of milk, so the hot liquid was thick and black and carried a welcome dose of caffeine straight to his brain.

The political connection slowly solidified, after a search for 'B Dennett'.

Specifically Brian Josiah Dennett III. One of the Gettysburg Dennetts. Republican senator, South Carolina 'good old boy', former cigarette baron and part-time Baptist preacher.

In other words, not exactly the type of person who embraced tranny lovers! The man's online presence spoke volumes, and there had been several scandals a few years back over Dennett's opinions on everything: women, blacks, the state of Israel, gay rights, abortion. You name it.

Gav took another mouthful of coffee and leaned back in his chair. According to Dennett's website diary, the good senator was meeting with a group of British businessmen at the Laurel Best Western on 25/06 to discuss Anglo-American trade relations.

Gavin pursed his lips. Nowhere was Derek Masters' name mentioned. But his anonymous informant hadn't steered him wrong yet. How many of Masters Industries' female shareholders knew their CEO had connections with a man whose views on domestic violence were... unconventional, to say the least? How many black investors were aware that their money may be about to be used by someone who had, last year, called an African-American interviewer 'boy'?

As his eyes scanned through an article in which Dennett had referred to homosexuality as 'an affront to God and all God-fearing people', Gav's own hackles began to rise.

He had to go. It was in the public interest that he go.

His eyes moved to the pile of fifty-pound notes that still sat on his desk.

And he now had the means to go.

While Gav was waiting in line at Heathrow's Continental Airlines check-in desk his phone rang.

'Gavin?'

He smiled. 'Hi, James. What's new?'

The normally unruffled voice sounded uncharacteristically ruffled. 'Oh, things are fine here – was just wondering how you're getting on.'

The smile broadened into a grin. 'Oh, getting on well, thanks.'

'Any chance of a rough draft?'

Gavin laughed. 'Don't you trust me?'

A laugh in return. 'I trust you about as far as I can throw you, my friend. But I do know you're a professional, through and through.'

The queue moved forward. So did Gavin. He said nothing.

'So – the article's still on target?'

'It is.'

'Finding lots to write about?'

'Some.' It made a change to hear the great James Delany have to fish for information.

The line fell silent. He could almost imagine James, on the other end, thoroughly frustrated that Gavin was refusing to give him a blow-by-blow of his progress so far. The idea was doing vaguely sexual things to his groin.

'Well, if you need any more money for expenses, just let me know – don't want you out of pocket on this one.'

'Will passengers please note that smoking is only permitted in designated areas of the airport.' A Tannoyed announcement drifted down from overhead.

'Where are you off to now?' The information was seized on.

Gavin smiled. 'Gotta go, James. I'll be in touch.' He ended the call and switched his mobile off. He was still smiling when he reached the check-in desk, and handed over his rucksack to the Continental Airlines girl.

She took his ticket. 'Business Class, sir?'

Gavin grinned and nodded: something about the irony of using Derek Masters' buy-off money to finance a trip to expose him was very, very appealing.

Thirty seven thousand feet above the Atlantic ocean, he stretched out in the extra leg room and stared at white, fluffy clouds.

'Another mimosa, sir?' The accent was American. The voice pure Oklahoma cornfields.

Gav turned his head and looked at the blond flight attendant. 'You know, I think I will.' He took the cut-crystal glass from the sliver tray. 'Cheers!'

'Er, cheers, sir!' The guy laughed and held Gavin's eye a little longer than was strictly necessary, even for a passenger who had paid £2,500 pounds in cash for an open, return ticket between Heathrow and Philadelphia.

Gav's gaze moved briefly to the man's name tag. Vincent. The guy had been all over him, as soon as he'd boarded. He'd helped Gav off with his jacket, insisted on storing it and the laptop in the overhead bin while Gavin tucked his passport into the back pocket of his jeans. He'd been round with nibbles. Twice. He'd personally checked that Gav's seatbelt was fastened before takeoff, taking much longer than was necessary to ensure that the nylon strap was smooth and snug across Gavin's lap. During the safety demonstration, lifejacket around his neck and whistle in hand, when Vincent's lips had closed around the damn thing in illustration, he'd looked straight at Gavin.

'I love your accent.' The cornfields voice dipped in pitch. 'You need anything else, you just call me, Mr Shaw.'

And now Gavin stared back into the fresh, open face and got a blast of CKOne and minty mouthwash. Vincent's hair was nattily cut and styled. Vincent's shoulders were broad, with a chest to match. Vincent's mouth was wide, his lips full and parted to reveal a set of the type of white teeth only Americans seemed to possess. 'I'll do that.' And, when the flight attendant moved away to offer a mimosa to the woman three seats in front, Gavin registered Vincent's firm rounded bubble-butt, amply displayed in tight grey Continental Airlines trousers.

Business Class was definitely a step up from the cattle truck of Economy. Bigger seats. Quieter. Free drinks and real knives and forks with the meal.

His eyes followed Vincent's delicious rear end as it ambled down the aisle: there was free eye-candy with every flight.

Chuckling to himself, Gav pulled down his seat-back table and sat what was left of his mimosa on it. Underneath the plastic surface, his hand was busy in his groin, repositioning the hard-on that had began with the phone call from James.

Five and a half hours...

His fingers lingered on the erection, then dipped to his balls.

Five and a half hours of Vincent's ministrations. There were worse ways to spend one's time.

He ate lunch, then dozed through the first in-flight film. When he woke up, the mimosas had reached his bladder. Unstrapping his seatbelt, Gav staggered to his feet and made for the toilet. A hand was at his elbow, in a flash. 'The executive washroom is this way, Mr Shaw.'

Gavin smiled and followed Vincent's arse down towards the cockpit. He could get used to this kind of treatment – he really could.

Ahead, a thick well-muscled arm was holding a small door open. Gav nodded his appreciation, easing his body past the American flight attendant's. Their crotches brushed. Gav inhaled sharply as a thick and very evident hard-on bumped over his. Then the door was closed behind him.

Gavin groaned audibly, then turned his attention to the matter in hand. Man, even the bogs were better, in Business Class – and bigger. No need to sit practically in the wash handbasin when you took a piss. Unzipping, he hauled now more than a half-hard-on from his fly, aimed it towards the toilet bowl. The other hand he braced against the wall, in case of any unexpected turbulence. As he stood there, his shaft bucked against his fingers. Gav rolled his eyes at the combination of circumstances that seemed to be con-stantly foiling his every attempt to take a Jimmy Riddle. He tried to think about something bland. He read the safety card fixed to the wall. He peered at the classy-looking soap dispenser – and the real towels. No nasty paper affairs for Business Class passengers.

His hard-on was just starting to subside when the door opened behind him and Gavin nearly fell onto the bloody toilet. He cursed himself: he'd forgotten to lock the damn thing. Turning, he moved the braced arm to push the door shut.

But Vincent was faster. The guy could fairly move, for an Okie farm boy. Sliding neatly into the confined space, he closed the door with his big, brawny body. Those clear blue eyes were now narrowed in desire. A pink tongue licked those full lips. And the hand that moved towards Gavin's crotch was obviously as accus-tomed to holding dick as it was to serving mimosas.

Gav grunted as the flight attendant's fist closed around his length. Blood immediately rushed to fill the fleshy shaft, and in less than a minute he was harder than ever. His own hands moved to the waistband of Vincent's uniform trousers.

Feet planted wide apart, the guy angled his hips, thrusting this crotch out.

The fist around his dick tightened and began to move. Gavin groaned, fumbling with belt, then button, then zip. When he eventually got the guy's trousers unfastened, he grabbed the waistband and hauled the garment plus underwear roughly to Vincent's knees.

The flight attendant moaned quietly, running his fist down Gavin's cock.

A pinkie stroked his balls. Gav gasped and closed the distance between them. His hands moulded themselves over two firm arsecheeks. The door handle dug into his knuckles. But, as his mouth dived for the guy's newly shaved neck, Gav barely felt it.

Trapped between their two bodies, Vincent's hand continued to move, dragging up to the head of Gavin's cock.

Gav squeezed Vincent's arsecheeks, fingertips slipping into the moist crack and parting those mounds of muscle.

The flight attendant moaned loudly, pushing back into Gavin's hands. The pad of his thumb rubbed over the head of Gavin's cock.

Gav's balls tightened. He kissed he smoothest of necks, licking the warm flesh, then taking the skin between his teeth. Nipping lightly, he started to suck. And an index finger stroked over the guy's hole.

Vincent was grinding against Gav's hands now, thrusting himself onto that finger. His other hand cupped the back of Gavin's neck.

Gav gnawed on, his mouth moving down inside the flight attendant's shirt. One hand gripping the guy's right arsecheek. He let his finger rest on that sweet, spasming pucker. Then he pushed. The hand in his hair tightened. The fist on his dick paused.

Vincent's moan of satisfaction was competing with the dull thrum of the aircraft's engines.

Then Gav was hauling himself away from the man's neck, easing him round, his free hand fumbling with his own belt.

Seconds later, Vincent's palms were flat against the toilet door. The trousers of his Continental Airlines uniform bagged around his ankles. And Gavin, cock in hand, was staring at that awesome, Okie bubble-butt. A coating of fine down caught the harsh fluorescent light, contrasting with the thicker hair on the man's thighs and the course blond tufts in his crack. Falling to a crouch, Gav kissed the base of the flight attendant's spine. His other hand moved to cup the guy's full, heavy balls.

Vincent was panting now. His lower body moved in wide circles, his arse pushing back, then his crotch dipping forward. The guy was grinding his dick against the toilet door.

And beyond that door passengers were eating, dozing, watching films or gazing out of windows.

Fumbling in the pocket of his jeans, Gav found a condom. He tore the foil packet open with his teeth, then carefully unrolled the latex length over his flexing dick.

He'd never done it in a plane.

He'd never done so many of the things he'd found himself doing over the past five days.

'Fuck me!' Vincent's wholesome, Okie accent had taken on a darker, more desperate quality. 'Do it hard and do it fast.'

Gavin shuddered, securing the condom in place. Both hands on Vincent's arsecheeks, he wrenched them apart and held them like that. His right hand moved to regrip his latexed length. Guiding the shimmering head to the entrance to the other man's body, he let it rest there and dipped his mouth to nuzzles the side of Vincent's neck. 'You got lube, pal?'

'Just fuck me!'

The urgency in the man's voice sent arrows of desire through his balls. Gripping Vincent's broad Okie shoulders, Gavin leaned back, then bucked with his hips.

The engine noise altered in pitch, covering most of the flight attendant's loud shout.

Gav's hiss of satisfaction was less audible. His lips drew back at the feel of the guy's sphincter, as it parted to admit him. One hand moving to the back of Vincent's neck, he spanned the neatly shaven nape and used the guy to pace his entry.

He savoured every centimetre, every millimetre of penetration that shimmered up his length as he pushed slowly into the steward's widening hole.

Vincent himself was pushing back now, trying to take more, trying to mount Gav's dick in his haste to get all of it inside him.

Gav's balls tingled. He paused, pushed the man firmly against the toilet door and stared down between their bodies. Four inches of his dick was buried inside the guy's arse, the remaining three curved up towards the stretched pucker. His knees trembled. The muscles in his thighs tensed. Against the back of Vincent's neck, his palm was sweating profusely. And he could feel the slick hair soaking under his hand.

The flight attendant was breathing heavily now, head turned and face flat against the door. 'Please! Come on, man!'

Gav's balls knitted together in their hairy sac. With one sharp buck of his hips he drove himself deep into the other man's body.

Vincent screamed.

Gav fell forward, releasing the guy's neck and gripping him by the hipbones. He bit Vincent's shoulder, grinding his crotch hard against the man's arsecheeks. His nipples impacted with Vincent's warm back. His balls snuggled heavy and full against another guy's nuts.

Gav closed his eyes. Around his dick, the walls of the flight attendant's arse were rippling and pulsing. And tight – tight as the second skin of latex. As Gav luxuriated in the feel of the man, an image suddenly burst onto the inside of his eyelids.

Derek Masters. With the beautiful lady-boy.

Derek Masters. With brutish Milo.

Milo. With the nameless, spread-eagled youth.

Derek Masters. And those dark, impenetrable eyes.

His cock flexed inside Vincent, who inhaled sharply in response. Then Gav was pulling out, easing back and dragging his dick down that tight, rippling tunnel.

A hand left the surface of the door, reaching round to grasp his arse and try to hold him there. Gav rebelled and continued to withdraw. Staring down between their bodies, he watched the way the thick, condomed head of his dick was stretching Vincent's hole all over again.

Beneath him, the man was trembling now. The flight attendant's body was slick with sweat and rigid with need.

Rotating his hips a little, Gav rolled the head of his dick around, just inside the man's body. He was vaguely aware of movement from Vincent. Another hand left the door and thrust down to the approximate area of the flight attendant's own hard-on. What had previously been trembling became rhythmic jerking movements as the guy began to wank himself off.

Gav's breath caught in his throat and he shoved himself roughly back into that hot, spasming hole.

It was a quick fuck.

It was the type of fuck Gavin liked best. And when Vincent came, his hole tightening vicelike around Gav's dick, it was a matter of seconds before his own spunk was spurting into the tip of the condom.

Gav left the toilet first, tearing off and knotting the condom before tossing it into the wastepaper bin. In the cabin, everyone was either dozing or entranced by the in-flight blockbuster movie. He slid unnoticed into his seat and leaned back. Spent, relaxed and a little sleepy himself, he let his eyes close and his mind wander off.

Inside his jeans, the skin on his softening cock tightened as Vincent's spunk slowly dried to powder. Legs splayed, eyes closed he drifted off, until—

'Mr Shaw?'

Gav's eyelids opened to low Okie tones and a smiling face. In crisp white shirt and Continental Airlines tie, Vincent was as pristine as ever. A slight flush to those cheeks was the only sign he'd recently been well and truly fucked.

'Fasten your seatbelt, please. We're beginning our descent into Philadelphia.'

Gavin smiled back. Their hands brushed as the steward helpfully righted the seat-back table.

'Thank you for travelling with Continental, Mr Shaw. We look forward to seeing you again very soon.' The words were rehearsed and formal. Then Vincent's voice dropped to a whisper. 'Welcome to the Mile-High Club, pal!'

Gavin laughed and winked. Beyond the window, habitation was visible through a thin layer of cloud.

Philadelphia. America. Land of the free and home to a certain Brian Josiah Dennett III.

While his body was pleasantly relaxed and heavy, his brain was sharper than ever. The right-wing congressman and Derek Masters.

What was in store for Gavin, here? What more would he learn about the mysterious entrepreneur? Mind buzzing with possibilities, he settled back to enjoy the landing.

Only when he joined the queue to go through US Immigration an hour later did he discover that something was missing from the back pocket of his jeans.

# Thirteen

It was every traveller's nightmare, losing one's passport.

Gav tore his rucksack from his shoulder and began to rifle thought its zip pockets. He had his boarding card – he even had the form he'd filled in on the plane, declaring that he wasn't bringing any fruit or vegetables into the country.

The queue in front moved on. Gav shuffle-rifled, digging past socks and shaving stuff and soap and everything else but what he was looking for.

Every traveller's nightmare – especially when entering the US. They were so damn picky. Europe was different: OK, there were still problems, should you be unfortunate enough to misplace the passport, but they were sympathetic – the EU, and all that.

Turning his attention to his jacket, Gav rechecked his pockets for the tenth time. He was sure it had been in his back jeans pocket. He distinctly remembered putting it there. But now that pocket contained only the remnants of a three-pack of condoms and a squashed packet of chewing gum. His heart sank, and he stared straight ahead.

Only three people in front of him now. Beyond them, seated behind a desk, a very large, very sombre-looking immigration official was giving a middle-aged man a very hard time. At either side of the desk, two armed women stood, equally stony-faced.

Gav knew the rules: no passport, no entry. At best, they'd put him on the first plane home and he'd never find out what went down at the meeting between Derek Masters and Brian Josiah Dennett III.

At worst? He'd be taken away, grilled for hours in dark rooms by grim-faced men who made the fat detective back at Hammersmith Police Station look like Dixon of Dock Green.

The queue moved forward.

Staring around himself, he racked his brain for the last time he'd seen the bloody passport. On the plane – definitely on the plane. He'd moved it from his jacket to his jeans when he'd put his jacket in the overhead locker. Had it fallen out then? Suddenly, it dawned on him – the toilet! The bloody toilet! In his mind's eye, he could see his British passport, probably lying on the floor inches from where he'd fucked big Okie Vincent up the arse. Then he remembered – no. He'd not been aware of the damn thing, when he'd been searching his pockets for condoms, so it must be somewhere in the cabin.

Beyond the immigration hall's huge plate-glass windows, various small aircraft took off and landed. Searching the recesses of his mind, Gav found himself watching one small plane in particular as it slowed.

A Lear jet, the craft carried six people at most. And in the kind of luxury that made Business Class look like a cattle truck.

He was next in line. Gav hurriedly stepped to one side, allowing the bemused person behind him to go first in an attempt to buy some time. The gesture did not go unnoticed. One of the armed women met his eye. Gav lowered his gaze and returned his attention to the Lear jet.

As it finally came to a halt, he noticed a distinctive and familiar logo etched on the plane's tail. The arresting design of an interlocked M and I, in gold lettering, gleamed in the afternoon sunshine.

Gav muttered under his breath: Masters Industries obviously had their own private jet – no commercial airline for *their* CEO. As he stood there, watching the aircraft, someone behind nudged him. Gav jumped, edged forward, and found himself crossing the painted yellow line to the immigration official's desk.

'Passport, please.'

Taking a deep breath, Gav looked the sober-faced man in the eye and opened his mouth. 'Um, I seem to have misplaced that, actually.' He cringed, watching the official's face remain impassive. Hoping they were used to ditzy Brits losing everything from luggage to hearing aids, Gav smiled his most appealing smile, and held out his international driving licence and customs declaration form. 'I do have these, though.'

The guy looked at him as if he were mad. 'Passport?'

Gav tried again. 'I've lost my passport.'

The official frowned. 'You mean you boarded your plane without it?'

'No, no – I had it then. Not sure where I—'

Then the immigration official was nodding to Gav's right.

His head swivelled. His heart began to pound as one of the armed women approached. Her right hand rested on her shoulder holster. Gav began to back away. 'Um, look – I'm not a terrorist. I'm not trying anything dodgy – I think I maybe left my passport on the plane and—'

'This yours?'

The London-accented voice at his shoulder made him jump. Gav spun round, and found himself staring into the thuggish face of Milo, Derek Masters' bodyguard. One huge hand held a burgundy-coloured object with faded gold lettering on the front.

'You dropped it, back there.' Milo nodded vaguely in the direction of the arrivals corridor.

Relief and gratitude drenched his body. 'Oh, thanks pal! Thanks a lot!' Gav snatched his passport from Milo, turned back and waved it at both the immigration official and the armed woman. 'Here it is – sorry, it's all been a misunderstanding.'

Both Americans eyed him warily. But the guy took his passport and the woman returned to her post. Gav's heart slowly returned to normal.

'What is the purpose of your visit?'

'Um, a holiday.' No point in muddying the waters. He smiled. And waited, glancing behind to thank Milo again.

But the brutish bodyguard was nowhere to be seen.

They gave him a thorough going over after the missing-passport incident. His bags were searched. His documents were inspected with a fine-tooth comb. He was body-scanned – twice. They made him take his shoes off. When they asked why he'd brought a laptop if he was on holiday, Gav told them he was a freelance travel writer and took a laptop everywhere. The open ticket caused some concern, as did the large amount of sterling in his possession, but finally a visa for two weeks was stapled into his passport and he was told to 'have a nice day'.

At last in the main body of Philadelphia airport, Gav headed straight for the Avis stand. One thing he knew about the US: you needed wheels. According to his map, Laurel was an hour's drive away – a mere stroll, by American standards.

In the cool air-conditioned comfort of the main foyer, a beaming girl with too many teeth took an imprint of his credit card, gave him the keys to a Ford Ka ('dark-blue, sir') and pointed him in the direction of an enormous car park. 'Section F, Mr Shaw.'

Outside, the heat and humidity hit him like a wall. Fifteen minutes later, he was still looking for the bloody car. And he was drenched in sweat. Pausing against a sign bearing the legend 'C', Gav wiped his forehead on his shirtsleeve and tried to get his bearings. The place was jam-packed with cars picking people up and cars dropping people off. Mere yards away, an enormous white stretch limo was drawing up in from of the arrivals exit. It made him think of Oscars ceremonies and movie stars.

As he lingered there, curiosity kept his eye on the oversized white car. But its passengers weren't in the movie business. Seconds later, Milo sauntered through the automatic doors, followed by the tall, angular form of Derek Masters. On his arm was another woman – not the lady-boy, this time, but a statuesque brunette in a smart pink business suit.

Gav watched their progress into the ostentatious vehicle, its door held open by a short, unformed chauffeur. Vague questions as to exactly where he'd dropped his passport edged into Gavin's overheating brain.

Then, bringing up the rear of the Masters party, was an unmistakable figure of blond, corn-fed Okie masculinity. Gav blinked, then continued to stare as Vincent the flight attendant handed his little wheeled trolley bag to the short chauffeur, then slipped into the car behind Derek Masters. The chauffeur shoved the trolley into the boot, got back into the car and drove smoothly away.

Wiping sweat out of his eyes, Gav continued to stare at where the car had been. Masters obviously knew Gavin was on his trail: the appearance of Milo with the lost passport had shown that. But when exactly had his passport become 'lost'? When hunky Vincent had insisted on stowing Gavin's jacket in the overhead cabin lockers? When he'd considerately checked, then rechecked, Gavin's seatbelt? Or in the aircraft's toilets, when a broad Okie hand had gripped his arsecheek, trying to pull himself more deeply onto Gavin's dick?

Two facts were now patently clear to him: Derek Masters had arranged for Vincent to steal his passport; he'd also arranged for Milo to return the bloody thing, just before Gav could be marched off by immigration officials. The means had been there for Masters to let US officials pack Gav onto a flight back to the UK. So why hadn't he merely allowed things to take their course? Why return the passport at all? And so blatantly?

'Mr Shaw?'

A bright, happy voice pulled his mind from another conundrum. Gav focused on the Avis girl, who was beaming at him.

'You forget your credit card, sir – and your car is right over here.'

Like a lamb, Gav followed her clacking heels towards a small, dark-blue vehicle. The second fact nagged at his brain. Who was sending him those texts? Who was making sure he as aware of Derek Masters' every movement? And what did they want him to find out?

Traffic was a nightmare, but Laurel was well signposted. Catching a glimpse of one of the world's most famous landmarks to his left, Gav ogled the domed roof of the White House and drove on. He'd never been more grateful for air conditioning in his life. Beyond the little car's dark-blue exterior, tarmac was melting – and summer had only just started.

Laurel itself seemed more town than the suburb of DC described in his guidebook. Wide roads, strips of shops, not a lot of houses. But masses of hotels. Of these, the Best Western didn't look particularly luxurious. As he parked his little car, he kept an eye open for the ostentatious stretch limo. Then he remembered that only the meeting was taking place here: neither Masters nor Brian Josiah Dennett II would necessarily stay in such a nondescript hotel.

Gav paid cash for a single room, dragged himself and his luggage up to the second floor, then passed out on one of two beds that looked built to hold four.

For the next two days, Gavin acquainted himself with the hotel's layout and conference suits. The bizarrely named MacPherson Room was indeed booked for that evening, in the name of Dennett. He also made a point of getting to know the cleaning and desk staff, tipping heavily and in general laying the ground for favours to come – the first of which had been the borrowing of a waiter's jacket, bearing the green Best Western logo.

There was little to see in Laurel itself, and the other guests seemed to be a mixture of families and travelling salesmen, so he spent most of his time in his room, with his laptop, poring over the steadily growing Masters file.

Derek Masters donated heavily to several charities. Masters Industries had been one of the first companies to boycott South Africa, back in the country's apartheid days. The conglomerate owned a few subsidiary companies in the West Indies, where it operated a scholarship policy for employees' offspring. Plus, there was also the question of his involvement in an infamous incident in Cuba.

Sprawled on the huge bed, Gav rolled onto his back and stared at the ceiling. What on earth could Masters have in common with someone like Brian Josiah Dennett III? Switching off the laptop, he hauled himself over to the window. Obviously, the meeting was secret – otherwise, why hold it in a crummy dump like this, in the American equivalent of the back of beyond?

As he stared out over the Best Western's grounds, Gav noticed a steady stream of cars turning off the freeway and heading in the hotel's direction. He gripped the windowsill, watching their progress.

Flash cars.

Chauffeur-driven cars.

And, right at the end, a great white stretch limo. Gav cursed himself and fled towards the shower. If his plan to gain access to the meeting was going to work, he had to be in place in the next fifteen minutes.

He got as far as the entrance to the MacPherson Suite, clad in white waiter's jacket, his hair tied neatly back in a ponytail, and bearing a silver tray of drinks. Through the double door, Gav could see Brian Josiah Dennett III's ruddy, grinning face just beyond the back of an iron-grey skull. To his right, he was aware of Milo's bulky form, clipboard in hand. Head down, Gav veered left, moving seamlessly between two suited businessmen.

'Oi! You!'

Gav moved a little faster. But not fast enough. Strong fingers grabbed him by the collar of his purloined waiter's jacket and hauled him back so hard he nearly dropped his tray of drinks.

'Don't you ever learn, Shaw?' The brutish bodyguard fixed him with a scowl. 'This is a private function.' Moving his hand to Gav's shoulder, Milo shoved him back out into the corridor, then moved inside the MacPherson Suite, grabbed the twin doors and closed them firmly.

Gav staggered. The tray fell, scattering glasses everywhere. By the time he'd picked them up, guests and official hotel staff were starting to stop and stare. Gav cringed, thrust his tray at a bemused waitress and made his way hurriedly back up to his room.

Plan A didn't work? Time for Plan B. Wriggling out of the jacket, he slipped his hand under the king-sized bed's mattress and grabbed a handful of fifty-pound notes. Down in Reception, he changed £300 into just under $500, then sauntered out into the car park.

It was just after seven in the evening, and the air hung like a sodden blanket around him. Gav surveyed the various cars – and the various chauffeurs lounging on bonnets or smoking in huddles as they waited for their respective bosses.

Gav sidled over to a likely-looking candidate. Flashing his NUJ card, he held out a crisp $50 bill. 'The London *Times*, pal – wanna earn yourself some overtime?'

The driver was in his fifties, and beefy-looking. He stared at Gav, regarding him like something that had stuck to the sole of his shoe. 'No comment.'

The second man Gav approached said exactly the same thing. Fifteen minutes later, he'd upped the money to $200 and been told to beat it, scram, and 'do one!', then been called a Limey muck-raking bastard and given the finger more times than he cared to dwell on. Over the far side of the car park, Derek Masters' white stretch limo sat alone. And empty.

Gav decide to take a break. Either this lot were incredibly well paid or their loyalty to their bosses was above reproach. Shirt sticking to his body, he headed for the bar and a well-earned drink. He didn't have a Plan C. But he'd think of one.

Gavin had barely taken a sip of his overpriced 'Bud' when he became aware of a presence at his elbow. Turning his head, he watched a short, stocky Italian-American in a shirt and tie order a mineral water. The guy paid for his drink and grinned at Gav's soaking shirt.

'Hot enough for you, pal?'

The accent was pure Little Italy.

Gav noted the guy's five o'clock shadow, a smudge of blue-black along his jaw line. 'I don't know how you stand it!'

The guy chuckled. 'This is nothing – wait till August.' He took a long drink of the mineral water, then stuck out his hand. 'Anthony Nardini – call me Tony.'

Gav gripped warm, stubby fingers and felt their strength. 'Gavin Shaw.' He noticed the thick covering of black hair just beyond Tony's shirt cuff. He was also aware of a thick thumb lightly stroking his palm.

'You're English – am I right?'

Gav stared into glinting sea-green eyes. And you're up for it, Tony boy. He smiled. 'That noticeable, eh?'

Tony chuckled again. 'Man, I love that Limey accent. You guys all sound like... kings and queens.'

A thigh pushed itself against his. Gav couldn't believe he was being propositioned by someone who looked like an extra from *The Godfather*.

Tony broke the handshake and thrust a fist into a pocket. Pulling out a packet of cigarettes, he offered one to Gav, then sighed deeply. 'Friggin' Maryland laws!' He withdrew the packet, then clapped a solid hand on Gav's shoulder. 'Gotta go outside for a smoke around here. Coming?'

Gav didn't need to be asked twice. It was almost too good to be true. All through their brief conversation, he'd had the impression he knew Tony Nardini from somewhere. And as he followed the short, solidly built Italian-American out into the car park, towards the white stretch limo, his hunch was confirmed.

Derek Masters' chauffeur chuckled again. 'The boss'll be in there for hours.' He pulled keys from his pocket and unlocked the passenger door. 'So we can have a bit of privacy, as you Limeys say.'

Cock already inching towards hardness inside his underpants, Gav ducked his head and got in.

He had hoped to get the opportunity to have a look around the vast, luxurious car, for anything he could use for his article. But Tony was unzipping before Gav had the chance to sit down.

'Talk dirty to me, Limey-boy.' Short stubby fingers hauled out a short, stubbier dick. 'Tell me how an English cocksucker's gonna blow me better than a New Jersey whore!'

His own length flexed against his sticky stomach. Gav knew he had to distract wise-guy Tony – and he knew the best way to do it. If the guy thought he was here for a quickie, he needed to think again. Moving towards where the man lay back on the sumptuous leather upholstery, legs outstretched and cock in hand, Gav settled himself between Tony's splayed thighs. 'Well, first of all, we need to get rid of this.' His hands moved on the buttons of Tony's shirt.

The promise of those hairy forearms was just visible on the guy's stomach. Gav wanted to see more.

Hands gripping the back of the seat, Tony smiled cockily as Gav reached up to loosen his tie, then each of the six shirt buttons. 'Attaboy – atta-good-Limey-boy!'

Gav smiled to himself, then gripped the edges of the shirt and pulled it open. He groaned.

The guy's chest was a mat of thick black hair. Gav leaned forward, lowering his face to a surprisingly large nipple, which was just visible through the dense forest. His lips were about to close around that pink nub when a stubbly hand left the back of the seat and clamped itself onto the back of his head.

'Suck it, Limey! Suck it good!' Tony pressed down roughly.

Gav groaned, and bit lightly.

Tony roared. 'You fuckin' English asshole, I'll—'

The hand released his head and Gav knew Tony's arm was drawing back for a slap. Lightning-like, he reared up and jammed a hand of his own into a muscular biceps. 'Shut it, ya bastard!' His other hand circled Tony's throat. Gav was aware the accent which had attracted the guy had just shifted from polished Kensington into the heavy East End brogue of his childhood. Moving onto Tony's lap, Gavin took advantage of the guy's shock to wedge an elbow into the muscle on his other arm.

He pinned him there, both with the weight of his body and the angle of his arms. Staring into the man's stunned face, he was very aware of Tony's stubby cock flexing violently against the inside of his thigh. 'Now listen here, mate...'

The chauffeur twisted sharply and tried to buck Gavin off.

Gav increased the pressure of his hand on the man's windpipe until he stopped. Which he did, gasping for air. Gav slackened his grip and ground down a little on the guy's dick.

Tony moaned.

Gav grinned. 'Better – much better. Are you gonna behave yourself?' Knees either side of the guy's waist, he tightened the muscles in his thighs.

Tony growled. His blunt, Italian face was a picture of frustration.

Gav laughed, then shook his head while tut-tutting exaggeratedly. 'Then I'll have to make you, won't I?' Quick as a flash, he reached over, grabbed one of the seatbelts and looped it deftly around the man's right wrist. Before Tony could react, Gavin had done the same to the left.

With both arms tightly secured, the Italian-American was back in his original position, arms wide against the back of the seat. Only difference this time was that he had no option.

'Ya cocksucking, motherfuckin' Limey fag, I'm gonna—'

Gav pulled the guy's tie free, balled it up and shoved it into that open, cursing mouth. The rest of what Tony was going to do having now been reduced to formless, furious mumbles, Gav returned to what he'd come here for. 'Now don't you disappear on me, right? 'Cos we're not finished yet.' With a wink, he opened the limo's passenger door, nipped out into the humid air and padded round to the driver's side.

If he couldn't gain entrance to the meeting between Masters and Dennett, maybe he could find out where the guy was staying.

In the front of the limo, Gav rifled through the glove compartment, searched down the sides of the seats – checked everywhere for some clue as to Derek Masters' base for the duration of his stay in the US.

Nothing.

Zilch, as Tony might say, if he hadn't had his own tie stuffed into his mouth. Raising his head, Gav glanced at the smoked-glass partition that separated driver's from passengers' quarters. Beneath him, the vehicle's suspension was being tested to its limits, as the trussed chauffeur bucked and struggled in his bonds. His eyes returned to the dashboard, and Gav found what he was looking for. Flicking a small switch, he listened to the hum as the smoked-glass partition lowered itself.

There, red-faced with effort, and with his hard dick still hanging out of his trousers, Derek Masters' chauffeur glared at him.

Gav winked. 'Be back for you in a sec, honey!'

Tony's fury increased with the epithet.

Ducking back down, Gav began to search under the seats. He knew guys like Tony back in the UK. He knew they knew gay guys gave much better blow jobs than 'New Jersey whores'. And he knew they never considered themselves gay. But the way Tony's stubby dick was as red as his furious face spoke volumes.

Suddenly, his hand came into contact with something, right at the back of the floor behind the driver's seat. Gav hauled it out. A cash box – a locked cash box, as he discovered when he attempted to open the lid.

Probably it contained only poor old Tony's float for the night, but there was a chance he kept his jobs schedule in here, too. Sitting back on his heels, Gav poked his head though the lowered partition. 'Do you have the key for this?'

Tony glowered at him.

Gav grinned. 'Tell me where it is.'

Tony's head shook wildly.

The idea that Tony believed he was about to be robbed by a 'Limey fag' had Gav's own cock up and around again. With a laugh, he opened the driver's door, got out and padded back round to the body of the luxurious car.

'You know you're going to give it to me sooner or later.'

Holding Tony's legs apart with his elbows, Gav tightened his hand around the man's hairy sac.

The chauffeur was crying silently now. Large tears rolled down that handsome, Italian face. But Gav knew they were tears of rage. Tears of sheer fury – and tears of frustration. Because he'd put money on the fact old streetwise Tony had never been harder.

He was getting off on this. The fact that some stranger had tied him up, gagged him in the back of his own car and was now fondling and probing every inch of that stocky, vulnerable body was killing Anthony 'Call me Tony' Nardini, who roared in protest as Gav, grinning, ran the tip of an index finger down to the guy's perineum. Half choking himself in the process of protesting, Tony continued, steadfastly, to refuse to hand over the key to the cash box. Gav was just about running out of ideas when something occurred to him.

What mattered most to men like Tony? Face. And, following on from that, what did Tony fear most – what did guys like Tony always fear most?

Discovery. Discovery by those whose opinion mattered to him most of what was really going through his mind when he was boasting about those 'New Jersey whores'.

Holding the man by the ankles, Gav wrenched Tony's lower body up off the leather seat and soundly slapped his arse.

No way could Gav invite the boys of the Nardini 'family' into the car to see their 'brother' trussed and hard at the hands of a 'Limey fag', but he could do the next best thing.

He could make sure his present employers knew – at least in Tony's mind – how Mr Oh-So-Straight Anthony Nardini really liked to get his rocks off.

With a sly smile, he leaned over, patted that flushed, humiliated face and winked. 'Last chance, Tony, mate.' Gav straightened up, then unzipped himself. 'Ever got come in your hair, my friend?'

The handsome face blanched.

Gav ran a fist down his ample hard-on. 'It's a devil to get out – and it stinks for days.' Feet planted wide apart, he slowly began to jerk himself off.

# Fourteen

Despite the limo's air conditioning, Gav's body was soon bathed in sweat. He took the wank slowly – as slowly as he could. Each time his damp fist slid down the curving length of his erection, he paused to bend his knees and savour the friction before allowing his hand to glide back up to the swollen, pulsing head.

Tony grunted and closed his eyes in horror.

With his free hand, Gav leaned forward and lightly slapped that scarlet face. 'The key?'

The eyes flew open. Tony yelp-mumbled, but shook his head, then began flailing with his legs – the only part of him over which he still had control.

Gav laughed and sidestepped easily. 'That nice glossy black hair of yours is gonna look great with my come in it, mate!'

The man's dark eyes smouldered with fury. He tried another kick.

This time, after he'd avoided another booted foot, Gav moved side on to the outraged figure and placed the sole of his own shoe firmly in the middle of Tony's hard belly. 'Naughty, naughty!' He could feel the muscle tense further beneath his foot, and, moreover, it gave him a better angle of impact from the spunk shower.

Tony glared at him, tugging helplessly at the seatbelts, which held him firmly.

Back on target, Gav chuckled and resumed the wank. He was enjoying this, thoroughly enjoying the look of total mortification on the Italian-American's face – and the fact the man's stubby dick was now leaking pre-come onto the dark velvety glans. With his free hand, he reached down and dipped the pad of an index finger into the clear, glistening dew. The liquid was warm on his skin. And the expression on Mr Nardini's face as Gav slowly painted a silvery line around the man's stretched lips, still jacking his cock, had to be seen to be believed.

Tony coughed with rage and spat out the tie-gag. 'Ya fuckin'—'

Gav caught the saliva-sodden item, balled it up and shoved it back in Tony's mouth. 'Watch your language, mate – the only words I want to hear from you are the whereabouts of the key to this.' He nodded to the cash box, which now sat at the far end of the wide limo seat, then sucked on his finger.

Tony made a retching sound.

Gav ignored it, tasting remnants of the salty sweet body fluid and rolling it around on his tongue. His cock flexed in his fist. His balls were sore, aching for release. Leaning forward, he transferred the balance of his weight to the foot on Tony's abs and stared into the man's eyes. 'Close them and I'll just slap 'em open again, mate.'

Lips straining and contorted by the gag, Tony for once did as he was told.

Gavin began to move his fist faster. He'd never seen anyone look quite as angry as this guy did right now. But beyond the fury, beyond the downright humiliation of his position, Gav could see something else in those eyes.

He didn't know this man. OK, he knew he was some chauffeur Derek Masters had hired for the duration of his trip. And he knew his name. But that was about all. He and Anthony Nardini had met – what, an hour ago? But as he wanked himself towards orgasm, and as Tony tugged and tore at his bonds, their eyes remained locked together and something strange passed between them.

Tony was fairly good-looking, but that wasn't it. Gav didn't even particularly like the guy – and he was damn sure Tony, at this moment in time, would give him the beating of his life if he had those strong Italian fists free.

But there was definitely something. Gav couldn't put his finger on it. Some sort of weird closeness? Some sort of nameless understanding?

Whatever it was, it was driving him on to new heights of pleasure.

Tony was writhing now. Sticking up out of the fly of his boxer shorts, his dick was as angry as the rest of him. Livid with blood, the shaft flexed and pulsed. Gav noticed that the guy's feet were back on the floor. The kicking had stopped, and Tony was now thrusting upwards with his crotch. Arsecheeks leaving the plush leather upholstery, the guy fucked the air-conditioned atmosphere in the back of the increasingly steamy limo.

The whole car was rocking now. Gav's nipples tingled. With his free hand, he pushed up the front of his shirt, took one hard bud between thumb and forefinger and began to squeeze. The sensation sent arrows of pain-pleasure deep into his guts. Under his foot, Tony's abs tightened further. And deep in Gavin's balls something twisted. Throwing back his head, he gripped his shaft as his balls began to knit together. Then his body was propelled forward by the force of the orgasm. Below him, Tony moaned and snorted.

One hand flailed for the limo's ceiling, to steady himself. Uttering a long, heartfelt groan of his own, Gav watched spunk fly from his gaping slit.

Some of it did hit Tony.

Most of it impacted with the limo's smoked-glass back window, where it slowly slid down like sticky rain.

His body shuddered again. Flexing against his cramping fingers, he pumped a second slitful right onto the Italian-American's flushed face. Lower down, Tony himself was still fucking the air, desperate for release. Trousers bagging around his own hips, Gav was mesmerised by the movement of Tony's.

Through the haze of orgasm, he was vaguely aware of something small and silver-coloured falling from the man's front pocket. But the key to the cash box was the least of his concerns right now. Plunging his free hand into Tony's mouth, Gav hauled the soaking tie from between the man's lips.

The first words from that mouth were the last he expected. 'My hands! At least release one of my hands!'

Blood pounding in his head, Gav slumped onto the panting figure. Shaking fingers loosened the belt on the guy's right wrist.

Tony's hand flew to his dick. With Gavin's body now heavy against his, the man began to wank himself furiously.

As the waves of release slowly receded, Gav curled one arm around the groaning man. His other hand snatched the key from the floor. Fingers shaking with the force of the orgasm, he fumblingly opened the cash box.

Tony was panting now, hauling on his cock so vigorously that Gav feared he might wrench the member off completely. Snatching a bundle of notes from inside the metal security container, Gavin tossed them aside.

Then stared.

Right at the bottom, a folded piece of paper. Gav grabbed it, hurriedly smoothing it out.

A list of dates, times. And places. Philadelphia airport. The Holiday Inn, DC...

He now knew where Derek Masters was staying.

... Arlington Cemetery. Then today's date: Best Western, Laurel MD, 7.30 p.m....

Gav's eyes flicked on.

... 11 p.m. Peabody Institute, Baltimore.

At his side, Tony's gasped and shuddered, crotch bucking up off the leather seat as he came hard.

Peabody Institute? What the fuck was the Peabody Institute?

And why was Derek Masters visiting it at eleven o'clock at night? Gav shoved the piece of paper back into the cash box, tucked his cock back into his trousers and zipped up.

At his side: 'You wanna have that smoke now, Limey boy?'

'Another time.'

Gav smiled to himself, glancing briefly at the spent, relaxed Italian-American. 'You have a nice day, y'hear?' Then he was out of the limo, jogging back to the hotel.

Ten minutes later he'd packed, flicked hurriedly through his map of the area and was now back in his little rental car. It was just after 9 p.m.

Whatever it was, it was closed. But at least the heat of the day was finally subsiding.

Having parked in a side street, Gavin stepped back from the impressive, Victorian frontage of the Peabody Institute and stared up at lightless windows.

Definitely closed: he'd hammered on the vast, boss-studded door for a full ten minutes, and roused not as much as a caretaker. He glanced at his watch: just after 10.30 p.m. In the cool of the evening, he wandered about a bit, taking in the faded grandeur of the area.

Baltimore was older than Laurel. More majestic. The pretty townhouses around here were neat and tidy, with painted shutters and granite doorsteps. After the faceless modernity of Laurel, this city had a very colonial feel to it.

And it was quiet. Very quiet. To pass the time, Gav strolled on over the brow of a hill, still admiring the buildings while wondering what was bringing Derek Masters here, at the dead of night.

Ahead, he spotted what looked like a church, and wandered over. It *was* a church. And attached to it was a fairly ancient-looking cemetery – ancient-looking for the US, anyway – surrounded by a firmly padlocked but low cast-iron fence. Gav glanced over his shoulder, then easily vaulted the barrier. As he did so, something from the guidebook stirred in his memory.

Baltimore was Poe county. And, if he wasn't mistaken, this very cemetery was the final resting place of the great Edgar Allan. In the still-humid half-light, Gav stared around at the monuments and grave markers and began to wander along the small, well-kept path.

'The Pit and The Pendulum', 'The Fall of the House of Usher', 'The Raven': he'd always loved Poe's stories. As he walked, Gavin examined each of the headstones. They were all from between a century and a half and two centuries ago: 1815, 1846 – there was even a 1798! In the midst of this very modern country, it was strange to find so much of the past.

The small cemetery was a silent as the graves it held. Crickets chirruped eerily. A few traffic sounds in the distance punctuated the quiet, and the odd squeal of a faraway police siren reminded him he was in the heart of the bustling city of Baltimore. But, apart from that, the place could have been in another world.

When he eventually found Edgar Allan Poe's grave, a single red rose lay in front of the faded granite monument. Gavin smiled, crouching to read the inscription. As he did so, the sound of a powerful engine took him by surprise. Turning his head, he glanced back onto the street.

And saw the, by now, familiar shape and colour of Tony's white limo.

Gav considered moving round to the far side of the little cemetery, scaling the fence there in order to find a vantage point from which to view Derek Masters' activities at the Peabody Institute. But something made him stay where he was.

And it was just as well. Because the limo was easing to a smooth halt. Still crouching, Gav watched Milo, not Tony, emerge from the driver's door and walk smartly round to the passenger door.

The burly bodyguard was holding something in one hand. He opened the door, and held it while the tall, angular form slipped smoothly from inside.

Derek Masters was also carrying something. Even from this distance, Gavin could see it was a red rose. He smiled: was this multimillionaire entrepreneur a fellow Poe aficionado?

What Milo was holding was identified as soon as the bodyguard stooped to insert a key into the padlock that held the gate to the small cemetery shut.

A gothic creak of ancient iron accompanied Derek Masters' progress into the gloomy, still-humid darkness. Ducking hurriedly behind a nearby headstone, Gav hid himself from sight and waited for a second red rose to join the first.

But he was to be disappointed. With Milo sombrely bringing up the rear, the silver-haired figure walked on past the Poe monument, heading deeper into the gloom. And Gavin followed.

At the very back of the graveyard, Derek Masters finally paused. Milo remained a respectful distance back, as his boss fell to his knees in front of a small – and as far as Gavin could see – unmarked headstone. The guy was talking, now. Talking to the grave! Ears straining, Gav tried to catch the words, but he was too far away. The whole thing took about a minute. Then Derek Masters carefully laid his single red rose in front of the headstone, rose smoothly to his feet and began the walk back.

A two-hour drive for this? There had to be more – what had happened to Brian Josiah Dennett III? And where was Masters off to now?

Waiting until the mourning party was a good distance away, Gavin darted forward and peered at the small grave marker.

No dates. No age. No epitaph. Only one word was visible, on the remarkably recent and very plain headstone.

'Johnny.'

The sound of a powerful engine once again revving into life

tore his attention from the enigma that was Johnny. Having run to the far side of the cemetery, Gav leapt over the fence and raced towards where he'd parked his car. He'd barely unlocked the door and got inside when the elongated form of the white limo cruised smoothly past the top of the side street.

After engaging the gears, Gav crept smoothly in behind the vast car. And the chase was on.

Over the next couple of hours, he saw a different Baltimore.

A city of vast docks and massive regeneration. A city of shopping malls, freeways and fish restaurants. A city of industry. A modern, pulsing metropolis of affluent, young glowing white faces.

Circling down from a hilltop cannonade, Gav continued to tail the limo towards one of Baltimore's more recent monuments.

There were less healthy-looking visages, too. Two in the morning, and the streets surrounding one of the largest housing projects Gav had ever seen throbbed with life.

But it was a darker, more desperate living these creatures were after. Literally with less light – most street lamps seemed to be out of order – huddles of thin youths, black and white, gathered around dim street corners in the uniform of the times: oversized trainers and Puffa jackets, despite the warmth of the evening. Nike swooshes were evident, shaved into seventeen-year-old skulls. Overturned trash bins and discarded pieces of furniture decorated these streets.

Gav gazed out of his window, slowing as the limo slowed. He met a few curious stares, but only a fraction of those that were directed towards the swanky car in front. Unlike the seedy backstreets of Amsterdam, these streets held little air of threat, only an ethos of hopelessness.

Seated in the middle of a discarded sofa, its stuffing disgorging itself onto the pavement, a young black man and a skinny white girl shared a crack pipe.

Gav could feel the poverty: if he were to wind down his window, he knew he'd be able to smell it. In the land of the free, some people were still chained. But, despite his pity, Gav was still glad the walls of the sky-blue car stood between him and Baltimore's underclass.

Unexpectedly, the limo turned left into a narrow, potholed alley and slowed further. Then stopped completely. Gav only just had time to kill his headlights. Ahead, he couldn't believe his eyes.

Derek Masters was getting out!

The sound of the limo's idling engine masked the sound of his own. Gav watched one of Europe's wealthiest men stride into shadow. Finally forced to roll down his window, he craned his head out into the dank humid air.

From the shadows, a skinny black boy in baseball cap emerged cautiously, caught in the beam of the limo's lights. Derek Masters lowered his head, and beckoned.

Dazzled by the glare, the black kid edged forward, one hand shading his eyes.

Gav continued to watch, spellbound. Some sort of brief conversation ensued. Masters rested a hand on the kid's shoulder, nodding while the kid talked.

Was Masters buying drugs? Selling them?

Before Gavin could indulge in further conjecture, Derek Masters pressed something into the startled kid's palm, then walked swiftly back to the limo. The engine revved and the car moved off.

The kid was still there when Gavin drove slowly past. Eyes like saucers in the gloom, he flicked through a bundle of hundred-dollar notes.

He'd have given his eye teeth to have heard whatever conversation had taken place between Derek Masters and the scrawny black kid

– just as he'd have sold his soul to have been a fly on the wall of the MacPherson Suite.

Maintaining a safe distance between himself and the car in front, Gav waited for Masters to head back to his hotel in DC.

But the evening obviously wasn't over. And, as the limo drove past a sign for the meat-packing district, Gav could only follow. Three in the morning, and Baltimore's slaughterhouses were still at work. Factory whistles blew. Hooters sounded. The streets were full of huge refrigerated trucks into which racks of carcasses were trundled. Vast, faceless warehouses disgorged groups of abattoir workers, their white overalls stained crimson at the end of their shift.

Gav was aware he was sweating again. Anticipation tingled on his skin, almost sexual in its need to be satisfied. As they drove, the area became more derelict. But still busy. Only now the groups of men were dressed in everything from suits to jeans and T-shirts. A couple of men in leather sauntered along the street, chatting.

Ahead, the limo swerved right and drew up in front of an enormous, aluminium-sided building. Applying his own brakes, Gav pulled in a little away. Sitting in the car for a few minutes, he watched the streams of men converge at a small door cut into the side of the building. One by one, they knocked. The door opened. They went in. Seconds later, Derek Masters, with the ever-present Milo, was doing the same.

And at precisely 3.07 a.m., so was Gavin Shaw.


Inside, the place was the size of an aircraft hangar. Bright lights dangled from a huge, curved ceiling.

And everywhere men. Short men. Tall men. Old men. Kids in their early twenties. Men on their own. Men with friends. Good-looking men. Ugly bastards. In the crowd, Gav could move more freely. He was fairly sure neither Milo nor Derek Masters had spotted him, but it didn't do any harm to keep a low profile.

Weaving his way through the throng, he nevertheless kept the silver-haired entrepreneur in sight.

Over the far side of the vast space, he could just make out... pens. Fenced-off, individual pens, like the enclosures he'd seen, years ago, when covering a cattle auction in the Scottish borders. Shouldering his way closer, Gav wondered if Derek Masters' portfolio of business interests included livestock. Then a bell rang loudly, and the crowd began to push its way over to the holding pens. Gav pushed his way through, one eye on Derek Masters. As he did so, he noticed that several largish men were now holding sticks and baseball bats.

Gav nudged someone out of the way for a ringside view. And realised that there were men occupying each of the four pens. Instinctively, he tried to back away, but the crush of the crowd behind him made any movement impossible. He glanced right.

A guy in his late twenties, with curly brown hair, stared at the pens.

Then he glanced left. This guy was older – forties – and was wearing a cowboy hat. Neither man as much as noticed Gavin. He swivelled his head wildly, looking for a potential route towards the door and out of this place. All eyes were focused on the cattle pens.

'All right, boys?' An amplified voice echoed up into the warehouse's vaulted ceiling.

Gav flinched, and glanced back.

A grinning figure with microphone and cattle prod now stood in the middle of the clearing, mere feet from Gavin.

The crowd mumbled.

The guy with the mike shook his head. 'We gotta bunch of pussies in tonight, or what?'

Someone sniggered.

'I said, all right, boys?' The voice boomed out once more.

'*All right!*' The responding roar was thunderous.

Adrenaline spurted in Gavin's veins. Pushed forward even more by the pressure at his back, his heart was hammering.

'Better – much better.' The guy with the mike grinned. 'Are we gonna have some fun here tonight, boys?'

'*Yes!*'

'Are we gonna enjoy ourselves?'

'*Yes!*'

Each time the crowd replied, the force of their answer shook Gavin's very bones. As he moved his attention from the guy with the mike to the four cattle pens and their occupants, he felt the massive sound as a physical force around him.

But he wasn't the one under threat. Beside each wooden enclosure, a figure holding a rifle had appeared. Gav stared at the four men inside the pen. They looked like ordinary guys, two white, two black – one wore a suit, two were dressed in jeans, while the fourth wore the uniform of the ghetto: padded Puffa jacket, trainers and baseball cap.

One thing united the captive quartet: they all looked scared half to death.

Gav tried to catch one of the black men's eyes. But three out of the four men were focused downwards at the straw-covered floors of their respective pens. The fourth guy – in jeans and plaid, short-sleeved shirt, his fore and upper arms thickly muscled – was staring at the man with the mike with undisguised aggression.

Something in the recesses of Gavin's brain told him that, given a room full of baseball-bat-bearing men, this was the wrong thing to do.

'Now, let's start with you.' The guy with the mike pointed over the four captives.

And something told Gavin he was right. An armed guard poked Plaid Shirt in the back of the neck with the barrel of his rifle. The crowd cheered its approval. Then, quick as a flash, Plaid Shirt reached behind, grabbed the gun and wrenched it free from the guard's hands.

The crowed booed loudly. From the back of the warehouse, someone fired a shot. Gavin almost leapt out of his skin.

Now armed, Plaid Shirt was circling his pen, eyeing his audience warily. Despite the newly acquired weapon, Gav could see that the man's hands were shaking, even at this distance.

'Quiet!' The order from the microphone was immediately obeyed. The silence was almost worse than the cheering. The eyes of everyone in the place were now on Plaid Shirt.

Gavin took in more of the man. His sweat-sheened face was finely chiselled. High cheekbones jutted beneath darting eyes. His chest was broad and deep, tapering down to a slender waist and strong thighs. And, to his own horror, Gav found himself checking out the guy's crotch.

A loud click tore through the unnatural quiet and drew Gavin's, along with every eye in the place, from the handsome man.

Two figures now occupied the pen of the kid with the Puffa jacket. One was the boy himself. The other was the MC, who now had a meaty arm curled around Ghetto Boy's neck. And a small, automatic pistol leaning against the side of the kid's head. 'Drop the rifle, son.'

Gav knew enough about guns to know that the click he'd heard meant that the safety catch was now off. He also knew enough about human nature to realise the MC wasn't joking. Or was he?

Every eye swivelled between the terrified kid and the armed man in the plaid shirt. The tension in the vast space was palpable. Gav held his breath.

'Drop it, or this boy'll never see his next birthday.'

Gav was close enough to see the MC's index finger tighten on the gun's trigger. Blood pounded in his head.

The MC dragged the boy around to face the plaid-shirted rebel. The handsome man stared at the boy, who was motionless with fear. The stand-off lasted ten seconds. Then twenty. Glaring at the MC, he spat and threw the rifle out of the pen. Gav was still transfixed by Plaid Shirt when another shot rang out behind him.

By the time he looked back, the kid in the Puffa jacket was lying on the straw floor. And the MC was strolling out of the pen.

Gav gasped audibly. He couldn't just stand here and watch this. He had to do something. His cellphone was in his pocket. If he could get to the back of the crowd, he could phone the police and—

'Bring him out!' The MC's voice echoed in his head.

So tightly packed was the crowd, Gav couldn't even get his hand into his pocket, let alone move. There was nowhere to go. There was nothing to do but watch. And pray.

As two armed guards gripped Plaid Shirt firmly by the arms and dragged him towards the MC, Gavin became aware of a new pressure behind him.

He could feel the outline of a hard-on digging into his thigh. The next time he glanced at the kid's pen, it was empty. And Plaid Shirt was standing directly in front of the grinning MC.

Handing his microphone to an associate, he gripped the handsome man by the shoulders. The crowd inhaled as one as he ripped the guy's shirt from his body.

The unclothed man clenched his fists, his face a portrait in fury. The plaid shirt now hanging off his arms in shreds, the sights of two rifles aimed at his head, his gleaming chest quivered with rage.

Gav stared at the finely defined musculature of the man's torso.

Unexpectedly, the MC stepped closer, and lightly patted that handsome face. 'I like a guy with spirit – let's see if your friends are as much fun. Jimbo? Markie?' The guards at the two remaining pens looked at their boss. 'Get the ladies naked – we're gonna have ourselves some real sport here tonight!'

# Fifteen

Ladies?

Gav swivelled his head in confusion. Around him, men cheered and hollered their approval. The stamping of feet shook the concrete floor beneath him.

No women appeared. But back in the clearing, the two remaining prisoners were being nudged and prodded from their respective pens.

The guy in the suit kept his head lowered. The other one, in jeans and a Chicago Bulls T-shirt, kept glancing around the crowd, searching for some way out.

Gav avoided the man's eyes, and focused on the MC. Maybe it was a blessing the kid in the Puffa jacket had got early release. Because the leering grin behind the mike hinted broadly at some further horror.

The MC grabbed the suited man's left wrist, peered at the gold band around the third finger, then held the hand aloft. 'We have a married man!'

The crowed said 'aw' in unison.

'Does the little woman know you cruise the docks, son?'

The crowd sniggered, as the guy's head hung down in shame.

'Does she know every time her lips fold around that fine cock of yours it's not her pussy you're thinking about eating out?'

The crowd whooped its approval.

'Does she know you're a faggot, son? Does she know you get down on your knees and suck thick dick when you tell her you're working late at the office?'

Gavin's face flushed up. And it wasn't just the heat in the crowded warehouse. He truly felt for the poor bastard in the suit. But, more to the point, the MC's teasing words, on top of the proximity of so many sweating male bodies, were having an effect between his legs.

'Leave him alone!' The disapproving shout came from the guy in the Chicago Bulls T-shirt.

The crowd oohed.

'Well, well, well.' Slowly, the MC turned his head to eye the objector. 'Looks like you found yerself a saviour, boy.' Releasing the suited guy's wrist, the MC wandered over to Chicago Bulls. He grabbed the guy by the back of the neck. 'A knight in shining armour, eh?'

The guy inhaled sharply.

The MC held him like that, bringing increasing pressure to bear. 'You volunteering your services, cocksucker?' Holding the mike away from his mouth, the MC brought his lips very close to the guy's ear.

Chicago Bulls' knees buckled. Whether it was the epithet or the grip – or the whispered threat no one else in the place had heard – Gav wasn't sure. But next thing he knew, Chicago Bulls was on his knees, in front of the burly man, and his hands were tearing at a zipper.

'Suck it!' The words came from directly behind Gavin.

The MC kept one hand on the back of the guy's neck and thrust forward with his crotch.

'Suck it!' The voice was to his right, this time.

Chicago Bulls was hauling at a broad, Western-style belt now. He shoved one hand inside the MC's trousers.

'Suck it!' The exhortation had been taken up by others in the crowd now.

Gavin stared at four fingers now curling around a thick cock. Despite his age and stature, the MC had a hard-on to shame men half his years.

'Suck it! Suck it! Suck it!' Two words became a chant, which grew in volume as it spread through the crowd like a disease.

The MC's hand slid up from Chicago Bulls' neck to the back of his head. 'Do the brothers know you like dick, boy? Do your smart ho-mo-sex-ual friends know you hang around truck depots? Do they know you love dirty, cheesy redneck dick?' The amplified taunt filled the warehouse.

'Suck it! Suck it! Suck it! *Suck it!*'

Around him, the crowd roared its desires. Gavin was panting now. He could feel his breathing speed up. The strength had left his legs. He was still on his feet only because of the closeness of the male bodies surrounding his. Gulping in air, he knew he was hyperventilating. As he slumped against a man wearing a leather waistcoat, a strong arm encircled his waist.

'Easy, son, easy.' Deep, breathy words caressed his ear.

Gavin moaned and tried to shut out the scene that was unfolding in front of him.

Chicago Bulls was now licking the head of the MC's dick. The pinkness inside his lips was visible, as was his tongue as he lapped and slurped saliva onto that fat red knob head.

Abruptly, the lights went out. Panic surged through Gavin's veins. In the thick darkness, claustrophobia wrapped its clammy arms around him. He couldn't see, he couldn't breathe. All he could register was the heavy smell of male sweat and the oppressive, aggressive heat of the crowd.

Then, equally abruptly, a single powerful spotlight flicked on, illuminating the activity just in front of him.

The MC had his hand on the back of Chicago Bulls' head, fingers tangled in the man's hair. Neck straining back at an uncomfortable-looking angle and throat open, the older man was steadily fucking the guy's face. Gavin shuddered, watching the MC's hairy sac bang off a newly shaved chin with each, violent thrust.

Chicago Bulls was making choking sounds. His hands scrabbling around the MC's waist, finally finding purchase around the leather, Western-style belt.

Behind this pairing, one of the armed guards was unfastening Plaid Shirt's jeans. A rough white finger hooked itself into the open fly and dragged out a long, flaccid, uncut length.

The crowd broke into hee-haws of derision.

'Any volunteers?' One of he guards took the mike from the MC, who now had both hands on Chicago Bulls' skull and was pounding himself between the other guy's sheathed lips.

Three guys broke free from the semicircle around the clearing, jostling each other in their eagerness to join in. On reaching the action, one grabbed Plaid Shirt from behind, holding him firmly. Another grabbed the guy in the suit, who had been in the process of trying to sneak off. The third was hauling at his own zip, watching the MC and Chicago Bulls pairing.

Gavin's head was spinning. In the now dark warehouse, there was nowhere to look but the spotlit clearing. And every nuance of every body was caught and magnified by the bright glare.

'Ya like cock, boy?' A blond guard raised a foot and placed it squarely behind Suit Guy's knees. In seconds, the guy crumpled to the floor.

One of the volunteers was now holding Plaid Shirt's dick by the root. The guy was still flaccid, but his gleaming black shaft was already responding to the pressure of the other man's fingers. His cock had to be nine inches, soft. Gripped by his tormentor's fist, it lolled over his thumb like some vast blood pudding.

The blond guard dragged Suit Guy across hard concrete on his hands and knees towards them. He stopped a mere foot away.

A sweating face and a thick cock were almost level.

Gav couldn't drag his eyes from that curving shaft, which was filling with blood as he watched. Like rumpled silk, the black cock smoothed out wrinkle by delicious wrinkle as the heavy foreskin rolled back. The cock was thickening by the second, plumping out and lengthening to reveal the startling rose-coloured glans. Far from lolling now, it fairly sprouted from the volunteer's fist, a stout stem of arousal.

On his knees, Suit Guy was also staring at the vast organ – difficult not to, since it was mere inches from his face now.

His neighbour's arm still firmly around his waist, a stranger's hard-on digging into the back of his leg, Gav watched through a haze as the volunteer tightened his grip on the great black cock. And slapped it soundly it across Suit Guy's right cheek – and Suit Guy didn't look too upset about the fact, either.

The crowd erupted. Hats were thrown into the air. Flushed with new-found fame, the volunteer continued to whack the increasingly engorged dick against the other man's face with more and more enthusiasm.

Gav inhaled sharply, noticing that several of the guys along the edge of the semicircle had unzipped. A variety of hard and half-hard members were being dragged from button and zip flies. Centre stage, the MC had just come, and was now wiping himself off on Chicago Bulls' hair. In the hot, humid darkness of the crowd, Gav could smell dick. He could smell the sour stink of male crotch, the meaty tang of a hundred aroused bodies crushed together.

The guy in the suit was whimpering with need. Plaid Shirt himself looked totally appalled. But his curving dick told another story. Meanwhile, Chicago Bulls had been grabbed by the third volunteer, who was in the process of positioning the man's mouth against his own erect knob. Around him, other men were unzipping, fumbling for their own cocks in the damp, dark warehouse.

Gav's head was spinning. His entire body was drenched from his own sweat and the condensing sweat of hundreds of other men's bodies. He had to get out, he had to get out of this place but the only part of himself he could move was his head.

He was hard. He didn't want to be hard. He couldn't decide whether the kid in the Puffa jacket had really been shot or he'd imagined the whole thing, but whatever had gone down with that gun he knew this whole thing wasn't his scene and he didn't want to be here.

But he was a professional, and this was an assignment – and Gav now had more than enough information to give his article that special Gavin Shaw touch. He scanned the crowd to each side, searching for a possible exit. Across the now-wanking throng, two figures stood motionless, eyes directed towards the main event.

Milo, T-shirted and with his heavy biceps bulging.

And the calm, immaculately attired, silver-haired figure of Derek Masters.

Gavin inhaled sharply. He had to get back to his car. He had to add this to the expanding Masters file, and get back to the UK fast. Holding his breath, he wrenched his body round, lowered his head and pushed his way through the groaning, wanking throng. He didn't look back. He just kept on going.

Only when he'd barged past the surly redneck doormen and reached fresh morning air did he stop. After sprinting back to his car, he collapsed over the bonnet, finally exhaling. Arms braced against the small vehicle, head lolling down between his shoulders, he breathed in deep, aching gulps. His stomach was cramping – he hadn't eaten since breakfast. Without the support of the crowd, his legs were rubber, his whole body useless. And he felt seriously unwell – literally sickened by what he'd witnessed inside that huge, aluminium-sided warehouse. The cramps moved higher, churning in his guts. Seconds later, he was throwing up over the side of the car. What little strength was left in his body left it then. Gav slumped to his knees, retching violently again and again.

'You OK, buddy?'

He'd never been as glad to hear a concerned voice, or feel a strong hand on his shoulder.

Weak as a kitten, Gav allowed his Good Samaritan – who introduced himself as Michael – to half-carry him over to a low wall. Michael produced a handkerchief, spat on it and methodically wiped vomit from Gavin's chin and lips while holding his chin steady in a firm and soothing grip.

'One too many, huh, buddy?'

Gav wasn't yet capable of speech.

The low, Southern-accented voice chuckled. 'Been there myself – once too often.'

Like a child, Gav submitted to the ministrations – and the ensuing lecture.

'You can use booze, buddy. Or booze can use you.' As Michael sat on the wall at Gavin's side, his heavily ringed hand plucked at the front of Gav's soaked and now puke-splattered shirt. He began to ease strong arms from the trapper's jacket he was wearing. 'I hate to say this, but you stink – get outta that thing, huh?'

Gav could only obey. But his arms wouldn't move. With Michael's help, between them they eventually got the drenched shirt off. Michael tossed it over the wall, then draped the worn, trappers jacket around Gavin's shoulders. 'Better?'

His only response was a low moan of pleasure. The garment was heavy and warm. It smelled of washing powder and green fields. Clean. Fresh. Safe. But everything that was still taking place on the other side of the narrow alley wasn't.

One of his saviour's arms remained around Gav's shoulders. Before he could stop himself, Gav was burrowing in against the man's strong body. Michael didn't seem to object. If anything, he way he curled Gavin closer beneath his arm said he was enjoying the closeness.

They sat there like that for a while. And slowly Gavin felt a bit better. It was getting light, now – had to be close on 5 a.m. He became aware of a pinkish glow around them that told him the sun was rising.

Then noises. Sounds. A door opening. Footsteps. First a few. Then more. And low voices. The horny, brutal activity that had been taking place across the alley had evidently climaxed. Car doors slammed. The sound of engines revving close by made him flinch.

Gavin began to shake.

'Easy, easy buddy. You're OK. Nothing can hurt you – I won't let anything hurt you.'

Gav continued to trembled. But Michael's words soothed him. Turning his body, he managed to wrap both arms around the man's solid, clean-smelling chest and clung on like a baby.

A hand moved to stroke his hair. 'It's OK. Everything's gonna be OK, buddy.'

Further reassurances, murmured from deep in his guardian angel's throat, draped him in a strong secure blanket. Snuggling in closer, Gavin found himself mouthing the front of Michael's T-shirt. Slowly, the sound of cars driving away and the echo of foot-falls eased. Apart from the occasional hooter from the meat-packing factories, the alley fell silent.

A low chuckle. The arm around him tightened. 'I love this time of day, you know?' Unexpectedly, Michael kissed the top of Gavin's head.

Gav whimpered, creeping closer until he was actually sitting in the other man's lap.

Michael showed no sign of objecting. He talked on. 'Summer dawn. It's so quiet – so cool. Makes you feel like you're the only person alive, you know?'

Gavin managed an affirmative mumble. Not the only person alive, though: the only two men alive. Held in these arms, his body still sore from the crush of the crowd, his mind still reeling with what had gone down beyond those aluminium-sided walls, he felt safe and secure and loved and cherished and—

Abruptly, as sensation began to return to his limbs, Gav became aware of something else.

He felt hard. He groaned in mortification, mouth open and wet against the front of Michael's T-shirt. The events of the day – the past three days – added to what he'd witnessed a mere thirty minutes earlier, topped off by the physical proximity of a caring but nonetheless very male presence, were bringing him to a peak of his own. A dozen different sources of arousal converged into a single point. A single urge.

Before he knew what was happening, Gav began to grind his crotch against his rescuer's thigh.

A single, undeniable urge. His eyes closed. He couldn't believe he needed to come so soon after the session with Tony. But his body was moving by itself, his erect cock itchy and demanding release.

And the strong arm was tightening around him, a leg conveniently pushing itself between his.

Gavin's fists gripped handfuls of Michael's T-shirt. His hips bucked against the solid muscle of the guy's leg. Eyes narrowed in need, face scarlet, he dragged himself up and down Michael's thigh.

The man himself was still murmuring soothing words in that deep, Southern voice. He was kissing Gavin's hair, his mouth burying itself in the soft skin of Gavin's neck.

Gav humped on, like a bitch in heat. It was hurting: the head of his cock had found the Y in his underwear and poked its way through. The sensitive glans was rubbing against the rough denim of his zip area, and, for each shudder of pleasure that racked his exhausted body, a parallel wave of discomfort echoed it.

His cock was so hard the skin on his balls felt tighter than a drum. He twisted handfuls of Michael's T-shirt in his fists, eyes screwed tightly shut and lips drawn back in passion.

As he humped his saviour's thigh, a million images fled through his sick mind.

Tony's pleading face as Gav had sprayed him with come. The

hunger in young Jordaan's eyes, back in Amsterdam. Brutish Milo's sneer of contempt, when he'd stopped Gavin sneaking his way into the MacPherson Room. And the cold, utterly calm smile that had played around Derek Masters' thin lips as he'd watched a crowd of sexually rampant rednecks as good as rape three defenceless men.

Gav rode Michael's leg like a stallion. He was vaguely aware of base, grunting animal sounds, and knew they were coming from his own mouth. The head of his cock was on fire, from the friction. But he didn't care. He couldn't have stopped if he'd wanted to.

One of Michael's hands found its way into Gavin's hair, and grabbed a fistful. The other arm was still around him, that hand holding the small of his back, and keeping him on course. He had no idea whether the man himself was aroused. That wasn't an issue. The only thing in his mind was a cold, selfish need for release.

He inhaled sharply, his body rearing back like a bronco rider's, and when he came a nearby abattoir hooter competed with his scream. His body was contorting. His hips bucked wildly as he shot into his own pants like some sex-starved teenager. He shot again, balls knitting together painfully, his glans burning as the wet come made contact with the grazed flesh.

And again...

Knees impacted either side of Michael's thigh. Gav could feel the rough brick of the wall beneath them.

And again...

He writhed against the other man's body, head thrown back, eyes open to the reddening sky.

And again...

Only when his balls were loose and empty did his body gradually stop jerking. Gav slumped into Michael's embrace, feeling warm kisses on his neck. And his guardian angel began to rock him.

They lay there like that, arms wrapped around each other, until Gav's brain began to clear. And embarrassment seeped into the warm sticky afterglow of orgasm. Sheepishly, he raised his head and looked up at the broad man who held him.

Really registering Michael's features for the first time, Gavin saw the man had a pleasant face, but was nothing startling in the looks department. A little careworn, a little battered around the edges, it was a face that had obviously seen a good bit of what life had to offer. Then the mouth smiled.

Heat spread rapidly over his cheeks. Gavin blushed furiously.

Michael chuckled and ruffled his hair. 'Better, buddy?'

Gavin nodded. He was aware he hadn't yet spoken to the man. Not one word had crossed his lips during the past hour. He didn't know what to say – had no idea how to thank this man for turning a terrifying night around, and providing a bit of that good old Southern hospitality Gav had read so much about. And it was pure chance Michael had happened to be passing when Gav reeled out from that terrifying warehouse. But now – as ever – his mind was back on track, and he didn't want to hang around. 'Um, listen, thanks for being here, pal.'

The smile broadened. 'My pleasure.'

Slowly, they disentangled and Michael helped him to his feet. Gavin found he could just about stand – in fact, he found he was feeling really good. 'I gotta go – take care, eh?' Bare-chested in the morning half-light, he took off the guy's trapper's jacket and handed it back.

Michael took it. 'You too, buddy – safe home.'

Fumbling in his pocket, Gav located the keys to the rental car and scanned the area for where he'd parked it. Which was when he saw that not all the cars from the disgusting goings-on within the warehouse had left.

On the far side of the space sat the white stretch limo. Its powerful engine was idling. The back passenger window was half open.

Gav blinked.

'See ya around, buddy.' Michael shrugged on the faded check jacket and gave Gav a mock salute.

He stared at Derek Masters' limo, wondering how long it had been there. How long it had been occupied. And how much of what had passed between himself and Michael had been seen. He felt violated. He felt spied upon.

But this was nothing to the mongrel emotions that coursed through his veins as Michael strolled over to the luxury car. He stretched out a hand.

A responding fist appeared through the limo's window. It held a bundle of green dollars.

Michael took the money, gave another mock salute to the car's unseen occupant, then sauntered away, whistling cheerfully.

Open-mouthed, Gav stood rooted to the spot as the engine revved and the great long white slug sped smoothly out of the car park to disappear back up the alley.

What was going on here?

What the hell was going on?

# Sixteen

Gavin drove straight to Philadelphia airport along deserted freeways.

He handed over the little car to another tooth-endowed Avis rep, then found the first flight bound for any UK airport. Only six hours later, soaring forty thousand feet above the Atlantic ocean, did he finally relax. Laptop open on the seat-back table, Gav entered his new information into the Masters file, with shaking fingers.

The meeting with Brian Josiah Dennett III – not illegal, certainly dodgy. Flowers on the grave of 'Johnny' – intriguing. A large sum of money given to a nameless youth – suspect. The shooting of a young guy in Derek Masters' presence – illegal. The abuse of three men, in Derek Masters' presence – illegal. The employment of 'Michael', to provide sexual services to a third party...

Gav leaned back in his seat and rubbed his eyes.

... specifically, a third party whom Derek Masters now knew was on his trail – just plain bizarre. Over the past five days he'd been arrested, sent ten thousand pounds and set up with someone Gavin was now sure had been a local, Baltimore call boy. Add to this Okie flight attendant Vincent's purloining of his passport on the journey out, and what emerged was a confusing mixture of stick and carrot.

'Drink, sir?'

He glanced at the pretty, albeit female trolley dolly, who was smiling at him and extending more mimosas. 'Water?' He wasn't taking any chances. Gav needed a clear head, when he landed in the UK, if he was going to make any sense of exactly what was going on with Derek Masters.

The trolley dolly returned with his mineral water. Gavin thanked her, unscrewed the top and drank deeply. Beyond the window, thick cloud shrouded his view, clearing only occasionally to show glimpses of a dark-blue sea. It made him think of Derek Masters: beneath the shroud of secrecy that draped the man's activities lay something even darker. The more he learned, the less he knew. And he more he wanted to know.

Gav dozed for most of the seven-hour flight home. His dreams were of scared faces, raucous redneck hollering. And Derek Masters' pitlike black eyes.

Coming though Luton airport's customs area, he switched his phone back on.

A slew of voice-mail messages demanded his attention. All bore James Delany's mobile number. One text bleeped its presence. Gavin ignored the calls from James and opened the text: 'Elkton Bugle. Archive 24/03/1996. Smith County crn. J Clark'

Keeping the message displayed on screen, he wandered out into the dark night. It was just after midnight. And it was raining. He'd lost five hours on the return flight.

But he was glad his anonymous informant had not forgotten about him. Hailing a taxi, Gav gave the startled driver the address of his office in central London.

'Can't do it for less than fifty quid, guv.'

What was left of Derek Masters' ten-grand buy-off money snuggled in the inside pocket of his Levi jacket. As ever, the text message was impenetrable. But Gav knew he'd soon make sense of it. He needed a web connection. And he needed it fast. 'Get me there in under an hour, and I'll make it a hundred.'

They set off at breakneck speed, windscreen wipers screeching against wet glass.

\*

Two hours later, Gav sat at his desk, peering at the website of the *Elkton Bugle* – the local free sheet of a tiny town in the north of Maryland. He was surprised that US free sheets kept online archives. He was even more surprised at the report, from five years ago, of the discovery of a man's mutilated body in a farmer's field.

From his fingerprints, he had been identified as John Clark, of Brooklyn, NYC. Ex-cop with NYPD, former security consultant, Clark had apparently been reduced to carrying out 'hits' for certain well-known New York criminal families. His death was no great surprise to the NYPD, on whose 'wanted' list the man had featured for some time. What was less easily explained was how he had ended up dead in a filed, in Elkton.

Gav narrowed his eyes.

John Clark, John Clark, John Clark. The name meant nothing. Grabbing his third mug of black coffee, Gav bookmarked the site, then flicked back to the Smith County Coroner's reports, for 29/04/1996, grateful for American public-access laws.

John Clark had been forty-four years old at the time of his death. He had enjoyed good health, although a degree of liver damage was noted, as were the remains of a barely legible, recently removed tattoo on the man's right shoulder blade. Intriguingly, the results of the autopsy were inconclusive. To this day, no one knew exactly how John Clark had died: his heart had just stopped beating.

Clark... Clark...

Gavin hmm-ed. It was a long shot, but he'd found it useful before. Typing the words 'John' and 'Clark' into his search engine, he leaned back in his chair and waited. He knew the results would be up in the hundreds of thousands, the bulk of which would be totally irrelevant to his present needs. But there was a chance – just a chance – they would throw up the connection he was looking for. Both hands clasped around the cooling mug of coffee, and with another dawn breaking beyond his office window, Gavin waited.

His land line rang twice. His cellphone beeped on and off.

Gavin ignored them both and stared at his screen. Finally, after two hours of wading through every John and Clark presence on the web, his search was paying off: 'Ex-Latvian soldier charged with the killing of John "Johnny-Boy" Clark.'

As his eyes scanned down the obscure court report from five years ago, Gavin's heart thumped against his ribs. The identity of the former Latvian soldier was revealed in the second paragraph, after a lot of stuff about Johnny-Boy Clark's mob connections and his time as a mercenary with, of all things, the Russian army. Back then, he'd gone by the name Deke Zenovich. But the photograph, showing a tall, angular man with a shock of silver hair, was unmistakable. 'Yes!' Gavin leapt from his chair and punched the air.

Deke Zenovich was Derek Masters. And the grave in Baltimore, marked only 'Johnny', undoubtedly belonged to John Clark.

He was almost too excited to read on, but he forced himself – and was glad he'd done so.

After their respective military careers ended, John Clark had been a partner in the then embryonic Zenovich Securities: a twopenny-ha'penny firm that supplied bodyguards to US dignitaries. There had been a falling out. Masters, a.k.a. Zenovich, had publicly threatened Clark, then manoeuvred him from the partnership with the help of clever lawyers. Motive had been seen in Clark's own very public assertion that he would 'tell everything'.

Gavin's hands shook. Lukewarm coffee slopped over his knuckles.

The case had been tried in a UK court, and halfway through the trial Zenovich had taken his British mother's name, and legally changed the Deke to Derek. Not that it had done him any good: through a combination of circumstantial evidence and top-drawer prosecution, the jury had found Derek Masters guilty of murder, and sentenced him to twenty-five years in prison.

Gav read on, fascinated.

A link at the bottom of the page led him on two years, to Masters' pardon and release from prison. His name cleared by a zealous investigative defence team, the now CEO of Masers Industries had gone on to great commercial heights.

Johnny-Boy Clark's 'real' killer had never been apprehended. The case remained open.

Gav exhaled noisily. What if Masters had killed Clark? What if the dark-haired blackmailer had proof of this? The international entrepreneur certainly still kept dubious company – what he'd seen over the last few days had convinced Gavin of that. However, it was only company.

But in Masters' position, mud – even clean mud – stuck, and Gav could well understand why the guy would go to any lengths to keep his past firmly in the past.

His phone rang again.

Gav ignored it, opening the Masters file in his word-processing program and began to type hurriedly.

Then his mobile rang.

His fingers flew like lightning. Somewhere in the distance, the door buzzer sounded downstairs. Gav barely registered it. His dossier on Derek Masters was growing. There was so much – so much the public had a right to know.

Then a pounding.

The thrill of the chase filled his veins. His head felt tight, his brain bursting with the thought of how great this profile of one of the world's most reclusive captains of industry was going to be.

The pounding was on the door to his office. Then a voice. 'Gavin? Gavin? I know you're in there – come on, open up!'

He groaned, immediately recognising James Delany's angry tones. Then a smile crept onto Gavin's face. He recalled an incident, from more years back than he cared to remember. He and James had just got together. It was the first of many, explosive arguments. Gav had stormed out. James had pursued him to this very office, pounded on the door, then kicked it in.

The smile took on an almost wistful quality: no one had ever kicked a door in to get to Gavin Shaw, either before or since.

'Gavin!'

A roar from beyond the office walls cut into his musings. He couldn't afford to lose a second door. Wearily, Gav saved, then closed, the Masters file, and walked towards the irate voice.

'Where the fuck have you been?' Dressed in his usual Hugo Boss, James barged past Gavin into the room. 'And why haven't you been returning my calls?' His eyes fell on the laptop and the coffee stains. 'What's—' James swivelled round. And stopped talking abruptly.

Gav smiled. 'Sorry, I just got back last night.' The smile faded.

James continued to stare at him, his expression changing. 'Have you seen the state of yourself?'

Gav rolled his eyes and ran a hand through his tangled hair. 'We don't all have butlers and manservants to take care of our every need.'

James coolly gripped Gavin by the chin, rasping immaculately manicured fingers over four days' growth. 'Ever heard of shaving?' He sniffed, and made a face. 'Or even a wash?'

Gav laughed and twisted away. 'I'm working – I've got better things to do than—'

'And you're losing weight.' James grabbed his shoulders and peered at him critically. 'When did you last eat?'

Gav shrugged. 'Yesterday.' Or was it the day before? He wasn't quite sure. 'I'll get something to take away, when I've finished this.'

'You'll come with me, for breakfast. Now.' James released his shoulders. 'Or at least after you've showered. Have you still got that ancient contraption through there?' He nodded towards the washroom Gav had converted when he'd been actually using the office as a bedsit.

The thought was appealing, if he was honest. But he had other things to do. 'Jim, I'm working – you know how I get when I'm working.'

The rugged face creased momentarily into a frown. Then the commissioning editor of *Financial Week* sighed. 'I know – look, at least take a break. You shower, have a shave – I'll nip down to that nice coffee shop at the end of the street and see if they can rustle up something.'

Gav yawned. 'No, I really can't. I—'

'And you're exhausted – have you been working all night?'

'I slept a bit on the plane.' Now that he'd stopped working, he did feel fairly grotty. A break might be good.

James arched an eyebrow at the mention of aeroplanes. 'I hope you don't think we're a bottomless pit as far as expenses are concerned, because I'm not sure *Financial Week* can stretch to—'

'Oh, I've got all that covered.' Studiedly casual, Gav reached into the pocket of his Levi jacket and produced a wad of notes. 'And I will have breakfast with you – but I'm paying.' With exaggerated nonchalance, he peeled off a fifty. 'Get the good coffee, eh?'

Both James Delany's eyebrows shot up. But he took the note. 'If you'll get a wash.'

Gavin nodded and smiled. 'Oh, and they do great Danish – remember?'

James laughed, then groaned, and patted his trim stomach. 'My waistline does.'

Gavin continued to smile. It was obviously the time for memories. In their early days – what James had wryly referred to as their 'courtship' – they'd spent the night here, from time to time, adjourning to the café at the end of the street for breakfast.

James smiled back. Not his business smile – not even his teasing smile. But the smile Gavin had glimpsed only occasionally during their tempestuous three-month fling. The smile he'd seen, lying in this man's arms, after a particularly energetic fuck.

They stood there, traffic roaring past outside, for what seemed like an age. Then James rolled his eyes, 'OK, I'll bring back the works – but you'd better be cleaned up a bit, right?'

'Yes, sir!' Gavin mock-saluted.

James shook his head, still smiling, and moved towards the door.

In the cramped shower room, Gav let the water heat up while he struggled out of his grubby, rumpled clothes, then dragged a disposable razor over his chin and cheeks in a cursory shave. He did need a wash: he stank of sweat, spunk and airport lounges. And, when he stepped naked under the hot, powerful jet Gavin knew the shower would do more than clean him.

For the first time in four days, he began to relax. Everything he'd seen – everything he'd done – on American soil slowly receded to the back of his brain. And his mind turned to James.

Grabbing the soap, he lathered it up between his hands and began to wash under his arms.

James Delany. Forty-eight and still a head turner. Cultured, educated at the UK's finest schools, then at Oxford. Rich, with impeccable manners, a brain like a razor and a wit to match.

He groaned, running the soap over his pecs then down to his stomach.

James Delany, one of the most powerful, influential figures in financial publishing.

Gavin braced one arm against the shower-cubicle wall, moving a soapy hand to his arse.

James Delaney – the hottest fuck Gav had ever had.

Standing there, with water coursing down over his head, Gav washed sweat and grime from his crack and remembered three glorious weeks.

They'd spent more time in bed than anywhere else. Or, rather, over James's Queen Anne dining room table, on the stone veranda of James's luxury's Wimbledon house, in the back of James's vintage Jaguar car, against the filing cabinet in James's office – everywhere but bed, in fact.

He let his head droop forward, jets of hot water pounding the tension from his tired body. Widening his stance, he ran a finger over his own hole. And shuddered.

They'd been unable to keep their hands off each other. They'd been at it like dogs, every time they were in each other's company.

Aware he was hardening again, Gavin let the pad of his finger rub the pink, puckered skin around his hole one last time, then leaned back against the wall of the shower cubicle. Knees bent, thighs parted, he grabbed his half-hard cock with both soapy hands.

He could still recall the way James smelled. The low, controlled sigh the man released when he came...

One lathered hand cupping his balls, Gavin yanked roughly at the full, wet sac.

... the feel of the man's hard cock deep in his body...

Gav grunted, his other hand moving soapily up and down his shaft.

... and the softness in those unsettling grey eyes afterwards. His own eyelids narrowed in desire, then closed completely. Gavin stroked himself slowly, enjoying the heat and the pressure of the water as it pounded over his exhausted body.

What had happened? When had things between him and James gone so badly wrong? When had the fights and the arguments outweighed the sweet surrender of making up?

He yanked at his balls again, sending jolts of pleasure deep into his arse. Gavin moaned, pushing away the bad times and hanging onto the good.

At the opera, with James. Picnics by the Ox, with James, followed by slow languid fucks in the long grass. Candlelight dinners *à deux* under the stars. Laughing at James's funny stories. Reading together in James's study. Being seen with the man in public, seeing the admiring – and envious – glances they drew as a couple.

Gav's fist was moving faster now, pulling his foreskin over the swollen head of his dick with each upward stroke, then pushing it back as his hand descended once more to the root.

The prestige had been part of it, he couldn't deny that. The sex had been most of it – even the kinky stuff.

He threw his head back, lips parting in a scowl of need as he remembered the mongrel sensations that had coursed through his body as James had tied his legs apart, then rimmed him into oblivion.

But there was something else – something unnerving about the way he'd slowly begun to feel that his independence was under threat. Oh, James never forbade Gavin from seeing other people when they'd been together – anything but. He'd actively encouraged it. They'd admired other men's bodies together. But all Gav had ever felt on these occasions was a slow-burning jealousy.

His cock pulsed in his hand. Standing there, leaning against the wall of the shower cubicle, he wanked himself furiously, part arousal and part anger. At himself. At James. At a relationship he'd wanted to commit to more than he'd ever wanted anything in his life.

But he'd been scared. Scared of James's insight. Scared of his ex-lover's ability to provide everything Gavin wanted from another man...

He came violently, thighs quivering and cock jerking in his fist.

... and a corresponding ability to withdraw it all, at will.

Gav's eyelids flew open, as warm milky spunk splattered his

upper chest and belly. The room was full of steam. His body jerked convulsively, and his head lolled forward, fist tightening and still moving to coax the last few drops from his gaping slit. The sound of running water filled his head.

And through the clouds of steam he met a pair of cool, vaguely amused grey eyes. And held them until the shuddering dregs of orgasm subsided.

James's expression was hard to read. They both stood there, silently watching each other. One naked, and with his own come still dripping from his knuckles. The other in a Hugo Boss suit.

Something beyond words passed between them. Then Gavin laughed, levering himself off the shower-cubicle wall. James's thin lips parted in a smile.

'You never change, do you my friend?' Those cool grey eyes glanced at Gavin's cock.

Gav chuckled. 'You get my breakfast?'

This time, the responding laugh was deep and warm. 'Your feast awaits you, my lord!'

Before he could think of an amusing reply, James had turned on his heel and Gav found himself staring at broad, Hugo-Bossed shoulders.

They ate on the floor, Gav with a towel modestly around his waist, James having removed his jacket. And, as they ate, Gav dropped a few oblique hints as to what he'd found out about Derek Masters. 'There's more to this guy than meets the eye – much more!'

James leaned forward, brushing crumbs from his lips. 'So tell me.'

Gav took a long gulp of his latte. 'Not yet – I want to get it all, first.'

James rolled his eyes. 'You're enjoying this, aren't you, you tease?'

Gav chuckled, and had to admit he was. Despite what he'd

witnessed over the past week – had it only been a week? – and despite the genuine feelings of fear and panic a lot of it had generated, he knew he was throwing himself into the Masters assignment with more vigour than usual.

'Can't I even see a first draft, at least?'

Gav shook his wet head solemnly. 'You know the way I work, James: you see it when it's finished, and not before.'

James sighed theatrically. 'I just hope you know what you're doing. Masters has some powerful friends, from the little I know.'

Gav felt a glow of satisfaction that he knew more. For once, the great James Delany, game player supreme and the toast of London's gay S&M scene did not have the upper hand. He winked. 'I will tell you something, though.' Tucking his towel firmly around his waist, he crawled over to where James sat.

James's eyes widened.

Pausing in front of the man in the suit and tie, Gav leaned forward, his lips brushing James's ear. 'This is gonna be so big – this is gonna be huge.'

James laughed, and unexpectedly ruffled Gavin's wet hair. 'Oh, I'm sure you're right.'

# Seventeen

James left half an hour later, having made Gavin promise to keep him up to date with his progress – and return his phone calls.

Stomach pleasantly full, Gav found an old blanket in a cupboard and curled up on the couch-cum-bed. He dozed off and on for most of the afternoon, finally falling into a deep sleep about 5 p.m.

When he awoke, it was to darkness – and the insistent buzzing of his mobile. Gav staggered up from the couch, switched on his desk light and grabbed his cellphone.

Another text. from the same number as before: '65 All Saints Road. Basement flat. Felicia.'

Gav rubbed sleep from his eyes. He knew the Westbourne Park area of London from years ago. It didn't sound like the sort of place Derek Masters would be seen dead in – even if the man had returned to the UK. And who was Felicia?

He grabbed his wristwatch, and saw it was just after 10 p.m. There was only one way to find out. Rifling through his suitcase, he located clean jeans – faded ones, his favourites – and a skin-tight black-mesh T-shirt he didn't seem to recognise. Gav groaned and held the garment up for inspection.

Too tight. Too obvious. Too tarty – definitely not Gavin Shaw. He rummaged about a bit, but there didn't seem to be anything else clean. Tomorrow, he'd find a launderette. For tonight, this strange creation would have to do.

Pulling on the jeans, he struggled into the mesh T-shirt, then hastily tied his hair back with the usual leather thong. Gav eyed himself critically in the mirror. And, to be honest, he didn't look half bad.

Gav smiled at the way the stretched fabric showed off his still-good pecs. He grabbed his denim jacket, sectioned off two hundred pounds from the Masters bribe money and shoved the rest under the carpet. Gav patted his pockets. Cellphone, keys, dosh condoms: he was ready for anything. It was time to hit All Saints Road.

He'd forgotten it was a Friday night. Out on Euston Road, he couldn't get a taxi for love or money, so ended up on the tube. Both trains were full of bright young things, heading for this club or other dressed in all their finery, to celebrate the start of the weekend.

Gavin hung onto an overhead strap and smiled to himself. Clubbing was for kids – he couldn't remember the last time he'd set foot inside one of those dark, hot, deafening establishments. Maybe it was a sign of age – or maybe he'd just worked out, a long time ago, that there were easier, more efficient ways of picking up partners for casual sex.

After all, that was what clubbing was all about, wasn't it?

On the opposite side of the train compartment, two late-teens boys were nudging each other and eyeing him with barely concealed admiration.

Gav grinned back and caught a glimpse of himself in the train window. He looked hot – fucking hot! Thirty-five and in his prime. As he moved his gaze from the two lusty boys, Gav met the eye of an older man. Then a well-preserved middle-aged woman. Chest swelling with pride, dick twitching, Gav preened happily in the train's dark window. Maybe, when he'd turned in this article, he'd have a night on the town.

When the train stopped and Gavin got off, at least eight pairs of eyes followed him onto the platform. Although he didn't normally like to attract as much attention when he was on an assignment, it felt good.

Fifteen minutes later, he was walking down All Saints Road. The area had changed somewhat, since his last visit. Several Isuzu Jeeps stood outside newly refurbished buildings. Ikea blinds were evident in double-glazed windows. Neighbourhood Watch stickers were visible. The old Afro-Caribbean grocers' shops had been replaced by smart café-bars and delicatessens selling extra-virgin olive oil. Gavin groaned.

The yuppies had moved in.

Turning down towards the bottom of the road, Gav continued on to Number 65. And discovered this section of the street was cloaked in scaffolding. Obviously, the refurbishment was still in progress. Swerving past a Portakabin and a chain-link fence around two cement mixers, Gav stared dolefully at the entrance to 65 All Saints Road. A large rectangle of corrugated iron sealed the doorway. Above it, a sign read DANGER: KEEP OUT.

The place was derelict. Gav frowned, pulled out his cellphone and rechecked the address. Definitely 65. Although no time or date was provided, his anonymous informant hadn't steered him wrong yet. More than a little disappointed, Gav stepped out onto the road and gazed up at six sets of sightless windows.

No sign of any life at all – not even a night watchman. Finding a wall, he leaned against it and looked at his watch. Coming up on midnight – what a bummer. He'd come all the way over here and—

The sound of heels clacking on tarmac made him turn his head.

A well-dressed man and woman were making their way down from the yuppie end of the street. Gavin watched them stride purposefully over to the boarded-up entrance to Number 65. From behind, he couldn't see what they did. But seconds later the section of corrugated iron was swinging inwards, and the couple disappeared into the derelict building.

Gav leapt off the wall and jogged over to the corrugated iron. He reached it, just as the makeshift door slammed shut again. 'Hello? Hello?'

Nothing.

He moved closer, pressing his ear to the rusting surface.

Nothing.

He took a step back. 'Anyone at home?' He felt like a fool, but the fact that he'd just seen two people admitted told him there had to be someone inside. And the fact that no one responded to his shouts made him want to be inside all the more – not to mention the obvious implication of the text message. Gavin frowned, banged hard on the corrugated iron with his fist. The metal rattled loudly and he hurt his hand. But no one came to see what was happening. Thoroughly irritated, Gav sucked on his fists, stalked back to his perch on the wall and sat down again.

Over the next hour, forty-odd people arrived at the boarded-up building. Some on foot. Some in taxies. Others emerged from Mazdas and Rovers, activating elaborate car alarms before leaving their vehicles by the kerb and entering Number 65. Several times, Gav darted over behind them. But the rusting door was always back in place before he could slip in.

None of them even seemed to bang or ring any bell. Maybe it was automatic – maybe there was a beam. A detailed inspection of the area around the door frame revealed no wiring or electronic eye or anything else from any James Bond-esque fantasy Gav could conjure up. He thought for a while that perhaps someone was keeping a lookout from one of the other widows. But they were all still either boarded up or covered by the same corrugated metal that screened the building's doorway. The basement evidently housed some private club or other – a club to which he was having no luck in gaining admittance.

He wasn't a member.

How did you become a member?

He hadn't noticed any of the people who had been allowed in showing any sort of card or anything.

Back at his post, Gav was at a loss. He was never going to get in – he would never find out what was happening inside, where Derek Masters fitted into it all and who Felicia was. In desperation, and hot on the heels of two burly men in bikers' leathers, Gav raced over to Number 65. As the door closed in his face once more, something suddenly occurred to him. He cleared his throat, and moving his mouth close to a crack in the rusting metal door, he whispered 'Felicia'.

Footsteps from inside. In moments, the corrugated-iron screen was moving inwards. Through the gloom beyond, a pale face appeared in the doorway. Just a face. No hair, no body. Gav inhaled sharply and stepped back as the disembodied apparition floated eerily in the darkness. As his eyes acclimatised, Gav saw it was a girl, with long black hair and clothing to match. Exhaling loudly, Gav coughed, and cleared his throat again. 'Felicia?'

'Lily, actually.' She smiled. 'Welcome.'

Gav entered the derelict building and heard the door slam shut behind him. The password had been a long shot, but it had paid off, and he was now on his way to discovering just what was going on in the bowels of Number 65 All Saints Road.

Lily led him along a series of winding corridors and down three flights of increasingly damp-smelling steps. The distant throb of a bass line drifted up to meet them.

'I had no idea the basements around here were so... extensive!' Gav laughed sheepishly.

In front, Lily giggled. 'Felicia owns this entire building. This is part of an old MOD bomb shelter and briefing suite – from 1943, would you believe? People say Winston Churchill himself planned the Battle of Britain down here.' Coming to an abrupt halt, Lily moved aside and stretched out an arm. 'Enjoy – I must get back to my sentry duty.' With another giggle, the gothic-looking girl had disappeared back off into darkness.

Gavin peered ahead. The music was louder now. And, as he ventured on, alone, he had a feeling Prime Minister Churchill would not have approved of what was taking place in one of his briefing rooms.

The walls ran red, pulsing with some sort of light show projected from a source he couldn't quite track down. The music was deafening, and seemed to consist mainly of drums and someone howling. The air reeked of cannabis, expensive perfume and stale amyl nitrite. And, underneath it all, a damp earthy odour that told Gavin this space was deep underground.

In every sense.

People milled around him, little more than exclusively dressed shadows in the flickering half-light. There didn't seem to be any seats. Or tables – or bar. To his right, Gav spotted a little cloakroom, staffed by a girl almost identical to Lily the Sentry. Surreally, he found himself handing over his Levi jacket and taking a red cloakroom ticket in return.

A passing waitresses offered him a glass of clear liquid. He took it, and was relieved to taste cold mineral water. Slowly, as he wandered around, his vision became accustomed to the gloom and he began to pick out faces.

Two men in bikers' leathers were locked in an embrace in one corner. A man in his sixties was stroking the thighs of a blond girl a third his age. Against one of the rippling red walls, a striking woman in her forties stood watching. A slender boy barely out of his teens knelt, eyes lowered, at her feet.

And the music pounded on. As Gavin explored further afield, the sexual nature of the activity increased and became more overt. In one of the darker recesses of the maze of tunnels and antechambers, a well-muscled man was tethered to a wall. His arms were secured to some sort of pulley above his head, his strong thighs tied wide part and quivering. Low gasps escaped his hidden lips each time a heavy cane descended across his buttocks. Gav paused, mesmerised momentarily by the purpling stripes across the guy's arse. He glanced at the man responsible for the damage. Big as a house, with a bulging crotch to match, the man with the cane paused between strokes. Sometimes he let the cane fall in a strict rhythm. Other times, he teased his captive by lengthening the gaps between the blows, smiling as the restrained man groaned in anticipation. Sometimes the cane fell so hard it looked as if it might draw blood from those quivering mounds of hard flesh, and Gavin himself winced in sympathy. Other times, it was more caress than attack. The touch of a lover could not have been gentler.

'Like what you see?' A low, husky voice cut under the pounding music.

Gav turned, and stared into the heavily made-up eyes of a statuesque brunette behind him. Part Betty Paige, part Joan Collins, the woman was of indeterminate age and was somewhat fierce-looking, in a severely tailored pinstriped jacket and pencil-skirt. But she smiled.

And he smiled back. 'Yes, I like.' Gav knew he'd got in here under false pretences. Hurriedly, he pulled together some sort of background to legitimise himself and yelled it at her over the pounding music. 'Of course, it's not... Judy's in Hastings.' There was no Judy's, and he'd never been to Hastings. But this woman didn't know that.

She arched a brow. 'Indeed?'

Gav nodded conspiratorially. It was easier than shouting

'You must give me Judy's address.' She held out a hand. 'Felicia, by the way.'

Gavin inhaled sharply. His hostess. With great aplomb, he took the offered hand and raised it to his lips. On her ring finger, a thick plain band of white gold caught his eyes. Not wanting to blow his cover, Gav lowered his eyes and softly kissed her ring, acolyte to bishopess. When he looked up, she was smiling at him with approval. Before he could move off, she'd tucked her arm inside his and patted his bottom. 'Now you must let me show you around – I'm sure we can outdo... Judy's, in Hastings, if you'll give us the chance.' She guided him forward towards the man with the cane, who was now stroking his victim's hair:

'Benjy, meet...' Felicia turned to Gavin. 'Why didn't I catch your name?'

'Because I didn't drop it?' Gavin smiled, and risked a wink.

Felicia clapped her hands approvingly. 'Touché, my friend!' Benjy laughed, deftly untying his victim's wrists. 'Good to meet you, whatever you call yourself, mate!' He stuck out a hand and gripped Gavin's in a bone-crushing vice. 'Ian? Meet Felicia's new... friend.' Benjy chucked again.

Gently flexing his previously tied arms, Ian nodded and smiled. 'Any friend of Felicia's is—'

'Popping up all over the place these days!' Gruff, familiar tones rumbled from behind.

Gavin cringed. He'd recognise that voice anywhere.

'Good to see you again, Shaw – what was all that about Judy's in Hastings?'

A solid hand thumped him on the back. Gav staggered forward. The last time he'd felt that hand it had been throwing him out of Masters Industries' headquarters in Canary Wharf. Slowly he turned round. He had to brazen this out – there was nothing else he could do. 'Just telling Felicia the provinces can still show the London... scene a thing or two, Milo.' He met the brutish bodyguard's eye.

Was this to be a replay of the Music Box in Amsterdam? Were these private parties something Derek Masters' right-hand man did on his nights off?

Suddenly, he was aware of a prickling sensation at the back of his neck. Beneath his ponytail, a shiver trembled down his spine. Milo's narrowed, bully-boy eyes flicked to a spot somewhere over Gavin's shoulder.

Felicia was saying something. Benjy the Cane Man was whispering something to him, and laughing. The music was louder than ever. But, as Gavin slowly turned and looked into Derek Masters' angular face, he heard only the thump of his own heart.

The rest of the evening passed in a blur. Felicia now considered Gavin her new 'discovery', and insisted on introducing him to everyone there. He caught the odd glimpse of Derek Masters' silver hair at various points. And, although almost everyone present ended up entangled with someone or other, by the time 4 a.m. came, the dark-eyed man only ever watched.

Masters watched Benjy beat some woman until she screamed with pleasure.

He watched Milo get a blow jobs from Ian.

He watched a variety of sexual interactions. But Derek Masters never took part. And Gavin watched the watcher.

Dawn was breaking over distant Notting Hill when he emerged from behind the corrugated-iron door. As he made his way back up to find a taxi, a hand tapped his shoulder.

'You doing anything next month, friend?' In semi-daylight, Felicia looked more drag queen than woman.

Before Gavin could reply, she was pushing a small card into his hand. It was the fourth invitation he'd received that evening.

'Here in London, we can outdo Judy's with our eyes shut.' Then she was clack-clacking over to the open door of a shining silver Mercedes, which sped off into the lightening sky.

Gav looked at the card: Skinner's Arms, Malvern Place, Upton Park. Jogging up towards the taxi rank, he felt vaguely exhilarated.

Over the next three weekends, he got into a routine. During the week, he slept and worked on the Masters file, tracking company profits and following up leads over the Internet. Fridays and Saturdays, he joined a variety of people at parties – held everywhere from derelict dog tracks to a private suite at the Gatwick Holiday Inn – at which Derek Masters was always present.

He got to know people. People got to know him. The more people he got to know, the more parties he was invited to. And the more offers to 'join in' he received. After a few pouts, Felicia finally accepted that Gav was gay and had no interest in her. She insisted, however, on introducing him to her friends.

He spent an hour talking to two older men from Islington, and turned down an offer to visit their dungeon the following week. He tried to avoid a very pretty bisexual boy and his young wife, who were interested in a three-way. A muscle Mary with a Tom of Finland moustache pursued Gavin all evening, in the back room of a Streatham drinking club.

Gavin had eyes for only one man – a man whose eyes seemed to be everywhere except on Gavin.

Milo had now taken to winking at him. And slapping him on the back like some long-lost friend. Which was what he did immediately they met outside the Skinner's Arms at the end of that month.

Gavin cringed and tried to return the brutish bodyguard's bonhomie. He always had the feeling Milo was playing some sort of strange game with him.

The guy knew he was journalist. He had to know Gavin was still going to write his profile of Milo's boss. Was the man stupid enough to think Gavin's presence at all these parties was mere coincidence? Gav had a feeling there was a fierce intelligence behind those heavily hooded eyes. Milo was far from dim. But Gav still couldn't quite work him out.

The Skinner's Arms was everything he expected from an East End pub. Filthy, badly decorated and full of skinheads. It also had the most eclectic jukebox Gav had ever seen. Everything from the worst of Doris Day to the best of punk rock shook the tatty establishment. But the atmosphere was very different from that of any of the other parties he'd been invited to. A definite air of menace hovered around the place. Feeling slightly out of his depth, Gav ordered a pint and looked around for Felicia.

No Felicia.

No Benjy.

No Ian – not even a solitary leather boy. With the exception of himself and Derek Masters – who wore another of those immaculately cut suits – Ben Sherman ruled in this pub.

Ben Sherman. Harrington. Bleached jeans. Braces. Zero-crops. And fourteen-hole Dr Martens boots.

Gav tugged his baseball cap down further over his eyes, edged along to the far end of the bar and tried to look inconspicuous. He was glad he'd dressed down this evening: faded jeans, white T-shirt and Levi jacket. And the Yankees cap had been a lifesaver. His head of shoulder-length black locks – whether tied into a ponytail or not – would have stood out like a sore thumb in this sanctuary of the shaven head.

For some reason, no one seemed to be giving Derek Masters' shock of silver hair a second glance. But Gav was aware of several predatory sets of eyes directed his way. He kept his head lowered and sipped his warm beer, waiting for something to happen. Over the next hour or so, more skinheads entered.

Big skinheads. Small skinheads. Skinheads with 'cut here' and a dotted line tattooed across their throats. Black skinheads. Asian skinheads. Apparently, all you needed to join this club was a pair of boots...

... and an attitude. On the far side of the pub, a scuffle erupted. A glass shattered. Loud male voices cursed various threats.

Along with those of everyone else in the place, Gav's eyes zoned to the area of the altercation.

A tall, scowling figure in a tit-hugging white Ben Sherman was lunging at a Japanese skinhead, fist clutching the remnants of a beer glass. Both were being restrained by separate friends. Both were hurling insults at each other. The Japanese skin produced a flick knife from the pocket of his Harrington jacket.

The object of the fight seemed to be a smaller, slighter man who stood a little away, arms folded in amusement. Across the back of the guy's neck, even from this distance, Gav could see what looked like a tattooed barcode.

Suddenly, the Japanese skin spat into the other skin's face, grabbed Barcode Boy by his barcoded neck and marched him out of the pub. His opponent charged after them, hurled the broken beer glass through the door, then stormed over to the bar, wiping spittle from his cheek.

'Pint of bitter, pal.'

Close up, Gav noticed a single silver hoop in the skin's right earlobe. Around them, guys were going back to their drinks, now the excitement had passed. Someone was pumping more money into the ancient jukebox. Doris Day began to sing to her 'lucky star'. Gavin glanced around, and saw that Derek Masters' dark fathomless gaze was focused in his direction. He felt vaguely unsettled. And vaguely flattered

'I need to drown my sorrows.' Earring Skin laughed wryly.

Then the truth dawned. Derek Masters wasn't looking at Gavin. He was staring at Earring Skin.

# Eighteen

'I'll get that.' Gav slid a ten-pound note across to the barmaid. 'And give me another pint.' He had no idea why he was paying for the skinhead's beer.

'Cheers, mate!' Earring Skin grabbed his glass, raised it and downed half of its contents in one.

Gav knew he was drawing attention to himself. He knew Derek Masters would now be watching intently.

The man at his side turned, and stuck out a hand. 'The name's Jake, by the way.'

'Gav.' Gripping the skin's fist in his, he got his first proper look at the guy.

The hair was cropped right into the wood, and Jake's cheekbones would have shamed Dietrich. But there the similarity ended. In sharp contrast to the shaved head, his eyebrows were thick and bushy. Below, a pair of piercing eyes blazed with an evil intelligence. At the corner of the right eye, a tiny crescent of scar tissue was just visible.

'Good ta meet you, Gav, mate – not seen you in here, before.' Jake released his hand and downed the rest of his pint.

He stared at the man's mouth. Large – too large. Almost girlish. Full lips framed a set of surprisingly white teeth. 'Um...' Gavin fumbled for a reply. 'Yeah, a friend told me about this place.'

On the jukebox Doris Day was replaced by Stiff Little Fingers. Behind them several of the skins started to dance.

Jake nodded in response, pulling out a squashed packet of cigarettes from the pocket of incredibly tight bleached Levi's. He stuck one between those too-large lips, then offered the packet to Gavin, whose eyes were now taking in the rest of the skinhead's lean, wiry body.

The white Ben Sherman polo shirt showed off a hard, well-muscled chest to best advantage. Red braces skimmed each nipple, attached to the unbelted and very battered jeans.

'Fucking lighter! Where the hell did I...?' Jake was patting himself down now, muttering under the raucous singalong that had started up to the Clash's 'White Riot' on the jukebox.

Gavin stared at the way the guy's zip bulged and strained over an obviously large package. He was just starting to admire Jake's thighs when a voice interrupted.

'Here.'

Something flicked at the side of Jake's ear.

Gav frowned, watching Milo – who had appeared from somewhere – smugly light Jake's cigarette for him.

'Ta, mate.'

Their eyes met. Milo winked. 'Evening, Shaw – bit off the beaten track for you, this place, eh?'

His frown slid into a scowl. Gavin ignored Milo, moving to close the gap between himself and Jake. 'Get you another?' He nodded to the empty pint glass.

'Nah, my shout – hey, you've not even touched yours.'

Using his body to prevent Milo from edging in on the conversation, Gav was vaguely aware that Jake was ordering more drinks. A myriad questions buzzed in his head. What were Derek Masters and Milo doing here, among this bunch of thugs? What had the fight been about? Why wasn't Masters again trying to warn him off? Why had Felicia, hostess of the capital's biggest and best kinky parties, given him the address of a grotty skinhead pub in the heart of London's East End? Then a large hand lightly touched the small of his back.

'Wanna go somewhere... quieter?'

Gav's eyes refocused.

Jake was holding his pint and nodding to a door marked SNUG. Over the door frame, the letter K in the legend SKINNER'S ARMS had been obliterated.

Would Derek Masters follow? There was only one way to find out. Grabbing his own glass, Gav fell in behind the tall, wiry skinhead and walked into the 'Sinner's Arms'.

There was no jukebox. No dancing. Fewer people. And definitely no singalong. They called it 'the snug' not merely because it was smaller than the pub's main bar: it more intimate in another way.

Following Jake past a lounging, younger skinhead who was talking in a low voice to a second, Gav tripped over something on the floor. Moving to avoid it, he saw a third man, face down among discarded cigarette ends and beer slops. The sole of the young skinhead's heavily booted foot was resting on the back of the guy's shaven neck.

Gav inhaled sharply, then raised an eyebrow as Jake paused, retraced his steps a little, then planted a solid kick into the kidneys of the skin on the floor.

The prostrate man groaned, but made no attempt either to rise or to retaliate.

Jake chuckled to the young skin. 'Evening, Andy!'

The owner of the foot broke off his conversation, and smiled at Jake. 'Think he's getting a bit thirsty down there?' Andy's hand moved to his crotch.

'Yeah, I think it's... rehydration time.'

Everyone laughed. Three pairs of eyes focused on the man on the floor. The sound of a zip dragged Gav's attention to Andy's crotch.

Hauling out a good six flaccid and heavily foreskinned inches, the young skin sank to a crouch. 'Want a drink, bitch?' He eased his foot from the back of the guy's neck.

Gav saw the length of chain around the guy's neck twinkle in the dim light.

The guy moaned, rolled over onto his side.

Gav flinched. Andy's 'bitch' was a well-preserved forty, and handsome as hell.

'Did ya hear me?' Holding his cock between thumb and fore-finger, Andy nudged his captive roughly with the toe of a highly polished Doc Martens.

'Yes… yes, I want a drink. Please! I want a drink.' The guy's lips moved to kiss Andy's boot.

Gav was very aware that Jake's wiry arm had, at some point, draped itself around his shoulders. He could also feel the warm hardness of the man's body against his. But he couldn't drag his eyes from what as unfolding before him.

With an unexpected gentleness, Andy trailed a finger under the chain around the guy's neck, then rose from his crouching position. Standing there, booted feet planted half a yard apart, he gripped his cock and aimed.

A trickle, at first, then a stream of yellow steaming piss splattered down onto the prostrate figure. It hit his head, the side of his face, running down onto the floor. Then the stream became a torrent and the guy on the floor was crawling onto his back, eyes closed, mouth open.

The arm around Gavin's shoulder tightened. Fingers played absently on the exposed mound of his deltoid.

But he kept watching. And as Andy shook the last few dribbles from his piss-slit, someone else took over. A guy Gav hadn't noticed earlier had unbuttoned the fly of narrow-legged, skin-tight Wranglers jeans and was now voiding his bladder onto the man at Andy's feet.

Another guy joined in. Then a third. Then everyone was unzipping. A tight circle was forming around the writhing, urine-sodden figure. Steam filled the air. The sour, alkaline stench of ammonia caught in the back of Gavin's throat and made his eyes water. The two pints of hideously warm beer he'd downed earlier in the evening – mainly through something to do – were pressing on his own bladder. And the sound of pissing was increasing his own need to urinate.

Jake's arm left his shoulder. Gav felt its absence in a way that surprised him. Then he was watching, open mouthed, as his new friend was unzipping too, hauling out a curving, heavily veined cock and aiming it, two-handed, at Andy's 'bitch'.

The floor was swimming. Gav stared at Jake's dick, the way it looked, held in two big hands, and with Jake's crotch thrusting outwards. A whisper in his ear: 'Your turn.'

Gav moaned and shook his head. The mouth moved closer. A warm tongue flicked out playfully, and licked the side of his neck. 'Come on – we'll do it together.'

He shuddered at the warm wetness on his neck. Something in the voice was doing strange things to his crotch. Behind the pressure of the need to piss, a new need was making itself known to him. Still staring at Jake's cock, he noticed it had become a little harder. Then Gav was unzipping himself, feeling his own fist around his own dick. Seconds later, they both stood there, side by side, dicks aimed at the now whimpering figure on the floor. The voice in his ear was back: 'One, two...'

On a whispered 'three', Gav relaxed the muscle in his dick and watched urine the colour of the beer he'd just drunk spurt onto the man on the floor.

Jake did likewise, and unexpectedly kissed Gav's neck at the same time.

Gavin's cock jerked, mid-spurt and sent an arc of urine over the intended recipient to splatter the legs of an oafish-looking skin with a huge beer-belly.

'Oi! Watch the gear, pal!' Oaf Skin scowled, leaping back.

'Sorry!' Gav regripped his cock and angled it downwards.

' "Sorry" doesn't wash me jeans.' Oaf Skin was tutting now,

batting at his soaked leg with a plump hand.

'It was an accident – and he's said sorry, mate.' Jake took a step forward, inadvertently kicking the guy on the floor as he did so.

'Who asked you to butt in, son? This is between me and him.' Oaf Skin lumbered forward, squaring up to Jake.

Gavin cringed. The atmosphere had been balanced on a knife edge all night. In a matter of seconds, good-humoured bonhomie had turned into thinly veiled menace.

Most of the pissing had stopped, although a good few of the tight circle were still holding their dicks. Some were holding one another's. Every eye was focused on Jake and Oaf Skin.

His heart began to race. Looking beyond the ring of unzipped men for a possible escape route, Gav met a dark, hooded gaze.

Locking eyes with Derek Masters, Gav did either a very stupid or a very brave thing: he moved between the two posturing men and placed a hand squarely on two very different chests. 'I'm sorry, OK? It was an accident. Let me buy you a pint, mate.' He stared at Oaf Skin's sneering, antagonistic face, his own expression studiously unapologetic but never wavering. With the hand pressing into Jake's chest, he rubbed slightly, pushing back against the pressure.

The room was silent. Gav's heart was pounding in his ears, now. Oaf Skin was built like a brick shithouse, and Gavin had no idea how he'd take to having his anger diffused. Nor could he predict how Jake would feel about having what he probably regarded as his fun spoiled.

Unexpectedly, movement from his champion's side. Gav suddenly felt his elbow pushed down. In seconds Jake, now with Gavin's arm twisted lightly but firmly behind his back, was standing directly behind him. Low words: 'The boy's new, Mikey – but ya gotta admit, he's got balls, eh?'

Jake's free hand slid swiftly between Gavin's legs to cup his crotch. Gav inhaled sharply, and released the chest of Oaf Skin, a.k.a. Mikey.

Then that oafish face was breaking into a grin. Skins were slapping Gav's shoulder – Mikey even shook his hand. And, beyond the now laughing ring of unzipped men, Derek Masters was still watching, those dark impenetrable eyes fixed on Gavin and Jake.

He'd never had a skinhead. But he had one that night in the Sinner's Arms, his fist wrapped around Jake's cock and those full lips sealed over his.

The last time Gav had fucked a woman he'd been thirteen and she'd sat next to him in geography class. But a week after the Skinner's Arms episode, as Derek Masters watched, Gavin Shaw, gay as a goose, was pushing himself between the legs of a raven-haired beauty at a party in Earls Court. He did a three-way with a bi couple, and then a gay couple.

And afterwards he subtly pumped each of his partners about the silent man with the shock of silver hair who always watched but never participated.

Rumours abounded. Most knew him as Deke – if they knew him at all. Some thought he was in the porn industry. Others swore he was a Russian arms dealer. As far as Derek Masters' sexual preferences were concerned, the gay men Gavin talked to considered he and brutish Milo an item, a pair of rich voyeurs who enjoyed slumming. The straight women went all cow-eyed and told Gav Derck Masters was bisexual, with a stable of women somewhere in deepest Hertfordshire. At another of Felicia's dos, one drunken heterosexual plumber leaned heavily on Gavin's shoulder and confided that, if he was ever going to suck cock, it would be Derek Masters' cock his lips would close around.

The man was an urban myth on legs!

Gavin recorded it all in the Masters file, matching insinuations with details from the man's past. The gunrunning was all too believable, given the entrepreneur's army background. But what finally clinched Masters' criminal side for Gavin came early in August.

In the middle of Epping forest, while a variety of partygoers coupled against trees, Gavin watched Milo palm something to a skinny boy in an artistically ripped T-shirt in exchange for a twenty-pound note. Minutes later, the kid and two of his friends were chasing the dragon behind a bush.

Gav's anonymous informant – who had been silent for over a month – sent a text the following day.

Three cities. Three dates.

Supposition and a rumour were about to solidify into hard proof. And this time Gav remembered to use his digital camera. Hidden behind a vast container shipment, with the Daugava river lapping against Riga's Baltic shores, he photographed Derek Masters and Milo in conversation with a nameless Latvian. As the crew of a Liberian-registered freighter loaded crates on board, Gav photographed the nameless Latvian prising open a wooden box and removing an Uzi automatic, which he raised to his shoulder and tried out for size.

Bluffing his way into a Moscow casino, he tailed Masters and Milo into an upper room. From the other side of an air vent in the office's wall, Gav got clear photographs of Derek Masters checking an attaché case stuffed with dollars while a burly Muscovite weighed and counted a number of sealed, heavy-looking packages of white powder.

The final city on the list was serviced by Abbotsinch airport. Bleary-eyed and hyper, Gavin waited for three hours in summer rain until Derek Masters' Lear jet landed and the usual hire car collected the entrepreneur and faithful Milo.

Murderer. Arms dealer. Purloiner of boys for men. Drugs baron. If any one of these details should reach the ears of shareholders, Masters Industries would crumble like the house of cards it was.

Tailing the nondescript vehicle in an equally unremarkable hire car of his own, Gav pondered myriad sources for Derek Masters' unknown blackmailer.

He followed Masters along the slick M8, noting that the car ignored the signs for Glasgow city centre. It stopped raining. The sun came out. While they'd driven past fairly affluent-looking areas initially, what framed the sides of the motorway now was growing increasingly dilapidated. Masters and Milo drove deeper into the badlands of Glasgow's East End. In his rear-view mirror, a setting red globe dazzled Gavin's eyes.

Finally, on the fringes of the city, Masters turned off.

Dalmarnock: what the fuck was Dalmarnock? Following the car past rows of red sandstone tenements, Gav avoided several groups of kids playing football in the streets. The area was a striking hybrid of regeneration and slum: new apartment blocks sat cheek by jowl with crumbling dereliction. In his role as chauffeur, Milo drove on, leaving the housing behind and driving towards a sprawling patch of waste ground.

In his role as investigative journalist, Gav followed, glancing at his wrist: just after 10 p.m. In front, Milo slowed the car, bumping it up over a grassy verge. Gav drove on, skirting the area to come to a halt a little away. Several other vehicles were already there.

Gavin switched off his engine and pocketed his keys.

Groups of men stood beside battered vans, spanking-new BMWs and the occasional motorcycle. There was even a fast-food truck, already dispensing steaming burgers to the growing crowd.

Gav opened the car door and got out. Strolling across to where whatever was going to take place would take place, he realised there was no point in trying to keep a low profile. The area was too open, too public, which in itself told him something other than that a gun or drugs deal was going down. As he approached, he could see Derek Masters leaning against the roof of his hire car, deep in conversation with a thin, unhealthy-looking guy in a shell suit. The ever-present Milo stood a little away, arms folded across his broad, heavily muscled chest. The bodyguard was looking rather more brutish than usual.

Pausing on the fringes of the gathering, Gavin noticed several bundles of money sitting on the bonnets of the cars. His eye was also caught by a number of men who had now stripped to the waist and were having their chests smeared with some sort of grease.

Snatches of conversation reached his ears, as he manoeuvred his way through the throng.

'Fifty quid on Liam.'

'Six to four, Johnstone'll eat him for breakfast.'

'Did ya see his hands after last month?'

'Aye, he'll never play the piano again, Jimmy.'

Slowly, darkness began to fall. And Gavin started to make sense of what was about to happen. The waste ground was far enough away from habitation to avoid both attention from passing police and light from street lamps. To compensate for the lack of the latter, two vans switched on dimmed headlights.

Between the beams, two bare-chested figures stood illuminated, face to face. Fists up, they waited patiently for the word from a smaller, thinner man with thinning grey hair who seemed to be serving as referee.

Gavin blinked. Something else about the two pugilists was unprotected. Their hands. Because this was bare-knuckle fighting. Illegal. Underground. And highly dangerous.

The bouts were merciless – and mercifully short.

The first pair of combatants lasted three, two-minute rounds before the ref physically stopped them. Blood was pouring from a deep gash just above the winner's eye. The loser could barely stand, never mind see his opponent.

But everyone cheered both men, and either collected their winnings or cursed their bad luck. The participants were paid, then moved off to lick their respective wounds.

Gav stuck his hands into his pockets and glanced over to where Derek Masters was again deep in conversation. The next two fighters moved into the headlights, eager to do battle. A few words, then a nod from the referee, and they were off.

He'd done a bit of boxing himself, years ago, but this was something else. There was something primal about the sound of fist on flesh. Without the padding of the boxing glove, it was almost as painful to land a blow as to be on the receiving end of one. But these game pugilists went at it with a level of ferocity that took Gavin's breath away. He could almost hear the delicate bones in the fighters' hands crack. On top of that, knuckles were sharp: bare knuckles broke bruised skin more quickly and more easily than gloved fists.

Gav moved behind a group of older men and continued to watch. Glare from the headlights illuminated details of each punch delivered, and the resulting damage achieved. The silence of the audience allowed every grunt, moan and rasping breath of the participants to be heard. On this desolate patch of Glasgow waste ground, Gav was held spellbound as pair after pair took to the informal ring and beat fuck out of each other. At the end of each bout, the fighters often embraced, each smearing the other with a very literal mixture of blood, sweat and tears. And, as the night wore on, something became clearer.

No hint of animosity could be detected in any of the contests. Yet each man fought as if his life depended on it, receiving – Gavin worked out – forty pounds of he lost, sixty if he won: a financial motive for ending up with a face like a side of beef was far from convincing. Participants were of all ages, exhibiting a wide range of fighting skills, but all shared a common purpose.

Maybe they were hitting each other, but the real enemy was elsewhere: in the slumlike housing Gav had driven past, on his way here; in the rising unemployment, and the dying industries that threw able men onto the scrap heap at thirty; in the dual temptations of alcohol and drugs. If, for one night a week, these Glasgwegians could vent their frustrations on a willing victim, who was to judge them? Gav felt an odd empathy for these strangers. And an even odder urge to stand between those head-lights himself.

Little did he know then, he would get that chance.

Gav inhaled sharply as blood from a split lip flew into the crowd of watchers, splattering his own cheek in the process.

After about an hour, a solitary figure strode between the head-lights. Mutterings of surprise swept the crowd like a Mexican wave. Gav blinked, then stared openly as the lone figure turned.

Shirtless, Milo's heavy chest gleamed. His low-slung jeans showed off his rippling abs. The muscles in his upper arms bulged impressively. Hands on hips, the bully-boy bodyguard seemed to be waiting for a signal.

Gav glanced right, and met Derek Masters' eyes.

For the first time in the three months he'd been tailing the man, Masters acknowledged Gav's presence.

It was only a nod.

But it spoke volumes. And it was all the communication Gavin needed to do what he'd wanted to do ever since Milo had thrown him out of Masters Industries' headquarters.

Struggling out of his jacket, he strode towards the glare of the headlights and began to unfasten the buttons on his shirt.

# Nineteen

There was a smattering of applause from the assembled onlookers.

Milo grinned and flexed his impressive musculature. Backlit by headlights, Derek Masters' bodyguard looked bigger and stronger than ever.

Cocky bastard!

Gav laughed and returned the grin.

Cocky, overconfident bastard! They stood there, eyeing each other while the referee gripped each of them by the arm.

'Clean fight, boys – nothing below the waist or to the back of the head. No biting, no gouging.'

The fizz of adrenaline in his head blanked out most of the man's instructions. He'd show Milo. Maybe he didn't have the muscle. Or the bulk. Maybe he was a good three inches shorter than the brutish bodyguard. But Gav was fast on his feet. And, in the end, that would see him right.

'Shake hands, boys.' Gav held out a fist, and felt Milo grip it with his own. 'And let's rumble!'

The small ref released their arms and moved back.

Milo continued to grip Gavin's right hand, continued to smile…

Gav tried to pull away.

… while smashing a left hook into the side of Gavin's head.

The sheer weight of the blow buckled his knees. The speed of the punch left his brain reeling. Gav shook his head to clear it, and managed to dodge a right cross more by accident than design.

The momentum of the missed punch carried the heavier man on past where Gavin stood, trying not to collapse. The look of surprise on Milo's face and the man's flailing arms were all the spur Gav needed. Torquing his body, he caught Derek Masters' bodyguard with a sharp uppercut to the ribs.

A cracking sound filled the air. Pain ratcheted through Gav's fingers and up his left arm.

But it was Milo who was clutching his chest, Milo who was on the ground.

The crowd uncharacteristically cheered its approval. Gav punched the air above his head, the discomfort in his hand now a shadow of its former self.

And it was Milo whom the ref was helping to his feet. Gav locked eyes with Derek Masters, bathed in a glow of pleasure. His victory was short-lived.

Roaring like a bull, and no longer grinning, Milo charged towards Gav and wrapped his arms around his waist.

Gavin oomphed. The breath left his lungs, squeezed from his body by a vicelike embrace. He staggered backwards, battering the only part of Milo he could reach – the top of the man's head – with both hands.

Bad idea.

Someone was pushing needles under his fingernails. The pain was like nothing he'd ever experienced, white-hot and ice-cold. It danced before his eyes, sparkling pinpricks of agony.

Very bad idea.

Milo's skull was like a rock. Throwing his arms into the air, mainly in an attempt to alleviate the pain in his hands, Gav veered right, trying to counterbalance Milo's weight left. And inadvertently brought his elbow smashing into the side of the bodyguard's lowered head.

The grip around his waist slackened immediately. But they both fell to the ground, nonetheless. Gavin flailed frantically, trying to free himself from Milo's bulk, which had landed on top of him. Through the excruciating pain in his fingers, he was vaguely aware of wet warmth spreading over his chest. But only one thing mattered.

Beating Milo.

Beating Milo, in front of Derek Masters.

Summoning every shred of strength in his body, Gav heaved mightily and threw the bulky, increasingly inert bodyguard off. He managed to get as far as his knees, one now numb fist balled to smash into the man's face, when strong hands gripped him from behind.

Gav moaned, flailing with his fists and his feet. To no avail. As he was dragged off Milo's motionless form, he noticed through spangling vision that his chest was a mass of liquid scarlet. For a moment, he panicked: had he been stabbed? Then he saw blood pouring from a wide cut just above the bodyguard's eye – a cut that the small, balding doctor was now hurriedly attending to.

Gav stopped flailing, and allowed someone to start wiping his face and chest with a wet cloth. Through the buzz of adrenaline, Gav became aware of cheers. People were slapping him on the back, growling good-natured curses at him for toppling the odds and losing them money.

Mere yards away, the doctor had managed to stop the bleeding, but Milo still hadn't stirred. A different type of panic spurted anew in Gavin's veins – the fear that he'd done the man some real damage.

Someone was cramming Scottish twenty-pound notes into his fist. Gav felt a distant discomfort as he closed his fingers around his winnings. It had dulled to a low throb as he crawled across the bloodied ground to where the bodyguard lay motionless.

The balding doctor had Milo in the recovery position now, and was slapping his face. The ref was standing over them both, looking worried.

What if he was dead?

What if he, Gavin Shaw, had killed a man with his bare hands?

He could taste blood. His ear felt the size of a melon. He couldn't feel his hands at all and his ribs hurt. 'Milo! Milo! Wake up!' His mouth felt funny and his voice sounded weird. Far away, and belonging to someone else. He stretched out a hand and tried to shake the man by the shoulder. He could only claw pathetically at the sweat-sheened skin on the bodyguard's arm. 'Please! Wake up!' Wet saltiness coursed over his cheeks. Gav bit back a sob, wiped his nose on the back of his hand and yelped.

Then someone was pulling him back and someone else threw a bucket of water over Milo. That seemed to do the trick. Gav watched in relief as the bodyguard groaned, coughed then retched violently.

Behind him, hands were under his arms, hauling him to his feet. The balding doctor had now abandoned Milo and was peering critically into Gavin's right ear. 'Can ya hear me, son?' he bellowed loudly.

Gav found himself laughing. Then someone seized his wrists and plunged his hands into what felt like a bucket of fire but which he could see was merely iced water. As his own injuries were tended to, he became aware that Derek Masters had appeared and was standing over him.

Milo was still throwing up, supporting by the thin man in the shell suit from earlier and an equally scrawny-looking associate.

The tall, distinguished multimillionaire stared at Gavin. 'Well done.' The voice was very quiet, and slightly accented.

Something twisted deep in the pit of his stomach. Before Gavin could respond, Derek Masters turned on his heel and strode back towards his car. In his wake, the two skinny men half carried, half dragged the unfortunate Milo.

Gav had no idea who would drive the entrepreneur back to the airport, now his driver could barely stand, never mind operate a car. But seconds later the vehicle was speeding away across the waste ground.

And Gavin was left standing amidst dozens of newly found fans.

The balding medic drove Gavin's hire car back to the airport for him, muttering about endorphins and giving instructions about having that ear checked out by a proper doctor in a thick, Glaswegian accent.

Head bursting with pride at those two words from Derek Masters, Gavin flew back to London. His luggage followed by plane. He felt like a million dollars! OK, the taxi driver – who took him from Heathrow to an all-night chemist – stared suspiciously at him in the rear-view mirror, and his fingers were a bit stiff. But his body burned from the inside. Sleep was a thousand miles away. And, after taking the three flights of stairs two at a time, he unlocked the door to his office and immediately plugged the digital camera into his laptop.

Hard-copy photographic evidence he'd pick up in the morning. But for now he needed to write up the details of the last three days. And download the digital images into the Masters file.

Sometime during the hours of darkness, Gavin fell asleep at his desk. The sound of a door buzzer woke him, drilling holes in his skull just before 8 a.m. Last night's euphoria had burned off with morning mist. He felt like death warmed up. Staggering to the office door, he took and signed for another package. The courier backed away warily as Gav tore at the cardboard-backed envelope.

Not money, this time.

Photographs. More photographs.

Derek Masters with various men Gav recognised from the Sunday tabloids. The pick of London's more glamorous gangland fraternity were shaking hands with the man. At the races. At a 'blackjack' table, with an assortment of beautiful, hard-faced women.

The implication was clear.

Added to his own evidence, this mud would stick. This mud would stick so fast the best layers wouldn't be able to scrape Masters free of it.

His desk was strewn with incriminating photographic material when Gav finally got back to typing up his notes. His head was splitting, but he couldn't stop. Not to piss. Not to eat.

His phone rang. Gav reached down, hauled the jack from the socket. The phone stopped ringing.

He definitely couldn't stop to take any calls. A full twenty-four hours later, he was stuffing more paper into the printer. The Masters file already occupied half of an A4 folder. Gav wanted hard copy of it all.

He wanted to be able to hold it. He wanted to be able to touch the man's name, where he couldn't touch the man. Last night's two-word recognition was tattooed on his brain. He could barely move his fingers. His right ear was huge. His whole body felt as if it had gone through a sheet-metal press. But for the first time in his life he felt properly alive.

Standing beside the printer, he caught each page as it appeared, carefully placing it on top of the growing pile. Gav scooped up the Masters file in his arms and carried it lovingly over to the couch. Curling his sore body under a blanket, he began to read though the dossier for the hundredth time. He was aware of the vague lob of a half-hard-on. It seemed to be his permanent state these days. But, as his lips moved soundlessly and he turned page after page, for the first time in his life Gavin Shaw had other priorities.

Nine o'clock Monday morning he was standing outside a building in Whitehall, waiting for the War Office to open. Documentary proof that Deke Zenovich had served in Her Majesty's Armed Forces was all that was missing from his dossier. More information on dead John 'Johnny-Boy' Clark wouldn't go amiss, either. A photocopy of the Masters File was locked in his office safe. The original was tucked under his right arm.

The doorman almost didn't let him in. His press card was submitted to minute scrutiny. Several phone calls were made. But Gav knew that the British Army's records were in the public domain and, even as a private citizen, he had every right to ask to see them. Eventually, he was granted a visitor's pass and led up to a large circular room by a wordless man in khaki.

Eleven a.m., and Gavin was wading through records for the period 1980–96.

One p.m., and he'd found the release papers of one Clark, J.

By 4 p.m. he was feeding ten pence pieces into a photocopier and the khaki-clad man from that morning was telling him the War Office was closing. Clutching his information, Gavin shambled from the building in a daze.

August sunshine draped London's West End in a haze of heat. Gav found himself on Oxford Street, wandering between groups of happy summer shoppers. He looked at their smiling faces. Did they know? Did any of them know what he carried in this innocuous-looking cardboard folder? Did they know a decorated ex-Gulf War veteran, a man of dual Latvian/British citizenship who was now at the helm of one of the world's most important corporations frequently fraternised with the worst of the UK criminal elements? Did they know he'd almost certainly either killed or had *had* killed Johnny-Boy Clark, with whom he'd served in the Royal Marines? Did they know he smuggled drugs to the former Soviet Union and imported arms from Riga?

Did they?

Shambling along Oxford Street, Gav suddenly lunged at a man holding a briefcase and grabbed his arm. 'Do you know?' His eyes blazed.

The man reared back in horror, shook Gavin's grip from the

sleeve of his jacket and walked swiftly away.

Something sparked at the back of his brain. Pausing, Gav closed his eyes, squeezing them tightly shut. What was wrong with him? What the fuck was he doing? He stood there, allowing the sound of traffic and footsteps and chatter to flood his mind. When he opened his eyes, several minutes later, the thick veil that had shrouded his thought processes for he last two days had lifted a little.

He found himself staring into a shop window. Reflected in the glass, a thin figure with wild, tangled hair, a dramatic-looking black eye and four days' growth stared back. The guy was wearing dirty and very dishevelled jeans and Levi jacket. Somewhere along the way he'd forgotten to put on a T-shirt.

Gav inhaled sharply. He sniffed. And he smelled like a pig. It was a miracle they'd let him into the War Office at all! Pulling himself together a little, Gav checked he still had what was left of the ten thousand pounds. Time for a little makeover. Smoothing down his messy hair the best he could, he strode into the first clothes shop he came to.

An hour later, he'd found one of those gentlemen's washrooms that had sprung up in the West End. He'd showered. He'd shaved. He'd washed his hair and thrown away his clothes. Now wearing new jeans, sweatshirt and jacket, he tied the laces of his trainers, then straightened up.

The man who stared back from the mirror this time looked more normal. Less of an animal. The jeans were a bit loose, and there was nothing he could do about the black eye, but at least he was once more fit for polite company. Gav's stomach rumbled audibly. For the first time in days, he was aware of hunger. Leaving a ten-pound tip, he strolled from the washroom and headed for a restaurant.

Over the best four-course meal he'd ever had, Gav drank a little wine and read the new additions to his dossier. *Financial Week*'s deadline was a mere four days away. What Gav intended to turn in, on Friday of this week, would blow the fiscal world apart.

As he sipped his coffee, he suddenly remembered he'd not checked his voice mail in days. Maybe his anonymous informant had left some other juicy titbit of a text for him. Fumbling in the pocket of his new jacket, he found and switched on the small grey Nokia, which rang immediately.

'Shaw.' He clamped the cellphone to his ear, checking for texts at the same time.

'What did I tell you about keeping in touch?' James Delany's cool tones seeped into his car.

Gav cringed. The cooler the voice, the angrier James was. 'Ah, yeah, I know.' No text messages. Gav sighed. 'I've been really busy and—'

'Where are you, Gavin?'

He smiled. 'Mal Maison, would you believe? Listen, don't worry about the profile, I'll have it on your desk by—'

'Mal Maison, in Soho?'

Gav laughed. 'Don't worry – I'm not putting it through as a business expense.'

'You OK, my friend?' A change in the voice. Anger gave way to something Gavin couldn't quite out his finger on.

'Oh, I'm fine, Jim – just busy. Listen, I'll—'

'On my desk, Friday, five p.m. at the latest, remember?'

'Didn't I say the profile would be—'

But James had already disconnected. Gav stared at the cellphone, then switched it off again and shoved it back into his pocket. Typical James: you never really knew what he was thinking, or where you stood with the man. What Gav had interpreted as solicitude for his wellbeing was merely concern that his precious deadline would be met.

He frowned, briefly, then shrugged. Fuck him! Fuck James

Delany! Any personal feelings he'd ever had for the guy were long dead and buried. And, when the next issue of *Financial Week* hit the newsstands, Gav knew he wouldn't even need James as a business contact any more.

Once more smiling to himself, Gav paid the bill, grabbed the Masters file and set off out into the balmy evening. Maybe he'd walk back to the office. It would be good to get some air.

He was halfway across Regent's Park when he heard the footsteps. Seconds later, something rough and hairy was thrust over his head and he was struggling to breathe.

Gav tried to scream.

Over the rough sacking, a hand clamped itself against his mouth.

He lashed out with his fists.

A pair of strong arms pinned his hands to his sides. More hands slipped what felt like a plastic luggage tie around his wrists, binding them in front of his body.

He kicked, and made contact – a low 'fuck!' told him that. Then someone else was grabbing his legs. Both feet left the ground. The same tight plastic encircled and dug into his ankles. And he was moving. Fast. Carried horizontally by at least three but possibly five attackers, Gav found himself racing sightless through the park.

He was being mugged. Just over five grand in cash, in his pocket, and he was being mugged. Panic spangled in his veins.

The file.

The Masters file!

As abruptly as he'd been seized, Gav stopped. He could hear sounds of something opening. A car door? He bit the hand over his mouth. It relaxed enough to let him gasp: 'There's money in my pocket. Take it and the cellphone, but please, that folder's—'

The hands threw him forward. Gav howled, impacting side on

with a hard, unforgiving surface. Before he could react, a door slammed shut. Silence for a few seconds. Then engine vibrations beneath him. The smell of petrol seeped through the sacking over his head. The possibility that this was just a mugging vanished when tyres screeched on tarmac and whatever vehicle he'd been bundled moved off at speed.

There didn't seem much point in shouting, even if his dry throat had been capable of generating any sound. He had to stay calm. He had to think. He had to prioritise. The sacking stuck to his face, filling his nostrils every time he breathed in. It smelled of chemicals. Panic had solidified into a deep, cold fear that he might actually suffocate.

Rolling onto his back, Gav raised his bound wrists and clawed at the hairy fabric that shrouded his head. His stiff unwieldy fingers were still raw and sore.

But the fear that gripped him at least let him act. Hauling the disgusting object up over his face, he gulped petrol-fumed air into his aching lungs. Gav blinked, and tried to open his eyes. He realised they were already open and the van in which he was a prisoner was windowless. Rolling back onto his side, he shuffled like a caterpillar towards what he hoped was the door.

The total darkness was almost as claustrophobic as the sack had been. Impacting with the side of the van, Gav dragged himself up it and probed with his bound and throbbing hands. Eventually, he found what felt like a handle. Grabbing hold of it, he pressed all his weight downwards, and uttered a silent prayer.

The bloody thing refused to move. It had been too much to hope for that his kidnappers had omitted to lock the vehicle. Gav released the handle, sliding back down the door and shuffle-crawling a little away. His hands were tied, his ankles were tethered. But he could still use his feet. Drawing his legs up as close to his chest as he could, he gritted his teeth.

And kicked with both feet.

A moan tore itself loose from his throat. Pain shuddered through his right ankle. But the door didn't budge. Gav fought the urge just to curl into a ball and let whatever was going to happen just happen. The pain brought the adrenaline, which in turn sharpened his survival instinct. Clearing his mind, he hauled himself over to a wall, propped his sore body against it and tried to listen beyond the van's walls.

He had no idea where he was being taken. They turned several corners, and Gav was thrown from one side of the vehicle to the other. His sense of direction left him. He didn't know up from down, left from right. But a good fifteen minutes later, as the tyres shrieked to a halt, he dragged himself to a low crouch and faced the door once more. Gavin Shaw did not intend to go down without a fight

When it was opened, he'd launch himself at his kidnappers and at least get the satisfaction of inflicting some damage of his own.

The van was stationary now. Gav crouched. And waited. Every muscle in his battered body was aching.

Finally, footsteps. The sound of keys in a lock. Gav shook his head. The sounds were coming from behind him. And, by the time he'd worked out he was facing the wrong way, it was too late. His shoulders grabbed, his body dragged from the van, Gavin found himself staring at four men in military fatigues. Two held guns. All four wore ski masks.

# Twenty

They made him hop at gun point, ankles still bound, into what looked like a disused factory. They made him stand, facing a crumbling redbrick wall while a pair of expert hands patted him down and went through his pockets.

'Take the money! Please, just take the money!'

A detached touch moved roughly over his arse, then between his legs. Gav inhaled sharply. The cellphone, keys and five thousand pounds in cash were ignored...

'Look, what do you want? Just tell me, and I'll give it to you.'

... as was every snivelling syllable from his lips. A hand turned him round.

Gav stared at the four, ski-masked figures. One produced a hunting knife. The other three, one of whom was holding the A4 folder, spread out to form a loose semicircle around him. Gav's spine tried to burrow into the wall behind. His eyes flicked between the Masters file and the five-inch blade. 'Please, come on, guys – I'm not worth it, really I'm not.' His voice echoed around him. No one else said anything: no one needed to.

The man with the knife walked up to Gavin and stuck the point of the blade under his chin. Gav closed his eyes and held his breath. The tip of the blade was razor sharp. He could feel the surface tension of the skin on his throat tighten. Then start to give. Just when he was sure he was going to die here, throat slit by four faceless men, the knife moved away...

Breath gushed from his lungs. His eyelids shot open.

... to rip clean down the front of his T-shirt. Gav whimpered as the guy with the blade delicately lifted each flap of fabric, drawing it back so that the garment hung loosely from Gavin's shoulders, exposing his chest and belly. Before he could start to plead again, the man slowly began to circle Gav's right nipple with the finely honed point. The tickle of steel was like the gentlest caress. Despite the danger, Gav was appalled to feel his body responding to the knife.

His nipple was hardening. Blood pumped into that tiny nub of gristle and sent a *frisson* of unwanted pleasure through his body.

Someone sniggered.

Gav's face flushed up. He lowered his head in shame, but continued to watch the tip of the knife as it traced around the centre of his right pec. Just when he thought he couldn't take it any more, the blade was withdrawn.

More blood was fleeing his brain. And heading lower than his blushing chest this time. Inside his jeans, his cock twitched.

But the blade now began the same process around his left nipple. Gav shuddered. The fine brown hair on his belly stood to attention. Staring down at his own chest, he watched delicate skin pucker and goose-bump under the twinkling tip of the blade. He didn't want to be, but he was hardening by the second. The type of terror that made normal men's dicks shrink and their balls scurry to hide inside their bodies was slowly and steadily swelling his shaft towards erection. 'I don't know what you want from me.' His voice was a hoarse whisper now. 'Tell me and it's yours.'

Again, no response. Only the continued tracing of the tip of a blade. His entire chest was crawling with the footsteps of a thousand tiny insects. He tried to slow his breathing – or at least lessen the size of each breath. Because the greater the inhalation, the more his vulnerable skin pushed against the pinprick point of that five-inch blade.

He was panting now. But relief surged through his veins as, abruptly, the knife moved away.

But at once it seemed to become a pen, which was drawing a

thin scarlet-coloured track down the middle of his hard belly.

Gav stared, fascinated by the faint scarlet line. He wondered why it was so red. He was so absorbed in watching the edges of the shallow cut slowly part and start to bleed more profusely that he wasn't aware of the knife slicing through the rough leather of his belt as if it were butter.

Or the deft twin hacking motions to the waistband of his jeans, which cut the garment into two sections.

But the feel of cold steel under his balls made an impression. Gav's eyes left the bleeding if shallow scratch bisecting his abs and stared at the knife.

Turned on its side, the flat of that vicious blade was now resting against the delicate skin of his bollocks. This time, his body reacted to the threat. His sac jerked up, fleeing the danger.

But there was no escape. The flat of the knife followed, pushing lightly into the twitching, puckered skin.

He felt no pain. There wasn't any pain to feel. Like the movement around his nipples, the touch was barely there. If he closed his eyes, it could have been a feather. Or a fingernail. Or the loving touch of a tongue.

But he couldn't. And it wasn't. This was a blade. This was a weapon that could, at best, mutilate and, at worst, kill. Depending on the whim of the user.

Gav was trembling now. In sheer desperation, he dragged his gaze from the activity between his legs and focused on his assailant's masked face.

Two eyes. A nose. And a mouth.

He tried to slow his breathing again.

They said the eyes were the windows of the soul. The windows into this soul were tightly shuttered. Gav gazed beseechingly into huge dark pupils, ringed by the faintest halo of hazel.

'Please!' One slip of that hand would have him a eunuch in seconds. 'Tell me...'

The eyes remained impassive. Expressionless. Unblinking. Gav had the feeling they belonged to someone not accustomed to slips or errors. The knowledge was both reassuring and all the more unsettling: if this man chose to castrate him, it would be no accident.

Only the dilation of the pupils conveyed anything about the emotional state of the man behind the ski mask.

Gav was sweating profusely now. His armpits felt clammy and sticky. Wet warmth was trickling down his sides. Between his legs, a fine sheen of perspiration coated his quivering balls. Then the blade was moving, easing from one nut to the other, as if the holder was weighing up possibilities.

He stood there, scared to do anything else. Ripped jeans at his knees, T-shirt hanging off his shoulders and with his hands bound at crotch level, in front of four masked men, one of whom was holding a knife to his balls, Gavin became aware of a nudging against his clenched and still-raw knuckles. Pulling his eyes from his tormentor's, he glanced down beyond his bleeding chest.

The head of his dick was curved and hard against his stomach. Something in the heart of him began to crumble. He couldn't move. He couldn't stop it. He could only stand there and imagine what was going through these four masked men's minds.

The knife slid abruptly out from under his balls. The man with the dead eyes raised the blade in front of Gav's face.

He stared at the blade. The mirrorlike surface fogged slightly, with the heat from his body.

The blade came closer. Gav backed away. And when he couldn't back away any further he tried to meld with the brick wall behind.

The blade kept on coming. Gav could see the reflection of his own face in the gleaming flat of the knife. In contrast with those of the man inches in front of him, his pupils were tiny darting dots, adrift in a sea of brown. The blade paused, directly in front of Gavin's eyes. A myriad nightmare scenarios scrambled through his brain.

Then the knife was lowering. Very slowly. Very deliberately. Held spellbound by the polished blade, Gav watched the surface fog, then clear, fog, then clear again in rhythm with each breath that left his lungs. And still his hard-on nudged the back of his tethered right hand. In fact, either his very cock was sweating or that was pre-come he could feel slicking his grazed knuckles.

A mirror was being held up to Gavin Shaw. He was being made to face what he was – some sick fuck who could be terrorised to orgasm by a bunch of psycho squaddies in ski masks with a beat-up van and a cheap knife.

The blade moved on, slowly turning in the dim overhead light. The edge now facing Gav was serrated. In each of the dozens of minute grooves a Gavin Shaw twinkled. Then, smooth as silk, the knife was turning in the air once more.

He barely had time to react when five inches of cold steel was pressing itself against his trembling lips.

He groaned through his nose, feeling the hard manmade surface sink into pliable flesh. He didn't move. He didn't want to risk a nick from that sharp edge – or that lethal tip. But neither did he feel motivated to draw back. So he stood there, letting this man in a ski mask press a knife to his mouth while another three men, two with hand guns, watched in silence

And he kissed it.

Involuntarily at first. Then intentionally. His lips parted over the smooth, slightly moist surface. His tongue flicked out, tasting the blade. Savouring it. He couldn't quite believe what he was doing – he couldn't quite believe it was he, Gavin Shaw, who was standing here, shaking and hard and half naked and licking the blade of a knife. He hadn't looked away from the weapon for a while now, but suddenly he felt the urge to raise his eyes to his tormentor.

From within the holes in the ski mask, the same cold unblinking stare met his. And, with a speed that belied his bulky camouflage fatigues, the hand that held he knife whipped it away.

Gav moaned, leaning forward for another kiss of steel.

But a hand was at his throat and the tip of the blade was tracing his hard-on. The back of Gav's head hit bare brick. Stars danced before his eyes. The weapon moved up his shaft, leaving tiny pricks of sensation in its wake.

He swallowed against the fist, Adam's apple bobbing against a rough palm. He didn't want to think about what was going to happen now.

Quick as a flash, the ski-masked squaddie was moving. Dragging him off the wall, the man repositioned himself behind Gavin, one hand still at his throat. The tip of the blade continued its menacing tracing of the veins on his dick.

But his line of vision had altered. The two men with the guns remained where they were. The soldier who was holding the Masters File now stood in front of him, one hand gripping the A4 folder, the other hand disappearing into a pocket of his military fatigues.

A small, rectangular silver object was produced.

As it sparked twice, then produced a flame, Gav identified it as a cigarette lighter. The knowledge ignited a new wave of panic. He could almost smell the acrid stench of burning protein. Or worse...

The man in front of him held the A4 folder in one hand, and slowly brought his other hand, gripping the lighted flame, towards it.

But what was taking place before his eyes had moved on to a different scale of horror. The palm around his throat tightened, threatening to cut off his air supply. And for the first time the squaddie with the knife spoke: 'Stay away from Derek Masters.'

Five low words echoed in Gavin's head. Flame licked around the corner of the cardboard dossier, refusing to catch for a few seconds.

Then the folder was alight. Slowly at first, then moving faster, the fire spread up the sides of the Masters file.

Inside, weeks of work began to smoulder. Then, in a whoosh of flame the whole thing went up. The squaddie in front of him continued to hold the blazing papers, then dropped the lot at Gavin's feet, where flaming bundle writhed and twisted.

The stink of melting celluloid joined with the odour of burning paper as the photographs burned and curled. A cloud of thick black smoke was making Gavin's eyes water. The hand around his throat was seriously affecting his ability to breathe. The knife at his dick was now tracing a semicircle around the root of his shaft. Tiny black dots floated before his eyes, carried up towards the ceiling by warming air.

Soot? Or was he losing consciousness?

Just at the point when he thought he was going to collapse, the squaddie with the knife laughed loudly, bit Gavin's earlobe and released him.

Only the man's grip had been keeping him upright. Gavin slumped to the ground in a coughing heap. While he struggled to get his breath back, he was vaguely aware of receding footsteps. Then doors banging. An engine revving. He continued to lie there on the blackened embers of the Masters file while the four squaddies plus the van that had brought him here sped away into the night.

Alone and shaking, he curled his knees up to his bare bleeding chest and hugged them. His body felt as if it had gone three rounds with Mike Tyson. He felt worse than he'd done after his fight with Milo on a desolate stretch of ground in the wastelands of Glasgow. The shadow of the knife was still there, under his balls. Around his dick. The hand was still gripping his throat – he could feel the imprint of the squaddie's strong fingers...

Stay away from Derek Masters.

Stay away from Derek Masters.

Gav retched, wiped bile and spit from his mouth with the back of his hand and managed to raise himself onto one elbow. Slowly, a smile spread over his lips. What was left of the Masters file lay smouldering, mere inches from his face – while a copy lay, intact and secure, in his office safe.

They thought they were so clever. They thought they could scare him off. The smile broadened.

And Gavin began to chuckle softly.

Part of him thought about phoning the police, as he staggered to his feet and lurched towards the door.

Kidnap. Assault. Intimidation. Destruction of private property.

But he had no proof. No one had witnessed his abduction. He hadn't been physically harmed – apart from the wound to his chest, which now looked exactly like what it was: a mere scratch, already starting to heal. And there was no way to confirm that what lay in ashes, on the floor of an abandoned factory, had ever been anything of value.

Gav continued to laugh as he wandered out into the night. But why tell the police, anyway? Why spoil the surprise? Better to wait until the next issue of *Financial Week* broke the news to an unsuspecting world.

Derek Masters used ex-army mates to intimidate anyone who dared to write the truth about him. Derek Masters was a murderer, panderer, drugs dealer, arms smuggler. When all that lot became public knowledge, the police would be on the scene soon enough.

Limping slightly, and holding his ripped jeans up around his hips, Gavin laughed all the way home.

Four days until his deadline.

Four days. Ninety six hours.

After locking the door to his office behind himself, Gav pushed the couch in front of it as a second barrier. He didn't switch any lights on: better his whereabouts remain unclear for the moment.

Gavin Shaw was a marked man. But with a bit of luck the squaddies would report back that he'd been well and truly frightened off. After plugging in his laptop, he darted over to the safe, entered the combination and withdrew the original Masters file. He sat patiently at his desk, face bathed in the glow from the machine, waiting for a new file to load. He didn't wash. He didn't change. He didn't even put on the coffee machine. He began to write his article.

Two thousand words James wanted. Gav could have written ten. Twenty. There was so much he wanted to include. So much that had to be said. And the words came so easily, flowing from his fingers.

He typed through till dawn, pausing only to pull photographs from his dossier. And occasionally to fondle himself. His nipples were still hard, twin buds of stiff flesh that rasped against the fabric of his jacket each time he turned to stare at another image of his subject.

Derek Masters' face floated before his eyes. The only two words the man had ever spoken to him reeled drunkenly in his mind.

Abstractedly, he played with his right nipple, letting the palm of his hand brush over the stiff tip. He pounded out another five hundred words in what seemed like the blink of an eye. The next time he paused for breath, he reached down between his legs to cup his own balls, feeling their fullness and remembering the touch of the squaddie's army knife. A shiver erected the sweat-matted hair on his lower belly. Altering his position, he leaned forward in his chair, inhaling sharply as his bollocks dragged against the curved seat and a second *frisson* tingled through his body. When he resumed typing, he continued to grind his balls against that curved edge.

Sitting there, the clothes hanging off his body in ripped rags, and with the imprint of a squaddie's rough fist already bruising around his throat, he typed like a maniac. And he jacked his cock more frequently. Parallel to the itch in his brain that demanded he fulfil this assignment, a yearning twisted in the pit of his stomach. Gav grunted and spread his thighs wider beneath the desk. His right hand left the keyboard completely, tightening around his heavy cock. While his left hand typed on, he tugged on his shaft. And his eyes remained focused on the screen.

Something strange was happening in his brain. He'd never been so focused. Intellectual hunger and sexual need were uniting towards a single distant vanishing point. He wanted to come. But he couldn't stop typing. Having dragged his wheeled office chair closer to the edge of the desk, he found that, if he leaned forward, his cock bumped against the metal desk frame.

The first touch was icy cold and made his balls jump. The second was a little better. His shaft located the head of a screw, which secured the metal frame to the desktop, and began to grind against that.

As he hunched over his laptop, his fingers flew faster than ever. And he pushed his dick against the metal desk frame, gasping each time the head of the screw came into contact with his body.

He had no idea what he was typing. Some new link had been forged, enabling the words to leave the deepest recesses of his subconscious and go straight to his fingers, without interference from the conscious part of his brain.

He rubbed himself more furiously now, eyes darting from the screen to stare at a photograph of Derek Masters at the Riga docks. His nipples ached. He ground down hard against the seat of his chair, spreading his arsecheeks, trying to brush his hole against the leather surface. He couldn't manage it. Frustration gnawed at his bones. So he shifted his position, moving his weight onto his feet and easing over to the edge of the chair.

Thrusting his cock against the underside of the desk, pushing back onto the side of the chair, he groaned with pleasure as the curved edge of his seat slid along his crack.

Touch-typing took on a whole new dimension: he could no longer see what he was writing. Staring at Derek Masters' gaunt, angular face, Gav fucked himself on the furniture, forcing his body on towards orgasm. The head of the screw dug into his shaft. The edge of the seat scraped against the delicate skin around his spasming hole. He fucked himself furiously, vision blurring until he no longer needed to see the photograph.

Every time he closed his eyes, Derek Masters' face was there on the inside of his eyelids, spidered with tiny pulsing veins.

When he came, warm spunk splattered over his nipples and he was propelled forward onto the laptop, his body writhing under the release. He knew his cock was bleeding. He thought he was blacking out. He'd never come so hard or so painfully.

Prostrate half over the desk, mouth open in a deep animal groan, sleep overtaking him like a sudden and unexpected onset of night, the last thing he saw before consciousness left him was a screen full of one man's name.

# Twenty-one

Gavin had no idea how long he slept. It could have been days. Or minutes. Waking with a start, he mumbled and tried to track down the sound responsible for dragging him from a dream in which Derek Masters was standing over him, stroking his hair.

His eyes zeroed in between the legs of the propped-up couch, the makeshift barrier he vaguely recalled erecting sometime last night, in an attempt to prevent unwanted intruders.

Lying on the carpet, a white envelope.

Scrambling from his chair, clothes hanging off his exhausted body, he threw himself on it and tore at the sealed flap.

Not money.

And it was the wrong shape for more photographs. As he ripped open the plain white envelope, he suddenly remembered that letter bombs came in all shapes and sizes. But it was too late. Even as he yelped, threw the object over the other side of the room and dived behind his desk, something fluttered to the floor.

Something made of paper.

Something totally innocuous-looking.

From behind his barricade, Gav peered over at the envelope's contents. It obviously had no intention of exploding. Unless it was on a timer. These things were very sophisticated. Ignition could be delayed until the unfortunate recipient had been lulled into a false sense of security. You couldn't be too careful. Not with men like Derek Masters.

So he waited. He hid behind his desk and counted to a thousand. Only then did Gavin emerge from his refuge and creep tentatively across the room. He grabbed a pen and kept one arm raised protectively in front of his face. Stopping three feet away, he reached out one hand and poked at the object.

It didn't explode. It didn't do anything, except reveal itself to be some sort of document. Gav crawled a little closer. When he finally found the courage to pick up the envelope's contents with the end of the pen, he saw that it was a one-way plane ticket. Issued by Lebanese Airways. And in the name G Shaw.

Destination: Beirut. Date: 3 August.

His head swivelled to his desk calendar. Today.

Departure time: 11 a.m.

Gav checked his watch: a little before 9 a.m. If he rushed, he could make it. Scrambling to his feet, he switched off the laptop then looked at the Masters file.

To take or not to take?

There was no time either to make a new copy or even to lodge it in a safe deposit box somewhere. His office had already been broken into once. It could be, again. But, if he took the dossier along, it could get lost – or worse.

Gav wavered wildly, tearing off his ripped clothes as he pondered the decision. Thankfully, he had another pair of jeans, although they were in need of a wash. He was reduced to wearing dirty underwear, too. As he stood up, he spotted a reasonably clean-looking shirt hanging from a hook behind the office door. Manoeuvring the couch-barricade aside, he grabbed the garment and put it on.

The cool cotton smelled of fabric conditioner. His fingers ached less as he hurriedly buttoned the shirt, then tucked it into his jeans. And he came to a decision.

The Masters file would come with him. He couldn't leave it here. And, anyway, even if it met the same end as the copy, they couldn't destroy what was in Gavin's head. He'd write the whole article from memory if necessary.

Grabbing the Levi jacket, he thrust his plane ticket into a top pocket and tucked the Masters file under one arm. No point in taking a bag. Everything he needed he was either wearing or already carrying. As he unlocked the door and stepped out into the hallway, he knew he must look like shit, despite the relatively clean shirt.

But it didn't matter. Nothing mattered except what new information on Derek Masters awaited him in that war-torn Arab city that might as well be on the other side of the world.

It was a seven-hour flight. Gav sat alone, in First Class, and stared into space. Lebanon was four hours ahead of London, timewise.

Ten o'clock in the evening, and he could still feel the heat of the day. Beirut airport shimmered in a muggy, humid haze. The clean shirt was a limp rag, sticking to his sweat-drenched torso before he'd cleared Immigration.

In the arrivals area, crowds of people were waiting for fiends and relatives. The place smelled strongly of cigarettes and melting tarmac. As he scanned the lounge for a way out, it dawned on Gav that he had no idea where to go or what he was supposed to be looking for here. Beirut was a big city. Lebanon was an even bigger country.

Suddenly he caught sight of the words 'G Shaw', scrawled in large black letters. Holding the sign was a small, smiling man in a pristine white djellaba, whose smile broadened as their eyes met. Gavin strode over.

'Mr Shaw?' The small man dipped his head respectfully.

'Um, yes.' Unsure what to do, Gav erred on the side of caution and mirrored the gesture.

'*Salaam alekum*, Mr Shaw. Welcome to the Lebanon. My name is Asif. I will be your driver and guide for the duration of you stay. You have no luggage?' The smiling face momentarily clouded.

'Um, no, only this.' He tightened his hold on the Masters file.

Asif's smile returned. 'Ah, good – then please follow me, Mr

Shaw.' And, with that, the small man turned smoothly on one slippered foot and led the way towards an exit.

Gav could only comply with the man's studiedly polite request.

Once inside the huge but battered black Mercedes, of which Asif was obviously the very proud owner, his guide kept up a barrage of general but insistent questions and comments in Oxford-accented English:

'How was your flight?'

'Are you hungry? My brother has an excellent restaurant, in the French quarter.'

'Please do not open the window, Mr Shaw. The air conditioning will not work if you do that.'

'If you would care for a drink, you will find bottled water at your feet.'

The last statement was the only one to which Gavin responded. The heat was overwhelming – in spite of the air conditioning. Fumbling on the floor of the ancient vehicle, he located the mineral water, unscrewed the top and took a long drink.

'Would you like the radio on, Mr Shaw?' A pair of almond eyes met his, in the rear-view mirror.

Gavin shook his head. There was one thing he did want. He wanted to know who had arranged for Asif to meet him. He wanted to know where they were going and what he'd find there.

The almond eyes smiled. 'It will be a short journey. Not much time for me to show you our beautiful city, with your schedule so tight.'

Looking through the window, Gavin watched Beirut flash past. At least he knew he had a 'schedule' – even if he didn't know what that schedule was.

'But maybe you will return someday, Mr Shaw. And maybe, if you do, you will permit me the honour of being your guide a second time.'

Gavin nodded. The guy's manners were impeccable. His English was flawless. He was obviously well educated and completely charming. So what was he doing chauffeuring Westerners around?

'In the meantime, if I can be of any further service to you, please let me know. I can bring you... boys, Mr Shaw. Or girls, if that is your preference. Everything has been paid for.'

Gav's gaze darted back to his driver's rear-view mirror. Paid for? By whom?

The expression in those beautiful almond eyes hadn't changed.

He almost asked, but was reluctant to disturb whatever fine balance had been established here. So he returned the smile. 'Thank you, Asif.'

The small man turned his head and beamed. 'My pleasure, Mr Shaw.'

Totally intrigued, Gav returned to looking out of the window and tried to be patient.

It was a short journey. Beyond Beirut, a hair-raising sprint along a motorway, then a turn off at a sign proclaiming Junieh led them towards a very modern building perched halfway up a steep cliff. Below, Gavin could just make out the Mediterranean sea softly lapping onto a wide stretch of beach. He looked at his watch: 2 a.m.

Asif waved cheerily at a sleepy-looking security guard, then steered the battered Merc into a car park full of spanking vehicles. 'Right on time, Mr Shaw – and we have a few minutes to spare.'

Gav tried to mask his confusion. 'Thank you, Asif.'

But the man in the gleaming djellaba was already out of his seat and racing around to open Gavin's door for him.

Clutching the Masters file under his arm, Gav scrambled out of the car. The heat hit him like a wall. Worst than Baltimore, the moisture in the air was almost visible. The cardboard folder that held his dossier immediately began to wilt. In seconds, Asif was at his elbow.

'If I may make a suggestion, Mr Shaw…' Gav nodded his assent, and watched his guide move softly to the boot of the antique car. Seconds later, he was back, holding four things. A black dinner jacket; matching black tie; the third, Gav could see, came in the form of a pair of highly polished shoes.

'I took the liberty of finding out your size and purchasing these, Mr Shaw – many of my customers are busy men and do not have time to bother with such things.'

But it was the fourth item that held his gaze. Taking the clothes and shoes, he let Asif help him into the jacket. The small man tied the black tie for him, while Gavin continued to peer at the solid-looking black briefcase Asif had also produced, which now leaned against the battered Merc's back tyre. Attached to the handle was a length of chain. And at the end of the chain a metal cuff.

Gavin stood there in 2 a.m. heat and let Asif efficiently brush him down and generally tidy him up. Waiting until Gav had removed the money and his cellphone from the pocket of his Levi jacket, he gathered up sandals and denim jacket to place them almost lovingly in the back of the Merc:

'And finally' – Asif produced a small key from somewhere in the folds of his djellaba, picked up the briefcase, opened it and held it out – 'perhaps this would be the safest place for your… documents, Mr Shaw.'

He hesitated, for the briefest second. But something made him trust this eager, open-faced Arab. So he placed the Masters file inside, allowed Asif to close the briefcase and deftly secure the metal handcuff around his left wrist.

His guide then laid the tiny key in the middle of Gavin's palm. 'Now you look' – Asif chuckled – 'like any other diplomat. And your valuables will be safe and sound while you play the tables and relax.'

The mention of tables took him by surprise. But it was short-lived, as Asif escorted him towards the squat, smoked-glass building. On the side, in contrastingly tacky lights, the legend CASINO DU LIBAN.

'*Bonne chance*, Mr Shaw – may your winnings be large and your losses light! When you have broken the bank, I shall be here to return you to the airport.'

And, with that, Asif trotted back to his battered vehicle. Gavin took a deep breath, and strolled into the casino.

The sumptuous gaming areas were full of men in sheikhs' headgear and dinner jackets, women in both burkas and spangled evening gowns. In air-conditioned luxury, heavy gold jewellery dripped from fingers, wrists and necks. The clientele were affluent and the stakes were high – too high and too rich for anyone other than a millionaire's blood. Gavin changed three thousand into chip, at the cashier's desk, just to blend in.

But half an hour later he was standing with a crowd of awed gamblers watching Derek Masters play vignt-et-un, a vibrant dark-skinned redhead on his arm. At the man's other side, Milo – with a bandage over his right eye – was holding a briefcase very similar to the one at present cuffed to Gavin's wrist. It was stuffed full of multicoloured chips.

This table took cash bets, too. Every currency in the world: yen, Lebanese pounds, German marks, sterling – all joined the growing heap in front of the steel-eyed dealer. Waitresses stopped to watch. So did other gamblers, who migrated over from the chemin-de-fer tables.

Three other men were playing. The heap of money continued to grow. Gavin watched, initially confused. The crowd clapped and oohed as some gamblers folded and others took their place. But, when the dealer smiled and pushed the enormous bundle of mixed currency towards a beaming Arab, things started to make sense.

The vibrant redhead kissed Derek Masters' cheek in commiseration. Phlegmatically, Milo closed his briefcase and strode over to the cashier. Following at a discreet distance, Gavin watched the burly bodyguard exchange his chips for US dollars.

Money laundering. It had to be. Casinos – particularly Lebanese casinos – were the ideal place to exchange whatever currency you liked for one what was easily transportable, and plausibly explained, should anyone ever wonder about the odd large influx of cash into Masters Industries' bank account. And of course, as long as tax was paid on it, no one looked too carefully. Win or lose, it didn't really matter. Because whatever you cashed in at the start of the evening, you could cash out in the currency of your choice at the end.

Gavin followed Milo back to his boss and the redhead. He followed them to the chemin-de-fer table, where Masters placed several large cash bets. Sometimes he won. Sometimes he lost. But Gavin would put money on the fact that any loss was worth it, if you were looking to move sums of money around and not attract attention. And you got an evening's fun out of it: after an hour or so, even Gavin felt himself drawn into the glamour and excitement of it all.

The chips in his own pocket were growing heavy. Finally, at the roulette table, as Derek Masters bet on 24 red, Gav sat a small pile of his own, beside 24 black.

The dealer spun the wheel and released the ball. Gavin watched the tiny object hurtle over the numbers. Every eye in the place was on that ball.

Gav looked up, and caught Milo's eye. The unbandaged eye. The bodyguard hurriedly averted his gaze. Gav blinked in surprise at the usually cocky thug.

Then people were clapping and the dealer was pushing a pile of chips towards where Gavin stood. He laughed, scooping them up and glancing to where he'd last seen Milo, the redhead and Derek Masters. The space had been filled by other eager gamblers. Then a soft, accented voice in his ear: 'Well done again.

You have a player's instincts.'

A shiver ran up his spine. His hands shook, and he dropped some chips. Like birds of prey, two beautiful women helped him pick them up, ensuring Gav got a good view of their ample cleavages as they did so. By the time he'd got himself sorted, Masters plus bodyguard were nowhere to be seen.

A player's instincts...

Shoving a couple of chips at his unwanted female companions to get rid of them, Gav made his way over to the cashier's desk. As he'd had to on the way in, Gavin showed his passport in order to cash in his chips.

Was this all a game? Was someone playing with him? If so, what were the stakes? And what was the reward for the winner?

'Ah, Mr Shaw – there is a message for you.' The pretty cashier pushed £5,000 in sterling through the space at the bottom of his reinforced glass screen, then produced a white envelope from somewhere.

'For me?'

The pretty Arab boy nodded, slipping the envelope through beside the money. 'You did well this evening, Mr Shaw – I hope we will see you back at the Casino du Liban in the...'

But Gavin was already moving away, hastily tearing open a second white envelope. Another plane ticket?

He stared at the slim document folder marker. It bore the legend 'Louis Cruises'.

No, a ship. Gav flicked open the ticket and scanned the details. Beirut to Famagusta, 9 a.m. sailing. This time, he didn't even bother asking if the cashier could remember who had left the envelope for him. He no longer cared.

Gav's mind was on Famagusta. Formerly one of the biggest commercial ports in the Mediterranean. And a one-time British army base, before the island of Cyprus was partitioned. As automatic smoked-glass doors parted to allow him exit, the dripping

Lebanese night embraced him once more.

He no longer felt the heat. Derek Masters was ex-army. Maybe he had even done a turn of duty on Cyprus. Raising his eyes from the boat ticket, Gavin scanned for Asif.

The slender Arab man was lounging against his battered car, smoking a cigarette, which he hastily extinguished under a slippered foot as soon as he saw Gavin.

'Profitable night, Mr Shaw?' Asif scurried to open the car's rear door for him.

Gavin stared at his chauffeur. Yes, the night had been profitable. But not in the way Asif presumed. But he smiled and nodded.

'Back to the airport, Mr Shaw?'

He slid into the ovenlike vehicle. 'Take me to the docks. Beirut's docks.'

Now back behind his steering wheel, Asif swivelled his head round. 'Mr Shaw' – the dark face looked unhappy – 'the docks are no place for a gentleman such as yourself. Why not allow me to take you to my brother's restaurant where we can—'

'The docks, please. Then you can go home.' He couldn't even think about eating. Gav glanced at his watch. Just after 3 a.m. He was hours early. But there was no way he was going to miss that sailing.

With a sigh, Asif started the engine and they were off.

Leaning against the bonnet of the ancient Mercedes, while ships hooted and overall-clad Thai workers lugged vast trolleys of goods past them, Gav inhaled marginally cooler, and definitely saltier, air.

'Can I do anything for you, Mr Shaw?'

A soft hand touched his arm. Gavin sighed and shook his head. Despite several tellings, Asif refused to leave his side. His guide had insisted on staying with Gavin until MV *Marissa*, the ship on which his passage had been booked, was ready to be boarded.

'You are a very handsome man, Mr Shaw.' Gavin laughed. 'And a very worldly man, if I may say so.'

His interest pricked, Gav dragged his eyes from the ship and looked at Asif. If it was possible to be coffee-coloured and blush, his guide was now blushing furiously.

'Our cultures are very different, Mr Shaw. Islam forbids' – the husky voice dropped to a whisper – 'congress between men.'

Gav rolled his eyes: Christianity didn't exactly embrace it with open arms, either. But he nodded, not quite sure what the guy was getting at.

Asif lit a cigarette. 'When I was taking my degree at Oxford university, there was... someone.' The flame flickered, between trembling hands.

'A man?'

Asif nodded. His almond eyes took on a dreamy quality. 'We had one summer term together.'

Gav found himself moving closer. 'You miss him, don't you?'

Asif sighed, his head falling to lean against Gav's shoulder. 'My country – my religion – turns a blind eye to sex between boys. Between boys with men is sanctioned, because it is seen as a way of keeping our women pure.'

Gav slipped an arm around the smaller man's waist. He'd seen enough in his time to know what was coming:

'But men with men – men loving men, and staying with them even after sex, is frowned upon. Making a life with another man, living with him, working with him – making him your life partner in preference to a woman is a sin in the eyes of Allah.'

He was rubbing Asif's back through the fine cotton of his djellaba. He could hear the sadness in the man's voice.

'I let my customers fuck me, Mr Shaw...' Sadness gave way to anger. 'I let rich Westerner tourists and diplomats come in my mouth in the hope that one of them will want what I want.' Then self-loathing. 'But they just give me money, then go home to their wives or their girlfriends.'

Gav pulled Asif closer. Something in the guy's words was striking a distinct chord.

'Do you have a... boyfriend, Mr Shaw?' The man slid an arm of his own around Gavin's waist.

Gavin opened his mouth to speak – but closed it again. Gerry was gone: he'd not thought about the guy in weeks, never mind considered phoning and trying to make things up with him. James? No, he'd ruined that too. There was no one in Gavin Shaw's life. No one. Except Derek Masters.

His head shook slowly.

'So you are like me, Mr Shaw: you are alone.'

His other hand reached up to stroke the smaller man's short, neatly cut hair. 'You'll find someone, Asif. I promise you.'

Unexpectedly, his guide pulled away from the attempted caress. 'But I am a sinner in Allah's eyes and I shall go to Hell!' There were tears in those almond eyes. Tears of sorrow. And tears of anger. Asif glared at Gavin, hurriedly wiping his wet cheeks on the sleeve of his djellaba. He looked away in shame and embarrassment.

Something inside him melted. Reaching out a hand, Gavin slipped his fingers beneath that fine chin and tilted the man's face back up to his. 'You're beautiful, my friend.' Before he knew what he was doing, Gav's mouth was on the other man's. He kissed him lightly, smiling. 'You're sweet and you're charming and' – he brushed his lips over Asif's again – '... and you're incredibly desirable.' It was true. Gav knew he was hardening. He didn't want to do what everyone else did with men like Asif. He didn't want to be just another Westerner who fucked and ran. So he took a deep breath and prepared to pull away before things went too far.

But Asif had other ideas. A soft brown hand curled at the back of Gav's head, holding their faces close. And he began to kiss back, opening his lips under Gavin's and pressing his hot mouth more firmly against a virtual stranger's.

Groaning, he could only return the passion. He pushed his tongue between the man's lips, tasting the warm, aromatic wetness of Asif's saliva. In seconds, they were moving. Gav eased the man onto the bonnet of the battered Mercedes, still kissing him, and manoeuvred his body between the Arab's splayed thighs.

# Twenty-two

It felt alien, fumbling in the folds of the pristine white djellaba rather than searching for a zip.

But alien was becoming the norm these days.

Mouth on mouth, and with the guy's arms around his neck, Gavin pushed the long flowing robe up until his hands made contact with the smooth silkiness of the other man's thighs.

Asif's tongue was in Gavin's mouth, now, twining with his own. Full sensual lips parted further, changing the angle to deepen the kiss.

Gavin shuddered, stroking the insides of the man's thighs and feeling the soft down there. His hands slid further up, pushing the djellaba roughly out of the way in his haste until his thumbs reached the moist V at the crease between leg and body. He was searching for hair. Gav inhaled sharply, finding only more smooth skin.

Asif broke the kiss. 'I shave, Mr Shaw – I shave to be more attractive, to be cleaner so that Western men will like me more and want to stay with me.'

Gav stared into the other man's almond eyes. His right hand moved up to cup hairless balls, a thumb stroking the root of the other man's cock.

'You like, Mr Shaw?'

To be honest, he preferred his men to look and feel like men. But he smiled, his other hand moving from under the rumpled djellaba to stroke Asif's cheek softly. 'I like! Oh baby, I like!' Then he was easing up reluctantly from his position on top of the man, and falling to a crouch, pressing his face between the Arab's dusky thighs.

Thankfully, they'd parked in front of a thick bougainvillea hedge. Even more providentially, at some point during that long, slow kiss, a large container truck had parked between the ancient Mercedes and the quayside. Sandwiched in between, in a little alley of darkness, Gav buried himself in another dark area.

The skin of Asif's crotch was like heavy satin. His balls were surprisingly large for such a slender man. Gavin nudge the bollocks with his nose, inhaling sweet oils and spicy scents.

Somewhere above him, the Arab was making quiet moaning sounds, tiny pants of pleasure that grew as Gav's tongue flicked out to lap at that strange, hairless sac. He held the man's thighs wide apart, feeling the tremble in the long, lean muscle, and continued to drag his tongue over every millimetres of the man's balls. Exploring. Tasting. Drawing the tender flesh into his mouth, while Asif gasped somewhere above him. Rolling each nut around his mouth, then spitting it gently back out, to feel the well fullness of it rasp against his own unshaved chin. Then he drew his cheeks over those balls, nudging them from side to side and feeling the exquisite heaviness flex and shudder against his face.

When he'd had his fill of the man's musky sac – when Asif's arsecheeks were thrusting up off the bonnet of the Mercedes in need, and Gav's mouth was as dry as the guy's balls were dripping – he slipped his hands under those arsecheeks and rose again to kiss the young Arab.

Asif was more passionate than ever. Maybe it was the taste of his own body in Gavin's mouth. Maybe it was the thorough ballsucking he'd just been subjected too. Maybe it was the magic of a brief encounter under the bougainvillea as the first rays of dawn split the sky to the east. Gav groaned deeply, sucking the spit from the man's tongue. Whatever it was, the guy was gouging at Gavin's mouth, biting his lips and trying to push his tongue down Gavin's throat. Both hands behind Gav's neck, Asif reared up off the Mercedes' damp bonnet. Their upper bodies pressed together. Chest to chest. Belly to belly. And, from under folds of pristine white djellaba, a hard insistent cock ground against an equally stiff member.

Gav's own hands were busy too. Asif's arsecheeks each resting in a sweaty palm, Gavin let his fingers play in that moist, hairless crack. He rubbed the pad of an index finger over Asif's hole. Asif moaned into Gavin's mouth, but continued the kiss.

Gav could feel that crinkled orifice give under the pressure from his finger. He wanted to be inside the man. He wanted to hold him and kiss him and make him come too, but at that moment in time Gavin Shaw had never wanted to be inside anyone more.

Abruptly, Asif shifted in his hands, wrapping bare brown legs around Gavin's waist.

His mouth slipped from the other man's, the kiss broken by the urgent movement. Then Asif was panting in his ear, licking it, kissing it, pushing his tongue into the delicate orifice.

Gavin roared and pushed his index finger into Asif's hole. The young Arab's head dropped back. He sat down hard on the digit, impaling himself on the intrusion. And started to grind.

Somehow, Gavin got his other hand free and began to fumble in the folds of the djellaba, which had become snagged on Asif's hard-on.

He wanted that dick. He wanted to take it in his mouth while Asif fucked himself on Gavin's finger. He wanted to feel the thick head batter off the back of his throat, then choke on the guy's hot spunk. He wanted dark, warm thighs wrapped around his head until he could hear the blood pulse in the man's veins.

Finally, his fist found what it was looking for. Asif's shaft was thick. Gav ran a thumb up the length of the man, finding by touch alone the thick ridge just below the head, then the velvety, blood-engorged flesh of the glans itself. Leaning forward, he kissed Asif's neck and inhaled the heavy scent of bougainvillea from the hedge behind them. The pad of his thumb moved over the head of Asif's cock, pausing to feel the slick wetness that was oozing liberally from the gaping slit.

The hands around his neck tightened, trimmed fingernails digging in under Gav's ponytail.

He grunted, biting Asif's neck now, biting, then sucking, the sweet-tasting skin. And easing a second finger into the Arab's tight hole.

Asif's happy scream rang out into the breaking dawn.

Gavin cut the sound short, lips moving from the man's neck to clamp over his mouth once more. He kissed Asif fiercely, a second finger sliding up beside the first, his other fist wrapping itself around the Arab's flexing shaft. With his Lebanese friend's arms still tight around his neck, Gav gripped Asif's cock firmly, and slowly began to move further into the man's hole. Hot, rippling muscle massaged his first finger joint. Pushing on, he felt the rippling walls of Asif's arse widen to admit knuckles.

Asif shuddered with each deepening penetration.

The guy's cock was swelling in Gav's fist, pushing against his hands the way his other fingers pushed into the pulsating lining of Asif's rectum. Sweat was running into his eyes, stinging them. Gav maintained the lip lock, feeling the Arab moan into his mouth. His knuckles moved past Asif's anus, widening the sensitive opening to the man's body, then letting the strained and stretched muscle clamp once more around the lower part of his fingers. When the V of his fingers impacted with Asif's arsecheeks, and his two fingers were deep inside the man's body, Gav slowly began to spread them.

Asif's entire body stiffened. His nails dug into the back of Gavin's neck. He seemed to stop breathing.

A sudden panic gripped Gav's mind. He paused, the walls of

Asif's arse pushing back against the widening. Under the pad of his index finger, a small rounded bump.

Then he found what he was looking for. Gently at first, then with increasing vigour, Gavin began to massage the Arab's prostate gland.

Asif broke the kiss, inhaling deeply to release a loud cry. Which became a torrent of fast, breathless Arabic syllables. Hanging off Gavin's neck, body bucking and writhing, his yells of pleasure were loud and unmistakable.

Just when Gav was sure dockers were going to come racing round from the quayside to see who was being murdered another, equally exalted, voice was joining in with Asif. Gav flinched, unsure of the source of the melodic, amplified sound.

Asif's cock flexed violently in Gavin's fist. The walls of the man's arse were a fleshy vice around his fingers.

The ululations from somewhere above their heads grew in volume as Asif howled his release. And, when the Arab came fast and hard in Gavin's fist, he finally placed the sound.

Almost in total sync with the muezzin's call to prayer from a nearby mosque, a young Muslim revelled in a celebration of his own. Staggering backwards under the force of the orgasm, Gav felt the boy's legs clamp around his waist. Fingers buried in Asif's arse, the knuckles of his other hand slick with warm milky spunk, Gav stared at the jubilant expression on Asif's face and uttered a silent prayer of his own.

God was indeed great, for creating a world in which such harmless pleasures could exist.

They ended up in the back seat of the battered Mercedes, legs tangled in crumpled folds of djellaba, and arms tightly around each other. While the exhausted Arab dozed against his shoulder, Gav listened to the sound of the docks just beyond.

He could smell the man – on his fingers, all over his body. Asif's saliva coated his lips. Gav smiled, kissing the top of the guy's head. A strange satisfaction draped his body in a rosy glow, despite the fact that he'd not come himself.

Asif murmured in his sleep, burrowing in against Gav's chest.

This hadn't been about him. Or rather, it had been about something more than him. He still couldn't quite believe that he, Gavin 'Fuck-'em-and-Run' Shaw, had just devoted minutes of his life he'd never get back to bringing this virtual stranger to orgasm.

The trust coming off the sleeping Arab in waves gave him an even weirder satisfaction. It was a trust he couldn't abuse, an open and raw need that spoke to something deep in the recesses of his own mind. Despite the fact that he and Asif could not be less alike, regardless of how little they had in common, Gav felt incredibly close to the young Arab, right now. And, for once, he couldn't put it down to the fact that he'd just come.

Because he hadn't. Gav wasn't even sure he was even hard. While Asif's release had been very physical, Gav's own orgasm was more mental. Even emotional. Feelings he didn't know he had were racing through his brain. The need to protect. The need to be protected.

The desire to hold. And the parallel urge to be held.

The need to possess. And the need to belong

The sound of a revving engine dragged his eyes from the sleeping face. Beyond the battered Merc's grimy window, the container truck was moving away. Beyond that, MV *Marissa* shimmered pink in the rising sun. In the dawn light, he could see more of the quayside now. Amid the picturesque palm trees and blooming bougainvillea, huddled groups of men in dirty djellabas smoked desperate cigarettes and eyed the docking ferries full of tourists. At their feet, shopping bags full of locally made souvenirs and novelties awaited the hard sell. Other men – men very like the one at present snoozing in Gavin's arms – waited beside vehicles even more ancient than Asif's, hoping to earn a day's wage by carrying the visitors to the casino, the historical ruins or the souks.

So much poverty among so much beauty.

A frown replaced his smile of contentment. Men like Derek Masters took advantage of countries like Lebanon. As they exploited post-communism Riga, depressed areas of Glasgow and the meat-packing districts of Baltimore.

He felt his muscle tighten with anger.

Men like Derek Masters, with their multinational, multimillionaire status, had to be exposed for the criminals they were.

His growing resolve woke the man in his arms with a start. 'What? What is it? What's…?' Asif began to struggle, arms flailing. Unfocused almond eyes looking up at Gavin in panic. Then recognition spread over the handsome face. Asif smiled in surprise. 'Mr Shaw! You are still here?' As he became aware of their entanglement, the Arab sheepishly began to smooth down the rumpled folds of his djellaba.

Gav laughed, his anger dissolving in the face of this sudden shyness. He kept a hand on Asif's warm thigh. 'Of course I'm still here.' He kissed the tip of the man's nose. 'My ship doesn't sail until nine a.m. And I hope you don't think you're going anywhere yet, because you're not.' He tightened his other arm around the man. 'I want to hear about Asif – I want to know about his hopes and his dreams.'

Asif laughed in return. 'Are you sure, Mr Shaw?'

Gav slipped a finger under Asif's chin and tilted his face up to his own. 'Of course I'm sure.' He had the feeling Asif didn't get the chance to talk about himself a lot. Moreover, Gavin couldn't think of a nicer way to pass the time than to hold this man in his arms and listen to that soft, Arabic voice.

Four hours later, the Masters file still locked to his wrist, Gavin was standing on the deck of MV *Marissa* and waving to the beaming figure on the quayside. Asif looked a lot happier. A warm glow still tingled on Gavin's skin.

Sometimes all it took was a friendly face, a sympathetic ear – and a good hand job! And as the slender Muslim had poured his heart out, Gav had got so much more in return. Nothing to do with Derek Masters. But everything to do with a world beyond his own experience, with all the parallels that world had to show.

MV *Marissa* sounded her hooter.

Asif raced forward from his battered Mercedes, hands cupped around lips as the cruise liner edged from her berth. 'I'll never forget you, Mr Shaw – thanks for everything!' The slender figure in the now less-than-pristine white djellaba leapt up and down, waving and smiling.

And I'll never forget you, my friend. Gav smiled and waved back. Somewhere, along the way, in the fucks and the blow jobs, in the hurried couplings with a myriad strangers, he'd lost sight of what he really wanted from life: a sense of peace, a sense of stability, in his own mind.

For all their differences, Asif and he were united on this.

Gav watched and waved until the white-robed figure on the quayside blurred, then disappeared completely. Around him, travellers and tourists heading back to Cyprus chatted and admired the fading Lebanese coastline.

Gav knew he had work to do. Now minus laptop, but with pens and plenty of paper, he retreated to a shaded spot, unlocked the briefcase and began to scribble. It was an eight-hour voyage – just enough time to bring the Masters file up to date.

He missed lunch. He missed dinner. He turned down two offers to buy him a drink. By the time the MV *Marissa* was docking at Famagusta, Gav's wrist was cramping and he had a pounding headache.

But he was back on track. And he was starting to work out how things were done. Even before the gangways had been lowered,

Gav saw the stocky, Turkish man with the bristling moustache, eyes hidden behind mirrored sunglasses, who stood beyond the Immigration fence holding a large white piece of card.

He couldn't read it at this distance. But he had feeling it bore the words 'G Shaw'.

The sun was a solid ball of fire just above the horizon by the time he disembarked, passed through customs and opened his briefcase for three different officials. In the car park, the night heat was worse than ever. A fine film of moisture coated everything, from the back of his neck to the roofs of parked cars. Back in sandals, Levi jacket, jeans and T-shirt, Gav knew he looked like just another a tourist – apart from the briefcase and the wrist cuff. When he reached the car park, he noted that his driver was wearing shirt and tie, plus full chauffeur's uniform: jacket, trousers and leather gloves. A peaked cap had appeared from somewhere. The guy had to be sweating to death under that lot.

But his new driver – 'Mehmet, at your service, sir! – smiled, cool as a cucumber, as he opened the door to a superior-looking and air-conditioned vehicle and ushered Gavin into the back:

'I understand you must be in Nicosia by eleven p.m., sir.' Bathing in the car's cool interior, Gav nodded. 'And do you wish me to wait for you while you talk to Zorn?'

Gav nodded again. His headache had moved to his temples, where it throbbed to a beat of its own. He was glad someone knew where they were going – and who he was supposed to meet.

Zorn...

Mehmet turned the key in the ignition. A powerful engine whispered into life.

Zorn...

The name didn't sound Turkish. Or Greek. On which side of Cyprus's divided capital was he to meet the owner of this strange-sounding name. And what more would he learn about Derek Masters?

The speedometer's needle rarely dipped below 90 k.p.h.

Gav dozed fitfully for most of the two-hour journey. He couldn't remember the last time he'd slept. Or eaten – or washed, for that matter. Derek Masters' blunt, angular features were dancing on the insides of his eyelids again when a tentative hand touched his shoulder.

'We are here, sir.'

His eyes snapped open. For the briefest of seconds he had no idea where he was. Or who he was.

'Zorn is working at the moment, Mr Shaw. I shall wait for you, just over there. I shall wait till morning if necessary, so take all the time you need.'

As Gav shook himself back into something approximating a conscious state, Mehmet held the car door open for him. His mind slowly cleared. Easing his body from the cool interior, he stared around.

They were in a narrow street, lined with dilapidated buildings. Somewhere nearby, another muezzin called the faithful to prayer from the top of another minaret. That meant they were still in the Turkish sector.

Mehmet inclined his head respectfully. 'I hope you find what you are looking for, sir.' And with that the man got back into his car and rove away, leaving Gavin standing in front of a small, domed structure.

A mosque?

He moved closer, peering at four steep steps, which led down from pavement level to an unremarkable-looking door. Then his eyes were caught by a peeling wooden sign, on which one word was barely legible: BUKKYAK.

Gav had no idea what awaited him behind that door, or who Zorn was. But there was one sure way to find out. Negotiating the steep stairs, he pushed open a scarred wooden door and entered.

*

'Zorn?'

In response to his enquiry, the skinny boy in a 'Nike' T-shirt who sat behind what passed for a counter extracted ten dollars from Gavin's mass of currency, gave him a towel and a pair of flip-flops and booked him in for the full massage. 'Zorn will come and get you, when he is ready.'

The sound of running water, the high domed ceiling and the presence of burly locals in various states of undress soon let Gavin know where he was.

A Turkish bath. A *hamam*.

In the changing area, he undressed quickly, shoving everything into a locker, which came with a key. The briefcase he kept locked to his wrist.

Contrary to what he'd expected, the *hamam* was pleasantly cool. And Zorn was obviously the resident masseur. Wandering through the various rooms and antechambers, towel wrapped modestly around his waist, he watched men of all ages wash, shave and stretch out on a huge, circular marble platforms by turns.

The only sound was the constant echoing trickle of water into the stone basins that dotted the walls of the rooms. Passing a curtained section, he was aware of a loud groan from within, which split the silence.

Gav flinched.

A young Turk who sat on the edge of the marble platform laughed softly. 'You can always tell when Zorn's working!'

A single droplet of apprehension slid from one armpit. Gav sat down beside the young man, who continued to chat.

'You booked a session?'

Gav nodded.

The man laughed again. 'He'll work you over – Zorn learned his

trade somewhere they know all about the power of a firm hand.'
He winked.

Gav's stomach churned. But he had little time to dwell on what
awaited him behind that faded curtain. Five minutes later, a heavily built figure lumbered out from the shrouded space. Towel held
in place with one hand, the man lumbered away, groaning and
scarlet-faced.

In his wake, a tall, Slavic-looking figure in pec-hugging black T-
shirt and the tightest of jeans emerged. Cheekbones glinting, cold
blue eyes scanned the area, and alighted upon Gavin.

'You!'

Gavin cringed and looked down at his feet.

'Yes, you!' The voice was deep, heavily accented. 'Come in
here!'

Every phrase was delivered like an order – in a tone that was accustomed to automatic obedience. That tone spoke to something
deep in Gavin's body. His cock twitched. While his mind rebelled,
his body was moving by itself, and was making his way across to
scowling Zorn.

# Twenty-three

'Listen, I don't want a massage, I just want to talk to you.'

'On the table!'

Gav held his briefcase against his chest. 'I want to ask you about—'

'On the table! Please!' Zorn's blue eyes narrowed impatiently. He pointed to a rickety four-legged structure. 'We can talk while I work!'

Every sentence came punctuated with an exclamation mark. And with every barked order Gav's cock hardened a little more under the flimsy towel. So he did as he was told and clambered onto the massage table. He could smell Zorn's previous client/victim. Gav was still tying to get comfy, half lying on his hard-on and wondering whether to continue to hold the briefcase or let it dangle off the end of the table when a pair of firm hands clamped themselves onto his shoulders.

'What do you want to ask me?'

Gav's entire body tensed. Braced for a pummelling, he remained rigid as the hands swept over his deltoids, palms moulding around the mounds of his shoulders. Then two parallel thumbs lightly dug into a nerve.

'Well?'

A series of electric-shock-like sensations shuddered through Gavin's flesh. He gasped, but it was the only sound he felt capable of making. His bones were melting. The skin was dropping off his body, taking with it most of the tension.

'Do you want to ask me things or not?'

The hands were moving now, back across his shoulders to meet in the middle. Slowly, they descended over each vertebra. With every practised motion of those expert fingers, a little more tension left Gavin's muscles. He barely felt the towel whipped deftly from around his waist. But he felt bone crack as Zorn's thumbs pressed into the tendons at the base of his spine. And he finally managed to speak, even if it was more of a croak. 'Tell me about... Deke Zenovich.'

The hands paused on the cheeks of Gavin's arse. He could feel the increase in pressure, in the tips of the man's strong fingers. When Zorn eventually answered, the voice was lower but still commanding:

'You have money?'

Remembering his winnings from the Casino du Liban, Gavin mumbled assent.

'I want two thousand dollars, and you didn't hear this from me, right?' As deftly as they'd removed his towel, the masseur's hands flipped Gav over onto his back. Lying there, naked and trembling, with his hard-on exposed to this man's gaze, he was incapable of movement.

Zorn loomed over him, blond cropped hair and Slavic cheekbones glinting in the overhead light. 'Right?'

Gav managed a blink of agreement.

One hand on his shoulder, the other covering Gavin's left pec, Zorn scowled at him. 'And if you mention my name, or tell anyone you found me, I will track you down, rip out your heart and eat it while you watch.'

He couldn't move. Whatever pressure points the man had used, he'd completely disabled Gavin's motor functions. He could only blink again, continue to lie there and listen to that cold, accented voice.

'First, you must understand that I am Serbian, and here under UN protection. I have papers to prove it. If and when I return to

Bosnia to face the tribunals, I shall tell them everything.'

Tribunals?

Maybe Gavin couldn't move, but his heart could still pound.

'I shall tell them what I saw Deke Zenovich – may God damn him to Hell! – do with his bare hands, and what atrocities were committed in his name. I was only obeying orders.'

As he talked, Zorn worked. His hands moved to Gavin's legs, which he lifted and parted as if they were featherweights.

'We all were, back then. But I shall never forget what I saw. War is war, and I have no love of my enemies, but what that monster Zenovich did to innocent civilians will remain in my mind for ever.'

The hands were moving up the insides of his thighs. Those thumbs were working their combination of magic and murder in the nerve endings and pressure points of his most vulnerable areas. But, while his body was numb, his mind seemed to have acquired a new dimension. As Zorn's low voice continued, recounting the crimes against humanity he'd witnessed committed by Deke Zenovich, a.k.a. Derek Masters, Gav was storing every word away for future use.

The rapes.

The tortures.

The massed looting.

The mass graves.

'Zenovich fled at the end of the war. He is on the UN's most-wanted list, and when he is found I shall return to my homeland.'

Gav's brain seized on this new piece of information: Zorn – along with the UN – was unaware of the name change. Was this what Derek Masters' blackmailer held over him? The threat of extradition back to Bosnia, to stand trial for war crimes? He was still digesting this possibility when Zorn ducked down, hoisted both Gavin's legs onto his shoulders and began to massage the backs of his thighs.

Arse in the air, strong Serbian hands running over his hamstrings, Gav could only stare at his own hard-on in disbelief. He gasped.

Zorn frowned, using his knuckles now to knead stubborn knots of tension. 'You doubt my word?'

Gav shook his head wildly – or at least tried to. But his neck muscles had dissolved.

His wiry body looming between Gavin's thighs, the Serbian masseur leaned down. Their faces were an inch apart. He could feel the man's breath on his cheeks, smell a vaguely menthol odour.

'I will give you proof – I will give you copies of photographs. Photographs which will make sure you never sleep well again. And dates, places – I have it all. Do you know what rank I held, under Sergeant Zenovich?' Zorn spat the name.

Gav closed his eyes, spittle raining onto his lips and chin.

'It was my job to record what happened. On film. So that Zenovich and his... perverted friends could relive what they had done afterwards. The man is sick. Truly mad, but his madness will be his undoing.' The anger subsided into a low, mocking laughter.

Gav risked raising an eyelid.

Zorn's smile was a million times worse than his scowl. The heels of his hands dug into the bands of muscle at the back of Gavin's legs. The man carried on the massage as if it were some function he'd learned to perform automatically. Now muttering to himself in some alien-sounding language, he hooked Gavin's right knee over his left shoulder, grabbed his other leg and yanked hard.

There was a sharp crack. He felt his hip joint jar. Gav howled, the power of speech firmly back within his grasp. The pain was short-lived but excruciating, and cut through whatever bizarre sort of epidural the Serbian ex-soldier had accomplished earlier with his fingers. Before Gavin could recover, the masseur was hooking his leg – which now felt strangely wonderful – back over his shoulder, and repeating the procedure with the other.

'Zorn... the photographs... I'll buy the... photographs.'

Delivering a sound slap to Gav's bare arse, the Serbian lowered his legs back onto the table, then hopped on behind him. 'I will give them to you free' – Zorn splayed his wiry legs either side of Gavin's naked form – 'if it will help find Deke Zenovich; I do not want any money. My hands are too stained with the blood of innocents to profit from their deaths.'

Gav shuddered. Those warm, strong palms were now covering his ears, gripping each side of his head firmly. He could almost hear the snapping of necks like twigs, which had accompanied Sergeant Deke Zenovich's inhuman commands.

Zorn pulled upwards violently, twisting Gavin's head sharply left, then right.

The crack was more gunshot than twig-snapping. Gav roared in another microsecond of agony. Then the same heat he'd noticed in his legs was swarming down his spine, spreading into his chest, arms and hips, where it seemed almost to hum like an actual sound. Gav slumped back against the man's stringy body. The briefcase still dangled from his left wrist. His other arm lay loosely in his lap. He felt dazed, disoriented, but surprisingly rejuvenated.

Zorn slapped him on the back and slipped from the table. 'I am good, no?'

Gav managed a laugh. 'You are... excellent.'

Zorn smiled that unsettling smile again, and held up his hands. 'What can kill also heals. What gives pain can also take it away.' Picking up Gav's towel, he threw it at him. 'You want those photographs?'

'Oh, yes, please!' Gavin veritably leapt from the table, wrapping the length of fabric around his waist. He followed Zorn's wiry form through the curtain and back out into the *hamam*'s reception area.

Ten minutes later, dressed in clothes that now felt two sizes too big for him, Gavin stood beside the Serbian war criminal in what was obviously the staff room. From inside a rusting metal locker, the man produced a tiny roll of microfilm. With great ceremony, he placed it in the palm of Gavin's hand and curled Gav's fingers around it. 'This will show you. This will show you the truth about Deke Zenovich.'

He could only nod, tightening his fist. His mind reeled with the possibilities of what he now held in the palm of his hand.

This wasn't some vague rumour about drug smuggling.

This wasn't unsubstantiated gossip about rent boys.

This wasn't conjecture about gunrunning, money laundering or any of the other illegal activities Gav had seen hinted at.

This was the real thing. This was the Big Time. Pulitzer prizes and Investigative Journalist of the Year awards floated before his eyes.

A snapping of fingers pulled him back to the here and now. 'Three thousand dollars, we said?' It was Zorn's turn to hold out his hand.

Aware the price had gone up by a grand, Gav fumbled for his winnings, stuffed more than enough into the ice-eyed Slav's hand. 'Thanks – thanks so much!'

Zorn shook his head. 'The money is nothing. You want to thank me, you help bring Deke Zenovich to justice, my English friend.'

Then he was standing outside the *hamam*, watching Mehmet steer the car to a smooth halt in front of him. 'Where to now, sir?'

He had to get home. He had to return to London, type all this up and get it on James Delany's desk by end of work tomorrow. Gav groaned and crawled into the back of the car. He had no idea how much money he had left. He had even less idea whether this part of Cyprus had an airport. 'Um, I need to catch a plane.'

Mehmet nodded. 'Certainly, sir.' The car moved quietly off down the narrow, twisted streets.

Turning his pockets out in an attempt to see if he had enough money to get home, he was surprised to see an unfamiliar white envelope among the crumpled currency. Gav hurriedly opened it, squinting at its contents in the dim light of passing street lamps.

Another ticket. A Turkish Airlines ticket, Cyprus to Istanbul.

Gav stared at the slim folder. When had he been given this? And by whom? Why did he need to go to Istanbul? He had everything he wanted now to blow Masters Industries out of the water.

Half an hour later, in the departure lounge of Kyrenia Airport on northern Cyprus, he found out. Someone had left a two-day-old copy of the London *Times* on a seat. As Gav leafed through it to pass the time, his eyes fell on a headline, on the business page: CEO OF MASTERS INDUSTRIES IN ISTANBUL FOR MERGER TALKS.

Gav smiled. What would a quick stopover in that most ancient of Asian-European cities hurt? And, if the worse came to the worst, he could fax the profile to James and meet his deadline that way.

When the call came to board, Gavin Shaw was first in the queue. It was only when he was sipping mineral water, high above the Mediterranean, and rereading the *Times* article that he noticed that his hands refused to stop shaking.

He landed at 4 a.m. No luggage, no customs or immigration area to pass through, so he was in a taxi by 4.30. He asked the driver to recommend a cheap hotel. At 5.30 a.m., to the sound of more calls to prayer, Gav was stumbling past a huge industrial vehicle, which was methodically hosing down the streets of the Sultanhammet area.

The Hotel Hali's receptionist looked at him strangely, but took his booking. Gav's room was small but clean. Sitting at the open window, while the sun rose over Aya Sofya's crumbling cupolas, he unlocked the briefcase from his wrist, opened it and took out the Masters file.

And he began to write. The letters and words strobed in front of his eyes. As he detailed the newest information, with Zorn's microfilm now snuggling in the hollow heel of his sandal, along with the cassette of the blackmail conversation, Gav knew something had happened to his handwriting. He tried to control the pen. But it refused to obey him. He scribbled on regardless, hoping it would all be legible later.

He wrote all though the morning.

When the chambermaid knocked, he sent her away and wrote on. The only time he moved from the small table was to leave in search of an English-language newspaper. A helpful desk clerk provided one. Gav scurried back up to his room and fumbled for the business section.

There, in black and white, was a photograph of Derek Masters shaking hands with someone who turned out to be the chairman of BJF Construction. This was the last day of talks, which were being held in the Turkish headquarters of Masters Industries, just off Taksim Square. Gavin grabbed the phone.

After interminable conversations with Istanbul Directory Enquiries, he eventually got a number for the Taksim Square office, where the press office informed him that a statement would be issued at 5 p.m. today. Still holding the newspaper, he sat down on the bed and stared at Derek Masters' angular face.

His profile of the businessman was finished. It lacked one thing – the one thing a Gavin Shaw article always included.

A quote. A few words directly from the man himself.

His whole body trembled at the thought.

Jumping up off the bed, Gavin lunged for the briefcase. The room spun around him. As he padlocked the whole thing back to his left wrist, two sets of handcuffs circled before his eyes. Two became three. Swaying slightly, Gav gritted his teeth and finally got the damn thing snapped into place. Then he was leaving his room, jogging past the desk clerk and out into late-afternoon Istanbul.

His NUJ card and passport got him into a plush suite on the second floor of a spanking new office block. Just. Two huge security men went over his body with a metal detector. The briefcase was

X-rayed, but he refused to remove it from his wrist. As he took his seat among a plethora of other journalists, Gav caught sight of a hollow-cheeked man in the mirrored wall of the press suite.

His hair hung around his shoulders in wild, messy tangles. Five days' stubble had become the start of a beard. The Levi jacket was filthy, and now two sizes too big for him. For the first time, he noticed his jeans were riding way too low on his hips.

Startled blue eyes stared back at him from within heavy dark shadows. Gavin tore himself from his own reflection and sat down between a Far Eastern gentleman and a guy who jabbered into a cellphone.

And his almost permanent half hard-on rubbed constantly against the inside of his right thigh.

After ten minutes or so, a striking woman in a dark suit appeared from a door, followed by Derek Masters, with a dejected-looking Milo in tow, plus the guy from the newspaper photograph. The female press officer addressed the assembly in Turkish, English, French, German and what had to be Japanese.

People around him clapped politely. Derek Masters and the guy from the newspaper photo stepped forward and shook hands, smiling at each other. Cameras clicked and whirred. The press officer took a few questions from the assembled pack of journalists.

Gav moved the Masters file, safe in its locked case, onto his lap. He stared straight ahead at the object of six long weeks' research. The others on the podium faded. The press officer's voice was barely audible over the drumming blood in his ears. The room seemed to clear as a silver-haired head slowly turned in his direction. And the rest of world slipped away. Gavin gazed into Derek Masters' dark, bottomless eyes.

They were the only two men in the room. On the face of the earth. Those eyes had seen a lifetime's worth of horror. Those eyes had smiled coldly, as money had been exchanged for guns. Drugs. And as desperate men fought bare-knuckled on Glasgow wastelands.

Those eyes had at least witnessed John Johnny-Boy Clark's murder, watched innocent Bosnian civilians die.

The head of his cock was pushing against the underside of the briefcase that held the Masters file.

And those eyes were now locked with Gavin's. This man had held his attention longer than any other man ever had. Some strange link had been forged over the past six weeks. And, although he had no idea why, Gav knew things were far from over.

Those eyes could give him something else. He had to know what it was. He had to find out.

When the press conference finally ended, Gav left the building and approached a taxi-rank.

'Where to?' The driver turned to stare at him as he got in.

Gav drew what was left of the bribe money from his pocket and thrust it at the man. 'I'll tell you when I know.' Hunched over the Masters file, he rocked slowly and felt his cock ache against the underside of the briefcase.


The Masters party had dinner in a swanky Thai restaurant; Gav sat outside and waited. They adjourned to a nightclub. The bouncers wouldn't let Gavin in without a tie, so he leaned against the side of his taxi, while its driver shook his head in bemusement. By midnight, Taksim Square was all flashing lights, clattering Turkish pop music and the smell of street vendors' food stalls. The Masters party were now having cocktails in the bar of a five-star hotel. Gav watched through two barriers of glass window while Derek Masters, Milo by his side, whispered into the ear of his Turkish business partner's fat wife.

At 2 a.m. the party started to break up. The Turk left, his wife smiling and waving to Derek Masters. The press officer hailed a taxi and departed into the night. Milo and his boss stood in the doorway of the hotel. Gav was looking around for their car, when the duo abruptly stepped out onto the bustling streets and began to walk. Seconds later, Gav had fallen in behind them.

This was it.

This was definitely it. All he had to do was lose Milo, and Gav would finally find what he was looking for. But that was going to prove easier said than done.

Away from the main drag of glitzy Taksim Square, the streets were darker. Narrower. But just as busy. Still scarred by the earthquake of four years ago, ancient Ottoman buildings stood half-demolished. Women in shawls huddled in doorways, selling exotic-looking vegetables. Men lounged in groups, smoking and listening to football on the radio. The colours of a local team draped their necks. Barbers' shops were still open. The buzz of hair clippers took over from the tinny noise of transistor radios. Packs of dogs ran wild among the ruins, scavenging in huge heaps of refuse, only to lope away, tails between their legs, at the sound of footsteps.

In front, Derek Masters and Milo walked on, picking their way over rubble and making their way deeper into the darkness. Overhead, a full moon illuminated their way.

Gavin trudged behind, fuelled on adrenaline and a week of sleepless nights. Need kept him going. Need for what, he had no idea.

Abruptly, the couple ahead of him veered left into an illuminated doorway. Gav picked up his pace, stumbling over a discarded five-litre can of vegetable oil in his haste. The sound echoed in the silence. Reaching the doorway, he craned his head to look in. A yeasty smell twitched at his nostrils. Some kind of illegal drinking establishment?

Another buzzing sound. Another barber's?

Gav's eyes zeroed in on a bare-chested man just beyond the door, and the instrument in his hand. The walls were covered in ink drawings – of naked women, dragons, anchors, hearts. At the moment, three boys in the uniform of the Turkish navy were sniggering as a fourth watched the buzzing needle-pen etch the word 'Galataseray' on his right biceps.

Slipping into the tattoo-parlour-cum-bar, Gav kept Masters and Milo in view while he found a seat. Unbidden, a surly waiter brought him a tiny glass of something clear.

Gav drank it without tasting it. When the second came, he drank that too, and felt it burn the back of his throat.

Sometime later, the three sailor boys laughed their way out into the night. And Derek Masters was guiding Milo, now shirtless, into the tattooist's chair.

# Twenty-four

Free of the white T-shirt, Milo's well-muscled chest gleamed with sweat. The massive shoulders slumped dejectedly. His closely cropped head remained lowered. There was a definite air of defeat about the bodyguard.

Derek Masters held out a bundle of Turkish lira and said something to the tattooist.

Gavin tried to catch it. On the jukebox, someone wailed soulfully in Arabic and drowned out everything. Masters and the tattooist stared beyond Milo's lowered head to the back of the bodyguard's left shoulder.

Gav heaved himself to his feet in order to get a better look. The clear liquid went straight to his head, where it exploded in a flash of white. He swayed, gripping the edge of the table to steady himself. By the time he'd managed to get his legs to obey him, the buzz of the tattooist's ink pen filled his ears.

What was Milo having done? What was Derek Masters paying to have tattooed on his right-hand man's left shoulder blade?

Slowly, Gav edged his way over, merging with the bar's other patrons. Someone tapped his arm. He turned. The surly waiter held a tray of empty glasses. He nodded to Gav's table, and held out his other hand. Gav dragged a handful of crumpled notes from his jeans pocket and thrust them at the man.

The next time he glanced over at the tattooist's corner, Derek Masters stood, hands clasped in front of his angular body, watching one the bare-chested men, who straddled a chair and held the tool of his trade, work on the shoulder blade of another.

The bar was busy and noisy. Groups of workmen knocked back glasses of the same clear liquid that now burned in Gavin's head. He'd heard about poteen – he'd heard about the risks of drinking the illegal spirit, which was probably produced in a bathtub in some filthy outhouse at the back of this grotty establishment.

His teeth were hurting. Something was eating away at his brain. Another tap on his arm.

Gav frowned, ready tell the waiter to fuck off. But this time, when he turned, a man in oil-streaked overalls stood there, grinning. He ducked his head, whispered something to Gavin in an alien language.

Movement made him looked down.

The guy's hand was at his own crotch, hefting and fondling his tackle abstractedly in that way older Turkish men did. Gav shrank back from the leering proposition, turned away and continued to push through the crowd.

Tattoos, tattoos. Something fluttered in his mind from his research. Something relevant. Something already in the Masters file. Something just beyond his reach.

The buzzing paused. Low chatter and the jukebox momentarily filled the space. Then the tattooist began again, and Gavin was moving closer to the source of that sound.

Finally, he reached the edge of the small circle of onlookers that had gathered to watch.

Tattoos, tattoos...

As he moved round to a point behind Derek Masters, Gav's eyes focused past the man's head. The area around Milo's left shoulder blade was a mass of blood and sweat. It was impossible to see what the tattooist was etching there. As he watched, the ink pen paused once more. The bare-chested man wiped roughly at his work with a small white pad of cloth before beginning again.

Gav stared at the man's work. In a blast of insight, John 'Johnny-Boy' Clark's autopsy report from the Elkton Coroner's

Office exploded in his head. Under the 'distinguishing marks' section, it had been noted that the illegible remains of a removed tattoo had been found on the ex-mercenary's left shoulder blade.

The buzzing was very close now – the sound of a tattooist's pen steadily erasing the immediately recognisable entwined M and I of the Masters Industries logo from the skin of Derek Masters' bodyguard.

Gav watched, entranced.

Milo slowly raised his head and glanced round at his boss. The tiny cut Gavin had inflicted above his eyebrow had almost healed. Neat black stitches held the edges closed. But, below the cut, tears ran freely from Milo's hard, brutish eyes.

Gav's gaze flicked between the man and his employer.

In contrast to Milo's pleading expression, Derek Masters' gaze was as cool and pitiless as ever.

Threads came together in Gav's poteen-sodden brain. The leaving of a single red rose on a grave in Baltimore; the so-called argument that had led to the so-called fallout between Derek Masters and his former army buddy and one-time partner Johnny-Boy Clark; the man's body discovered naked and lifeless in a field.

Those cold eyes drew Gavin, a helpless moth to an icy flame. There was more to this than boss and employee – much more.

In a sudden gesture of something like affection, Derek Masters stretched out a hand to brush a tear from Milo's cheek. The tattooist's pen stuttered as Milo grabbed that hand in both of his and kissed it.

Were Masters and Milo also lovers? Had Johnny-Boy Clark fulfilled a similar role in the multimillionaire's life? Did the man kill himself, rather than live without Derek Masters? Or had, as a jury five years ago concluded, the ex-soldier played a more direct role in John Clark's death?

Gavin watched as Derek Masters allowed Milo the gesture.

Something was ending here. Some subtle yet strong relationship was being brought to a close. You could feel it in the air, even in a rundown bar in the backstreets of Istanbul, at three in the morning.

But what?

And why?

Milo had never shown Masters anything but unquestioning loyalty – hell, he'd even fought at the man's behest!

Under the tattooist's pen, more and more of the Masters Industries' logo was reduced to a raw, smeary wound. Gavin swayed, watching, until Milo's tattoo had been gradually obliterated. Vaguely aware of a form at his side, half propping him up, Gav continued to stare.

When the buzzing finally stopped, Milo dragged himself from the chair. A bloody pad taped to his left shoulder blade, he grabbed his T-shirt and began to make his way through the crowd. His cropped head was still lowered – in shame now more than respect.

Gavin followed the departing figure with his gaze, brain full of questions.

Just before he reached the door, the ex-bodyguard glanced around. Red-rimmed eyes met Gavin's. Something suddenly made sense. Then Milo was pushing his way out into the night, towards whatever lay ahead of him.

Gavin's mind raced. In that briefest of glances, at least one question had been half answered: maybe the loyal bodyguard hadn't been so devoted after all. Was Milo Gav's anonymous informant? Had Derek Masters' right-hand man been tipping a journalist off about his employer's activities, both past and present?

Heart pounding at the implications of it all, Gav returned his attention to Derek Masters. For the first time since he'd begun this assignment, he saw that the man was now alone.

The tattooist had another customer.

Another soulful song of lost love played on the jukebox.

Over at the bar, the group of workmen were laughing with a scantily dressed girl. Other men lounged and drank, lounged and smoked foul-smelling Turkish cigarettes. Lounged and watched.

And Derek Masters looked straight at Gavin. This was his chance! This was the reason he'd followed this man halfway around the world. This was why he had a locked briefcase chained to his left wrist. Taking a deep breath, Gav began to move towards the guy who ruled his world. But someone was preventing it.

'Hey, hey, my friend – what about a drink?'

Gav stared at the grinning guy in the oil-stained overalls. The man was still fondling himself, still leering.

'A nice warm drink?' The hard mouth twisted suggestively, the fondling hand now cupping overall-clad cock and balls. The other fist slipped behind Gavin's neck, gripping him roughly.

His eyes were focused over the shoulder of the mechanic's grease-smeared work clothes.

Cold eyes stared back. That silver-grey head nodded almost imperceptibly.

Then Gavin was on his knees, pushing his face into the mechanic's crotch and feeling the man's hardness against his cheek. The overalls stank of sump oil and days of toil, piss, sweat and nameless filth. Groaning, Gav opened his mouth and began to nuzzle the outline of the mechanic's cock.

A harsh, mocking laugh. 'Hey, hey!'

The grip on his neck increased, dragging his parted lips from where they wanted to be. Gav groaned. A slender thread of spittle continued to link his hungry mouth to the front of the mechanic's grimy overalls. The silver strand stretched, then broke, as the guy's hand angled in Gav's hair and wrenched his head right back

'Let me get it out, my friend.'

Pain shuddered through him as the muscles in his neck strained.

The mechanic kept his grip tight. His other hand hurriedly unbuttoned the one-piece garment. Gav could see that the man's nails were caked in slime and other dirt. The yellow discoloration of nicotine stained the sides of work-hardened fingers.

The unbuttoning continued. The mechanic was naked beneath the overalls. Tufts of bristling body hair appeared, as the fastenings parted. The Turk's chest and stomach were a black sea of matted swirls.

Gav lunged, wanting to drown in that sea. But the hand on the back of his neck held him fast.

The last two buttons snapped open to reveal a fat, uncut cock, curving up from a jet forest.

Gav lunged again.

The mechanic yanked his head back hard, sending more agony ricocheting down Gavin's spine. Then, sliding his hand down inside the crotch of his overalls, the guy dipped his knees and hefted his balls free.

Gav stared at the heavy sac. Somewhere in the distance, the tattooist's ink pen buzzed on. Somewhere slightly closer, men sniggered to each other, watching the show.

Movement to his left dragged his eyes momentarily from the vision of hair and dick and bollock.

Derek Masters sat down at a table just behind them. Cold bottomless eyes glazed into Gavin's.

Then the hand at the back of his neck was pushing his head forward and he was closing his eyes and sheathing dry lips

The mechanic's crotch stank of the very city itself. Clutching the briefcase to his chest, Gav let the guy's cock slip into his mouth. The workman controlled the face fuck – with the hand on Gavin's neck, the hand round his own balls, and with the motion of his hips. Sinking forward to accommodate the thick, uncut cock, he allowed the mechanic to angle his head.

The swollen glans impacted with the roof of his mouth.

Gav coughed but tightened his lips. His gag reflex kicked in, throat muscles spasming wildly. The mechanic's balls buffeted his chin. His nose was buried in the man's bristling pubes. The cock was thickening further, filling his mouth.

The hand at the back of his neck pushed roughly, slapping Gavin's face onto that thick shaft. Then the swollen glans was sinking past his soft palate, over the back of his tongue to impact with the hard cartilage at the back of his throat.

The mechanic bucked his hips. The motion knocked Gavin backwards. Hands releasing the briefcase that contained the Masters file, his fingers scrabbled for purchase. He gripped handfuls of oily overall and held on tight. Just when he'd regained his balance, the mechanic withdrew a little, then bucked again, harder than ever.

Gav was choking. Saliva filled his mouth. The guy's pubes cut off his breathing. The angle of his neck was hurting. The head of the mechanic's cock was in his throat. And the hand had moved to the back of his skull, holding his face there.

He couldn't stop swallowing. He couldn't get any air. His eyes were watering and he knew he was going to vomit or drown. Retching around the cock that filled his mouth and throat, he struggled in panic. But his stomach was empty. He had nothing to throw up.

Then the cock was withdrawing, leaving his windpipe and the back of his throat, and receding past his tight lips.

Gavin moaned and opened his eyes. Gazing up at the man who was fucking his face, he met another pair of eyes. Not the mechanic's, which were squeezed shut in pleasure. Dark, bottomless pits stared back at him.

And, when the mechanic pushed back in, Gav held the stare and allowed the fuck. He felt every centimetre of that thick white shaft. Every raised pulsing vein. Every tightly stretched fold of foreskin. He laved the underside with his tongue, as the mechanic's shaft slipped towards the back of his mouth. He tightened his lips and heard the Turk grunt in response.

And he stared into those pitlike eyes.

The mechanic altered his stance, leaning back and pushing side on to thrust his cock deeper into Gavin's mouth.

Tight dry lips parted in submission. Gav opened his mouth wider and sucked on the guy's left ball. The head of the mechanic's cock curved further up into his windpipe.

Gav sucked on, revelling in the feel of the heavy, puckered sac. As he explored the dimpled flesh with the tip of his tongue, blood fizzed in his ears. Stars danced in the air between his eyes and Derek Masters.

He couldn't breathe. It didn't matter.

He was about to pass out. He couldn't care less. Mouth slack, throat tight, Gav let the mechanic manoeuvre both balls between his sore dry lips. The man ground himself against Gavin's face, using his grip on the back of Gav's neck to control his own pleasure.

Using.

Being used.

Gav tried to suck on both balls, but the mechanic withdrew them suddenly and was now banging furiously against the back of Gavin's throat

Gav felt a jerking of the cock in his mouth, and something alien at the top of his windpipe. He didn't even taste the man's spunk when the mechanic shot down the back of his throat. Derek Masters' dark eyes opened up and almost swallowed him into blackness.

He felt barely conscious of sudden movement around him and on top of him, as one cock was removed from his mouth and another was inserted. Different cock, different position. Flat on his back, and with someone holding his head steady, Gav tightened his lips automatically to increase the pleasure of this stranger who straddled his chest.

He had no idea who the man was. But his cock was smaller. Stubbier. Gav could taste pre-come. He could taste stale piss. His eyes refused to focus. He stared at the swimming outline of some-one muscled and tall. And then he found them again.

Those eyes. The eyes that haunted his dreams and plagued his days. Eyes belonging to someone who was always with him. Gazing dreamily into Derek Masters' emotionless face, Gav let the Turk astride his chest fuck his face as roughly as he wanted to. He let the man dig his knees into Gavin's ribs, when his lips began to slacken. He let the hands of the nameless man who held his head tangle in his hair and keep his throat angled wide and open. And as the second man spurted in his mouth, Gavin flailed with his hands, grabbing onto folds of another filthy work overall, and felt hot come trickle down his throat. For a moment, he lost sight of Derek Masters.

The cock pulled out. Its owner wiped smears of come in Gavin's hair. Gav whimpered with longing.

He was empty.

Without a cock in his mouth, he was nothing. Without those dark, unforgiving eyes on him, he was less than nothing. Tears ran down Gavin's face, flowing over his aching lips to join with the salty thickness of the spunk. He tried to move his head, but the hands held him firmly. Just when he thought he'd never felt as empty, the eyes were back. And in front of them the blurring out-line of another man unbuttoning another set of oily overalls.

The third was fast, pounding hurriedly into Gavin's face. Then there was a fourth, maybe a fifth.

He knew Derek Masters was enjoying this, that his cold eyes were soaking up the spectacle somewhere on the periphery of Gav's confused vision. But Gav was enjoying it, too.

Soon he became aware that the weight on his chest had gone. Somewhere in the background, men were laughing and slapping each other on the back. The soulful jukebox played on. Gav blinked a couple of times, then managed to prop himself up on one shaky elbow. He coughed, wincing as the movement tore the skin from the back of his throat.

His body was wet paper. His mouth was raw, lips puffy and swollen. He looked around.

The grotty bar hadn't changed. Men still drank, and flirted with the scantily dressed woman. In the far corner, the buzz of the tattooist's ink pen was still audible. Gavin dragged his legs in as the surly waiter stepped over him, delivering drinks to a table. It was all the same.

But he was different. He had changed. Somewhere in that morass of cocks and bodies, some subtle alteration had taken place in Gavin Shaw's head. Scrambling unsteadily to his feet, he scanned the crowded drinking den for what he needed most.

The man he craved.

The man he'd craved, Gavin now acknowledged, since he'd first set eyes on Derek Masters, all those months ago, in an anonymous office down at Canary Wharf.

Panic spangled in his veins. No silver-grey head. No sober, conservative suit. No dark, bottomless eyes.

Then movement, just behind him. Gav's head swivelled, just in time to catch a glimpse of Derek Masters' tall, angular form disappearing out into the night. Desperation gave strength to rubbery legs. Gav lunged towards the doorway. The briefcase trailed behind, still chained to his wrist. It was now the least of his worries. He'd come so far. He'd done so much.

For Masters. For Derek Masters. It couldn't end now. Not here, not like this.

As he pushed open the door, only one thing mattered now. Gavin had to talk to the man. He had to know it all. He had to know everything.

*

A chilly dawn was breaking in the sky above his head. Great industrial vehicles hosed down the streets. Seagulls screamed their doleful cries somewhere to his left. And in the distance a ship's hooter sounded.

Gav shivered and staggered on, tripping over rubble and trying to make up the distance between himself and the man who was everything to him.

Derek Masters walked briskly.

Gav followed blindly, trailing after the man through unfamiliar alleys and now deserted streets. Over the stink of his own body and the stench of several men's come and sweat, he could smell the sea. They were walking towards the Bosphorus. Abruptly, the buildings gave way to the vast bridge that spanned that most ancient of rivers.

Gav quickened his pace, snatching at the briefcase's handle and curling his fingers around it. They crossed the bridge together, the distance between them remaining constant.

Back in the European part of Istanbul, Gavin followed the gaunt multimillionaire down onto the riverside. Ferryboats were tied up, swaying the morning tide. Further along, fishing vessels unloaded the night's catch onto the quay. Gav watched Derek Masters raise a hand in salute to a couple of fishermen, who smiled and returned the greeting.

He had no idea where the man was going. Gav knew only that, wherever it was, he would go too. Ahead, he could see the glow of a brazier, around which several seamen were warming their hands. His own teeth were chattering, and he exhaled in relief as Derek Masters slowed his brisk stride. Beyond the brazier, he could just make out some sort of loading area, in which trucks and lorries were drawing up to collect the night's catch.

Gav pondered what Derek Masters had caught in his own net

– a net that spanned the world and the past endless weeks.

Abruptly, the man in front paused. Turned.

Gav moaned and broke into a run. By the time he got there, Derek Masters was chatting amiably with several fisherman in what sounded like Turkish. Skidding to a halt, and unsure what to do, he stood there, clutching the Masters file to his chest and staring into the glowing brazier.

If the man wanted proof of Gavin's adoration, had he not already got that, back in the bar? It was all for Derek Masters. The cocks, the come. Lying on his back on a filthy floor and taking the seed of nameless men into his stomach – it had all been for Derek Masters.

As the previous weeks had been – or should have been.

Gav's fingers tightened on the edges of the locked leather case. It contained his future. His passport into the Big Time. As an investigative journalist, he'd waited a lifetime for a story like this.

Suddenly, Gavin knew what he had to do. If the man wanted proof of his devotion, he'd give him proof. With Derek Masters' cold gaze glittering beyond the flaming fire, Gav stuck a hand into the pocket of his jeans. He found the key. He unlocked the briefcase from his wrist. Then, opening the leather security case, he lifted the Masters file from its container and slowly began to feed its pages into the brazier.

Weeks of hard graft. Endless hours and sleepless nights spent poring over research material ignited in a flash. Photographs burned brightly, flaring up only to sink back into smoulders of smoking celluloid. Finally, Gav fell to a crouch and unfastened his right sandal. He twisted the heel and shook two tiny objects into his hand. Then a mini-cassette and a roll of microfilm were joining the blaze. It was gone. All his proof. All his evidence. All his work.

One of the fishermen chuckled, rubbing his hands together to enjoy the heat of Gavin Shaw's labours.

Raising his head, Gav looked into that pale, angular face. Derek Masters nodded his approval and beckoned.

Gav did the only thing he could do. He moved slowly round to the other side of the burning brazier and stood directly in front of the man who dominated his world.

# Twenty-five

Beside them, the Bosphorus glinted orange in the rising sun.

Derek Masters gazed at Gavin and rested a hand on his shoulder. Those thin lips smiled. 'We've come a long way, you and I.' The voice was quiet, but deep and resonant. 'Shall we walk a little further, Gavin?'

His cock leapt to attention. Some invisible string was tugged every time he looked at this man. But now that he was being addressed directly the movement in his groin was fast and hard. Gav bent his neck in assent and let the voice fill his head. This man's every whim ruled him. Gav knew he'd crawl over fire if that was what it took to belong to Derek Masters. But the journalist in him refused to lie down: he still had a few questions. 'How long have you... known about me?'

'From the start, Gavin.' The hand patted his shoulder. 'From the moment I first saw you, outside my office, with your' – a soft laugh – 'little tape recorder in your pocket.'

His face flushed up. But Gav continued: 'What will happen to... Milo?'

'Oh, Milo will be taken care of, don't worry about that.'

The phrase 'taken care of' circled in his brain. Would the bodyguard end up dead somewhere, all reasons to live taken away from him with the erasing of that tattoo?

They walked slowly into the lorry park, Derek Masters gradually easing Gavin ahead, but maintaining the hand on his shoulder. A little in front, he could see the outline of a large black car.

'What happens... now?' He was suddenly afraid. 'Now that

I'm… yours, I mean.' Gav tried to turn, but Derek Masters just kept pushing him on.

'Just little longer, and everything will become clear.'

Everything he'd seen – everyone he'd met over the past few months – filled in his head. Then the thought came from nowhere. There was one person he'd not considered in all this. The man he was working for. The man who'd commissioned him to write the profile of this strange, wonderful, enigmatic entrepreneur. Gav bit his bottom lip.

Would he be able to tell James why he wasn't going to write the article?

Would he ever even see that wry, handsome face again?

The prospect clutched at his guts, twisting knots in the pit of his stomach. For eight long years, James Delany had been in his life, in one way or another. Half the time they fought like cat and dog. Gav had squirmed at his ex-lover's interest in his personal life, the man's sarcastic if insightful comments always tinged with just enough home truth to let them bite.

James. Rich, powerful, irritating, infuriating James. He'd miss the kinky bastard, with his head-fucks and his handcuffs.

Fingers tightened on his shoulder. Then pushed. Gavin moaned and fell to his knees. 'Fuck me!' The head of his dick impacted with the waistband of his jeans. 'Fuck me, please!'

No reply.

Gavin groaned. 'If you won't fuck me, then give me to someone who will.' His hand moved to his crotch, and he began to stroke himself through the filthy denim.

Still no reply.

The longing in his balls was a physical reality. 'Let dogs fuck me, if that's what you want. Anything – I'll do anything!'

'Then say it, Gavin.' At last a reply. From directly behind him.

Gav leaned back, feeling his spine brush the front of Derek Masters' legs. 'Tell me what you want me to say – just tell me.'

A low laugh. 'I think you know, Gavin.'

And deep in his heart he did. Shuddering, Gav addressed the ground. 'I want to be used. I want to be owned. I want to be—' The hand left his shoulder and grabbed his hair. Words previously aimed at the ground were now shouted into the dawn sky. 'I want to belong to another man! I want to be his property.' As each word left his lips, his cock echoed the truth of it all. 'It's what I've always wanted!'

The hand left his hair. Gulping in lungfuls of salty morning air, Gav was aware of Derek Masters moving in front of him. He threw his arms around the man's legs and slumped into a heap at his feet. 'Make me yours – take me, and make me yours!' His mouth was open on the toes of Derek Masters' pristine shoes. Gav covered the fine leather with wet kisses.

'Gavin?'

He moaned, licking the dust from the polished hide.

'You are not mine to take, tempting though you are. You belong to another.'

The words cut through his happy haze.

'But there is one thing you can do for me.'

Gav dragged his face from the man's feet. 'Anything. Just tell me.'

'Take off your clothes. I know your mind inside out, but I've never seen you naked.'

He didn't need to be asked twice. In the very public lorry park, Gav tore at his filthy Levi jacket and jeans, hauling the grubby T-shirt over his head and scrambling to his feet. Kicking the sandals off, he stood there, head lowered.

His hard-on flexed in front of him, clear sticky pre-come oozing from his slit. Derek Masters' words circled in his head:

You belong to another.

You belong to another.

He could feel those bottomless eyes on his naked form.

Inspecting. Appraising. Admiring?

'You're very handsome, Gavin Shaw. You are a strong, attractive man. I would be proud to own you.'

He began to shake.

'But that's not what this is about.'

Gav closed his eyes. He would have clasped his hands over his ears if it would have shut out the words he didn't want to hear.

'And I think you know that.'

Maybe his eyelids were squeezed rightly shut, but something else had opened somewhere along the way. The raw vulnerable sensation of standing naked before his virtual stranger was nothing compared with the exposure of his soul. But, along with the stripping away of all pretence, a great weight had been lifted from his body.

So many years of hiding from himself. So many years of covering up what he really wanted beneath casual fucks and a refusal to commit. So much lying – to other people, to himself. So much wasted time.

'Gavin?'

He whimpered.

'Gavin, touch your cock.'

His whole body shuddered. He didn't want to – he couldn't have cared less about his own dick. It was a mere barometer of the power other men held over him. But, if it was what Derek Masters wanted, he'd do it. Hesitantly, his hand moved over his thigh.

As soon as his fist made contact with that throbbing rod, Gav felt the first stirrings of incipient orgasm deep in his balls. He grunted like the nameless animal he was.

'Now masturbate yourself.' The voice was low, without emotion.

Gav inhaled sharply, tightening his fist, and gave his dick a couple of hasty strokes. His balls knitted together. Somewhere deep in his arse, something spasmed violently. Knees trembling,

Gav threw back his head and prepared to come.

'Now stop.'

Gav growled and kept wanking himself.

'I said stop.' The voice barely increased in volume.

With supreme effort, Gav's hand left his dick, which continued to flex in the air in front of him. Both fists curled into balls of sheer frustration, clenched at his sides. He could feel his nails digging into the palms of his hands. But the pain went a little way to distracting him from the need to shoot his load onto the dusty ground of this lorry park.

Somewhere nearby, a cab door opened, then slammed shut.

Derek Masters chuckled and moved back behind him. 'Good – good boy.'

The small words of praise filled his heart and sent it soaring into the dawn sky. Then the hand was back on his bare shoulder, and they were moving again.

Slowly, as they walked across the emptying lorry park, Gav became aware of men approaching from all directions. Fishermen and dock workers, he presumed – or ferry staff, making their way down to the quayside to begin the day. In the half-light, he caught a glimpse of a face. Gav did a double-take.

One guy was the spitting image of big Okie Vincent, the flight attendant Gav had fucked in the toilets of the plane that had taken him to Philadelphia. His mind was playing tricks on him. More men appeared, from behind bushes and out of cars. Was that Jordaan, from the Music Box?

A rangy figure with cropped hair sauntered past, flashing Gav a smile. That was definitely Jake, from the Sinner's Arms. A shortish shape with ropy arms in a sleeveless T-shirt was the image of Zorn. And that was Asif with him! Head now swivelling wildly, Gav took in the group of men who had now formed a loose circle around himself and Derek Masters.

Tony. The lady-boy from the Blue Lagoon. The fat detective

whose name he'd never been given. Two of the men he'd watched suck redneck dick in an abandoned warehouse in Baltimore's meat-packing district exchanged smiles with each other – and the kid in the Puffa jacket Gav was sure he'd seen shot! Even the floor cleaner from Schipol airport, along with Mehmet, his Turkish driver, the security guard from the office block at Canary Wharf and half a dozen others. Plus Milo, who was grinning in a most unsettling manner.

The hand on his shoulder tightened, easing him to a halt. What was going on? What the fuck was going on? Before he could voice the question, a car door was opening in front of him. Gav peered at the sleek black vehicle he'd noticed earlier. The first figure to emerge he recognised straightaway. 'Gerry! What the hell are you—' The sight of the second cut short the enquiry, mid-flow.

James Delany stepped from inside the car, leaned an elbow on the roof and chuckled. 'So you don't like playing games, my friend.'

Behind Gavin, someone began to clap slowly. Others took up the signal, and the applause spread like wildfire. Gav barely heard it. Derek Masters' hand left his shoulder. Gav didn't notice. He stared at James's calm, handsome face. 'What's going...?'

The commissioning editor of *Financial Week* walked slowly into the middle of the circle to join Gavin. 'I trust you found the... assignment challenging?'

Gav's jaw dropped, along with a very obvious penny. He stood there, surrounded by men who had fed him information at every twist and turn, men who had sucked his cock, blown him and let him fuck their arses. Men he'd thought he'd been using. But who had, in fact, been using him – on the instructions of a master game player.

James stretched out a hand. One immaculately manicured finger stroked a lock of tangled hair back from Gavin's face.

The applause was dying away. The circle of men crowded in on the two of them. People slapped Gavin on the back and shook James by the hand, smiling their congratulations and best wishes.

He stood, naked and silent, through it all. When Gerry moved forward, something like shame spread over Gavin's skin. He looked at a man whose affection he'd toyed with, whose good nature he'd exploited – a man whose feelings Gavin had definitely hurt.

Their eyes met. Gav had no words to say how sorry he was. But Gerry just smiled. 'I've met someone, by the way – your surf-bum trick.'

Gav goggled.

Gerry laughed. 'Turned out to be one of the managers at our Hong Kong branch. We got together at a team brunch last month.' The futures dealer winked. 'And he keeps the place tidier than you ever did.'

Gav managed a weak smile. His mind was still trying to make sense of the whole thing when a silver-grey head entered on the periphery of his vision. He watched James and Derek Masters embrace warmly. He had to be sure. 'Um, you're not a war criminal?'

The head of Masters Industries chuckled. 'I'm afraid not. I don't deal drugs, smuggle guns or launder money, either. I'm just a boring businessman.'

'What about all that... web stuff? What about Johnny-Boy Clark, and the prison sentence and the—'

'A boring businessman with an HTML expert for a submissive!' Milo's gruff voice interjected, from behind. 'The web's so easy to tamper with. It was just a matter of tacking on some links and letting you read what you wanted to read.' The brutish-looking man slipped an arm around Derek Masters' waist and grinned at Gavin. 'Helluva left hook you've got there, by the way.' Milo fingered the small cut above his left eye. 'But no hard feelings, eh, Shaw?'

It had all been planted. It was all a game. He'd been led by the nose by everyone involved, and Gavin had fallen for it, hook, line and sinker. He'd been set up. He'd been set up and knocked down.

Gradually, James's partners in deception made their way back to their respective cars. The lorry park emptied. Only two men remained.

One naked and still hard, the other rich and powerful enough to organise a game on a worldwide scale.

Confusion trembled in his fists. Gav was no longer sure what he felt. Part of him was angry. Part of him felt stupid and unprofessional. But a greater part of him felt lost – lost and so lonely.

Something churned in the pit of his stomach.

His mask had been well and truly ripped off by James. But what was underneath? And who would want him now? Summoning what little strength he had left, Gavin turned away and looked around for his clothes. A semi-amused voice called to him from the far side of the lorry park.

'And where do you think you're going?'

Gav continued to walk.

'Gavin?' A note of concern had entered the voice. 'Gavin!' Then footsteps were pounding across towards him and James's hands gripped his shoulders turning him round. 'Baby!'

The new affection in the voice was the last straw. With a sob, Gavin tumbled naked into James Delany's strong arms.

'Shh, shh, baby.'

James's lips were on his neck. Those strong arms were tight around him. Gavin burrowed in like a child, smelling James's smell and never wanting to leave that embrace.

'I'm sorry it had to be this way – I'm sorry you had to... go through what you did.'

The words were gentle. Soothing. Full of regret and very reassuring.

'But you were so fucking stubborn! I wanted you so much eight years ago. And not a day has gone by since you walked out when I haven't wanted you back. This was the only way I could think of, to make you understand, baby. I only play games with people who matter to me.' Gav buried his face in James's chest. 'And you matter to me, Gavin. You were meant to be with me. And I was meant to be with you.'

His arms slipped up around his ex-lover's neck. Gav crushed his naked body against the fully clothed one. 'You never said you loved me.' The reproach was half sobbed, half mumbled into the front of James's shirt.

A wry chuckle against his ear. 'I think we've moved a bit beyond that, but if it means that much to you' – warm lips brushed Gav's ear – 'I love you, Gavin Shaw. Happy now?'

Gavin laugh-sobbed and raised his head. Staring into those odd grey eyes, he saw his own reflection there. 'You own me. That makes me happier.' For the first time, he meant every word of it. 'But no... collars, eh? No handcuffs?'

James nodded. 'I don't think we need them anyway.' He moved one hand to rub a thumb along Gavin's bottom lip. 'So will you come home with me now?'

Gav licked at the thumb, then drew it into his mouth and nodded.

James groaned. 'That drives me wild, and you know it!'

Gav sniffed, laughed and kissed the man's knuckles. 'Take me home, James. Take me home and fuck what's yours.'

Slowly, arms around each other, the two men made their way towards the waiting car. It was the end of one game. And perhaps the beginning of another.